Joolz Denby is an award-winning novelist, poet, spoken-word artist and illustrator with an international reputation. She has published four collections of poetry and short stories and ___ novels, and made numerous recordings; she has appe_____ ly on radio and television all over the world. Her i_____ ___ from the study of body modification practices (of whic_ _____ ered a _ading expert), mythology, theology and _____ ogy, through to workin_ with underground c_____ _ Model Army, Hatha Yoga, gardening, and being an obsessive reader with over three thousand books stored in a very untidy house which is also stuffed with cats, people and curios. When not travelling, she lives in Bradford and never quite manages to get enough sleep. Please visit www.joolz.net for further information.

BILLIE
MORGAN

Joolz Denby

Library of Congress Catalog Card Number: 2004103040

A complete catalogue record for this book can be
obtained from the British Library on request

The right of Joolz Denby to be identified as the author of this work has
been asserted by her in accordance with the Copyright, Designs and
Patents Act 1988

First published in 2004 by Serpent's Tail,
4 Blackstock Mews, London N4 2BT
website: www.serpentstail.com

Typeset at Neuadd Bwll, Llanwrtyd Wells

Printed by Mackays of Chatham, plc

1   2   3   4   5   6   7   8   9   10

Dedicated unreservedly and with deep gratitude to Justin Sullivan and Warren Hogg, and to the memory of my beloved companions Finn MacCool and Little Egypt.

Acknowledgements

I would like to thank the following for their invaluable help and support: John Williams, Pete Ayrton and all at Serpent's Tail, Kate Gordon, Dr Christine Alvin, Nina Baptiste, Kulbir Singh, Tracie Critchley, Jodie & Chris, Sheila McLean & Isaac McLean-Swain, Donelda McKechnie, Nic Sears, John Connolly, Julia Wallis-Martin, Spotti-Alexander & Miss Dragon Pearl.

All those readers of my previous works whose continued loyalty, encouragement and support have been extraordinarily touching.

All those persons whom I cannot name, but who know who they are: thank you, brothers. To those no longer with us, rest in peace.

My gratitude and respect, as ever, to the Goddess.

These are my memoirs; the truth as I remember it. BM

Prologue

I KNOW THE WOMAN at the window is me, although she doesn't look like me. She's flushed and fair, skinny, with wispy blonde hair knotted up in a clip. She looks tired and unhappy; lines score down from the sides of her compressed lips. My hair is dark brown, threaded with silver and springs back from a small widow's peak into a short, wavy crop. I am strong, stocky, and my skin is yellow-white, almost nacreous. My eyes aren't her red-rimmed, faded blue, but sea-grey, the iris flecked with green around the pupil. My father's eyes.

But I know she's me; I know it's really me gazing out at the furious rain that pelts down outside the window while I – she – washes up the dinner things wearing pink rubber gloves, something I never do. I'm back in the old house in West Bowling and I'm looking out at the stone-flagged back yard, at the narrow, six-foot-long flowerbed filled with struggling roses and grey, dispirited city soil. It's a poor, run-down area; a slum. The yard is battered and the outside walls graffitied. I sigh, and push a strand of that lank yellow hair off my flushed forehead with the back of my wrist.

I see myself from outside, from slightly above. Part of me is floating in the rain, watching my mouth open in a silent, horrified scream, watching my eyes – those alien, blue eyes – fly open in appalled disbelief turning to dreadful recognition as the downpour washes the earth off a hand that protrudes limp and bone-white from the flowerbed. Slowly the soil is washed away and the terrible, lifeless form of a man lies exposed, his mouth stoppered with mud, his eyes clotted with muck, staring. Although I know the body has been there for many years, like some kind of hideous saint's relic, it's not decayed. I sag against the sink, weeping as I realise that the dreadful secret I've hidden for so long is now revealed for all to see and that my life is over.

The silent sobs turn into hoarse crying as I wake up. I always wake up at that point. Always.

My name is Billie Morgan. *My name is Billie Morgan.*

I am a murderer.

Part One

Chapter One

Y**OU KNOW**, the fact is I have no bloody idea why I'm doing this. Writing this stuff down, committing it forever to black and white in Times sodding New Roman fourteen point (yes, that's huge, but I'm a bit short-sighted). Perhaps I need to confess, like they always do in crap films '*before I shoot you, Bond, I'll tell you why I assassinated the president and...*' Bollocks, I always thought. Off the smarmy sod and leg it with the diamonds. But then, look, here I am, tapping away at the keyboard. And it's not safe, anyone could get hold of it. I mean, you read about criminals – criminals, Christ, that's a laugh, like I'm not one, of course – being hoyed up in front of the courts because 'incriminating evidence' was found in their computer after they thought they'd gotten rid of it, thought they were safe. Leckie always says, her glossy lips pursed judiciously, that people who don't understand computers (meaning, she does) assume if you delete things they're gone, vanished into the ether like wind-blown ash. Then she pauses for effect, her head wobbling slightly and a knowing expression on her broad, brown face. *But*, she says, her eyes widening, but *no*. Not a bit of it. Along comes a spotty young whizz-kid cyber-Plod and casually retrieves the stuff from your hard-drive where it's been crouching, hidden, amongst the burblings and twitterings of your computer's innards all along. Oh yes, says Leckie, bridling happily, people can be very stupid.

That bit always makes me smile. She thinks I'm smiling along with her wisdom and perspicacity, her incisive grasp of the human condition. Actually, I'm grinning mirthlessly at the grotesque memory of my own, unspeakable, blinding stupidity; my error, my colossal, terminal fuck-up.

Poor Leckie. I am fond of her, I really am, but as they say round here: *bless her, she knows nowt.*

You see, every time I had the urge to confess, to talk about stuff, regardless of the risk I got it out of my system in print, or before I got computerised, in a notebook. But this particular manuscript or whatever you call it, the one you're reading now whoever you are, is the big one, my attempt to get it all tidied up, sorted out. You know, before I die, or leg it to Tahiti like Gaugin and vanish. It needed sorting, too. There's a steel lock-box under my bed crammed with tatty notebooks, all different sizes, shapes and colours full of my illegible scribble. Now there's various types of disks in there too, that chart my acquaintance with PC culture, also full of scribble, only print scribble. All locked away, the key stuffed in a scruffy little Chinese silk baggie too knackered even to put in the sale and shoved between the mattress and the bed-base. The obvious place, I know, but God knows I wouldn't want the coppers straining themselves searching. Sometimes I think I'll hide the damn thing somewhere better; maybe in the cavity behind the light switch plate, where the lads used to put their stash in the old days. But I can't be arsed, I'd have to unscrew the plate every time I wanted the key and I know I'd just not bother.

Increasingly these days, I can't be bothered. I'm forty-six, why should I bother? Sometimes I think it's a miracle I'm alive at all, never mind Leckie going on at me about dying my hair to get rid of the grey and having manicures. Pampering, she calls it. Like I was a baby, if babies went in for facials and aromatherapy.

I like the lock-box, anyway, it belonged to my grandfather. It's army issue, with his name stencilled on it: Major W. E. G. Morgan. William Edward George Morgan. Bill Morgan. He was the first Bill, then my dad then me, Billie. It's not Wilhemina or anything like that, either. It's Billie on my birth certificate. My father insisted, against my mum's wishes, that I was named Billie; partly for the family thing, and partly after Billie Holliday. She was his favourite singer, *the* jazz singer with a voice like lazy, ruined velvet. My mum wanted to name me 'something feminine' like my older sister, Jennifer – but for once, Dad stood up to her. Mum wasn't impressed and when she's pissed off – well. I had a cold entry to this world and no mistake.

I love that battered old box, it reminds me of childhood, of comfort, of the safe, sweet past, of my dad. His father was gone before I was five, and Gran shortly afterwards; Mum's dad died when she was a teenager and her mum, who she never got on with, was in a Home in Scarborough for years until she died, probably of boredom, when I was sixteen. There was Mum's brother, Uncle Arthur and his family, but they live down South so we never see much of them, or want to, really, they're a social-climbing lot to be honest. Ashamed of where they're from – Uncle A was once heard to tell someone that no, he wasn't from Bradford, actually, he came from Harrogate; you can't get snobbier than that. So Mum, Jen and me were virtually on our own; a sealed unit with all the inturned vision that implies.

The box is all I have of Dad; he had it for his papers and he would get sealing wax out of it, and a strange brass stamp to push into the fragrant, melting pool of red and we'd write out 'certificates' for things like being a good lass, or growing an inch, or helping Mummy. Then he'd light the sealing wax, drip it on the paper and let me push the stamp into it, to make it official.

I loved him so much, so much. I loved Mum of course, but Dadda... Dad was everything to do with dreaming, and being Welsh, and him reading me *Narnia*, and poetry I didn't understand by someone he called Mr Thomas and the smell of whisky and cigarettes and his aftershave – *a bit of Old Mice, eh sweetheart, never fails, y'can't go wrong with a bit of the Mouse* – and his grey eyes fixed on far horizons and loose women.

Then he was gone. Ran off with his secretary when I was just turned nine. Classic really, the secretary thing; a dolly bird, Home Nana used to call her when we went on an infrequent visit and mum would try to shut her up and scold her about 'dragging that old stuff up again'. Home Nana would cackle wickedly and thwart Mum by drooling her stewed institutional tea through her naked gums and repeating over and over, *'He ran off with one of them dolly birds, the swine, men are all pigs, pigs I tell yer.'*

I never saw her, the DB as I called her secretly, but I imagined her as a blonde, buxom, with long legs clad in knee-high black kinky boots like Emma Peel in *The Avengers*, only Yorkshire, of course. Mini-skirts and plastic 'fashion' earrings; white rabbit-fur 'coney' shortie jackets and a PVC handbag on a gilt chain. False eyelashes and long frosty nails for evenings. Tanned like a kipper in summer. Flashy, but always playing the lady. Gin and tonic with a slice of lemon, thank you. Ooooh, Bill, you are awful, really, the things you say.

Not unlike Mum, in fact, though Mum's never tarty. She's always very smart; real cultured pearls and a medium tan wool-and-cashmere coat with a genuine Mongolian lamb collar and cuffs. But the principle's the same. Blonde, big pointy breasts, little waist, round hips, high heels, sexy-but-actually-frigid. The DB was younger, naturally. Men always run to type, they get hooked on a certain look and seldom stray from it their whole lives, though they get narky if you mention it. It's usually the image of their first love, so I shouldn't think Dad legged it with a skinny brunette. I had a mate who got always got goosebumps about Scandinavian-looking girls with that bright blue kohl-liner in their eyes, all on account of that blonde out of Abba. He had a soft spot for Lady Di because of that, too. Sad, I call it, but there you are. Oh well, women are just as bad. We're all fucked up, one way or another.

Dad and the DB went to live in Torquay, the English Riviera and all that. Were they happy? Probably. Dad liked to be happy, when he wasn't filled with that cursed dark Celtic melancholy. The Black Dog, he called it. *The Black Dog's bitin' me, sweetheart, give yer poor old Dadda a kiss, that's my girl; I love you, Billie, I love you best, you know, a chip off the old block you are and that's a fact...*

I never saw him again. He died in a car crash when I was twenty. Drunk. Head on into a tree they said. Never knew what hit him. I didn't go to the funeral, none of us did. God knows what had happened to the original DB, left him years before probably. There was no estate, just a few bits and pieces. He'd been living alone in a bedsitter in Brighton. Someone sent his pitiful bits and pieces up to us – I got the lock-box before Mum chucked it out. Rubbish, she'd said fiercely, rubbish, he just left some rubbish.

Mum and Jen say I look just like Dad. I think that was the problem.

Chapter Two

I LIVE IN BRADFORD, in West Yorkshire, the bit of England Southerners like to think of as grey, dead and it's-grim-up-North: '*Ooh, is it near Manchester? God, I mean, I've, actually, well, I don't…*' No, they don't know where I live, where we, the bloody barbarians, *live*.

They miss so much, silly buggers like that; they miss the pungent, intense flavour of the town, the beauty of the great nineteenth-century buildings, fretted and laced all over with the finest stone carving in the country. They miss the light, so thick and golden just before dusk it ignites the crystals in the sandstone and fires them into glowing amber. They miss the food – fantastic food from everywhere in the world and cheap as you like: mangoes, persimmons, sugar cane, okra, tattered petticoat bunches of fresh-cut coriander held together with old elastic bands, you name it – all for tuppence in the corner shop. Bread like God's true gift to humanity made by stand-up Ukrainian blokes in a bakery on a pony-town estate. Curries from every part of the subcontinent and some that are pure Bradford. People who sneer at us miss the great skies, the vast blue air above us that swirls with flying clouds as the wind whips them free across the valley. They miss the fifteen-minute drive into the country, to the crag-studded moorlands washed with the purple veils of heather or rusty, ice-dusted cloaks of winter fern, echoing with the coughing barks of foxes and watched by kestrels wheeling on the swirling thermals.

Oh sure, it's a poor place; when the textile trade all but died poverty crept in on naked, rotting feet and soured things; clabbered the milk in babies' mouths and put a blighted fury in our young men's hearts that leads them to rash and brutal acts. I won't pretend it's *nice*. Sometimes it's ugly and cruel; sometimes it drives me crazy with frustration and despair at how people go on. But it's not grey; it's not dull – it's as fiery and drenched with colour as a Turner painting. It's a stone maze; a trap for the unwary – I'm not surprised poor old Londoners get culture shock…

I've always lived here, me and Mum and Jen and Liz, we've never lived anywhere else – I don't count Jen emigrating because in her head, she's still Bradfordian. We don't live in the city centre, mind you, it isn't that sort of town. My shop's there, that's how I make my living – I have a gift shop on Carlsgate by the shopping centre, called Moonstone. It used to be Moonstone Gifts but after Leckie came to work with me we redecorated and dropped the 'gifts'; more modern that way, goes with the pale blue metallic paint job and blonde wood floors. If I could just get Lecks off the idea of flogging all her precious New Age folderols, it'd be great, but hey, everyone's got their pet obsessions. I just wish she'd leave it out with the stinky joss and thin, pastel-covered books called *Beyond God* and *Discover Your Inner Sacred Clown*. I put my foot down sharpish about *them*.

I specialise in gemstone and silver jewellery, good pieces, lovely stuff. I do art cards, unusual gifts, fancy wrapping paper and the like too. It's a nice place, the shop, a nice working environment as they say and I'm proud of it. There's a tiny flat above it, but it's used as storage, no one lives in it anymore. I did for a while when I first got the shop and I was skint and desperate but I got out of there as soon as I could. No one really lives in the town itself; at night it was strangely lonely, curled up in a doss-bag on my mattress on the floor, listening to the drunks singing.

Mum still lives in the terraced house she moved into first with Dad, in Saltaire; then it was nothing particular, maybe a bit picturesque what with the canal and the dinky toy town look of it, the whole village having been built all of a piece, complete with miniature hospital and alms houses by Titus Salt, nineteenth-century mill-owner and social visionary, for his workers. Nowadays it's very hip and increasingly overrun by what used to be called Yuppies. There's organic cafés, boutiques, art galleries, a harmonium museum and a whole building dedicated to local-boy-made-good artist David Hockney. It's a sort of pre-mortem shrine, complete with hushed, sepulchral atmosphere and giant votive vases of lilies. Very un-Yorkshire.

So Mum lives there, and I lived with her until I got wed, and so did our Jen until, as I say, she emigrated. Now I live right across the other side of town, in another satellite village, Ravensbury, also very pretty but possibly a tad more countrified. I live in a cottage; two small bedrooms, living room, kitchen, bathroom. There's a bit of a garden I've made nice and colourful, it's got a lovely old weeping willow, tangled masses of old-fashioned roses, a tiny frog pond fringed with yellow irises, and a Gaudi-style mosaic-tiled bench I made in the curve of the old stone wall. There's even a rather dilapidated garage for my old estate car. I bought it before house prices rocketed – it was a snip at twenty grand – oh yes, you could get stuff like that back then.

It's just me and the cats, Ghenghis and Cairo. Gheng is a very old, arthritic, night-black former hellraiser with mauled ears and sulphurous yellow eyes full of malevolence and violence, but he likes me as well as he likes anyone. Cairo is younger, a slant-eyed, heavy on the eyeliner, Sophia Loren of a cat; a part Siamese tabby slinky whose operatic caterwauling could wake the dead in the cemetery next door. I love my animals; I mean, I really love them. I don't care if that's soppy, or middle-aged, they mean more to me than most humans. I've lived with them now for years, smelling the clean, primitive scent of their fur and feeling its silk ripple beneath my blunt fingers. I've listened to their conversations and arguments, seen them kill and kiss with equal satisfaction. I've watched them change from tottering babies, through springy, elastic adolescence to melancholic, grey-muzzled maturity. I've nursed them and slept with them, the rise and fall of their breathing the rhythm I drop off to, their hungry morning calls my alarm clock.

I love my home, too. It's a nice house now, I've spent time on it, mended it, repaired the damage done to it by the demented former owners who painted the oak beams lilac with emulsion and glued purple PVC onto the floor into the bedroom. Now it's light and open, with a lot of natural wood and stone and a big, cushioney red sofa to curl up on in front of the living flame gas fire. It's unashamedly cosy, I suppose, not very minimalist or modern. And I like the tree-studded cemmie and the little lichened stone church being so close; it's peaceful. I'm not frightened of the dead; it's the living that put the shits up me, no mistake.

I put my dad's framed photos up on the walls; I got them off Mum, she was glad to see the back of them. I don't hang my own stuff, I can't do that, it's like begging for compliments to me, I suppose. You know, that cringemaking bit where someone goes '*What a lovely painting, who did it? It's yours? How super...*' It's like, ooh, look at my cleverness, I'm an *artist* – but maybe if I'm honest, it just tweaks a bit to think what I could have been. Not top-flight, not Britart, but I could have made a living at it, I'm pretty sure. But I'd probably have had to leave Bradford; go to London or St Ives; by the sea, that would have been perfect.

But I never left town. That's not my fate. So it's Bradford; strange, contrary, truculent, kaleidoscopic Bradford – the backdrop of my life, part of me, of what happened to me, of what I became.

It would be easy to say I'd had an awful childhood, to use that as an excuse, but it wouldn't be true. I lacked for nothing material. Mum had a good job in local government as a – yes – secretary. A proper one, she always insists, not a jumped-up typist like That Woman. Mum serviced the work needs of a couple of 'gentlemen' in the Architectural Department. Artistic gentlemen, apparently, given to musings about baroque churches in York and imitation classical facades in Huddersfield. After her retirement, she joined every club, class and activity going – bridge, charities, pottery (not for long, that one, too messy), literature (as long as it was Catherine Cookson or similar – no swearing, no shagging, and every book exactly the same for comfort), golf, coach trips to famous gardens and, God help us all, salsa dancing for the over-fifties. She bought new shoes for that one, silver, with a two-and-a-half inch heel – what she thinks of as a 'practical heel'. She could ascend bloody Everest in that sort of heel and a nice Revlon lipstick. No, there's not a spare hour in her day, and that's how she likes it. Basically, as you might have gathered, she doesn't like thinking.

Jen, being older than me by nearly eight years (I wasn't 'planned' like her, I just happened after one too many G&T's) had work as soon as she left school at sixteen. She lives in Canada – Calgary – with her husband Eric and the girls, Cheryl Anne and Tiffany Jayne, my nieces. I've met the Girls exactly twice on their two visits to 'the old country'. On the first occasion, Cheryl was nearly three and Tiffany a babe in arms. Cheryl screamed like a banshee whenever I went near her that time, while Mum, Jen and Liz (like, she was all of a sudden the baby expert) pursed their lips and nodded in unison like a bunch of chrysanthemums in a breeze. Or chrysanthemums with a dead rose-stalk stuck in with them in Liz's case. The second time, some eight years later, the Girls were polite. I'd like to say something warmer but I can't.

Jen emigrated almost directly after the colossal meringue of a wedding, with him, Eric, the Chinless Wonder. They're doing very well, thank you. She takes after Mum – a classic blonde, with a curvy figure, tiny hands and feet, big blue eyes and a genuine peaches-and-cream complexion. Like Mum, she'll get plump and a faint tracery of red veins will marble those smooth cheeks – but Jen will know how to deal with all that: she's a top Chanel Lady, now, at a huge store in a vast mall in Calgary. She'll whip out the green-tinted concealer to counteract that cruel flush of decay, or Crème de la Mer at a million bucks a pot to smooth out those creeping wrinkles. If all else fails, as it always does, there's always some unctuous plastic surgeon wielding his magic scalpel; North America, home of the umpteenth face lift, the grinning death's head crowned in straw blonde wreaths. Like a cosmetologist King Canute, Jen will stand foursquare against the tide of time.

For Jen, beauty therapy is a religion, a breathless mantra; her first job was as a 'beauty consultant' – a counter girl for Estée Lauder – in the long-since-closed department store in town. She was – there's only one word – ecstatic. She looked like St Theresa; transfigured.

I think she got the job because her bosses could see the redemptive fervour in her glistening eyes as she convinced them that for her, this was a vocation. In Jen's superbly manicured paws the old, the acned, the T-zoned and the desiccated would be saved. These poor, desperate women would recover that holy grail of beauty culture, their lost femininity. Men would admire them, women envy them. They would be loved again. *Sancta sanctissima – bless you, Jennifer*, those women would breathe as they dared at last to confront that tyrant devil, the mirror, and saw their dewy new facades freshly painted in a uniform beige (Jen doesn't do black women – 'not her line'), their eyes a graduated masterpiece of autumnal browns, their lips so thick with russet grease they look like they've been smacked in the gob – *bless you*. Saint Jennifer intercede for us, renew our womanhood, give us back our femininity…

That was what it was all about. Femininity. Mum and Jen were obsessed by it. The worst thing they could say about someone was that she wasn't very *feminine*. Their lives revolved around this rigid construct of womanhood – all the more, I expect, because mum never remarried after the divorce.

It was a house of women, even the dog, Sweetie – a Yorkie that Mum top-knotted with tartan ribbon – was female. Men did enter the sanctuary, but they didn't stay. Not even the night, as far as I know. At first, I was her excuse – *'My youngest, she'll be upset, thought the world of her father, poor thing'* – I could hear them in the hall as some love-sick Lothario struggled to grasp Mum's generous curves clad in a peach cashmerette twin-set, her precious pearls gleaming like drops of light in the becoming pink-shaded gloom while Sweetie yapped piteously round her nyloned ankles. I'd put my hand over my mouth so as not to giggle out loud, remembering what she'd said about the man before he arrived, his rep's saloon pulling up outside the house in the fine mist of rain that turned everything outside grey and soft.

'Well, I don't know why I'm bothering, that I don't – Jen love, hand me that chiffon, it's damp out.' Heavy sigh and much finger-fluffing of perm. 'He's not all that and I swear, it'll be a bunch of nasty carnations and chase me, Charlie, all night. Men! Still, Liz is right, I can't stay in all the time, I'll go mad. Is Dickie coming round? Well, mind you don't get up to any hanky-panky, young lady – you know where that ends up, look at poor Stella Parrish, big as a house and I don't see a ring on that finger, do you? No, Billie, not now. You'll find out when you grow up, they're a woman's cross to bear, men. Oh, hear that? Bipping his horn like a bloomin' taxi driver – see what I mean? Common. Well…' Peck, peck of kisses. 'I'm off, don't wait up, girls, it's a week day, remember.'

They never lasted. Mum would go out with them either alone or in a foursome with her friend Liz, whom she'd palled up with since school, for a few dates then shrug them off like a worn cardi. She was much happier going to the pictures or a discreet dance with Liz, both of them gussied up to the nines. Liz had divorced her husband Ted after four scant years of marriage when she came home unexpectedly and found him shagging her sister in the marital bed – *wearing outfits*, apparently, though this was hissed in a sibilant undertone accompanied by pursed lips and intense, meaningful looks. I have wondered all my life what the poor bastard and Liz's unmentionable sister had got themselves up as. The mind boggles. Anyhow, the general awfulness of men was a bond between Liz and Mum, it was their battle cry. The gay divorcées, the called themselves. A pair of gay divorcées.

In those days, gay meant happy – but I really think Mum would have been much happier if she'd married Liz in the first place. Liz, with her solid, matte soot-black helmet of wiry hair, simian tobacco-brown eyes, faint moustache and sallow 'Spanish' complexion, complemented by jangling gold slave bracelets and matching cross on a chain (no Jesus on it though, continental she might look, Catholic she wasn't, thank you), was a constant presence in our house, though she supposedly lived severely alone a few streets away in a neat-as-a-pin cottage that reeked of ashtrays and air-fresheners. In those days, fags equalled sophistication in a woman; the height of seduction was taking a deep drag whilst eyeing your quarry, then exhaling cruelly and saying '*Go on then, if you must*' to some smoke-dazed swain.

And by God, Liz was sophisticated all right. She had been legendarily compared (by a blind fella, presumably) to that other Liz, Liz Taylor, and always managed to let it drop that unlike La Taylor, she wouldn't have let Richard Burton slip, oh no. A man like that needs a firm hand, not being let to run mad. But there you are, that's theatricals for you – no common sense, no backbone. Arty. Personally, I always thought Liz's severely girdled-and-Cross-Your-Hearted physique had the stiff, sculpted contours of Queen Victoria in her later, monumental years rather than the dangerous curves of her violet-eyed, fish-crazy namesake.

Liz's ivory, nicotine-stained, be-ringed hands flew about as she spoke like tainted doves, a habit she attributed to her cosmopolitan, foreign outlook. She favoured 'smart' Leeds styles which Mum admired but couldn't wear due to her hips and tits getting in the way of the uncompromising tailoring. It was well known round by us that Liz Hodges could have married anyone she chose, what with being so passionate and superior, but she chose not to wed anyone, she chose Mum.

They loved each other; Mum and Liz, they were each other's biggest fans. Liz had loathed Dad, despised all men on principle in fact, but she had a mania for 'not interfering' in family business. She'd just purse her lips and glance heavenwards if Dad's name came up. It 'wasn't her place' to comment but you'd have had to be blind not to read her body language. I'd heard her *comment* quick enough when she thought I couldn't hear, in the kitchen late at night over a last, lingering cuppa before she strode off into the sleet. '*You're better off without him, Jeanie love, the creep, he's made his bed and by God, he'll lie in it now.*' I ground my teeth as I shivered on the stairs in my flanelette nightie and bunny slippers. Mum hung on Liz's every word like they were gospel; Liz was smart, no one *ever* got one over on Liz Hodges. No wonder the poor lumpy-suited, receding men who wooed Mum's buxom charms foundered on the rock of Mum and Liz's iron devotion. When Liz died suddenly of a heart attack four or five years ago, Mum was devastated. Dad's desertion wasn't in the same league.

But at home, closeted away from the harsh world, Mum loved the cosmetics, the skin-care things she shared with Jen. She was, after all a Beauty, as everyone agreed, and as such, was obliged to keep up her standards. It was her duty – that frightening old song always makes me think of her:

> '*Keep young and beautiful,*
> *It's your duty to be beautiful,*
> *Keep young and beautiful*
> *If you want to be loved...*'

Beauty treatments were the rituals that structured her time outside work. The names of her beauty gurus were like a hymn to real, proper, film-star Glamour – Helena Rubenstein, Max Factor, Elizabeth Arden, Guerlain, Estée Lauder; none of your trendy Mary Quant or scary Biba. Then there was the hairdresser, the manicurist, the hours in the tiny bathroom plastered in free samples from whoever Jen was working for at the time. I particularly enjoyed the rock-hard bright blue face-packs that left the three of them speechless, their eyes rolling meaningfully like frightened horses as I struggled to understand their wants – tea,

Nescafé, tissues, cotton wool – without them speaking and 'ruining' the mask, cracking them into furious Methuselahs.

And the endless, useless diets, too; every mouthful of nice, interesting non-diet food accompanied by the chant *'two minutes in the mouth, two inches on the hips'* and a massed rolling of those hyacinth eyes. We had calorie counters in every room and the only books apart from romances in the front room were diet fad books. My favourite, due to its need for a leap of faith equivalent to believing in the Virgin Birth was the Grapefruit Diet. If, apparently, you ate half a grapefruit (disgusting things) before a meal – all the fat in the food just dissolved! Cor, fantastic, eh? Oddly though, despite the kilos of tongue-shrivelling, acidic grapefruit Mum and Jen bolted before pork chops and mash, it didn't work. Shame, really, Mum used to say – *we must be doing it wrong, Jen love.*

The concept of exercise and eating in a balanced way was far too boring and potentially unfeminine due to its unpleasantly sporty possibilities to get a look in at our house. Femininity demanded a crazed illogical need for blind, cult-like rituals, rather than anything like reason or method. Men thought like that. Women had sensitivities, temperament, were swept by shuddering storms of emotion, wept at *Gone With the Wind* and would most definitely have run a frock up out of the old-gold Lister's velvet curtains in the front room if necessity and a dinner dance demanded.

Mum and Jen were – are – what's now called high maintenance, alright.

It all made them feel precious, cosseted – 'cherished', Mum's favourite word – and despite my lack of enthusiasm, it did leave me with what Jen always calls a 'beauty routine'. Without fail I remove make-up (though I hardly ever use it these days), wash face with cleanser, not any old soap, apply suitable grease, use sun block, brush hair with a Mason Pearson. Drunk or sober, stoned or straight, tired or not. Jen says she feels she at least managed to do that for me if nothing else; the despair in her tone is palpable.

So, then, between Mum and Jen and my paper round and Saturday car-wash service, we did for ourselves nicely, thank you. Nothing fancy, not much spare, the occasional package to the Costas for Mum with Liz in tow like a fag-happy dressmaker's dummy. Me and Jen stayed at home during the holidays, since it was considered a waste taking us abroad. But Mum was wonderful about the house, always clever with remnants and perfectly able to paint and decorate – though it required industrial-strength rubber gloves and huge scarves. And wrapping presents for birthdays or Christmas was her forté. She'd spend hours making foil paper chrysanthemums or sticking sequins onto the most trivial of gifts – at work, no leaving present or maternity offering was complete with Mrs Morgan's 'magic touch'. *'My magic touch – well, I don't like to blow my own trumpet but really – it's just a gesture, you know, just being nice, making things nice.'* You should have seen the carol singer's paper lantern she made me for the school concert one year. Mine was fantastic, a masterpiece in cardboard and metallic wrapping paper. Everyone else's was a wonky knock-up their mum or dad had done their best with. I was mortified. I should have been thrilled to bits – but I wasn't; it just made me more noticeable than ever, more sticky-out.

I just wanted to be like everyone else, you see. More than anything. I used to pray to Baby Jesus every night to make me like everyone else, not this cranky, black-browed kid who always said the wrong thing. He didn't answer me, by the way, even though in a fit of childish sympathy for His awful life (as I saw it, aged eleven) and having watched *The Nun's Story* that Sunday afternoon with Mum and Jen sobbing at Audrey Hepburn's impossible Sister Luke and even Liz setting her lumpy jaw and not making her normal cutting remarks, I – don't laugh – left a box of hankies with 'J' embroidered in the corner on the altar of St Peters after school. He wouldn't have had hankies, you see, in Palestine, back then. It wasn't fair, poor Jesus; no one got Him a useful present, just asked Him for stuff all the time. So I got Him hankies out of my pocket money. I can't imagine what the vicar thought when he found them labelled in my big childish italic scrawl: 'For Jesus, Love B'. That was as far as religion went for me personally after that. It's an interesting thing to study in a lazy way, but believe in God? The Christian God, or the Buddha, or Yahweh, or Allah? No, not really. As Liz would say, just another man trying to boss you about.

Still, when it came to our house, my school friends were green with envy. Mum loved playing hostess with doilied trays of biscuits and lemonade and the warm, pink-and-gold living room was a million miles away from their kid-ravaged, gerbil-stinky utilitarian houses. *You're so lucky*, they'd sigh. *Your mum's fantastic, like an actress or something, like on telly*, and I'd feel proud and pretend I didn't care about it at all, myself.

If only Mum would love me like she loved Jen, it would be perfect.

If only Dad hadn't left, it would have been perfect.

If only I'd been blonde, been buxom; if only Dad hadn't bequeathed me the Black Dog and his damned Welsh contrariness.

Chapter Three

I WASN'T UNHAPPY, you see; not at first. Certainly not when I was little and the world was all finger-painting and sucking my teddy's paws bald. I have lots of happy memories: the time I was asked to sing a song at nursery school and the only one I could do, for some unknown reason, was Lonnie Donegan's 'My Old Man's a Dustman'. I remember eating squares of cooking chocolate, Kake Brand, that tasted like chocolate-flavoured candle wax, the nursery school tortoise pissing on the table to the scatologically delighted squeals of us infants; I remember the smell of the cupboard under the stairs (old shoes and mice) and Mum's perfume – Blue Grass by Elizabeth Arden. I remember Dadda bringing me a toy panda one Christmas that was as big as myself and my doll Becky who I tortured horribly by lashing her with string to the gate and shooting sucker-tipped arrows at her whilst playing Cowboys and Indians. I remember being Red Feather, the courageous Indian Brave for weeks and saying '*how*' to people in what I thought was a fierce, warrior-like way. I was fine, just like any other child; every day a brand new wonder, every night a dreamless pleasure of untroubled sleep in my little bed with a family of ducks stencilled on the headboard.

Then slowly, I began to understand what adults were saying. Like a damaged film soundtrack where you hear snatches of things that tear into incomprehensible babble, then reappear, then fade again. Slowly the sounds, the words, the ideas expressed in those high-up conversations began to come together into sense and I started to see my place in the family, to understand that the world didn't revolve around me but that I was part of a bigger whole. Eventually, the gabble fine-tuned enough for me to realise that things weren't as they seemed and that I was not the unconditionally beloved baby I'd thought I was. I drifted into being not happy. Nothing definite, nothing you could quantify or dissect, just – I wasn't happy, like Jen was. She and Mum are mirror images of themselves, as the Girls now are of Jen and their Nana; everyone trots out the same comment they used to say about Mum and Jen '*ooh, more like sisters than mother and daughter*'. 'My bevy of blondes' that self-styled smoothie Eric wrote in a postscript to one of Jen's letters. Right. All that fair girliness drove me nuts, but I felt guilty too, as if in some inexplicable way I'd let them down by being myself. My father's daughter, dark-haired, heavy-browed, angular with 'moody' grey-green eyes and – spots.

Oh, you can laugh if you like. I mean, every teenager gets spots, it's comical, right? Not in our house it wasn't. Mum and Jen's complexions were always fine-grained, translucent, pinkly perfect as shells. The fact that I grew blackheads and pimples like crops of night-sprouting weeds was cause for, literally, shrieks of horror. It wasn't – you guessed it – *feminine* to be an awkward, acned teenager, there must be something wrong with me. Medically wrong. I got taken to the doctor's by Mum, who dabbed at her eyes in the surgery as if I'd got VD. I remember the doc's expression, it was partly fascinated by Mum and partly disbelieving anyone could make such a fuss about a few spots. But Mum wasn't going to be fobbed off with some *man* telling her what was or wasn't important to a woman, oh no. She went on and on, her face a mask of refined tragedy until he gave in and sent me to the Dermatology Department at the Infirmary. I was officially diseased.

I persuaded Mum not to go with me to these appointments, she didn't object too strongly. She hated hospitals because the slab-sided buildings were so ugly and smelt so awful. The overworked, unkempt docs were kindly but bemused as I tried hopelessly to explain my family's obsessive interest in appearances, but you could see they didn't get it. They'd just raise their wild eyebrows and do that catch-all doctorey '*Hmm, I see*' thing, while I blushed beet-red and muttered disjointedly about beauty care and femininity.

Then they put me on Tetracycline for a year. It was supposed to be the latest thing in acne cures, the big bomb. For twelve months I dutifully swallowed enough full-strength antibiotics to cure a small country of infection for a decade. I had no spots. I had no bloody innards either and fungal infections in every orifice. I looked like pressed cheese and felt like shit – wan, lethargic and depressed. I was the most biddable kid you've ever seen, I simply didn't have the energy to play up. But in those days, doctor – and your mum – knew best. It all combined, along with my cuckoo-darkness and mystifying lack of femininity to confirm my opinion that I was a freak.

I knew I was weird from the age of eleven or so. I knew it in a deep, cellular way that was as natural to me as breathing. I didn't try to be a rebel, rebellion was thrust on me; in fact, I hated it and rebelled on several occasions against being a rebel and tried as hard as I could to be normal. It didn't work – people sense an outsider like a dog-pack knows you're scared. It's atavistic, chemical; it's the tribe against the strange – or the stranger. School, from primary onwards, was a nightmare of not fitting in. I suppose I had what they now call 'school phobia' but then wasn't called anything except skiving. I dreaded every school morning and learned how to fake a temperature at will to get a day's breathing space. Not that it worked often, and when it did it only brought down Mum's wrath on my head for causing trouble. Now they have government directives against bullying; then it was dog eat dog and the devil take the hindmost. I remember one fat girl with puffy scarlet cheeks and slitty, bitch's eyes who stuck pins in my arms during sewing, then wept to the teacher that 'Billie Morgan give me a Chinese Burn, Miss, she 'urt me'; I got lines and detention for the umpteeth time and a ton-weight rep for being difficult and doing something called 'dumb insolence'. I still can't stand the sound of school bells, or the thought of school.

I think my 'weirdness' was taken for granted because from an early age I'd loved to draw and paint, to make mermaids out of felt and sequins, or 'sculptures' out of papier mâché painted with poster colours. I was Arty. This, to my mother, Jen and Liz, accounted for a lot of my apparent oddity, even though it was obvious to me I'd got at least some of it from Mum. She brushed this aside on the grounds that her famous magic touch was a sort of social fairy blessing and not in any way connected with the morbidity and uncomfortablness of actual Art. Nudes and things. Abstracts. Van Gogh – now, don't tell me *he* was all there, didn't you see the film with Kirk Douglas? No, my interest in 'all that' was firmly attributed to my dad, who liked to write poems and read books other than pulp thrillers, did his own picture framing and kept the family photo albums neat as a pin, everything stuck in properly with corners and labelled. I once caught Liz whispering an aside to Mum as they pored over the pictures of Mum in a daring two-piece bathing costume on the beach in Blackpool, or in a flame-coloured tulle formal and diamanté for the office Christmas do at the Burnsyke Hotel, that it was a pity Billy-boy hadn't been so neat-handed with his life as he'd been with them bloody pics – then she'd cawed her hoarse, choppy laugh, like a crow choking.

It took an enormous effort of will not to chuck a what-not at the old cow; only the thought of the uproar that would ensue prevented me. I could picture the scene so vividly I quailed. Because the flip side of Mum's soft womanliness was her – and Jen's, not to mention Liz's and probably Sweetie's – iron-hard, unforgiving temper if crossed. It was why I wasn't able to be happy, in the conventional sense; it was why I could never fully relax with them after I'd grown.

They never tolerated anything that caused 'upset', or 'made a scene', you see, and their outbursts were terrifyingly random. Sometimes I could venture a mild joke about a beauty product or Mum's beehive hair-do in one of her old pictures and they'd giggle and say oooh, I was awful; if I tried it the next day they'd round on me and say what a nasty piece of work I was. You could never tell. I expect it was hormonal, or to do with sexual frustration, but I was a kid, I didn't know about that stuff, I thought it was all my fault.

Their weapons were formidable, too; the iris-blue eyes grew steely, the painted pouts thinned to slashes and their round chins jutted like a bulldog's ready to bite. Sarcasm came next, lots of 'oh, and who does madam think she is' and 'So sorry, I thought this was my house, my mistake, obviously' or if it was a beating offence, it was a grab and wrestle for my ponytail to hold me by and a few hard slaps round the face, pointed nails curved inwards for best effect. Then there were the silences that could last literally for weeks and if I asked what was wrong it'd be 'If you don't know, it's not for me to tell you' and a gleam of tears along the averted eyes. They would taunt me with baby-noises if I cried; 'Nyah, nyah nyah, *cry-baby Bunting'* and Liz would ostentatiously go and put the kettle on, sighing deeply. My faults were picked over in voluptuous detail: my hands too big and bony, my breasts the 'wrong shape', my hair too coarse, my colouring suspicious (a 'touch of the tar brush' on Dad's side – thank God Jen was so fair), my expression too moody. They told me I was mentally unstable, that there was tuberculosis and madness in my father's family and that no man would ever be interested in me if I went round being so know-it-all. They said I had been the cause of my father's desertion (never explained satisfactorily, that one, but logic didn't enter into anything at our house) and my mother not remarrying (who'd have a woman saddled with a sullen brat like me?). Liz forced herself to admit she'd heard I was the talk of the street, if not Bradford, on account of my behaviour. They'd join together into a pastel-tinted Greek chorus that wailed in a discordant chant that I was born wrong, made wrong; I was blood, bone and gristle wrong, wrong, wrong.

But the worst thing they said, the thing that really fucked me up seems so trivial that I don't suppose anyone else would understand how devastating it was to me as a child. I'd be pottering about with my paints or something, everything would have the fragile film of apparent content stretched thin and taut over it, then I'd do something like spill my paint-water. Mum would furiously swab at it while I waited, frozen, brush in hand – then she'd say it.

'For God's sake, Billie, why do you always have to spoil things, *you can go off people, you know.*'

You can go off people, you know. Nothing – it's nothing, is it? Stupid, just a stupid saying, a silly…There it sticks in my head, a poison fish hook, a splinter, a spell. A wicked little incantation, neat and effective as a barb that killed trust in me stone dead because, if your mum can randomly stop loving you because you said or did something totally trivial, then what about the rest of the world? *They'd* stop loving you if you *breathed* wrong.

And nothing makes that feeling unsnag, nothing makes that terror diminish. *You can go off people, you know*. I know it in my bone marrow, in the cells of my body; I'll look in my friend's or my beloved's face and see the love vanish from their eyes, see indifference wash over them like a receding tide leaving a scoured emptiness behind it. Nothing I do or say will make it OK again…Dadda will never come back, *Dadda went off me.*

Was it me? Did he – oh God – did he leave because of me? Was Mum right? In my childish way did I do something that snapped the bond between us forever? What did I do to make Dadda go off me? Like all children, I lived in a self-absorbed little world where I believed that I was the cause and centre of everything. For years I'd cry myself to sleep in the dark (no night-light, they made you soft, Liz told Mum, who believed her) going over and over in my mind every word, every movement, every action I could remember regarding Dadda, to try and find the fatal flaw that had caused him to go.

I couldn't talk to Mum or even Jen about my terrible guilt and fear because 'that man' was of course a taboo subject. It brought on one of Mum's 'heads'. It was typical of me to 'bring it all up again'. I learnt to keep my mouth shut; physically, as well as mentally. A number of people have remarked that I keep my lips pressed together and don't do toothy smiles in pictures. Loosen up, they say, relax – big smile, now! But I can't. What might get out? So I dragged the burden of what I truly believed was the responsibility for Dadda going along behind me like a rucksack full of bricks.

Even now – yes, adult though I am, logical, analytic, all that crap – even now it prickles like nettle rash at the edges of my consciousness: *what did I do to make Dadda go? What did I do to make him go off me?*

Why did he never write, never call, never try to see me, ever again? As a kid it crucified me, that guillotine drop of abandonment. Not a birthday card, not a Christmas phone call, nothing. Every year I'd wait, not saying anything, hoping with all my heart, at the same time scolding myself under my breath for hoping, because when nothing came, it was worse if you'd hoped, half convinced yourself this was the birthday he'd write. If you'd hoped, looked for omens in things like the postie being ten minutes late, or it being a beautiful April day, or you'd got a good report from school, anything, the pain when nothing came was unbearable. Better to be hopeless, not to expect anything but disappointment. Then it wasn't so bad.

I used to write to him at first. I tried giving the letters to Mum to post, like I had done with my letters to Santa, but unlike then, Mum didn't smile indulgently, wink at Liz and say, *Of course, love, I'll post it from work, don't you worry.* She'd frown, then unfrown quickly in case of lines, but retain the clouded, angry gaze. If I persisted, she'd take the grubby envelope from me and tear it up, throwing the pieces in the bin while scolding me for being such a little show-off, always trying to get attention. In the end, I stopped trying but it killed me thinking Dadda was all alone somewhere, not knowing how I was, or that I hadn't forgotten him.

I couldn't stop thinking about it, it still haunts me. Did my dadda die, alone, thinking I didn't want to see or speak to him? Oh no, no, that's too awful to bear; Dadda, Dadda, I never stopped loving you, or thinking of you, or wishing we could be in the dining room together, with my namesake playing quietly on the record-player – maybe 'Stormy Weather', our favourite – doing some drawing or mending a broken picture frame, the light from the ruffled lamp pink and cosy, the gas fire flickering. Your blunt-fingered hands deft and sure, your breathing stopping and starting as you held your breath while you did a tricky bit of glueing or painting. Your deep, husky voice humming along to the tune and sometimes singing absently along '...*there's no sun up in the sky, stormy weather, since my man and I aren't together...*' Then pausing to listen properly, your head cocked, a lock of black hair falling over your broad forehead. '*Listen to that, Billie, beautiful voice, eh? Beautiful...Heartbreak in that voice, I tell you, real heartbreak...*'

Ah, ah, it still hurts me, even now, as I write this bloody, this... whatever it is: story? Confession? Diary? It hurts and tears are dropping on the keyboard as I pound the keys one-fingered, my heart swollen and sore.

I don't think Mum or Jen thought for a moment they were being cruel, or even nasty. They were too unthinking for that. They were just reacting. Their behaviour was reflex, knee jerk; like I said. If he didn't want them, then he couldn't have me. Tit for tat. Sorry, Bill Morgan, but you've made your bed, now lie on it. How could he want me, and not them, anyhow? They were the pretty maids all in a row – I was the changeling, the elf-child. It must have driven them mad with incomprehension. I became the scapegoat; so instinctively, they took their hurt, jealousy and rejection out on me, Dadda's living image.

I grew up believing that I was ugly, socially incompetent and utterly unattractive to the opposite sex. That I was unlovable. I never questioned this. I never fought against it. It was accepted fact in our house.

So, it's true I didn't lack for toys, art things, clothes or a nice house; I didn't lack an education or a hot dinner. My mum was admired by all and my sister the belle of Saltaire. There were kids I knew who had it real bad, beaten, abused, neglected, but not me. I had everything material a child could want, on a pretty china plate.

It was just that I had a big, roaring hole in my spirit; a maelstrom of pain and black rage that no love, no kindness, no admiration or compliment could ever assuage; it ripped like a blunt blade in my heart and left me raw inside; I had no shields, no barriers against other people's suffering, either, because if I felt like this just because my family didn't love me like they should have in an ideal world, what about those poor bastards out there who really had it bad? What must they be feeling? It was too terrible to contemplate and I felt it like it was my own flesh. Dadda's legacy, the Black Dog, howled like a demon beast in me until its feral cries almost deafened me.

That, in the end, was all I had of him, the thing he least wanted me to have. The curse of the Morgans. The hell-hound of depression, dark as night, unstoppable and always at my heels, its stinking breath hot on the back of my neck, its killing fangs snap, snap, snapping...

So when I was around eleven or so, as a kind of defence, I closed my face over it all, sealed it away, steadied my gaze and stood up straight, kept those lips firmly pressed together; looked at life dead on and swore no one would ever find my weakness, because weakness had destroyed my dadda and I was going to survive no matter what. I would make myself strong, I was a fighter. I was so good at this, that years later a guy I knew who was a counsellor commented – after a long night's dope-smoking and talk that he assumed would lead to bed, him being so sympathetic and all – that usually, people with my kind of 'challenging' background were very angry, confused people with low self-esteem; he was, he said, amazed at my tremendous strength and like, um, you know, resilience.

I was amazed at how thick he was and decided not to sleep with him after all. He never got why, either, and never understood what he'd said or why I was laughing so hard tears tracked down my cheeks and why I was still laughing when he picked up his shoulder bag and huffily strode out the door, poor sod.

Chapter Four

I STARTED TAKING DRUGS – other than antibiotics, that is – when I was about fourteen-and-a-half. Halfs mattered then, they meant you were nearly fifteen. Well, almost. Anyhow, I began with acid, those big pale-blue Sandoz tabs that you split into quarters. I didn't start with dope like most people, because I didn't smoke. Liz had put me off fags for life. Anyway, anyone who was anyone, all my mates at that time, dropped acid at the weekends and if you were really cool, during the week, too. You may gather I was hanging around with a bad crowd; or at least, that's what everyone said.

People like to say that, don't they? A bad crowd: drop-outs, weirdos and worst of all back then – motorcyclists. Bikers. The Wild Ones. Hells Angels. Sub-human Neanderthals who dope and ravish weeping maidens and carry them off strapped to their roaring machines to a life of unremitting sin in sleazy, untidy dens of filth and unwatered plants... Well, you could see why I was attracted to them.

Actually, at first I just hung out like any teenage goof at the record shop, lounging in what I fancied was a cool way round the listening booths – remember them? Those strange, smelly wall-mounted hoods not unlike those transparent phone bubbles in airports, only constructed out of plywood with silvered punchboard inside to give that modern acoustic look. There was a shelf for your handbag and you stood in the muffled stinkiness, leaning casually against the back wall, while your honest-to-God vinyl record of choice (for example, 'Lay Lady Lay' by Bob Dylan – rather racy that one, with its growled references to 'Lay across my big brass bed') was played for you from the counter.

Sometimes all your mates came crowding in with you, giggling and shoving, but I didn't like that, I thought it childish. I was big on 'childish', because obviously, at fourteen (and-a-half), I wasn't. *I* was a music fan. I bought singles and played them on my very own second-hand powder-blue and cream Dansette portable (the size of a small suitcase, believe me) record player. I kept my singles in a bizarre, gilt-wire object like a toast rack that I'd got at the jumble for a few pence due to it being a tad rusty.

I bought lots of singles, what happened to them, I wonder? All my pocket money went on them – those saucer-sized black disks of pure escapism, the warm plastic smell of them, the wisp of strange fluff that always gathered on the needle as it tracked relentlessly round the magic groove, the lurid neon paper covers...

A few older lads nibbled at the edges of our little troupe of go-go girls: me in the beige hand-me-down maxi coat and long parted-in-the-middle hair, the rest – Gillian, Mandy, Sue, Claire – in minis and knee-high stretch PVC boots. All of us smothered in make-up, frosted lips, chalky-blue eyeshadow with a brown socket line and white highlighter on the brow, heavy gobbets of black spit-cake mascara, reeking of cheap perfume like Aqua Manda or Kiku. These were my pre-drug friends, my childhood schoolie pals. Innocent, under the tarty slap. Still children.

I remember the afternoon, in the silvery-grey endlessness of a northern winter, when I'd pinned my hair up in a wildly sophisticated chignon and Dunc Peters, that bony, desirable Older Man of eighteen with his long shiny brown hair, hipster loons and appallingly odorous Afghan coat sidled into the booth where I was listening to something by Curved Air and murmured in my burning ear, *'You should let your hair flow free, man, don't be so uptight...'* And as I blushed redder still and felt a strange electric buzz run through my entire body at his musky closeness, he pulled all the pins from my hair one by one as the whole of the record shop crowd pretended not to look. He ran his dirty, nicotined fingers through my loosened hair, his bangles jangling, and I couldn't raise my eyes to return his doped-out, green-eyed gaze as his face came close to mine.

'Ur, yeah,' I croaked, my throat dry. Was he – no, it wasn't possible – God, was he going to kiss me? I mean, like, *me*? The freak? Surely he should be doing this with long-legged, feather-cut Gilly whose precocious bosom was a genuine marvel of nature. I wasn't, boys didn't…Not me, things like this didn't happen to me…Oh my *God*! What should I *do*?

'Hmmm, you look OK, nice. Wanna come to the Concord, maybe?' His sexy fat lips hovered millimetres from my cheek; his warm breath was untouched by toothpaste but beneath the nicotine-and-hash smell had a sweet, almost perfumed scent. It was pure sex. My heart pounded so hard I was sure he could hear it. The air was glutinous with patchouli and teen angst.

Did I want to be publicly squired to the Concord Café, the hippest and coolest low-down and dirty pothead's coffee house in town by Dunc, a genuine A1 hippie pin-up and snake-hipped heartbreaker of the first water? My trembling lips began to form the word *oh-yes-please* but then I stopped short.

Gilly, Sue and Co. were forbidden to enter the Concord on pain of terrible punishment from their parents, such as not being allowed out for a month or pocket money stoppage. I wasn't – well, nothing had actually been said but presumably if I'd been seen going in there, the dive of dives, all Hell would have broken loose. But I mean, *technically* I could…Loyalty won out. I'm big on loyalty. Only in those days, I wasn't so choosy about who I was loyal to; in this case, my honour was bound to the lasses. I felt a wave of Sister Luke-like nobility wash over me and I knew I was doing the decent thing. I forced myself to turn towards Dunc.

'C-can't. Me mates. I can't…'

He wasn't there. In one fluid movement he'd slithered across to the record racks and was deep in conversation with Malc Oulton and Barry Ferris – actual musicians who played at the Friday night dance with their band Genesis. Not the real, famous Genesis, obviously. The Bradford one with Ade Salter from Keighley singing: the one that played covers of Free and Led Zep, man, while we girls undulated round the church hall dance floor in what we thought was a hip, sexy way, but in fact made us look like dying squid.

I was gutted. My hands were shaking. I'd blown it totally. I'd turned down Dunc, *Dunc*. It was a bad dream. I'd never get a date in my whole life. No lad would ever ask me out, ever. My life was over.

'What did he say? Billie, Bill-*eee* – what did he *say*? The lasses pressed round me, the virgin martyr, their faces all bug-eyed and pink with incredulity.

I regarded them with the wan face of a broken woman. 'He asked me t'go t'Concord with him.'

The collective intake of breath was like a flock of geese hissing.

'No! No! He never! He never asked yer…And yer *hair*! See what he did t'yer hair! What did y'say, what?'

Plump little Sue, her figure bursting the buttons on her skinny-fit white silky shirt, American Tan thighs straining her mohair mini, her eyes like saucers, sighed heavily, and somewhat asthmatically. 'I thought he were goin' ter kiss you, right out – I did. Are you goin' with him, Billie? With…*Dunc*…'

'Don't be soft. Fellas like Dunc don't kiss girls like Billie, she's only a kid.' Gilly bridled, furious with envy.

That stung. 'Kid', indeed. 'As it happens, Gillian, I give him the brush off, he's not my type. He's so – so – obvious. Anyhow, how could I go when you lot can't? It wouldn't be fair.' I was flushed with righteousness.

Gilly looked at me, her eyes narrowed. 'If that's so, yer plain soft. I would've gone like a shot, any of us would, wouldn't we, lasses? Honest Billie, yer so *weird*. Yer livin' in a dreamworld or somethin', yer such a baby.'

And turning on her stack heel, she stomped off, shoulder bag swinging crossly.

'Yeah, honest, Billie – sometimes…' The others followed Gilly while I struggled not to burst into loud, hot sobs at this betrayal.

Sue put her pudgy, starfish paw with its bitten-to-the-quick nails on my arm. 'She don't mean it, Billie, she's just jealous 'cause he don't fancy her; come on, we'll go t' the Wimpy, eh? 'Ave a milkshake – a chocolate one, yer favourite. Come on, else she'll know she's upset yer…But, y'should 'ave gone with him, yer really should – I mean, when he took yer pins out, it were so romantic, honest…'

Six months later I was walking into the Public Bar of the Crown Hotel with five hundred trips and the best part of a handgun in bits in my Greek handwoven tote bag, grinning my head off and high as a kite.

Chapter
Five

I T WAS BROODING that finally tipped me over the edge into badness. Brooding – like Leckie always says, does no good at all. Makes you morbid. The devil makes work for idle…Well, idle brains or something, I suppose. Leckie, when she's inclined to dwell on anything negative, 'clears her mind', 'centres herself' and 'thinks beautiful thoughts'. If only I'd learnt that technique when I was fourteen, eh?

But I didn't know about the power of positive thinking then – in fact, I'm not exactly adept at it now, despite Leckie's exasperated coaching. No, I brooded about Dunc, about what the lasses – especially Gilly – had said, about what I considered their lack of the proper appreciation of my sacrifice. I brooded about the cruelty of the world, about how no one, but *no one* had ever, ever, ever felt as bad as I did now, it wasn't possible. I was unique in my suffering. I gazed at myself in the mirror trying to arrange my features into an expression of interesting melancholy but only succeeded in looking more sulky and heavy-browed than ever.

It was then I started writing a journal – not one of those poncey little pocket diaries with a centimetre of space per day – they're only fit for noting down the dates of your period. I had an A4 hardbacked notebook, with blue marbled covers and thin, ripply pages that I got at the discount stationers in town and I either wrote nothing for three days or did five hours solid whilst listening to 'Whole Lotta Love' again and again. I filled every page with my spiky italic writing (OK, yes, I do 'write big' as they used to say at school, but none the less) then I bought another one. Nothing and no one escaped the scorching breath of my scorn. Naturally, hiding them from Mum, who believed firmly in a parent's inalienable right to nosy round their child's every drawer, nook and cranny, was an operation of James Bond proportions involving loose floorboards and gaps behind the wardrobe.

I've still got them, those books, as I said, in the lock-box under my bed; very battered now, that flimsy paper friable and almost transparent, like dead insect's wings. I get them out and read them sometimes and wonder at how I've changed – and not changed.

And still I brooded. I brooded like a female Heathcliff as I walked to school, the wind wuthering round my hunched figure, whipping my hair into greasy elf-locks and setting cold fire to my cheeks; I brooded through assembly even when the hymn was 'Onward Christian Soldiers', which I liked, and still like a lot, not for its religious sentiments but for the chance to open your lungs and belt it out. I brooded until during break one Friday, as I drifted moodily round the icy playground ignoring the wastrel brats who foamed around me like a winter sea, Sue rushed up, wheezing as usual.

''Ere, 'ere, Billie – Bill-ee, guess, guess what? Guess, guess!'

'What?'

'*Guess!*'

'Dunno. *What?* What, what, what. What?'

'Gue...'

'Oh Su-oooo, for God's sake, honestly, what *is* it?'

Heavy asthmatic sigh and rolling of covertly mascared eyes. 'We're off t'Concord termorrer afternoon! We *are*. Gilly says she don't care. Says she's a nadult now an' she can do what she likes. Her parents are *getting a divorce*. They don't care what she does no more, they don't notice nothin' 'cause of 'em goin' at each other all the time 'cause her dad had an affair *with her mam's hairdresser* which, y'know, meks it worse, Gilly says, on account of her mam an' the hairdresser knowin' each other an' women outghta stick t'gether an'...So she says she's off t'Concord an' we all are too an' you can. Maybe Dunc'll be there...'

'Dunc? *Dunc*? Honest, Sue, I mean, *Dunc*? God, huh, who *cares*?'

'You do, Billie. Everyone knows that.'

'Oh – *Sue*. Oh, no I *don't*, I...'

'See yer termorrer, then, at eleven, by t'bus stop like usual. Shall y'wear yer maxi? I want to wear my red Christmas dress wi't buttons but it's that cold I dunno cause I'd 'ave ter wear a jumper an' that'd look *awful* so...Oh, if my mam sees me goin' in there, I'll get such what for!'

'Sue...'

'See yer!'

My fate was upon me then, in a beating of sleety wings and the salty music of the playground – the high-pitched moans of little boys being beaten senseless by other, bigger boys. I sighed heavily. The bell went and I trudged into double Maths with a suitable expression which caused that wizened old bitch Miss Carter to tell me to 'buck my ideas up'.

I did, but not how she meant. Throughout the impenetrable complications of numbers I dwelt on one thing alone: the thing that occupies ninety per cent of an average teenage girl's mind – clothes. I decided that if it was to be the Concord and the path to Hell lit by the lambent possibility of Dunc – not of course that I was interested – then, by God, whatever it took, I'd look the part. No one would be trendier or more with-it than me.

Certainly not *Gillian*.

That's how it started; I wanted to be more fashionable than poor old Gilly, whose parents did get a divorce and who after a brief spurt of furious rebellion got caught out with twins and married at seventeen to a complete twat from Shipley. What's she doing now, I wonder?

I did myself proud that Saturday. I wore my maxi-coat, and under it my new look – a long, black, hooded kaftan embroidered with chain-stitch flowers in primary colours round the hem, neck and sleeves. It had cost me the best part of my Christmas money and with it I wore a pair of ankle-strap round-toe suede wedgies that had, during the previous summer, been dusty pink but were now, rather wonkily, dyed black and had gone weirdly shiny and lacquered-looking. My wrists chimed with masses of Indian bangles and my neck was yoked in beads and pendants strung on thonging; I had a ring on every finger and one thumb. My hair, freshly washed in Boots Herbal shampoo, rippled in gleaming waves on either side of my Clearasil pale face. My eyebrows were plucked as bare as I dared and my eyes were gummy with stick khol. My lips were defiantly and modishly bare. I reeked of ylang-ylang. I was too much, y'know? *Oh* yeah.

I was fourteen, but I looked twenty – which, in view of my future life of depravity and vice, was very useful.

Chapter
Six

WE GOT AWAY with going unchecked to the Concord for about three Saturdays; then fate in the form of Sue's Auntie Betty intervened. She saw us – we were sat in a window seat like fools, though I was at the back, somewhat hidden – and she told. That Sunday morning the air was full of the sound of teenage girls weeping, protesting at how unfair it was and shopping each other.

Gilly was grounded for a month and her mother – according to gossip – was heard to scream at her dad that this was what a broken home was doing to her daughter, you bastard – comments that were heard right up the street. Sue was to be kept in too and so were the rest. I waited for my punishment in as martyred a way as I could muster, even going to the lengths of patting talc into my cheeks and rubbing the crusty remains of my eye-black round my eyes so they'd look hollow. All that happened was that Jen ticked me off for bad beauty habits that lead inevitably to enlarged pores, blackheads, tired skin and spinsterhood, while Liz muttered about consumption. I allowed myself to imagine I'd somehow, miraculously, got away with it.

Then Mum struck. After tea on the Sunday night as I was desultorily packing my satchel for school the next day – boom; she went straight into it without any warning.

'I hear,' this with a knowing glance in Liz and Jen's direction, 'I hear you and your little friends have been seen in that place in town, that Concord Café – what d'you say to that, Miss?'

'Dunno.' I maunged sulkily, frantically trying to think of a way out of this horror. The thought of being stuck in the house for a month with no 'privileges' like my records or TV made me feel sick. It was an eternity, a life sentence. A trickle of sweat ran down my back as I felt myself blushing furiously.

'You don't know. You. Don't. Know. Oh really? I think you'll find you know full well what I'm talking about, young lady – doesn't she, Jennifer? Well, is it right? Did you go to that – that *place*? I dread to think what people are saying – Mrs Letts was near tears on the phone and I can hardly blame her. What the neighbours must think, I cannot imagine, the shame of it. You're a disgrace to...'

'I didn't.'

'*What?*'

'I didn't go to — to that place, Mum. The others, not me. I went to the library, for some new art books – those ones, see? I never went to the Con – that place, honest. I went to the *library*, but Gilly...They went, not me.'

It was the first time in my life I had told my mum, my family, a direct, absolute, out-and-out lie. A big lie, a colossal, adult-type lie, in fact. It jumped out of my mouth whole and in one piece like a fat, croaking toad. Sure, I did have the books – one on Van Gogh, one on Art Nouveau – I'd run in and picked them up before I'd gone to the Concord. There they lay: big, plastic-covered alibis as I stood by the kitchen door and stuck my jaw out. Mum's mouth dropped open and for the first time ever she was robbed of speech. Jen gawped and Liz narrowed her nicotine eyes. Even poor old Sweetie panted nervously in her basket, her tartan-tied topknot quivering and her shiny blackberry nose whiffling in alarm.

And in that moment, as the kettle started its rising whistle and the washing-machine pounded away, in the warm, frilly gingham kitchen with the radio droning out golden oldies on 'Sing Something Simple', everything changed. I felt it in my body, as if a draught had crept into the room, putting the hairs up on my arms and making me blink. As if the devil had stirred my blood with his glittering claw and I'd been shivered into the future, into a whole other place in the world. I couldn't have named the feeling, I but I knew nothing would ever be the same again and I waited without breathing while Mum processed this new information.

'Well, I — well. I see. At the library. But...'

'The others, Mum. Not me. I mean, I'm sorry, I...'

Mum swallowed like a python gagging on a baby goat and bridled furiously. 'No, no, if this is true — yes, yes, *obviously* it is, it's not you has to be sorry — *this* time, at any rate. Oh, those gossiping old cats, Liz – anything to get a dig in at me, it's the old green-eyed monster, it really is...No, I'm not finished with you yet, Madam...'

And she gave me the works regarding obedience, decency, goings-on, how Jen had never been such a torment to her, how I took after my father, how I'd be the death of her, how I dressed like a drop-out and was determined to make myself ugly and I let the whole family down.

Liz didn't smile with her mouth, but I knew she was grinning like a crocodile inside. Jen's flower-face was pink with concern and sorrow, especially about the ugly bit.

But I didn't care – I'd won; they were straights, they were squares, what did they know anyway? From the lofty heights of my coolness I looked down at their sad little lives and felt a sweet pity for them (but not Liz). I was an artist, I was going to go to art school, I had to be free to live my crazy life to the full, to *be*, you know, to *experience* things. Otherwise, how would I ever be a great painter, like Vincent? *He* didn't let his mum dictate to him about where he could go and what time he had to be in – he lived his life to the full, come what may. Anyway, they didn't know the Concord crowd like I did – how could they? They were so scared of people who looked different, who thought differently they'd never even listen if we tried to explain it all to them. Mum and Jen and Liz. Pathetic, really.

I never told my mother the truth again. I felt – and I still feel, if I'm honest – I was saving her and Jen from things that would only upset them; that would frighten and confuse them.

Maybe I was right to shield them – I'll never know. Maybe I was dead wrong and my lie had opened Pandora's Box and all the flittery badnesses, the whining insect sins, the fuzzy, moth-heavy mistakes were fluttering round my head in a dusty swirl, sucking into my lungs, laying their eggs in my blood, their grubs and maggots crawling through my veins, filling me with an unsatisfiable itch.

Bad blood; that was me, I thought dramatically, with an inner smirk of self-satisfaction. The bad seed. Bone bad, moon bad: I wanted everything bad and crazy and cool. I wanted to strut my stuff at the hippest love-ins, happenings, rock shows and superstar parties. I wanted to be the one-and-only freaky-deaky far-out foxy baby Venus glittering in my satin and rags. Swinging hipsters would kiss my jewelled hand and murmur my name with cool reverence. I'd be the Face of Faces, the chick that men wanted to ball and women wanted to be. Oh, every kind of bad and fascinating thing going – I wanted it, and I wanted it *straightaway*.

Chapter Seven

I ACTUALLY WENT OUT with Dunc for a while. Well, I say 'went out', but all that meant was we both went to the Concord and the record shop, and to see faux-Genesis at their church hall residency where he'd slope off into the dark to skin up with his muso mates, leaving me – a mere chick – to fend for myself. As the weather got nicer, we went for walks in Peel Park. Wow. It was hardly a deathless romance and in relationship terms it meant snogging behind various buildings and under bushes. On one memorable occasion I remember nearly having an epi when his claggy chewing gum fell into my mouth during a particularly intense kiss.

Dunc wasn't the talking kind, really, which was a signal disappointment. I wanted to talk and talk and talk about everything – especially art – and he wanted to fuck me. Or anyone, really, it wasn't personal. So as I rabbited on about Alphonse Mucha or Aubrey Beardsley he tried manfully to get my knickers off, without success. At first, knowing no better, I thought he was the strong, silent type. I worried that he might have a mighty brain whirring away behind his normally stoned, slightly dense but deeply sexy face and that I was doing him dreadful harm by not letting him have his way with me. Several times he indicated that fellas suffered terrible pain in the lower regions if they couldn't ball the chick of their choice at will, that I was nothing but a cock-tease and oughta be, like, more co-operative.

But I wasn't co-operative and I was a virgin; some instinct told me I didn't want to Do It the first time with Dunc, so guiltily, I let him suffer. Poor Dunc, he was only a lad, even though I thought him impossibly worldly and knowledgeable, there was nothing in his boy's head at all – well, there was no room, it was full of hormones.

But I was moving up the social ladder fast. I began to see less and less of Gilly, Sue and the lasses; they had been thoroughly cowed by their punishment and stuck to the excruciatingly safe Youthie and the Teen Disc Club held on Friday nights by the Methodist Youth Group. Sue tried to woo me back to the fold a couple of times, saying I was getting a bad reputation (yes! result!) and people were talking, but I didn't care.

Mum had decided after that fateful Sunday evening, that if I wasn't bothered about how I looked, neither was she. I was a living disgrace, but then, what could she expect with a father like mine? She washed her hands of me, she said, in regard to where I went and who I was with, as long as I was home by whatever time she considered fit and didn't show her up in our street or Get Into Trouble. If I did Get Into Trouble, by the way, I'd be out on my ear and could expect no help from her, thank you. After all, she had Jen to consider, and she wasn't going to waste her precious time arguing with a stroppy madam like me about every little thing. Her nerves wouldn't stand it – the doctor had offered her tranquillisers when she'd gone last time and she'd told him how I went on; Mrs Morgan, he'd said, Mrs Morgan, you're not strong, no one would blame you if you needed a bit of help to calm down – but she'd refused, proudly. I was the cross she had to bear, apparently, and she constantly reiterated that nothing I did anymore would surprise her.

It would have, it would have sent her into screaming fits, but she never knew about it. Like the five hundred trips and the gun thing; now, as I look back, I cringe at my stupidity, but then – it was cool, OK?

I was sat in the Concord, sipping a soapy, frothy coffee, waiting for some new Concord pals of mine, Cathy and Nikki, when Jakey Reynolds, bad boy *extraordinaire* and thoroughly disreputable sleaze, slid into the seat opposite me, his weaselly face twitching with malice.

'Now then.'

I looked up uncertainly. Jakey was far above me in the strict pecking order of the café and wouldn't normally have exchanged so much as a nod with the likes of me. Also, I didn't like him – he was skinny, undersized and peaky-looking, almost albino and had wet, sloppy lips. But none the less, he was a mover and shaker, so I kept my face blank, a trick that has stood me in good stead over the years.

'Yeah. Uh, hi.' I replied with as much nonchalant *froideur* as I could muster.

'You know Sam, dontcha?' he rubbed his corpsy hands together twitchily, his lank, whitish hair falling over his face.

'Yeah, I mean, I know him by sight, y'know. I don't, like, y'know, know him to talk...'

'Yeah, yeah, but y'know him, right?'

'Yeah.'

'Wanna do us a favour, then? Tek this to him, he'll be up at the Crown, in the Public, an' say how as I sent it him, and this'll mek it right, right? 'Ere, there's a trip in it fer you if yer'll do it – 'ere, I'll break it for yer, just 'ave the half, I don't want yer wanderin' off all ovver or nowt. Go on, tek it, get it down yer neck like a good little lass.'

I swallowed the half tab without blinking. I couldn't have done otherwise, everyone was covertly watching our conversation. Part of my brain reminded me Cathy and Nikki were on their way, but after what had happened about Dunc and the lasses that long-ago and far-away day, I wasn't quite so rigid about things. They could have the remaining quarters anyway, and we'd all go off giggling round town together.

Jakey slid a plastic carrier bag containing something lumpy and heavy under the table to me and I stuffed it in my shoulder bag.

He smiled, his teeth yellow and tiny, like rats' teeth. I knew I was doing something foolish, if not very stupid, but I felt like a dreamer caught in treacle, struggling to get clear but strangely weak.

'What is it? What's in the...'

'Shut up, shh, doan want the whole café ter hear, do we? It's nothin'. Just a few trips, y'know, an' a broken — a broken — well, it's a busted up old pistol, nothin', just a bit o' fun. Sammy-boy collects stuff like that, it's a present, like. He'll be happy ter see yer, he will, happy as owt'.

'But aren't guns illega...'

'Not busted ones. No, not in bits, like — come on, you wanna be a sport, don't yer? Yer won't get no hassle, no one knows yer face, see? No one's gonna look twice at yer, I swear...'Ere, you an' them chickies you hang round wi – wanna come ter a party tonight? Up at Fred's? Yeah, you can come – say I said yer could – yeah? You get off now, an' yeah, yeah, I'll tell ter yer pals you'll be back in a bit – wi' summat for 'em, eh? Eh?'

He winked. A party at Fred's – the ultimate. We'd been scheming for weeks to get an invite to one of beautiful Fred's weekly psychedelic freak-outs in his legendary pad up Manningham and here it was, handed to me on a plate. Just wait until Cath and Nik heard this, I'd be Queen For A Day.

Proud of my maturity and with the drug very faintly beginning to twinkle round my system, I strolled up to The Crown where Sam was indeed very glad to see me.

It made my rep; I was the chick who took the biggest stash – plus a *gun* – in town up to the biggest, most connected dealer in Yorkshire and smiling bold as you like, handed it over bang in front of everyone. It was official; young I might be, but I had brass neck. I was one ballsy chick. I was safe, I was made.

Re-reading this, I suppose if you're a stranger to the drug scene and get your information about the nation's chemical hobbies from the newspapers or the 'serious' programmes on the goggle-box, my fall from grace might sound a bit weird. Unlikely, even. I mean there I was breathlessly making my debut into alternative society and within weeks, whoops-a-daisy, I was a 'drug-runner' as they say in the *Daily Mail*. Well, sorry, but in real life, that's how it is. Random. You just happen to be in the wrong/right place at the wrong/right time and you get lucky/unlucky.

The fact that I had no fucking idea what I was doing, who scruffy, spaced-out Sam really was, or that the gun was a real, actual gun when assembled didn't come into it. The thought that if I had been stopped by the police – and Sam and Jakey were usually under DS surveillance – I would have done serious Borstal time at least and had my whole life, and my family's lives, ripped to bits by the Social Services didn't enter my tiny, acid-fried brain. Nor did I even begin to understand that I would never have been able to return to Bradford in my life after shopping – and I would have – a major player in the local drugs war.

I was innocent, you see. Not of the crime itself, obviously, but in myself. Jakey saw that and it was useful to him. Under the kaftan and the kohl was a child desperate for acceptance and he smelt it. I'd have done just about anything to get in with the In Crowd and he knew it, he'd seen it many, many times before, of course. So I was the perfect mule, while I lasted. And when I was banged up, or nodding out or just too well known a face, there were plenty more where I came from.

But it was that innocence that protected me. Like the Fool in the Tarot, I wandered about tra-la-la-ing to myself with never an inkling about how dangerous stuff was. I was cocooned in ignorance and too short-sighted to know I was lollygagging around on the brink of the abyss. I had the idiot's unfounded confidence and I was plain old lucky. Others I knew from that time weren't; sometimes, when I'm sentimental, I light a candle for them in my window. Maybe their lost souls will see the flickering light and feel comforted that someone remembers them not as fucked-up wasters, or drug death statistics, but as children who weren't taught the rules, who lost everything in a game they weren't up to playing, who died even before they got a good taste of life.

But not me. I survived everything.

Chapter Eight

THE PROBLEM IS, as I read back, it all sounds a bit glam and interesting in a yahoo druggie kind of way; like those bloody awful films about the seventies. Lots of glitter, silver stars and black eye make-up, girls in floaty smock dresses flipping their long untrimmed blonde hair in watercolour landscapes and smiling wistfully with glossy lips. Lots of living the dream, man.

It wasn't all that fabulous, let me assure you. In fact after the first big thrill of thumbing my nose at Mum and being, like, er, wild and free, I began to see the darker side of hippiedom.

People nowadays, after watching the TV programmes where jeering young celebs get ironic about the fashions and the music and seeing those rock'n'roll movies, think hippies were harmless love and peace freaks. Well, they weren't. They were just people, with all the mental dross and baggage that people have and all the stinking attitudes of the time – especially towards women. Like punk and Goth and every other youth movement, for most people it was a fashion, not a cause. A way of separating yourself from your parents' generation. That's all, nothing more, nothing deep.

I found that out quick enough. Oh, there was a lot of guff spouted at Fred's weekly love-ins about freedom and how sex was a natural, beautiful thing, baby – and you can guess why. No one used condoms, *ever*, it wasn't cool, it 'spoiled things', and no girl could ever possibly carry them because only prostitutes did that. So unless you were on the Pill…Not to mention the epidemics of clap, crabs and NSU that swept like plagues through the chick-sharing in-crowd.

In fact, the Pill didn't set women free, it set the lads free. It meant they never had to worry about getting some chick up the duff again; as far as they were concerned it was the chick's responsibility. They never asked if you were on it, either, they assumed you were, mostly because in those days no one talked about that sort of thing. Stuff like that was embarrassing.

I realise this vision of loon-clad hipsters too mortified to talk about anything real clashes with the rosy-tinted nostalgia for a lost Golden Age currently so in vogue. There's a sort of hip mythology about counter-culture Aquarians, their hair flowing as freely as their ideas, all in tune with nature and living in the Now, no barriers, baby, no regrets. But it wasn't a Golden Age, unless, I suppose, you were beautiful, wealthy and lived in Swinging London, none of which applied to the vast majority of the country. As usual. Nothing changes, does it?

But one thing bugged me more than anything else. Hippies didn't stick together, they weren't loyal to their mates. If it came down, it was every freak for himself. There were a lot of predators drifting through the crowd, too, out for what they could get despite wearing the Love Generation uniform. As a girl, you had to be careful; we all knew that, but again, rape was something no one mentioned. Now they call that sort of thing date-rape, as if that makes it not so bad.

It happened to me, along with nearly all the women I knew at that time. At some point or other, you'd get into a situation – and to use the slang of the time, wham, bam, thank you, ma'am. I was raped by a man I knew vaguely called Steveo; the bastard, may he rot in hell.

It's not much of a story; like one of those endless, whinging folk ballads, it's been repeated over and over down the centuries, you just change the frocks and the drugs to fit the times. Girl gets careless, girl gets drunk or stoned, girl gets raped.

In my case, it was acid that proved my undoing, as usual. I was in The Crown, tripping. I was sixteen and in my foundation year at art school living the art student life to the full and happily off my bonce listening to the chemically improved sounds of 'Walk on the Wild Side' (which I still can't listen to properly without that trippy little squeeze in my chest). The music wavered in and out of phase, embroidering the air with three dimensional curlicues of light and up strolled good-looking, long-haired

Steveo, his Liberty-print voile shirt open to the waist, a tangled skein of love-beads bouncing off his smooth brown chest and his skin-tight, button-fly flares grazing the ground round his silver-sprayed baseball boots. When he smiled at me, I smiled back gormlessly, when he sat next to me, I grooved on the smell of patchouli, incense and fresh sweat that fluttered from him in pastel wreaths like tattered silk scarves.

I was whacked. Out of it. Solid gone. Anyone could see that, everyone in the pub knew it, after all I was the Acid Chick, wasn't I? I was known for my conspicuous consumption of those pale-blue pills. Only, no one knew that I never had more than a half, that really, I was faking how much I took to look cool, to look *grown-up*. But yeah, I'd had my half, it was strong gear and I was susceptible. That was a fact.

So, anyway, no one said a dicky-bird when Steveo – who everyone knew was a one-man chick-hammer and who literally notched up his kills on his bedpost, snick, snick, snick – made like he was worried about a poor little thing like me in that condition; why, he'd take me home, make sure I was alright – but we'd just have to stop at his flat first so he could pick something up…

When we got there he locked the door and beat me, to make me pliable. Then he fucked me.

Steveo punching me, hitting me in the stomach where it wouldn't show. Me falling onto the filthy bed, winded, gasping, as the drug fractured the streetlight through the old sash window into shattered prisms. Him grasping me by the throat as I felt my heart bulging, pounding and I felt my face swelling like a cartoon character's, my eyes squeezing out of their sockets. Him pushing, pushing into my dryness, my skin tearing in a rip of fire. My head banging on the headboard, his hands sharp as pincers, twisting my nipples; pain transmuted into sounds and the stink of his unwashed dick gagging and foul as decay. Him with his head between my legs, his unshaven face rasping me bloody. Him telling me what a fantastic lover he was, how I should be grateful, how women begged him for it as he ate me and the remembrance of a picture from one of my art books – an Art Nouveau jewel, the ivory torso of a woman emerging from being devoured by a great insect – swelled in my head…The sound of his laughter and the last thing he said to me – you'll be ruined for other men now you've been with me, you loved it, didn't you, you slag.

Then he threw me out. Snick, went his big old clasp knife against the serrated edge of his bedhead. He threw me out like a piece of garbage and all I remember is a confused acid memory of looming hallways and the brilliant luminescence of the lichen on the stone steps I fell down. And the sound, curdled air, of his insults and his laughter as I was on my hands and knees on the gravel drive in the rain. After that, nothing.

I came to in the park, freezing cold, my make-up all over my face, shaking uncontrollably, big bruises on my throat where he'd held me down and my eyes all bloodshot. I couldn't walk or speak properly for a week. I told, or rather, croaked to Mum that I had a terrible cold and sore throat and I wore a long crepe scarf wound fashionably Isadora-style round my neck until the marks faded. Mum never questioned me and it was just another lie. I'm just eternally grateful I didn't either catch on or catch anything; I think I'd have killed myself if either of those things had happened.

And everyone knew about it. He told everyone. Joked about it. Boasted about how he'd balled Miss High-And-Mighty Billie Morgan. The lads had a myth in those days – if you forced a lass who wasn't a virgin, it wasn't rape, and I'd finally lost my virginity to a sweet, rather dim French exchange student with deep-set brown eyes and a mouth made of smiles that summer. It had been nice, it had been right, a good, sunny memory full of laughter and kisses and I cried sentimentally when Xavier went home to Paris, vowing his eternal love in letters that petered out mildly as the leaves started to turn gold.

Now that pretty memory was overlaid with the thick, tarry stamp of Steveo who thought what he'd done was a hoot, a real laugh. I saw him in the pub a while later and I saw the fucker smirk and nudge one of his cronies. Rage blossomed in my heart as I stood there, long tremors shaking my legs and hands, my belly roiling; fury wailed up out of those dark, hidden places in my soul and I thought about killing him. Not just hypothetically, but actually; about stabbing him to death with his own knife, his dirty, copper-stinking blood soaking my hands, the look of disbelief on his handsome face, the soaring, singing beauty of revenge. I wanted to hurt him so badly he would beg my forgiveness as he crawled abject and destroyed on his broken knees and went away, or died, or just was gone, gone, gone off the face of the earth forever, and ever and…

But I did none of those things because I was young and without protection. Without tribe, without family or gang-brothers to fight for me, and I promised myself I'd find my own tribe, and nothing like this would ever happen to me again. So I threw a drink over Steveo as he sat there grinning, it was all I could manage because I was too furious to speak. He was outraged. And so was everyone else; making a scene, causing a fuss, it wasn't on. It wasn't *cool*.

I learnt a number of things from that experience.

I learnt that you can never trust a hippie; they're in it for themselves and they've got no honour. I was done with them, finished.

I learnt that I had a black streak of temper in me that I could barely control, that it felt like a weapon and stank of death and that when the fit was on me, I'd do and say anything, hurt anyone, hurt myself and that afterwards, I felt as scoured out as a dead shell washed by a thousand tides and all I wanted to do was puke. I learnt to wait for the crushing self-hatred that followed the blood-red release; the trembling, hopeless belly-crawling disgust with myself that took days to recede while I swore I'd never, ever lose my rag again.

And from that lesson, I decided not to take acid anymore, or to smoke too much dope, snort too much whizz, drink too much or put anything into me that caused me to lose control.

But lessons are easy to invent and sometimes, as I found out, very hard to do, especially when it came to whizz – not coke, the rich man's toy, but cheap, brutal Billy Whizz, the only drug I've ever really loved. Oh, that feeling when those coarse, crushed crystals shove you into the light, it's like being God on a rocket, like being full of bright, scintillating frosted stars, like feeling you could do anything, make anything, pull down the universe and dance on the broken shards. It's a proper drug, a drug that makes you think you're more than yourself, full of hot blood and boundless confidence, beautiful and clever and witty: not something that turns you into a grinning, half-asleep vegetable or a useless, whinging nodder begging beside the cash point, despised by everyone who pretends not to see you. I know, I know, whizz robs your body of years, of health and eventually, robs you of your reason; turns you into a shrivelled-up, desiccated, liverless mummy with rotting brown stumps of teeth ground down to the gumline, stinking breath and a brain that can't hold a thought for longer than two seconds, but when you're young and someone at a party says *Here, help yourself*, the future isn't exactly on your mind...

I fought hard not to become a speed-freak, not to be a waster or a user, to try and live honourably and to get control of myself and I succeeded, but that battle wound me up tight, tight, tight and no amount of lavender bubble bath or bloody yoga could ever make me ease that tension. It's there for a purpose. It's my shield, my defence system, my comfort.

Also, I learnt not to tell anyone about the rape; obviously, back then, there were no Rape Crisis Centres, or Helplines, or counselling. If you went to the coppers they treated you like a sub-human whore. Like as not, even your family would blame you and many's the fiancé who broke off the engagement after his tearful bride-to-be 'fessed up her dark secret in a moment of loving weakness. But times change and eventually, I told Leckie, Micky and Johnjo.

I told Leckie a couple of years ago, after we'd been out for a meal and I'd – against my rule – had a couple of glasses of wine. We were at her flat. She cried. God bless her soft little heart, I loved her for that, for her feeling it for me. She wept for me as I'd never let myself weep for that wronged girl, for myself. She hugged me – and I'm not a big hugger, but I hugged her warm, scented softness back without reserve – and she said all kinds of things about men being bastards and how brave I was and how much she admired me.

I made her tea as she gulped and bubbled and blew her nose on a tissue printed with gold cupids. I tried to tell her I didn't hate men, or anyone really, because hating a whole swathe of people because a few of them are rotten is pointless and takes too much energy. I mean, people are sound, or they're unsound, right? Gender, race, religion, that's all bollocks, really. Sound, or unsound, that's all there is. She laughed a bit at that, said I was awful, a dreadful old biker chick, and I laughed too, but it's true, really. I got it from them, from the gang, that minor philosophy, and I stick to it because I think it's a good way to live.

Then I told her how I'd taken the thing Steveo had done to me and cut it out of myself, because under no circumstances did I want that fucker to have power over me. If I'd let him scar me with what he'd done, he'd have won. And he wasn't going to win, end of story. It was what I told myself, over and over. My mantra.

Then she cried again and said I was a real example and I couldn't make her understand I didn't think like this out of bravery, or strength, it was out of fear.

I was so afraid, you see. So mortally, horribly afraid that if I let Steveo win, if I got addicted to the misandry and bitterness that beckoned to me with their withered, scraggy claws, I'd never be real again, *I'd just be the rape*. Nothing else. Everything I did would be defined by that act. I'd never be happy, or loved, or love anyone, ever again. My life would pivot sickeningly on that one horrible thing forever.

It scared me stiff, I'd seen it happen to girls I knew and as I got older I saw women who sat in the unhealing sore of their victimhood and fulfilled nothing but the prophecy of their brutalisation and the pitiful, cruel self-hatred it brought with it. I was too much of a coward for that. I wanted to live so much, to travel, to see everything, to be alive. Like Frida Kahlo said on her deathbed – *Viva la Vida*. I wanted life too much; I wanted to be somebody.

Viva la Vida. God, it makes me laugh now. *Viva la* fucking *Vida*. Long live Life.

I told Leckie about the rape, and what I'd done to repair myself, but I didn't tell her everything, because it's only lately, after all that's happened, that I can admit to myself the whole truth. Because I may as well, mayn't I? Jesus, I can hardly bear to put it down, my hand is hovering over the keyboard as if some part of my mind can't let this come out. As if by keeping it in I'll be safe – no – I'll be whole. But I'm not whole. There's a bit of me gone forever, the bit I cut out. Not my 'purity' or any of that drivel, no, it's to do with flashbacks, it's to do with not forgetting even when you've willed yourself to forget for years. It comes back when you don't expect it; or when you want it to least. Like herpes. Like a recurrent virus. A relapsing fever of the spirit.

Sometimes, not always, but sometimes, when I'm having sex, making love, fucking, call it what you like, what's actually going on gets imprinted with those older, malevolent images. As if there were two films running at once. In one film, it's a perfectly normal man and woman – me and whoever – doing what men and women do, then it's not. A dark, chaotic set of visions, feelings, smells, noises gets superimposed. I become terrified, panic-stricken. I want to scream and hit the man I'm with, force him off me, away from me. I want to run and hide, to get away from the juddering swoop of memories that rip through the present from the buried past.

I didn't tell Leckie, or anyone else, that bit.

I told my husband about the rest, though, like a silly cow. My young, innocent, loving husband, Micky. Oh yes, I've been married, properly, with a certificate and everything. I told him after we'd been married a few weeks, in a foolish moment, like one of those abandoned fiancées. I let my guard down, since we were so in love. I confided in him as I lay wrapped in his strong arms in our big, battered old mahogany bed on the lumpy mattress under the smart, new-fashioned duvet we'd got as a wedding present and the icy moon shone in the deep window. I told him and with a sickening lurch in my stomach, I felt the warmth leave his embrace like the cold drop in a summer's night.

I shouldn't have said anything, he didn't know what to do. There was nothing in his life of *Boy's Own* adventures and fun with the lads that had prepared him to deal with the knowledge that his new bride had been violated whilst on drugs at the age of sixteen and that no one even tried to help her. And that the man who'd done it was walking free somewhere and had probably done it to other girls and that this was possible, and there was nothing he could do about it, no one to fight. Just ghosts, dancing and jeering as he swung at them blind with frustration and anger. Just ghosts in the moonlight. Poor Micky.

Johnjo took it better, but then, we weren't kids anymore and times had changed. He just held me closer and rubbed my head with his big, callused knuckles while I talked. I knew what he felt and I knew he'd never say or do more than that rare gesture of tenderness. We're not married; he is, to someone else. Has been for years, he's got a grown-up daughter. Leckie calls him my 'outside cat', you know, not tame, like Gheng and Cairo. Johnjo's the cat that walks by himself, the feral cat you leave food for by the door, that once in a while lets you rub his scruffy, handsome, wild head, then saunters off, without a backwards glance. Johnjo comes and goes when he likes and it's what I like. No strings, no attachments, no pain. Just sometimes, comfort and someone to sleep with through the night. No pain, you see, no more pain, I can't do that anymore. In the twenty-five-odd years I've known Johnjo, as a pal, then as a lover, he's never said he loves me, or that I'm pretty, or that he's bothered about me. But he always comes back, we always talk through the night, we care about each other, in our way. We have the past, you see, we have a lifetime of memories, of shared laughter, of disbelief at our own youth and foolishness back then, all those years ago, when I was married to Micky and he and Johnjo were prospects.

Me and Johnjo have the Devil's Own.

Chapter Nine

DUSTY MILLER STARTED it. He was doing tech drawing at the college, and I knew him a bit through some mates, so when he offered me a lift home on the back of his Bonneville, I said, sure, why not? I was seventeen, at the art school and up for just about any new experience.

I didn't fancy him or anything, he was a blocky-headed, tow-haired lad with a nice smile and one of those old sheepskin flying jackets I'd always wanted. He was a mate. I always had lots of male mates, I got on with lads at that level very well. More so than I did with girls, who I still didn't quite feel at ease with; sure, I wished I had a fab best pal with whom I could share my thoughts, giggle and always rely on (I'd read *Bunty Magazine for Girls* a lot when I was very young, it was formative) but the actuality of the cliquy, bitchy, intensely competitive lasses I knew who hid their brutal drive under fluffy jumpers and googly eyelash-batting seemed a smooth wall built to repel outsiders like me. I seemed constitutionally unable to do the simpering thing most men seemed to want. Secretly, I called girls like that 'barracudas' – all slim, silvery and attractive with big round eyes on the outside and predatory on the inside. Big teeth. Snapping jaws. A quick side swipe in the canteen and whoops! You were missing a big lump out of your confidence while they swayed smoothly to the counter and wriggled at some drooling bloke who would pay for their tea and bun. Ouch.

Anyway, fortunately (or unfortunately – if I'd had a skirt on, I might be a nice hausfrau with a brood of kids living in a tidy little house in

Bingley now), I had my jeans on that fateful day, and you could ride a motorbike without a helmet then. I'd never been on a bike before, though someone's uncle had once taken me round the block on the back of his moped when I was little and I'd enjoyed it so much and got so over-excited begging for more rides that I'd been sent to bed in disgrace. Had that homely moped ride sown the seeds of my eventual downfall into ganglife and goings-on? Any mothers reading this take note: letting your darlings have a quick twirl on a 50cc leads inevitably to Sin and Ruin, I'm living proof.

Dusty assumed an expression of hard-nosed rebellion and gunned the engine in a fair imitation of Marlon Brando in *The Wild Ones* and I swung my leg over the seat and scootched in behind him, fumbling to hook my stack heels on the back foot pegs he'd kicked down for me.

In that moment of seamless happiness, the smell of his sheepskin jacket mingling with engine oil and greasy denim, the liberating joy of being astride a machine that would carry you like Odin's eight-legged horse in a whirl of noise and disapproving stares from straight folk, was beyond my wildest dream. I knew right then and there I was destined to be a Greaser.

'Ere, you keep your 'ead level with mine an' don't fuckin' wriggle, right?' Dusty yelled.

'Righ...'

My reply was lost as we set off, me nearly falling off the back and Dusty nearly knocking down the Head of College who happened to walk out of the side door as we thudded off in a cloud of summer dust.

It was love at first ride, honest to God. I can still feel the sheer bliss of it. How brilliant it was, how *real* I felt as we chugged out of town towards home. I hugged his teddy-bear back and blinked the wind-tears from my eyes as we swooped round corners and passed cars, their drivers glaring at us.

At the top of our road – I dare not let Mum see me on a *motorbike*, with the likes of Dusty, whose sprawling family of hunky blond brothers was the talk of the neighbourhood – I dismounted awkwardly, hopping madly on one leg while struggling to pull the other leg over the seat.

My knees were wobbly from gripping the bike and my cheeks tingling from the wind and the sandy Bradford dust it carried. I felt *wonderful*.

Exhilarated, excited, every cell of my body jumping. I felt somehow as if I'd been set free.

'Thought you ad'nt bin on a bike before?' Dusty pushed his goggles up, revealing how gloriously dirty the rest of his face was in comparison to the space they'd protected, and let the Bonnie idle, grinning at me as I stood there, dazed.

'I 'aven't.'

'Well, you're a good pillion, then, a natural. Wanna lift in termorrow?'

'Yeah, ever so, can I — will yer, I'll give yer some gas money, I'll…'

He laughed. 'Oh, you're hooked, ent yer? A right little grebo – see yer here then, at eight-thirty, right?'

And that was it. From then on, I was a biker – in my head, anyway. Out went the remnants of my hippie gear, in came the skin-tight jeans that threatened to sever my bits every time I clambered on the Bonnie, cowboy boots with bean-can heels, tight T-shirts and skinny-ribs, and eventually, after much begging and pleading, for my birthday, the money to buy a black, lancer-front Lewis Leathers jacket with six-inch fringing across the back and down the arms. I loved it so much I slept in it for a week. I've still got it and frankly, just cremate me in it, please. I've never adored an item of clothing like I worshipped that jacket, never – just the smell of it, the musky incense of old leather threaded with a faint tang of motor oil, transports me back to those days, to my youth, instantly.

Mum and Jen were disgusted with me, of course. In their minds, bikes were dirty, dangerous (what if you fell off and your face was *scarred for life* like the girl in *Woman's Own* they'd read about, who went to be a *nun* because of it, dreadful) and worse, symbols of poverty. A proper lad had a car, only poor boys rode scooters or bikes. Working-class lads, the type who went to the Mechanics Institute and biggest sin of all – worked with their hands. I didn't understand then the deep-seated, almost cellular drive of Mum's generation to 'better themselves'. To me, she was just being snobbish with her constant harping on Jen's nice, white-collar beaus. I didn't see how terrified she was of losing her precious, hard-won gentility and 'letting herself go'. Motorbikes and the Dustys of this world were a living affront to her years of struggle and there I was, throwing it in her face…Oh, Mum, I'm sorry, I am, but it's too late now, isn't it?

So, in Mum and Jen's opinion, you couldn't possibly go on a *date* with a boy on a bike – your hair, your make-up, what would you wear? You couldn't look nice tearing around with your face all dirty and your perm ripped to bits by the wind even if you wrapped it up in a pretty scarf like Audrey Hepburn in a sports car. They shuddered. It was unthinkable. As to a girl having her own bike, which was my dream, it wasn't natural. Mum allowed she had known a girl, years ago, who'd had a bike, but she'd been a bit funny, mannish, one of 'them', you know. Flat shoes and smoking roll-ups. A lezzie.

But they let me get on with it, what could they do? Lock me in my room? I'd only have got out and they knew it. They just kept up a stream of caustic remarks, mostly under their breath. They were somewhat distracted anyway, as Jen had recently become engaged to Eric, her long-time sweetheart. She wore the diamond-chip ring as if it were the Koh-I-Nor and Liz was ecstatic, there being nothing she loved better than a wedding, no matter how far away in the future it might be. Think of the shopping, the dressmaking, the flowers, the invitations, the crazy castle of the cake, the whole insane juggernaut crushing everything in its frilly organza path.

Mum wasn't so thrilled. She turned mulish and weepy. The usual smooth, flowing intimacy of their relationship was interrupted by the thought of Jen's leaving home, even though both Jen and Eric (rather too enthusiastically, in his case, I thought) assured her they believed in long engagements, saving up their money to get a good start, not rushing things. Still, when Eric, the great fool, brought up the idea one Sunday lunchtime of their emigrating to Canada after they got wed, Mum fled the table sobbing and it took hours to calm her down.

I didn't know about the menopause, then. I never thought that Mum might be wrestling with her body, swept by hormones and mortified by hot flushes. Or that she might be frightened of being alone (I didn't count) in her old age without Jen, or that she might be jealous, her marriage having failed and her youth and beauty, as she thought – not being one to see beauty in age – waning.

I just bumbled along in my offensive leathers and grubby jeans, my hair in a braid – like a bloody squaw, as Mum put it – so I could tuck it down the back of my jacket and wondered if I was going to have to be a bridesmaid. I shuddered at the thought of a lemon, or shell-pink, or powder-blue nightmare frock, complete with matching dyed satin shoes, pom-pom bouquet and ringletted chignon.

As it turned out, I got married before Jen and Eric. No bridesmaids, no frills. And no, I wasn't pregnant.

I met Micky Kendall at the SDMCC: The Sykebeck and District Motor Cycle Club. It was a straight bikers outfit who met in a Working Men's Club just out of town. By straight bikers, I mean bikers who weren't in a gang, who weren't what we call outlaws. They just liked bikes, beer, rock music and greasy nosh. I suppose to the average Joe they were indistinguishable from a real bike gang, but to anyone in the biker world the difference was enormous and insurmountable. To use an analogy Mum and Jen would understand, it was the difference between Diana Dors and Marilyn Monroe. And the SDMCC were definitely Diana, bless her coarse British charms.

I started going to the club nights with Dusty and his girlfriend Tracie, plus anyone else who could squeeze in her car. You could go in a car, if you swore blind (this only applied to lads, mind you) that your bike was temporarily off the road for mods or repairs. Not that, looking back, anyone really gave a shit, as long as you looked the part and sometimes turned up on two wheels. In fact, I knew lads who never came on a bike all the time I went there and no one said a dicky-bird.

But it was a nice club, though after a while, I felt restless there, somehow. I couldn't have said why exactly, I just felt it was a bit tame and samey. The bikers there were a little too straight for my taste; ordinary guys who thought ordinary thoughts, who had stepped out as far as they dared or wanted to. That's not to say I didn't enjoy it, I did – I felt at home in a way I never had with the hippies. This crowd felt more honest, they were what they seemed: scruffy, beer-bellied blokes who liked the bikes they rode and tinkered with endlessly and enjoyed a night out with their long-suffering but good-humoured girlfriends in a dark little barroom filled with the raucous laughter of their own kind. Where they wouldn't be judged. Where they could relax. They might not be intellectual, but at least there wasn't all that tedious love-and-peace cant the hippies regurgitated between tokes without actually understanding it.

As you can see, I was right off hippies.

Mostly we went to the club on Fridays, disco night – though actual disco music was definitely off the menu. I met Micky during the scene of what could be called my greatest social triumph. I won the annual Miss SDMCC. Yes indeed, I am a genuine Beauty Queen – though perhaps not the type my family would have understood. None the less, I stand by my claim. I've still got the engraved cup, and the sash. They live in my bottom drawer wrapped in my threadbare Ogri T-shirt along with my beloved leather jacket.

I hadn't meant to enter, in fact, I didn't – Tracie entered me, for a joke. She thought it was hilarious since she expected to win herself. I was supposed to be a sort of background for her; my lumpy darkness a perfect foil to her frosted prettiness. It was me and Jen all over again, I could feel my cheeks burning and my fists clenching. I'd known that for reasons that escaped me, Tracie didn't like me much, but this was the sort of cattiness hidden under smirking false flattery that always left me speechless. You know, like when some woman says how lovely she thinks your eyes are and wouldn't they look nice with some proper make-up? Or isn't it smashing to be tall, *some* men really go for tall girls, don't they? That was Tracie. It never occurred to me she was jealous of me and Dusty's casual matiness, or that she thought we might be having it off behind her back. Dusty was my pal, we talked about bikes, he was teaching me mechanics, we had a laugh.

Maybe that was it, the laughing. Tracie didn't have much of a sense of humour, though she reckoned she'd outdone herself on the comedy front, entering me in the contest.

I was furious when I found out, five minutes before the parade, in which we trembling maidens would mince round the dance floor to the genial hoots and catcalls of the beered-up crew of bikers who bet heavily on the outcome and cheered on their favourites with the enthusiasm of Grand National punters.

I could have refused to do it, but I didn't. Pride rose up in me and I unbraided my hair, which fortunately was freshly washed, and ran a borrowed brush through it, pinched my cheeks and bit my lips, like Jen had advised me to do 'in an emergency'.

To this day, I don't know how I won. I mean, there were plenty of nice-looking lasses wearing proper girl's clothes in the biker style – tight stretch jeans, high-heeled boots, scoop-neck T-shirts or pastel sweaters, their make-up tending towards pale pink lips and pearly blue eyeshadow. I had on my patched old jeans tucked into a pair of fireman's boots with thick white socks turned down over the tops, a heavy old leather belt, all my favourite chunky silver jewellery, bitten nails and a black vest. *Très chic.*

Later, Micky said he fell in love with me the moment he saw me; he thought I looked very fierce and proud, a biker princess. Well, I don't know about that, all I remember is my hands shaking and the swirl of faces like bobbing balloons scattered through the thick blue fug of cigarette smoke. If I looked fierce, it was because I was too nervous to smile. As I reached the judges' table, I did manage a grin and a wave out of relief it was over, which provoked a bout of cheering and table thumping. I thought that was because they admired my courage – the Plain Jane with brass neck.

In the Ladies, as we waited – or the other lasses waited, I knew I hadn't won – I re-braided my hair. Tracie said she hadn't realised it was so long. I hadn't realised you could say something like that and it sound so nasty. I felt sorry for Dusty, who thought Trace was a real lady, too good for the likes of him.

Then they called us out: *'Come on, you lot, lets be 'avin' yer.'*

The club president called for hush and the noise subsided. I waved at Dusty and he gave me the thumbs up. I felt, rather than heard, Tracie hiss.

'An' in third place – no, no shame in that, shut up, you lot – in third place, Miss Elaine Bartle!' Big cheers and a knot of folk in the far corner jumping up and down raucously. I clapped hard as a tiny blonde in five-inch heels teetered up to get her smacking kiss and box of chocolates from the president and his wife.

'Now then, this year's runner up, in second place – Miss Sally-Anne Prescott! Again, I applauded as a willowy redhead swayed up for her prize, rolling her big, lumpily mascaraed eyes and making 'oh, honestly' faces at her mates. I waited to congratulate Tracie as she smoothed her hair and bridled beside me.

'An' this year's Miss SDMCC is – steady, lads, I 'appen ter know she's single – by a u-nan-imous vote from our judges – shut it, now – *Miss Billie Morgan!'*

The place erupted. People cheering and banging the tables, then everyone was hugging me and slapping me on the back. I felt dazed. It must be a mistake, I began saying, it must be a…I was shoved up to the table and soundly kissed by the president and then his plump wife. I was draped in the sash, which she had embroidered by hand, and given flowers, the cup, a big box of chocolates.

I looked across to Tracie. She looked like Medusa. Her hair was practically writhing on her head and her livid gaze turned me to stone. But I didn't have time to think as I was dragged to the bar for a drink and the DJ put on 'Tiger Feet' by Mud and everyone started dancing and shoulder-bopping, grebo-style.

I'd be lying if I said I wasn't chuffed. Me, a beauty queen – it was a huge laugh, I was buzzing. I grinned so much my face ached, it was wonderful. It was only when the slow number was played, and the big fella I was dancing with finished steering me round the dancefloor like I was made of porcelain, did I realise something was wrong.

Tracie and Dusty were nowhere to be seen. I made my excuses, a wave of cold anticipation drenching through me and ran outside. The car was gone. Trace had had her revenge; she'd left without me and I was stuck in Sykebeck at gone midnight, miles away from home and the buses long finished for the night.

'Sod, sod, sod, fuck, bastard, *fuck*…' I could feel tears squeezing from behind my eyes as my high collapsed like cold ashes in the hearth.

'Er, you OK, there?' It was the big fella, the one I'd been dancing with.

'Shit – sorry, shit, no, I mean, my lift, they've, they've fucked off without me, oh bollocks, I…' I was crying now. I could feel the happiness I'd felt so carelessly seeping away into the cold, foggy night air.

'Er, look, I've got the van tonight, I could — can I take you home? I'd — look, I won't, you know, I wouldn't, you'd be safe with me — I'd like to…I mean, it wouldn't do fer Miss SDMCC ter walk home, now would it? What would the committee say?'

He was smiling like a person approaching a wild animal; his big hands outspread, his broad face determinedly calm. I looked at him properly for the first time.

Ah, Micky, Micky, my poor boy. He had the placid, open countenance of a child, his blue eyes the colour of faded cornflowers, his long chestnut hair caught into a shining ponytail with a nasty old rubber band. An old scar cut his left eyebrow in half; he did it playing footie as a lad, he told me later as I traced it with my fingertip.

He was six-foot-two of sweetness, a boy's innocent dreamy soul in the body of a rugby full-back; muscles popped from his arms like cantaloupes and his legs were long and strong enough to hike the Three Peaks in a day without complaint.

Was he handsome? It sounds as if he was, but no, not really; his nose a tad blobby, his eyes a bit too deep-set, his chin a tiny fraction too Captain America. But definitely nice-looking, and my absolute hero and saviour as we stood in that grotty carpark in the chilly mist. I felt like kissing him I was so grateful; later that night I did more than that in the back of his old van.

We started dating. Even Mum, Jen and Liz grudgingly liked him; you couldn't help but like Micky, he was so – so – *nice*. Loved animals, was brilliant with children, handy round the house and always polite. I can't say I fell in love with him head over heels like in the films, my eyes full of stars, my knees gone to jelly; but I grew to love him slowly, like everyone who knew him did. I called him Little Buddha, because he was so big and calm; he always called me Princess. Anyone else using that as a nickname would have sounded naff; he didn't because he meant it. I was his princess and that's how he treated me, with kid gloves, like cut crystal, nothing too good for me, like he couldn't quite catch hold of me.

And he couldn't, but then I couldn't catch hold of myself, either, as I rollercoastered through my life without brakes.

But that was my Micky – hardly the Evil Mother-Raping, Babby-Eating Filthy Grebo of straight-world legend, but there you go. I know people often want things to fit the mould because it's comforting to think bikers are all hell-hounds and say, golfers are all charming outdoorsey types with an eccentric taste in sweaters, but anyone who knows either group knows that it isn't so, either way.

My Micky was a good boy through and through. Perhaps if he'd been a bit harder, stronger, our lives wouldn't have been ruined.

But he was just his gentle, weak self, and it cost us dear. Not that I blame him, understand that: I did it and I forced him to help me deal with the result of my action.

It was my fault Terry Skinner died. I killed him, not Micky. I won't have him blamed. I killed Terry, not Micky, *me*.

Chapter Ten

ABOUT EIGHT MONTHS or so after Micky and I met, the Devil's Own came into the SDMCC on disco night like creatures from another dimension materialising from the leathery dark. One minute we were all chattering and bouncing around like usual, the next silence fell like a guillotine dropping.

Naturally, I'd heard of them, we all had. Some claimed to know them, to have mates who'd become members but they never brought them to the club or were seen with them in the pub. The Devil's Own were, in our eyes, a genuine, bad-to-the-bone outlaw biker club, one-per centers, the real deal. Everyone knew those guys kept to themselves, had their own world; if one of our lads had once palled up with one of them, that was in the past and that 'pal' would have renounced his former life entirely. Our worlds didn't overlap much.

I'd seen them riding round town on their rigs (what straights used to call 'choppers') the low-slung, surreal bikes with their strangely organic forms a glittering mass of custom paint and chrome, engines bulging, front forks extended into infinity like a Dali painting. The long-haired, bearded, earringed riders, their hands lumpy with huge silver rings, were impassive and menacing in their filthy embroidered gang colours – a denim jacket with the sleeves cut off, a lurid devil's head design on the back and a semi-circular 'rocker' patch above and beneath it, the top one reading 'Devil's Own', the bottom one

'Bradford', and a small MC patch on one side. It was worn over a leather bike jacket – and, of course, mirror shades were *de rigueur*. I'd stop and watch them cruise by, thinking in a confused way that they were cool, and way out of my league. Naturally, I had no way of actually becoming one of them, since I was a girl and no girls were allowed to become members, like, *ever*. No chicks flew colours, the crops would fail or something. The sun would go out, eternal darkness would fall, the Fimbul Winter would come upon us etc., etc. Dicks would shrivel and the world turn upside down. You know the kind of thing.

It was a guy thing – no, it was *the* guy thing. The ultimate bloke-fest. I'd sigh and curse my gender and add it to the long list of 'things girls can't do' and meditate upon how very, very much I hated being told what to do.

So when they came to the club I watched them fascinatedly as they sauntered in a block of grimy outrageousness to the bar, led by a thick-set man with a broad, brown, cunning face, black curly hair and a mammoth, rock-solid beer gut.

Micky came out of the bogs just as they settled round the long table usually reserved for our club's officials like ravens settling down to dine on a hanged man. No one said a word. People looked away, or looked into their beer. The DJ played 'Silver Machine', Lemmy's vocals sounding like a man who ate gravel mixed with amphetamines for breakfast, dinner, lunch, tea and snacks. Some of the outlaws hummed along or drummed their fingers like actual human beings.

'Oh, bloody Nora,' said Micky, his eyes wide and a grin on his face, his Yorkshireman's talent for understatement stretched to its limits by the appalling sacrilege of the long table colonised by outsiders; what would our dearly beloved president Albert say to this?

We waited, with baited breath. Albert said sod all. When June, his missus, bridled and made as if to speak, he shoved her into the side room. You could hear her chuntering from where I was sitting. The outlaws smiled slightly.

Nothing much happened. Later I found out they liked to drop in on little clubs sometimes, just to put the wind up them in a general kind of way, unless they were wannabe outlaw clubs. Then they took their sad little wonky colours away and scared them stiff. Violence wasn't usually required with the likes of the Coniston Valley Hell Pigs, the Ullthwaite Marauders or the Tarnsyke Iron Riders. They knew they were chancing it and they knew well enough to pack it in when the time came. The strong lads in those outfits went to the Devil's Own to be prospects when they'd recovered their pride; some made it, some didn't, that's the way it goes. No one from the Hell Pigs *ever* made it, though – but, man, that's another story...

But the Devil's Own weren't bothered about a solid citizen's outfit like the SDMCC. They were just being sociable.

I watched though, and so did Little Buddha. I watched how they spoke, walked, drank, acted with each other and, most importantly, towards the big man who was obviously their leader. In a weird parody of Da Vinci's 'Last Supper', he took the place of Christ, his men on either side of him, talking in his ear, his deep-set, sloe-black eyes full of a Machiavellian intelligence, his florid face ugly and compelling. He didn't miss a trick, that was obvious, nothing escaped him.

Not even me. He saw me watching and he smiled. I immediately looked away, went bright red and felt like the biggest fool ever, a rube lollygagging at the circus folk, a mark, a punter, an *amateur*.

'Bollocks, he seen yer; God, he's wicked, that 'un. That's Carl, that is. Carlo. Italian he is, well, 'is family were – from down south, London. That's what Rick says, says he killed a bloke down there an' had to get out fast so 'e come up here ages ago now, like. He's bin their prez fer years, he's a right bastard, they say. Hard as nails, fights with his belt. Nasty.' Micky stuck his jaw out and nodded knowingly.

I elbowed him as hard as I could then waited until he finished complaining.

'Well, you could have said. How come you know so much about them, Mr Big Know-It-All?' I felt unsettled, cross for no real reason I could think of. Perhaps I was still embarrassed about being caught googling; but I don't think so. More, it was like something dark and golden was coalescing in my brain, like when you push the heels of your hands into your eyes and those serpentine, gleaming patterns form in your blind eyes. A plan was unfolding in my head but I didn't want to put it into words so it just irritated me.

'That 'urt, that did,' Micky complained. 'Give up, now. OK, OK, Rick told us. Well, you never asked, did yer? Princess, no – don't you – you little…C'mon, nougies int fair…Look, they're off – 'ere, that Carl, 'e's lookin' at you, wave goodbye like a good little…Pack it *in*, Bill…'

By the time we got to my house, defrosted (it was a bike night on Micky's trusty 750 Norton Commando) and lay sleepily on my single bed (still with the ducks on the headboard), Led Zep on and the house empty on account of Jen being at Eric's and Mum and Liz being at a Rotarians dinner dance, I knew.

'Miiiiiccckkkeeeee' I wheedled, twirling a strand of his silky hair round my finger and partially wondering how come it was always so glossy when all he did was dunk his head in the dirty, lukewarm bath water and wash his hair with a bar of Fairy soap.

'Mmm.'

'Miiiiicccckkkk – what d'you want ter do with your life?'

'Errr, dunno; get a BMW fer Sundays, go ter America, have a big win on the Premium Bonds what I haven't got an' tell 'em ter stuff their shitey fuckin' job…Why?'

'I was just thinkin'…'

'Oh blimey, now we're fucked…' he said, kissing my neck.

'No, I mean it, listen, them Devil's Own, that's proper that is, y'know, not pissin' around pretendin' like the club, we could – you could…It'd be summat like, wouldn't it? Bigger'n all this – this…' I gestured wildly at the ducks, and the flounced floral curtains.

Micky was silent. I held my breath; if he made like he wasn't bothered, didn't know what I was on about, thought I was nuts, I'd – well, it'd be over, it would. We would.

'Rick goes up The Swan on a weekend. That's where they go – he knows a couple of 'em ter nod at, like. He's said before I oughta – we oughta go up. We could go tomorrow night, if you like…'

I jumped on him and kissed his homely face.

''Ere, get off, you're worse than that bloody dog, I'm all ovver slobber…Bill, Billie, it's nowt, nowt'll come of it, you mustn't get yer hopes up…'

Nine months later, along with Johnjo who had turned up a week later, coming in from the night like an unspeaking wraith from no one knew where, Micky was a prospect for the Devil's Own, his newly finished rig, Lady Blue, parked outside The Swan, its sapphire hi-pearl paint and daringly modern custom murals based on Hokusai's 'Great Wave Of Kanagawa' being admired by the lads.

And I was Carlo 'Carl' Verradi's pet.

Chapter Eleven

I SAW A FOX today, as I stared gormlessly out of the window cradling my strong black wake-up tea and getting my head round going to work. There he was, bold as you like, loping through my garden and disappearing into the cemetery; a grey-muzzled old dog fox, lithe and wick as a dusty russet flame. For a split second he looked at me, and his wild eyes were as distant and unforgiving as only nature can be. There was no relationship with humanity there, no pussy-cat domesticity, no doggy love. I've seen that look before, in the eyes of men now long gone, some long dead. Feral. Fixed on horizons so far away that only God knew their savage hearts and only He could forgive their trespasses.

And something else; you could see it in every line of his battered old body. That quality of tenseness, that awareness of mortality. He knew damn well that his little moment of peace in the sun could end forever at any moment. With the sound of horses and dogs thudding and baying over the brook, with the sickening crunch of a car hitting him – too slow, old dog – with the taste of bitter poison from that tempting carrion in the back of his throat. He knew his life was finite, that his enemies were waiting, that he could never, truly, be off guard.

Never be weak.

I withdrew out of his view; a little gift to my fox brother. One threat less for him to deal with today, at least. I drank my tea but I couldn't settle. The fox had disturbed me as much as I'd disturbed him. The muddy depths of my mind stirred, sending detritus up through the thick waters. Memories, like glimpses of carp twining through weed, gleamed in the dark then vanished.

Why did Carl take to me like he did? I don't know. I think, in his way, he really cared about me, not that I realised that at the time. It was a gradual thing – the sense that he was looking out for me, defending me against the criticisms of some of the lads. Johnjo once said Carl had a soft spot for intelligent people and despised the stupid, and that gender was meaningless to him in that respect. He'd once said to Johnjo that in the wild, it was the lioness who did the hunting, not the lion; then he'd laughed, as if, Johnjo said, he was amused at some private joke. But for whatever reason, he quietly shielded me against trouble because looking back, I cringe at the way I went on, I really do.

I didn't know when to put a sock in it, that was the problem. I was so gung-ho, so infatuated with the whole idea of the outlaw life, I – as Carl's wife Rita put it so succinctly – didn't know my fuckin' place.

Not knowing when to shut up is what brought me into contact with Terry Skinner, and Jas, his heavily pregnant girlfriend. I told him to leave her the fuck alone, to pack in winding her up in her condition.

I didn't like Terry. I thought he was – and don't laugh – not the sort of person the club should associate with. But he was a petty dealer; he sold gear at low prices to get in with the lads and live out his fantasy of being in the club, though everyone knew he never would be. Carl said to me, after he took me aside with a heavy sigh and an expression of mild despair on his face and told me to shut up in future and watch what I said in case my blathering led the lads into serious bother defending me, that I needn't *worry* (his Cockney accent heavy with a drawling sarcasm), Terry would never fly a patch. He wasn't a good soldier, Carl said, and tapped the side of his bulbous nose. Know what I mean, gel?

And I did know, because my Micky was the best soldier in the world and he was going places, I knew it.

But Terry and Jas. The odd couple. He was tall and gangly, his long lantern-jawed face embroidered with acne, a scrubby mess of yellow dandruffy hair falling into eyes the colour of sulphur gas, or dirty copper pennies depending on the light or his mood. He had a mirthless haw-haw laugh and never forgot a slight, or let go of a grudge. To Terry, the world was his enemy, society out to get him and while it was obvious he wasn't thick, there was something weaselly cunning in him, something greasy and predatory that was repellent.

Unless you were Jas. It was all too obvious she genuinely loved him and believed all his garbled speedfreak conspiracy theories utterly. If anyone scoffed – and they did – she'd murmur, *'No, he got it from a book, dint yer, Terry'* as if getting it from a book was a God-given guarantee of truth and accuracy. Maybe it was to her, since she could neither read nor write. She thought Terry was brilliantly clever, a counter-culture intellectual; that it was a miracle a bloke like him could tolerate, as she saw it, an ugly half-caste whore's daughter like herself.

To say, in modern psychobabble, that Jasmine came from a highly dysfunctional family and had very challenging self-esteem problems would be the biggest understatement of the millennium.

When I think of Jas back then, I think of a dandelion clock, delicate, fragile, about to blow away in the slightest wind, only weighted down to the earth by the colossal swollen dome of her belly. Skinny little Jas, her spidery, spatulate fingers, their chewed nails blotched with the bitten-off remains of burgundy-coloured varnish splayed protectively over her unborn child. Jas with her satiny, rose-brown skin sprinkled with freckles and stretched over high cheekbones that slanted her eyes and gave her an ageless, archaic look like one of those compelling little goddess statues dug from ancient graves, and her halo of weightless, floating weak-tea coloured curls. Jasmine Pearl Savage, half Bradford, half St Kitts, those enormous green eyes framed with the faintest smudge of eyebrow and heavily fringed with curling black lashes fixed on Terry with uncomprehending hurt, her soft, full-lipped pink mouth trembling as he taunted her in order to make himself seem hard, to give the impression he didn't give a shit about her carrying his child. Maybe he really didn't care – with him, it was hard to tell.

''Ere, Jassie, get us a pint in – whadja mean, yer too tired? Too fuckin' tired? Ooh, is it yer belly? Boo hoo. Fuck me, I ain't never seen such a fuckin' whale as you, eh? Fuckin' enormous, fat as a pig, ugly cow...Get yersel t'bar, go on – aw, look at fuckin' lip on it, are you gonna blub, eh? Eh? You lot don't get tired, what about all that working in the fuckin' cotton fields then fuckin' poppin' it out where yer stand, all that Mandingo shite? Tired? I'll give yer fuckin' tired...'

So I told him to shut the fuck up. Well, I couldn't bear it, someone had to. Jas seemed so pathetic, so completely bloody useless, a born bully-victim with the IQ of a dormouse. It broke my heart watching her, the awfulness of her background and her self-hatred made something tear inside me and I felt bound to defend her because, to be honest, no one else would.

I don't know why they wouldn't. At the time it drove me nuts, I mean, OK, it wasn't a vicar's tea party and everyone got ribbed and teased, but it toughened you up, you learned to put on a good face. But if it got really vicious, it was stopped. Someone would tell the person dishing out the crap to pack it in.

But not when it was Jas. No one said anything, they just turned away as if it was too painful to watch; maybe that was it. Jas took it all to heart so much, it cut her to the quick. Every time Terry got pissed and tried to play the hard case and impress the lads by abusing Jas, those great peridot eyes of hers would fill with tears that spilt out down her cheeks in crystal tracks. She cried soundlessly, like a saint, she didn't screw her face up, go red or get mad. She just gazed at her beloved tormentor and murmured her perpetual little mantra 'Sorry Terry, sorry...' It was unbearable so people looked away, embarrassed, uncomfortable; like the bullied kid at school, sometimes people just make like it's not happening.

So I went at him. Not because I'm some sort of hero, or any of that nonsense. It was because I felt sorry for her and I loathed him so much I wanted a reason to confront him.

There was a right barney. He went ballistic, chuntering on about lippy women – I said he was a wanker. On it went until he found out lippy I might be but I was part of the Devil's Own (albeit a lowly part, being a prospect's bird), and he wasn't. The lads told him to fuck off out of it. They didn't get up from their seats though, or get that narked for two reasons – one, he sold them cheap blow and whizz, two, they couldn't believe he'd really do anything. But I could see what he was, like all the other lasses in the place – a bone-deep woman-hater.

Terry looked livid, then mutinous and grabbed his empty beer glass. The atmosphere notched up a gear and out of the corner of my eye (I was staring straight at Terry, I wasn't going to be the one to drop my gaze) I clocked Micky leaving the pool table, slow and steady like always and I stepped back. Micky walked up to Terry, in his face, and told him to shut the fuck up, to leave me alone, right? Johnjo came over from the bar, moving with a silent, sinuous grace like water turning in a riverbed and stood with Micky. The whole pub was watching, waiting for Terry to be stupid; there was a breathless moment when you could see Terry, drunk and not thinking straight, heft the glass in his hand...

Then Carl was behind him, like one of those giant Easter Island totem figures, as if he'd been there forever and always; not speaking, just terrifyingly, enormously *there*.

Terry went white, the colour drained out of him as his fury ashed to cinders of fear. He didn't turn around but gingerly stepped sideways, put the glass down, grabbed his jacket and shouldered his way out of the pub. I felt the tension ebb away and that's when I noticed Jas was holding my sleeve.

She struggled up, clutching her coat and bag with the other hand. She smelt of vodka and orange, and fags and faintly, of jasmine, her namesake, the night-blooming flower of the islands, sweet and faintly decayed.

Her voice was little more than a breathy whisper. ''E don't mean it, he's just a bit drunk, y'know, he don't mean nowt by it, love. But – thanks, like, thanks, you're kind, you are, it were good of yer...'

And a tiny smile, like the shadow of a hummingbird, passed over her face.

I could have wept, from rage, from frustration – and from pity. With Jas, it was always pity and that was the first night I felt her power, the inverted power of the brutalised and what it really meant. 'The audacity of the weak,' as Edith Wharton, Dadda's favourite author once said. He'd read the story with that phrase in it to me, mulling the words over as if I wasn't there. Then he'd seemed to recollect himself and giving me a smile had said, 'Clever woman, eh, Billie? Very clever...Now you go to sleep, fy annwylyd, my dearest, an' I'll finish the story tomorrow...' I remember the moment because he spoke Welsh – he never did that unless he was distracted. He never finished the story, either, and I puzzled over the idea that weak people could be strong, or strong people weak, for some days, until I forgot all about it, like kids do. I hadn't known what he meant until I met Jas, when it jumped into my mind like a fish on a hook.

Had he also meant it applied to himself? Were Dadda and Jas cut from the same cloth? No, not my dadda, he wasn't like Jas – was he? I felt tension yoke my neck and shoulders with unyielding iron, my head aching with the pressure of it.

All that night, as I shifted and turned uncomfortably in my chilly bed, I thought about what I'd done. It had been incredibly stupid to mouth off at Terry even though he was a moron. Jesus, all my careful hard work undone in one burst of irritation and anger. Oh, why couldn't I control my bloody temper? I'd suppress it for months and months then, boom, it'd pop out sideways, like a balloon filled with fire, it would escape when I wasn't expecting it. To barrack a bloke in public, to draw your man and his brothers into it for no good reason other than your narkiness and lack of self-discipline – mortal sins. Had I really got away with it? What would it mean to Micky's career as a potential gang-leader? Round and round it all went in my head until I had to get up and make myself a cup of tea.

It was nearly dawn. Through the living room window an ashy light was blooming. Mum and Jen would be getting up for work in an hour. I crept back upstairs to bed; I couldn't face them, I just couldn't. I felt exhausted. There was always so much to think about, so many people to consider, be careful about, not offend. Like walking on eggshells day after day after day, no rest, no pause.

A sudden thought drifted into my mind as I shut my eyes and tried again to sleep. An image from a holiday brochure: white sands, blue seas, warmth. Then I saw myself, barefoot, my hair in a loose plait, a beautiful flower tucked behind my ear, wearing a pair of old, salt-faded jeans rolled up to the knees and a bikini top, strolling along the water's edge, smiling.

Suddenly, I was wide awake again. Oh, please, please, *please*…Let that be me, let that be real…But people like me didn't have the cash or connections for that sort of life. It was so impossible it was a joke. A bitter, nasty, painful joke.

This was my life. I'd chosen it. I'd stick with it.

I sighed and wriggled deeper under the covers, bunching myself up to get warm. Jas though – that's why I'd yelled at Terry. Poor little Jas. Poor kid. Jesus – I might feel shitty, but at least I wasn't *Jas*.

Chapter Twelve

MICKY MOVED UP the ranks fast. Partly it was to do with his undoubted mechanical skills (he was, after all, a proper City and Guilds mechanic who came first in his class). He was generous by nature and happily worked on other people's bikes – Carl's great black monster 'Widowmaker', Doc the vice president's candy-apple red 'Wolfsbane', Knobby the sergeant-at-arms' hideous purple metalflake trike 'Satanica'.

He even made my pride and joy, my lipstick pink street scrambler, created out of a 250 BSA Barracuda, with its peanut tank, wide cow-catcher bars, tiny flat seat and knobbly tires barely shielded by cutaway minimal mudguards, 'Pinkie' was my pride and joy. She was Micky's love for me made concrete. Needless to say, I was the only bird with a bike in the club and while I thought I was the dog's bollocks, others did not. It was me being uppity again, being a clever cunt. But I didn't realise this, like I never realised so much of the general disgruntlement against me that would inflate my rep to monstrous proportions without me noticing. Looking back, if it hadn't been for Carl's patronage, I would have been in deep shit; but his eye was on me and that was enough.

Anyway, there we were, the perfect biker couple. Along with his unruffled calmness and sunny smile, his mechanical creativity allowed Little Buddha to quickly leave prospecthood behind. He got his top rocker, and after a romantic trip to Whitby, as we stood by the Abbey watching the sunset, we decided to get married.

Mum was absolutely livid. It wasn't that she disliked Micky particularly, despite his being a biker (she didn't have a clue about the

Devil's Own and I didn't enlighten her), it was the fact I was, as she put it, just trying to upstage Jen and Eric. There was nothing I could say that would convince her I wasn't getting wed in order to annoy her personally and I could feel that tightening across my jaw that always came when we were set to get into a big, stupid fight; sometimes when this happened I'd wake in the night with my teeth locked solid, a big pain in my face and jaw muscles like bags of walnuts. We'd been at odds for so long that I no longer knew how to talk to her calmly, everything I said turned in its own iron track that led, like the grooves in my old singles, inexorably back to the central argument of our lives. I was like my father, my father was a waste of time and cruelly self-centred. Mum was the injured party and I was just fulfilling the curse of my blood and trying to ruin her life – but she wasn't going to let me, oh no, she wouldn't make that mistake twice.

I just wanted her to love me. I mean, to show me she loved me as much as she adored Jen, but I didn't know how to ask her to do that, I didn't know how to break through to her. It was a Mexican stand-off, a war of attrition. Now I think how alike we are in our pig-headed stubbornness, but then I felt like a monument to illogical rejection.

Jen was cross too, though not very, as being cross solved nothing and gave you lines. She just sighed and kissed me on the cheek saying 'congratulations' in a voice that made it sound like 'condolences', then glanced at Micky and sighed again, more heavily. She didn't approve of long hair on men, she thought it was effeminate, even when the man was over six foot of bulging muscle like Little Buddha. Actually, I thought Eric, with his fish-pale sloping face, wine-bottle-shaped body and black Brylcreemed coiffure was definitely swishy – but hey, maybe he was a tiger in the sack. Jen thought he was a real gentleman, with lovely manners because he crooked his little finger slightly when he drank from a teacup and said, '*I don't mind if I do*,' in a nearly inaudible voice when offered a biscuit. I know for a fact he liked to paint her toenails for her, but I suppose that's not actual proof of weirdness, is it?

Liz simply lit another fag, pursed her lips and raised her pencilled eyebrows to her stiffly dyed hairline. I knew she'd be suggesting to Mum I'd probably missed a couple of periods. But I didn't rise to her bait as I used to do; she seemed more and more like Joan Collins or the Wicked

Witch of the West, a spent force spouting her worn-out clichés, ageing and increasingly mummified-looking in her frozen past-it glamour, her power waning. I half expected to hear her hiss, *'I'm melting, I'm melting,'* and dissolve into a puddle on the Wilton.

I wanted Mum to – to, I don't know. Be happy for me, make a fuss, get excited. Something. But she just told me not to expect her to pay for anything as she had enough on with Jennifer. She didn't forbid me to marry poor Little Buddha who loomed uncomfortably in the door frame and looked like a man about to be shot; she just sucked her teeth pityingly and wished him the best of luck.

Six weeks later we did the deed at the Registry Office. Me in a black velvet trouser suit from Boodlam in Leeds, stack-heel boots from Sacha and a bouquet of cascading Madonna lilies and maidenhair fern I'd ordered myself. Micky was in his colours and leathers. Mum and Jen came, my few other relatives having been too busy at such short notice and anyway, what with Jen's do coming up…They sent telegrams, though. Mum stayed long enough to comment that she was glad none of the family came, with us in those get-ups and those funeral flowers. Jen was gracious enough to tell her lilies were all the rage but Mum was unconvinced and told her she could think again if she thought her bouquet would be anything other than decent pink roses and gyp. They left as soon as they could and didn't even bother speaking to Micky's family, what there was of it.

Micky's mum came dressed in a eau-de-nil crimplene two-piece, a rusty black floppy felt hat (Micky said it was her church hat) and a big cross on a chain round her neck. His dad, in a shiny navy marriages-births-deaths suit and spit-shined black shoes, was as sweet as his son. I think he'd have liked to stay and have a drink with us but Micky's mum was having none of it. She thought I was the Scarlet Woman and Micky a lost soul doomed to eternal damnation. She dragged his dad off as fast as she could. I wasn't surprised his older brother had gone to Australia.

I don't know. I'd like to tell you what a lovely day it was, all the romance and sentiment, but I can't. It was just quick, I suppose. Leckie once asked me why Micky and I didn't just live together like everyone does these days but then, it wasn't done so much. Personally, I'd have been happy to 'live over the brush' as they say round here, but Micky was dead set against it, he thought it was disrespectful and he wanted to do things properly. He was so sweet and when he'd asked me to marry him, he'd looked so anxious, I'd cried and kissed his face over and over like a child kissing its favourite teddy. But the thing itself, the droning, disinterested registrar, the over-heated grubby room, the faint smell of dirty washcloths and dust – no.

We got on 'Lady Blue' and rode the fuck away from the registry office and the straight world as fast as we could, back to our six pound a week stone wall flat over a hairdressers in Sykebeck village just outside of town. In front of the blazing gas fire (which just made the walls sweat and did nothing to take the damp off) I buried my face in Micky's chest and wept.

'Micky, Micky, why? Why do they hate us? Why? Why's my mum so – and Jen, I mean, I didn't want to upset her, I didn't – oh, Micky, Micky, why? Why am I so wrong all the time? I wish my dadda – he'd have understood, I want my dadda…Micky, d'you love me? Do you? I mean really? Properly? You're not going to go off me, are you? Oh…'

'Shush, shush now, Princess. Here, my lot are just as bad, aren't they, eh? Hmm? Look at my mum with that bloody great cross round her neck an' me dad too frit ter say a word to her? Come on now, come on, stop cryin' now, we've got each other, int we? You're my wife now, Princess, my wife, legal. Of course I love yer, I always loved yer from the first time I set eyes on yer, so wild and fierce like a little kestrel in with a load o' canaries. I love yer. I love yer, nothin'll split us up, I swear. I'll tek care of yer always, I'll mek it better…'

It was the longest speech he'd ever made to me, or ever would again and the look of tenderness in his face was unbearable. I loved him so much, it broke my heart. I turned the wide gold band on my finger as if I could screw it on tighter, so it would never come off and we'd never be parted, like he said.

If the straights didn't want us, fuck 'em. They understood nothing, they were cruel and bigoted, their petty prejudices iron shackles that would weight them to their lonely graves. We were free, we were young and we had each other. It would be fine.

I had no doubt on that score, God help me.

That night we went to the pub and had our wedding party, with our real family. Increasingly, that's how we felt – we'd talked and talked about it. Our blood families didn't seem to care, but the Devil's Own did; they were our brothers and sisters, our clan, our tribe. We all stuck together, you were never alone and undefended and the straight world seemed to recede further and further away, like a long tide leaving the shore, leaving us on an island of what was to us, sanity.

I know to an outsider we were violent, dirty, ignorant and anti-social, but naturally, we didn't think of ourselves that way and making the straights – or cabbages, as we called outsiders – flinch was a great game. I especially liked the epithet 'anti-social' because what did society offer me? A life of grovelling subservience to some marketing bloke's capitalist ideal of a 'good little woman' and years of kow-towing slavery to some boss for Micky – a boss who'd lay him off without a second thought if finances demanded. We'd all seen our parents' generation, we all smelt their terrible fear of going against the norm, that terror of being outside. We *wanted* outside. Sure we took our wages from the world, we bought food, clothes, paid gas bills (eventually) but we didn't have to think like they did, we didn't have to waste our precious free time being good citizens – or as Doc, the Trotskyite put it, patsies for the system.

But this was my wedding party, I was a bride, I had the ring to prove it. The landlord promised us a lock-in and everyone got drunker and more stoned-crazy as the night went on. Knobby told long, interminable shaggy dog stories he made up on the spur of the moment about the other club members, Chalky and Cochise being his favourite targets.

'...So after they – wait, wait, I'm gettin' there – so, after they like, staggered cross all this desert right, boilin' hot, no water – no, no beer neither – they sees this like, palace, all white an' glitterin' in the distance. Come on, Chalky lad, says Cochise – yeah yer did, in this yer did – just a bit further, you can do it, and they gets there – mek mine a pint while you're up there, Maur – an' it's like, room after room of gold an' jewels an' fountains with wine instead of water, fan-fuckin'-tastic. So they staggers on ter biggest hall like, an' at the end of it is a be-yoo-ti-ful statue of a like, nekkid woman, life size, in pure ivory an' gold an' big blue sapphires fer eyes just winkin' at 'em. So Chalky, he's eyeballin' the fuckin' jewels in the walls an' drinkin' the wine an' then he hears this noise – ugga ugga ugga – yeah, you heard, I aint doin' it again – an he looks round, an' there's Cochise shaggin' this statue! Fuck me, he goes, fuck me – I allus knew that Cochise were an idle fucker! Get it? An idol fucker! Here, get off, it's true is that, as I live an' breath…'

Still laughing, I went out into the filthy yard to the toilets, but before I went into the rat-infested cubicle, Carl stopped me.

''Ang on a minute, I want a word.'

'Er, sure, I mean, yeah, fine.'

I hadn't got over my feeling that Carl represented something profoundly darker than I fully understood. It was common knowledge that he *was* the Devil's Own; he'd founded it and it was his charisma – there was no other word for it – that kept it going. He was our leader and there wasn't a man among the club members who would have challenged him. There was something about him, something powerful that drew people. I often thought what a brilliant politician he'd have made if he'd been into that kind of thing, if he'd come from the kind of background that would have enabled him to go that way. Carl had had a stint in the army, then joined the teddy boy gangs of the fifties before becoming a 'ton-up' greaser with a fast café racer bike and a hair trigger temper. Then he pulled a blade on the wrong man for what reason no one ever knew, and – though no, he hadn't killed him as legend had it – he'd put him in intensive care. So he'd run up north, and over time, formed the Devil's Own because he liked and understood the things about the American Hells Angels he heard, read and saw. Not the things you might think, either – but the sense of comradeship that the first Hells Angels, mostly army veterans, felt. The discipline and structure of a gang that made them feel secure in a world that no longer had a place for them. Carl understood the value of family and tribe. He understood people and what they wanted and needed and he had the true instinct of command.

Now you never saw Carl's temper and you never saw a blade. Just his gaze, compelling and calm, and that slight smile that often moved across his face like sun coming out from behind a haze. The dark anger that had boiled in him as a young man was banked now, it was an energy he used, instead of it using him. I envied that.

'Congratulations. I thought you might like to know, I got plans for your boy. He's steady, honest. I like that.'

'Oh, er, thanks…'

'You though, you gotta watch your mouth, Billie, no more of this business like wiv Terry. He's a wrong 'un, I know, but I don't want you making enemies. Not him, but there's club members, an' their old ladies, wot don't like a mouthy bird. See?'

'Oh, sorry. I'm sorry, Carl. I won't...'

'You will, gel. But listen – an' don't you never tell no one this, not ever – I got your boy in because of you. I seen you that night at that poxy club, I seen you watchin'. You gotta brain in that thick head you 'ave. If you was a bloke – *if*, I say – it'd be you flyin' a patch, not him. He's a good boy, but he's weak. You remember that, he's weak an' one day you'll know it, see? But look, right – if you was a lad, I could use you, because you believe, dont' ya? You believe more'n any of them in there. You got loyalty an' you understand duty. You got balls. But it ain't gonna happen – no, gel, it ain't, so take that look off yer face. I just wanted you ter know, an' ter know I'm lookin' out for yer – *if* you can keep that fuckin' gob shut. Right?'

'Right. Right – I – I mean, I'll...'

But he'd gone, with the curious gliding grace of the fat man.

And for the second time on my wedding day, I felt my eyes fill with tears, but this time, the hot tears of anger and frustration. It was so unfair and cruel. The thing I wanted most I could never have. I could never really be in the Devil's Own, never really belong. And Carl was wrong about Micky – he wasn't weak, he was gentle but underneath he was solid as a rock, definitely.

I hovered, thighs aching, over the appalling toilet and tried not to inhale the dreadful latrine odour; then I pulled myself into some semblance of order. Running back into the pub, I sidled up to Micky, who was chatting away with the faintly glazed expression of the amiably drunk. I tugged his sleeve.

'So I goes, I don't fuckin' think so, mate, but he just...Oh, Billie love, what is it, Princess? Scuse me, my bride wants a word, eh? Eh?' He winked broadly at Dog, who was bottle-nosed from drink and slowly slipping beneath the bar, then stepped aside carefully.

'I love you, Micky.'

He smiled, puzzled. 'Well, I love you too, Princess. Are you alright? Owt up? We won't stay much longer, I'm bushed. You must be knackered – *Mrs Kendal...*'

He arf-arfed like a kid.

'No, Micky, I love you – I mean I really, truly love you. Like, forever. You know...'

He put his beer down and wrapped me in a big bear hug, provoking a few wolf-whistles and remarks from the lads. I felt his breath warm on my ear, smelling of beer and dope; not unpleasant but familiar, safe.

'I love you too, Princess. Don't go frettin' yourself like you do. I love you an' I always will. Till I die – an' after. Always. Now, don't go blubbin', wipe yer eyes...'

He gave me a squeeze and, tucking me in the curve of his elbow, turned back to the bar.

''Ere, a Britvic Orange for the missis – nothin' stronger, mind, she's got a long night in front of her!'

Everyone cheered and raised their glasses to us. I glanced across at Carl. He touched a finger to his brow in a kind of salute. Family. You can't beat it.

Chapter Thirteen

S O OUR LIFE in the club progressed. I tried harder to get on with everyone and to keep quiet – or at least quieter. I even avoided Terry, when he slunk back into the pub with the air of a yellow mongrel dog just waiting to bite the foot that kicked it. Jas, more enormously pregnant than ever, seemed to have decided I was her guardian angel. She was always confiding in me in the Ladies and asking my advice about everything from hairstyles to proper nutrition for a mother-to-be – like, should she, did I think, eat vegetables? Since her current diet was chips, chips-in-curry-sauce for variety, pork scratchings, vodka-and-orange and Mars bars, I didn't think it was pushing it to say, yeah, it'd be a sound idea. She beamed up at me from her full five-foot-three in rope-sole wedgies and said she was sure she had a tin of Marrowfat peas in the larder and she'd scoff it that very night. Anything to ensure her baby was fit and healthy; already you could hear that blissfully self-sacrificing mother-tone in her gentle, husky voice.

Then, after an horrendous labour, her baby was born, and she sent a message that she'd like me to visit her in the hospital.

Rather unwillingly, I went. I felt faintly uncomfortable about getting more involved with her but that tug of pity made me lecture myself about being mean and selfish. If it made the poor little cow happy to chat for a few minutes about her new kiddie, why not go, it would be plain old cruel not to. I didn't feel the tentacles of Jas's power twining deeper and deeper into me as I reasoned with myself and tried to squash what I considered ungenerous thoughts.

She looked like Hell, her face ashen and huge dark circles under her eyes which made them seem more enormous than ever. I made desultory conversation for a bit, horrified by the state of her, then she told me the gruesome details of her birth experience. What could go wrong, had. She was so small, so narrow, the baby had virtually ripped its way out. Her voice was still raw from the screaming. She'd lost pints of blood, and the doctors and midwives had despaired of her, she said. More children were out of the question, her insides were trashed, like a mess of bloody spaghetti. It was like a Victorian melodrama, I wouldn't have believed it if I hadn't seen how awful she looked; she was crushed and desiccated, like a dead leaf, her head barely denting the pillow. I shuddered – if this was childbirth, spare me. I'd thought in this day and age it was all perfect and painless. All the Johnsons adverts showed glowing mums cuddling adorable babies, no mention of this horror; Jeez, how wrong had I been?

It made me shudder and I felt something turn in my stomach, not like being sick, but like a deep revulsion about the whole process. Not to do with the looks thing like some people have accused me of – you know, not wanting to get 'fat' or 'lose my figure', which is ludicrous, but of turning your physical self over to another creature not just for the term of pregnancy, but for the rest of your life. I was, I am, too selfish. I'd have made a terrible mother, moody, narky, you name it. All power to the mothers of the world and all that, but I wasn't at all sure I'd ever be brave enough to try it.

But Jas was, and there she lay, her drawn face lit from one side by the pallid light from the grimy hospital window. She smiled. It was as if someone had lit a beacon in her heart.

'But see, Billie, you've been that good ter me, I wanted yer ter see my babby, my boy. He's lovely, so beautiful, honest, it were worth it, wait till yer see him…I'm gonna call him Nathan, d'you like it? And Terry, after his dad. Nathan Terry Savage. I think it's dead classy. A real classy name, eh?'

'Terence, love. Terry's the short version.'

'Oh – but – no, it's Terry, not Ter – Terrunce, honest…'

There was no point arguing, if she wanted Terry, then Terry it was and anyhow, Nathan was a very nice name. Unusual, but not weird like the names some folk burden their kids with. I personally knew fully baptised kids called Ringo, Zebedee, Crystal Moon and best of all, Caramel. Not Carmel, Caramel. Her mum had been mad for Cadbury's Caramels apparently and thought 'a sweet little babby wanted a sweet name'. People beamed at that one – how cute, eh? I managed a tight smile and nod – well, be honest, you may as well call the poor little sod Fruitandnut and have done with it.

But Nathan was good – Natty. Natty Savage. A strong name, a lucky name; it had a solid, decent ring to it.

And then the nurse brought Nathan to his mother, and he *was* beautiful. I looked at his perfect face, his tiny hands with their rosy nails, his little mouth like the curve of a damp petal. I put my finger in his palm and he curled his fingers round it and I felt a sharp pain in my heart; bending down I smelt the sweet, inexpressible scent of his little head, the most powerful, magic, binding smell in the world and I kissed him, just brushed his downy head with my lips. Maybe it wouldn't be so bad, having a kid, maybe... Then I looked at Jas again as she gazed at us, exhausted, and in too much pain to move.

'I knew you'd like him, I knew yer would, an' when you 'ave babbies, they can play tergether, can't they? My Natty an' your little 'un. Like brothers. An' Billie, I want – if yer don't mind like, I want yer to be his godmother – will yer? Please? It'd mek me feel easier like, knowin' you had summat ter do with him, would tek care on him if owt happened ter me...'

I swallowed a lump that had suddenly appeared in my throat and I looked down at Natty as he snuffled and burped. 'Course I will, Jas, don't you worry, love, it'd be an honour, really.'

Two of those diamond tears trickled down her wasted cheeks and she smiled like a Madonna in a renaissance painting – possessed, consumed by love. I wiped my nose surreptitiously and smiled back while Natty gurgled and waved his tiny paw.

What else could I have done – her being so ill? What would you have done? Only a complete bastard would have burst her bubble at that moment. And anyway, I did feel rather proud to be asked, no one had ever asked me to be a godmother before. It was grown-up, responsible. I was really chuffed. So I was Natty's Godmother, his Fairy Godmother as he used to say later. *Auntie Billie's my Fairy Godmother she is, int she, Mam?*

And that was how Natty Savage came into my life, like sunrise, like a breaking wave, like a flower; irresistible as nature.

Love at first sight.

That night, as Micky and I lay on the battered sofa and watched TV, we talked about having kids. We decided one day, we'd have two despite my fear of it; after all, the future seemed safely nebulous and far away. We agreed to wait a year or two – a year at that age seemed a lifetime – until we'd got ourselves properly settled. We even picked out names (yes, very fancy ones) – Storm for a girl, Kai for a boy. Or Hester and Dylan. Or maybe Emerald and Rory…Life was good and it was going to get better. Maybe I could never wear a patch but I could be the power behind the throne and the throne was what I had my eye on. Nothing was impossible, nothing too high to aim for.

True to his word, Carl kept Micky close and soon he became treasurer. This was a position which carried a terrible weight of responsibility because of the money involved. Notoriously, the last bloke to be treasurer, Lenny, had succumbed to temptation, absconded with the cash and fled in a VW combi to Europe, never to return. Carl had taken the job over for a bit but now it was Micky's and he took it dead seriously. Every week, club members paid subs and the accumulated funds paid for lawyers, and parties. Micky laboriously wrote everything down each Thursday night in a school exercise book accompanied by much grunting and pen chewing. His first big accounting was due for the annual Easter run, the first mass outing of the year, which this spring would culminate in us going to a big party in another club's territory.

A lot has been written about outlaw biker parties and most of it's shit because the straights who write it have either never been to a biker do or have and were so intent on making themselves appear daring and 'authentic' they didn't bother with a paltry thing like accuracy.

I won't pretend the parties were Sunday School picnics or the kind of gathering most people would enjoy, but then, they weren't set up for people other than those who knew what they were letting themselves in for and were prepared. So no, there wasn't any of that guff about biting the heads off live chickens, sorry to disappoint. There were more drugs than you could shake a stick at, though – and booze, guns and knives; biker party favours.

People getting beaten up? Well, yeah. Of course it happened. There was the usual gang stuff between rival outfits or the town hard men, but there were other kinds of fighting, too. Some people had – still have, probably – a kind of demented desire to bring it on themselves; I call it Gunfighter Syndrome. They'd see a large, probably armed biker (think Western Gunfighter propped up against a bar) and they *had* to go up to them and tell them *exactly* what they thought of them. Or chuck a beer over them. Or slap their face. I've seen all that and more. Men, boys, women, girls, anyone. And not always drunk, either. Like moths to a flame, some people long to crash and burn by being as stupid as is humanly possible.

But none of the bikers I knew personally were truly evil. I know this, because I've seen real evil since. It's not wild and hot, crazy and high like those men were, it's sly and gloatingly stupid, it's cold and brutish. Real evil starts small, in little cruelties that excite and grow exponentially. It's secret and dirty, sewer-stinking and without hope, light or redemption; its puke-green eyes hold no spark of human love and it's so repulsive when you meet it, you will yourself to forget as fast as you can – but you can't because it taints you forever and thickens the darkness of your dreams until you die.

We were lots of things, and not all of them good by any means, but we were never that.

Also, and very importantly, people forget or don't realise that human nature being what it is, there's a terrible amount of politics involved in gang life. It's worse than the bloody Masons in that respect. The manoeuvring and game-playing would have shamed the court of the Sun King. Which brings me back to the parties. They were the great ceremonial events in our calendar, where deals were negotiated and reputations made, or if you were stupid or unlucky, ruined. So you had to be very, very careful. *Very*.

Sometimes these parties, or territorial meets, were held at one of our club-member's homes. More worrying were the ones where we were invited to party with another gang, on their territory. The houses where these exercises in mayhem took place always seemed to look the same though – big, dirty old Victorian places, with backyards full of discarded machinery and the carcasses of dead bikes and cars.

They were always cold, damp places too, like our flat – except for the front room, where a gas fire with broken ceramic elements would be hissing on full blast and glowing a furnace orange. I'm sure half the feeling of being horribly stoned was actually carbon monoxide poisoning.

But there was one party I'll never forget because it marked a turning point in Micky's and my time with the Devil's Own. It's a tale I can tell now because all the major players are dead or gone out of the life; not, I imagine they'd care much whether I recount it or not but, like all men, they don't like their goings-on discussed in public, or in this case, whoever finds this memoir after I'm dead. Leckie, probably, I think I'll leave her the old lock-box along with all my other worldly possessions – why not? She's the nearest thing to a true sister I've ever had. What will she make of all this, I wonder? I expect she'll just sigh and shake her head, her thick black hair dancing like a pony's mane.

Anyhow, I was talking about this party with Johnjo only the other evening as we ate dinner and even he remembers it as out of the ordinary – and there's a fella who's not easily impressed, believe me.

This particular do was held at the house of a Biker Legend – a man so terrifying that even hardened old bikers spoke of him in a tone of marked respect. He was extremely handsome, very Clint Eastwood, and had his own gang that operated from a small village on the moors near the north west coast. The only noticeable difference between the Legend's house and any of the others we partied in was the huge incongruous fire surround in the front room. It was carved from white marble – now much stained and battered – and above it was an ornate, tarnished mirror framed in peeling rococo gold. They were obviously relics of the house's former days of glory. Now the mirror reflected the chaos of the party, the discoloured silver lending a curious, hellish distortion to the images it contained.

I must admit, now I don't have to keep up a good face anymore, I never enjoyed these parties. They reminded me of going to the Christmas dinner dances and dos Mum's work organised. I'd packed in going as soon as I could, but Jen always went, she loved all the dressing up and playing the part of a sweet loving daughter, flattering Mum's idea of her perpetual glamour and Jen's careful self-image of beautifully groomed sophistication. Sullen and uncomfortable in my itchy party frock, I'd hated those evenings of being on my best behaviour *or else*, and these parties – despite the outlaw trappings – made me feel the same. I knew one false move, one word out of turn and I'd let Micky down, just as I knew I'd let Mum down.

This time, I felt really nervous for reasons I couldn't properly explain. True, I'd been struggling with depression for some weeks; carefully putting on a calm, happy face each morning to see Micky off to work, then feeling it slide off my bones like melted wax when I was alone. The Black Dog, prowling round me, his eyes glowing like the Barguest. But was it just the depression that made me not want to go to this do? I didn't know. OK, maybe I should have confided in Micky more, but that haunting little voice, '*People can go off you, you know*,' chanted its cruel song in my heart and I'll be honest, I was afraid. Afraid he'd be bored of my moaning, afraid he'd go off and find a nicer, prettier, happier girl. He deserved to be loved and cared for, to have children by a nice, ordinary, normal girl. Not me. I didn't deserve his love. I didn't deserve anyone's love. It tormented me and I was getting raggety and weird. Things like not eating for two days then bolting half a pound of ham or six rounds of buttered toast and feeling nauseous and tearful. Biting my nails to the quick. Crying hopelessly at sad adverts on TV. Micky was puzzled, sure, but he was working all hours and, frankly, was too tired some nights to even speak. One night he fell asleep in the middle of his dinner, head back and snoring, the macaroni cheese congealing on his plate.

So come the day of this particular party, I felt unsettled and jumpy from the off. Perhaps, with hindsight, I should have pleaded illness, and stayed in bed that day with a hot water bottle and a cheap novel. But I didn't want to let Micky down. Duty called. And once we'd set off, come so far, I could hardly turn round to Micky and say, '*Take me home, I've lost my nerve, I don't like it, I'm not up to it, I'm scared*.' We'd done so well on the run, too – not too fast, not too slow – no stops other than the mass ones, no breakdowns. We'd ridden like princes in Carl's wake, us and Johnjo on his newly finished lowrider, 'Witchqueen', a black twin to Micky's beautiful, much admired 'Lady Blue'.

So I controlled myself. Like always. But I was strung out and exhausted.

I was – *weak*.

Eventually, we arrived at the house and the sound of Deep Purple's 'Child In Time' could be heard a street away. It was a done deal, no sneaking off, and it wouldn't do to be caught napping. I tried to pull myself together, shake off the weird feeling, but I felt sick with fatigue and tension. I thought maybe my period was due or something, I did feel a low, dragging ache in the pit of my belly and a clammy, chill shiveryness goosebumping my flesh. Still, there was nothing I could do now but see it through. Careless of the etiquette that said all the women should sit together or with their man, I sat on a sagging sofa that reeked of cat piss next to Doc, his crumpled gnome's face lazy with drink and cheerful cynicism. I hoped he'd provide camouflage and maybe take my mind off my nerves with one of his yarns, or political rants while Little Buddha and Johnjo sloped off to inspect some marvel of engineering in the yard.

'Want some acid? Plenty acid round 'ere – blotter, mind you – wouldn't care for it meself, like, it's cut wi strych. Fuckin' hard on the guts, in my opinion, but there you are, youth of today, fucked, the lot on 'em.' He gestured at a cadaverously thin boy dressed in skintight greasy black leather, giggling through rotting green teeth at nothing *I* could see. 'Fucked in the head, eh, bolloxed – silly cunt. Still, if yer want some…'

'Yeah, see what you mean – no, I don't like it anymore meself, actually…'

'Don't yer, *actually* – ho, pard-on *me*, milady,' he said in a 'posh' voice. I froze – was he in a bad mood? Was he on a paranoia speed thing like last week? He was smiling, but that didn't necessarily mean he was OK. He caught my look of confusion, laughed hoarsely and passed me his beer.

'Get yer gob round that, Bill, guaranteed blotter free, the only fuckin' one in ere, believe me.'

I drank the warm, sweet-sour fluid and tried to relax as I gazed around the room, being careful not to linger too long on one person. I didn't want anyone to think I was dead-eyeing them. There were outlaws from all over the country, plus hangers-on of all varieties. A couple of baby Grebos had sneaked in and were fucked on free acid. One of them had tried to pet our host's German Shepherd and it had bitten clean through his upper lip which was hanging half on, half off in a swollen, blackened mess. *He* thought it was some sort of badge of courage and kept repeating the story at the top of his voice. There were some older, mean-looking guys in one corner, with sharp, pallid prison faces and concealed guns that everyone knew about, but elaborately ignored. And there were unattached women, too – some confident, long-time party girls hoping to score a steady fella and a boost up the social ladder – some pitiful, drunken losers with 'victim' written in block capitals on their raddled, cacky foreheads. And there was also Knobby's Fuck-of-the-Month, a middle-class art student unaware that Knobby was so riddled with the clap his dick-end looked like a leper's fist. He wasn't called Knobby for nothing, not that she was to know that. She was thrilled with her bit of rough and her slumming expedition and her voice cut like a buzz saw.

Inch by unsaveable inch I watched with horrible fascination as she crept closer and closer towards disaster. Then it happened – in the blink of an eye.

'Knobby – Knobb*eeee*, don't be such a *wanker*, give me a fucking *drink...*'

Her voice sliced through the noise cleanly and fatally as she took the whisky bottle from Knobby's lips in front of us all. Without a second's hesitation, Knobby punched her in the face with the economical action of a man used to winning. Her high bridged nose broke with an audible crack and a red blossom of blood. Her world fell apart like a badly stitched frock. Knobby turned away while she stumbled, sobbing from the room and out of the house. He was done with her, and he didn't give a fuck. I looked away – it was bad luck to see these things.

Then, suddenly, the Legend himself was sitting companionably on the arm of the sofa, talking to Doc. I tried not to stare. He was a major celebrity, famed for exploits such as biting a bloke's nose off in a fight *and swallowing it*. Tasted of blood, snot and gristle, he'd say cheerily. He rode a dragon-green rig with much-admired – but rather crudely done to my mind – artwork on the tank and in every way, behaved like a star. Doc made careful compliments about the party and the beautiful rig, which was parked in the kitchen, while I tried to look keen, yet cool. I must have succeeded because the Legend addressed me personally, a thing normally unknown in the social annals of Outlaw Bikerdom.

'I int seen yer before, who's yer Old Man?' he enquired affably.

I froze with terror. Doc answered for me, as was the custom, that my Old Man was Little Buddha, their new treasurer, and a good lad. I nodded, mute. The Legend nodded, too. Again, I felt that sense of confusion rage through my mind and inwardly tried to give myself a stiff talking to. I snapped out of my reverie to realise I'd broken my cardinal rule. I hadn't been on the ball – and that had been a very bad mistake. The Legend was smiling in a wolfish sort of way and Doc looked worried. Something was amusing the Great Man. He spoke.

'Doc 'ere says you're a bit clever, like, a bit arty, eh? Eh? Tell yer what, you come wi me, an I'll show yer summat a bit *artistic…*'

He uncoiled himself from the sofa arm and wove through the party with me in his wake. I had no choice but to follow him after a direct request. The noise quietened and all eyes followed our progress, the men grinning and their women nudging each other. It was like a bad dream from which I could not escape, and all I could do was tell myself not to panic, or I was done for. We neared the ruined mantelshelf and our dank, distorted reflections wavered in the flyblown mirror as if it were a dirty pond. The atmosphere was thick and hot with expectation. The Legend gestured languidly to a large domed birdcage draped in a cloth on the mantelshelf. I heard Doc whisper '*Oh shit*', but I felt a wave of relief. A birdcage – wow – it was obviously some sort of exotic bird, a big old parrot or something – I mean, a *birdcage*, well…

The Legend swept off the cover.

'That *arty* enough for yer, eh?'

It was not, after all, a birdcage. It was a very large, thick glass jar. In it, immersed in a murky fluid, was a severed head. Its eyes were half shut, its mouth – a soft, small mouth – partly open. Long hair floated around it like weed. It was the head of a young girl. I heard the men's laughter echo in the white, sweaty coldness that enveloped me and I heard, as if from very far away, the Legend proudly boasting he got her off a bent mortician for over a hundred quid. Then a woman started screaming shrilly, '*God, God, God,*' over and over and the Legend grumpily covered up his prize. With careful deportment, I walked to the stinking toilet and threw up in private.

It had been a test. Had it been a set up, contrived by Carl and his long-time compadre, the Legend, designed to show the Devil's Own I was fit to be among them? I don't know – maybe, though; it was the kind of thing Carl liked to do, a public ordeal, the ritual, the initiation rite. It was more politics. But whatever his intent, I had passed the test. Carl was pleased with me and I hadn't shamed him or Micky, or let my club down. I wiped my mouth and ran cold water from the rusty faucet over my wrists like Mum always said to do when you felt faint. Mum, Jen – dear God in heaven, what would they have done? How far away from them I was, and not just in miles; we were on different planets. I felt sickly and feverish, as if seeing that dreadful, pitiful thing had pushed and pushed and strained me up against some membrane in my head and then with a wet splitting feeling I'd ripped through it at enormously accelerated speed into another part of my life. The world was not the same place it had been only minutes before. I tasted the vomit in the back of my throat and swallowed convulsively.

Wiping my mouth I walked back into the room. Carl caught my eye and nodded. I nodded back and that fleeting smile of his told me he was proud of the way I'd managed things. But it couldn't warm the fever-cold inside me and I longed to go home. I didn't feel triumphant, or clever, or anything like that. I just felt different.

Micky noticed it straightaway. Though he couldn't be seen to be concerned, because it was all supposed to have a been a bit of casual fun, his blue eyes spoke volumes. He draped his arm round me, the beer bottle dangling from his hand in a carefully careless way and slowly we drifted out to the bikes, as if he was just going out to check everything was OK, though traditionally, that was the prospect's job. But everyone knew Micky was mad about 'Lady Blue' and so they just joked with him about how he should be married to her, not me. We laughed, like automatons, until we found a safe place across the road, on a little bench under a big old chestnut tree.

Micky sprawled, drinking his beer, apparently without a care in the world while I struggled to look calm and maintain that hieratic, impassive look favoured by the gang women.

Micky looked away from me, as if surveying his surroundings in a lordly manner. 'Jeez, Princess, are you OK?' he said under his breath.

'No – yes; yes, I'm – Oh, Micky, Micky, can we go? Can we go home? Please?' My face didn't move as the weak, pleading words tumbled out of my mouth.

'You know we can't, love – y'do, don't yer? We can't. If we do, that's it. I'll 'ave ter hand me colours in. That'll be it, done. Over.'

I pretended to wipe my nose on the bandanna I was twisting in my hands so I wouldn't look nervy. 'Yeah. Yeah, I know. I know. It's OK, I'm – I'm OK, just – can we sit here for a bit? Just a few minutes, just till I get mesel together.'

'Aye. Course we can. Billie – I'm that proud of you, I am. Not cos o' this, not just cos o' this, but like, generally.'

'Micky...'

'Now then, youth – how y'doin?' Micky greeted a square-jawed fella, one of the Gypsy Jokers, who had a thick mop of tow-coloured hair almost obscuring his eyes. The man sat next to Micky and began an earnest conversation about gearboxes while I cursed him roundly in my mind.

I managed to stick it out until we could go home the next morning but I made like I had flu and stayed in bed for the next two days, and to be honest, I was running a bit of a temperature. Micky never mentioned what had happened and neither did I, but I found the stick I got at the club levelled off a bit and more than once, I felt Carl's gaze on me though he never spoke. I laughed and joked with the rest like normal while they sat about in the pub grumbling and yarning, playing endless hands of brag and interminable games of pool. But though I felt my face working to produce mechanical smiles and my mouth speaking the acceptable platitudes, I had the feeling sometimes of swimming through deep waters, dark currents swirling beneath me; monstrous creatures white as leprosy, with eyes like dead pearls, their ropy tentacles coiling and uncoiling in mindless hunger, stirred in the far depths below as I concentrated on swimming as hard as I could towards some distant shore and safety. I felt blind and deaf, muffled and distant, as if some terrible fate was gathering like a storm far out to sea – only I couldn't see what it was, I could only feel it in my nerves that sang through my body like thin sizzling filaments stretched to breaking point.

Nowadays they'd say it was post-traumatic stress syndrome, the combination of the assault in my youth and the incident at the party, the sheer energy it took to live the life I was in. My nana would have called it brain-fag, or brain fever and I would have been packed off to some quiet convalescent home in Sidmouth or somewhere – a change of air, the rest will do you good, dear. It would have, too, but Micky and I were far too skint to have a holiday, and it never crossed my mind that I was actually ill; over-tired, maybe, but nothing serious. Nothing that couldn't be cured as usual, by my will-power and determination to keep rushing forwards, like a freight train out of control.

I lost weight, but I was pleased about that; even then, women thought losing weight for whatever reason, including actual illness, was a blessing (*Well, I may have had a gippy tummy all the time we were in Spain, and I suppose it did spoil the trip, but I lost ten pounds! Oooo, lucky you!*) and a few people complimented me on being so slim. Mum was very happy, but assuming I was on one of her crash diets, warned me not to get 'gaunt' – men don't like it, she said, they like a bit of an armful. Quite how that titbit married with women's obsession with becoming human broom-handles, I don't know, because if we're not doing it for men, why the fuck are we doing it? I mentioned this – without the swearing – but just got a head-wobble, pursed lips and comments about being contrary for the sake of it.

But I felt contrary. And jumpy. If there was a sudden noise I jerked as if I'd been electrocuted and often, I found tears welling up for no apparent reason. I was sallow, and my hair a heavy, limp mass that seemed to drag my head back with its weight; I thought about cutting it short in some fashionable style, but Micky forbade me on the grounds he loved my long hair – and glad of his attention, I just wound it into a knot and changed my shampoo from Vosene to something almondy-smelling by Vidal Sassoon. I permanently had dark circles under my eyes; my periods got more painful, heavier, the thick dark blood clotted and glutinous. I thought I might be anaemic, the catch-all excuse for all 'women's problems' in those days and bought some vitamins that I never took. Even Jas asked me if I was feeling alright, and told me some of the women thought I was expecting which they considered would settle me down a treat and 'be the makin' of me'. When I told her I wasn't pregnant, just tired, her face fell; she'd so hoped for a buddy for Natty, who was fat and thriving on cold curdled Cow & Gate and fag smoke.

My heart beat so hard sometimes I thought it would burst; but I never thought I might be spinning out of control, getting spattery and mixed up like a Jackson Pollock painting made flesh. I never lost control, me. Never. Not ever.

And out to sea, the thunderheads doubled and re-doubled in gravid masses while I fretted over nothing I could understand and chewed my fingernails to the bloody quicks.

Chapter Fourteen

I WAS SMOKING a lot more dope than I usually did. OK, it wasn't the hideously strong GM skunk that's popular nowadays, but none the less. Like I've said, I don't like to get blind wasted, unlike some. I was never a big drinker, so I can't say I missed that; being drunk isn't a sensation I've ever enjoyed. I still occasionally succumbed to a bit of whizz, but since my life had become more settled, whizz meant tons of energy and nowhere to put it: after all, there's only so many times you can rearrange the spice rack into alphabetical order.

Sometimes smoking was the only way I could get some sleep, though. But I paid the price; the freaky dreams that surged through the heavy nights left me groggy and disorientated the following day, and I'd sleep late and then not be able to sleep that night…And so on and so on. People like to say dope's not harmful, it's just herbs, but that's not true; if it is, why are so many regular hash-heads so bloody twitchy? The fact is, it makes you paranoid, if you smoke enough.

I did try to get some sleeping tablets from the doc's, just a few to sort of kick-start me into a more regular sleeping pattern. I'd tried to explain to him how I felt, I suppose I tried to ask for help, but I couldn't seem to express myself properly, and his pink, doughy face only registered impatience and irritation as I stumbled through some disjointed phrases. In the end, he'd barked out a few comments

about going for walks and not drinking coffee or alcohol at night
and refused to give me any pills, saying I'd become dependant on
them, or he implied, I'd trade or sell them on the street. I left the
surgery, my face burning with frustration and humiliation. When
the receptionist (cow) raised her eyebrow at the sight of me I nearly
bit her. That would have been fun; it would really have confirmed
what they thought of me – the scruffy weirdo in patched-up faded
jeans, Norton T-shirt and black leather jacket. I wonder what they
think nowadays, those straights, now all the things they loathed are
commonplace – girls with scarlet hair and belly-button piercings,
boys with footballer mohicans and tops with FCUK emblazoned on
them and everyone and their auntie tattooed. Those poor straights,
they must be livid to think all their petty power trips and prejudice
came to nothing in the end.

It was a joke anyhow, what the doc said – like he didn't hand out
Valium to every pissed off, trapped housewife in the village, just to
keep 'em quiet. Prozac, now, isn't it? Sure, he chucked tranquillisers
around like sweeties, but not to me. He wouldn't give me a script.
He wanted to punish me – and he did, but not how he thought.
In a way, it's his fault, what happened, because if I'd been happily
necking my legal gear, I wouldn't have begged Micky to run me over
to Terry's that night to get some blow to calm me down. Stupid to
blame the doctor, I know, but I can still see his smug, judgmental
face patronising me, dismissing me as street scum, unworthy of his
real attention. It made me grind my teeth, it tightened the screw
inside me another few turns.

I'd had such a bad day, you see. I don't mean that as an excuse but
I had. In fact, I'd had a bad few days, the sort where the world seems
to conspire against you, the littlest thing is a mountainous effort,
when everything I touched fell apart. I burnt dinner twice because
I forgot about it, staring out of the window at the wind ripping the
russet leaves off the tree across the road, plastering them wetly
against cars and knotting them into gutter-blocking masses. The sky
was a leaden, unrelieved grey, pregnant with rain and each morning
it was a struggle to crawl out of bed into the unheated room from
under the warm quilts. I broke a glass and cut myself. I spoilt a

drawing I was doing for someone's tank mural. Nothing was right, it was all off kilter.

I knew I wouldn't sleep and my body was screaming with fatigue; even Micky allowed I wasn't looking too good, but when he went to his stash to roll us one, like the proverbial cupboard, it was bare. I felt unreasonably, unaccountably frantic.

So I begged Micky, really pleaded with him, to go get me something – something a bit stronger than blow, something that would knock me out, drop me into blissful unconsciousness for a few hours. Just this once, really, just for tonight.

'I can't do tonight, Micky love, I can't...Please, love, please, sweetheart, it's only half nine, not so late, you've got the van, please, please...'

He sighed heavily and rubbed his forehead hard with the heel of his hand, then scratched at his beard. 'OK. But...'

'But what? What? Look, here's some money, my money, not housekeepin', just this once...'

'Yeah, I know, no, don't fret about the money, it int that, I just can't think who might...Oh, well, Terry would I s'pose...'

My dislike of Terry seemed a small thing in view of the white, cruel night of sleeplessness and twisting, raw unnameable terror that faced me. I felt as if tonight would be the last straw, that I wouldn't possibly be able to get through it. Terry...Fuck it, what was he there for, the shithead, if not to be of use to us? I didn't like the thought of owing him a favour, but I was secure in my position, I couldn't imagine he'd dare push it. Talk about tunnel vision.

'Will you? Will you go? Micky, please, Micky?'

'Yeah, yeah, OK, OK, it's alright, it'll be alright. But you're comin' with me – no, I mean it. Come on, it'll do yer good ter get out the house an' anyhow, I won't leave yer here alone. Get wrapped up warm, come on.'

If he had left me – oh Jesus – if he had left me...Micky, my poor boy, you should have gone without me or better still, not gone at all. We should have taken off on a little holiday instead, just packed a bag and driven off to Whitby, stayed a few days, walked by the sea, anything. But I can't be thinking like that. I can't.

The drive to Haleshaw was uneventful. The wind was getting up a bit and there was a near-full moon. As we drove through town and out the other side, it started to spot with rain fitfully. It was cold in the old van and I was glad I'd put my big black jumper on. I pulled the sleeves down to cover my hands; they were shaking, but not from cold. Micky was humming 'Black Betty' under his breath and I stared out of the window at the drunks skittering around the gleaming pewter streets.

We passed a bunch of punks coming out of their favourite pub – the only one that would let them in; they huddled under the streetlight sharing a tab. Micky made a rude comment but I liked the way they looked. I turned my head to watch the little scene as we passed: the girls with their heavy Cleopatra eyeliner and black lips, dog-collars and holey mohair sweaters in neon shades over mini-kilts and ripped fishnets, the boys practising their sneers in raggy combat trousers and leopard print bum-flaps, Clash or Pistols shirts and spray-painted DMs. I liked their explosions of coloured hair, blue, green, pink, orange. It put me in mind of 'Stingray', my favourite TV puppet show from when I was a kid. There'd been a beautiful mermaid puppet called Aqua Marina with floating, spangled dresses and long, sea-green hair; her smooth, lovely face had been a cross between Julie Christie and a seal. Maybe I could dye my hair turquoise, maybe I could start again, have a new life…I remembered watching kids' TV with Dadda, all excited about 'Vision On' or something, and hearing his gentle, husky smoker's voice saying it was smashing, absolutely. *'Lovely, Billie girl. Clever stuff, now, eh?'* Oh, Dadda, I've inherited your Black Dog, haven't I? Never mind, it wasn't your fault, just my bad luck, my fucking awful luck.

I kept thinking about the punks as we drove up the long road out through the high-sided old mill buildings towards Haleshaw village proper. I could paint those punks, just as I'd seen them, I thought. A real painting, on canvas, work it up into something special. I was sick of doing fantasy stuff in the style of Frank Frazetta for bike murals; how many roaring dragons and naked sorceresses with enormous tits and bums and the faces of big-eyed children could one woman do? No, I'd get some decent paints from Daley's and stretch a canvas and really go for it...

The rain was coming down good style now, as we got out into the countryside. Bradford's like that; one minute you're in a raw, ex-industrial canyon swirling with rubbish and the ghosts of dead machinery, the next it's all Dales-like and hobbity, a soft, hilly landscape stitched with knots of trees and the amber lights of grey, lichened cottages nestling like tired pigeons under the lee of a hillock.

Just before the village itself, we turned up a farm track to Terry's cottage. To my surprise, it was all ripped up; great tree-roots, their snaky black tentacles dripping in the wet heaped together by the bumpy road. Mounds of earth chunky with stone spilled across the ruts.

'Jesus, what's goin' on here?' I queried. The only other time I'd been to Terry's it had been in an idyllic setting, the tussocky grassland cropped by some horses from the nearby livery stables, shaded by old trees and hedges. I'd been jealous that a tosser like Terry could live anywhere so pretty, but to be honest, bucolic fantasies aside, his cottage wasn't much: an old cold-water, outside netty, three-roomed place – stone built, stone flagged and damp as buggery despite the ancient Aga. I suppose if you'd been of a mind to do improvements, it could have been made nice, but Terry lived in it like the pig he was. I think he paid a pound a week for it or something ridiculous.

'Yeah, a right mess, int it. All them trees, it's fuckin' criminal. They're buildin' some houses, bought the land off the farmer an' it's all goin' to them houses like boxes. An estate, like. Smart. Everythin' the same, all neat an' tidy. Shit. Terry's place is comin' down. He's been paid off – a tidy sum. Fuck me, he's a jammy bastard that un.'

As I pondered why anyone in their right mind would want to live in a ticky-tacky new Lego house we pulled up into Terry's yard. It was a repository of old engines, scrapped bikes, dead cars and what appeared to be an old steam engine in bits. The lads used to joke that all this twisted metal was just decor, to give Terry the correct bikery look, because he was about as good with an engine as a trout would be.

The light was on in the front room, it lit the dark heaps of junk with a yellow gleam, like a Caravaggio.

'Stop here if you like,' said Micky as he zipped up his jacket. 'I'll not be long.'

'No, I'll come, it's bloody freezing in here.'

'Fuck me, you wait till winter sets in, you're getting soft, my lass – you shoulda put on that Damart Thermalwear stuff I got yer for yer birthday, lovely an' warm that is, nice pair o' long johns – sexy...'

I reached over and tugged his hair, smiling. I felt better, the drive had relaxed me. Maybe if I felt crap in future, I should just get out of the house; even, though it pained me to admit it, do what the doc said and go for a walk. I was excited by the painting I was going to do, too. It would be good, I felt it. I nursed a little warm feeling of anticipation in my belly. Plans and ideas flitted through my mind as I picked my way through the rubbish behind Micky. Alright, Micky wasn't big on punk rock, but he'd see what I was trying to do with the picture, he'd appreciate it because he was open-minded, unlike some – huh, Terry for example. Well, he'd never see it, and anyway, what did I care about the likes of him?

The door opened. Terry stood there in his leather jacket, check shirt and filthy Levis, dirty, mud-crusted steelies unlaced over grubby fisherman's socks. He smelt terrible, a thick sweat-sour funk overlaid with the whiff of rancid bacon fat. My nose wrinkled at the odour and something prickled in the back of my mind, something... I knew that smell, what was it? I mean apart from BO, no, it wasn't just that, it was...

Terry grinned mirthlessly like a death's head. 'Fookin' hell. Royalty, eh, eh? Fook me. Ha ha fookin' ha, well, well, don't fookin' stand there, come in, welcome ter my 'umble fookin' abode, yer majesties, don't mind the mess, I say, don't mind the mess, it's the maid's day off! See? The maid's day off! Fookin' hell...'

He was speeding off his tits, his weaselly face blanched to a bloodless fish-belly white and drawn, his nose red raw, his eyes brilliant and pinned. He must have been up for days; spending his compensation money, no doubt. That's why he smelt like that, it was the typical whizz-head's stink, the by-product of his liver and kidneys overloading, unable to process fast enough. I coughed. Jesus, to smell like that he must have been on a king-size bender and no mistake. Faintly, at the back of my mind a warning bell sounded and I heard Carl's voice; *'Never trust a speed freak, eh? Fucked up bastards, all of 'em – you never fuckin' know what they're gonna do next...'*

I felt a prickle of nerves run through me and I began to say something to Micky about forgetting the whole thing, no worries, I felt much better; but it was too late, he'd gone in.

I stepped over the threshold.

It had begun.

Part Two

Chapter Fifteen

I SUPPOSE I SHOULD do headers for this story, you know, like put the date and 'Dear Diary...' Apparently writing a diary is all the rage these days, especially in America. 'Journalising' they call it. All the gen on what frock you wore to the Prom, what Bobby-Joe said at the Dairy Queen, stuff you'd look back on with a nostalgic smile years later and wonder, with a gentle sigh, where the years went.

Well, I'm not going to put in all the insane stuff I got up to in the years between that night at Terry's and now. It's now, by the way; present day. We're up to present day. I only wish the actuality of going from there to here had been as painless as writing that phrase was. What shall I tell you? Shall I give you a précis of how screwed up you can get without actually killing yourself, taking excessive drugs or drinking yourself insensible? People believe you need to be smashed to really be self-destructive but that's *so* not true. I didn't even have the comfort of chemical oblivion. I knew what I'd done, those mornings after as I stared at the crusty fizzog of some unsuitable bloke I'd hoyed back to the flat over the shop for some mind-numbing shagging, or nursed my bruises after a brawl in some dodgy club.

So I'd like to say, '*The intervening years were a blur, dear reader.*' But I can't, because they weren't. So let's just get on, eh? I have a feeling – ha ha – time's running out for me.

But anyway, eventually, things did improve – I mean, we all grow up, don't we? It gets too bloody tiring, all that drama and nonsense, in the end. One night you don't go out, you stop in and watch telly and some part of you goes – ah, the relief, and that's that. So, things had been pretty hunky-dory for some years; my life had settled into a routine. Not exactly thrilling, but frankly, I was cautiously happy to relax a bit, to imagine my future; keep saving, get Natty and Jas settled, retirement, perhaps go live abroad, Spain, somewhere like that. I might even be able to persuade Johnjo to come, he was always complaining about the winters here. I remember being, feeling, very ordinary, very normal. Positively chilled – for me. This summer had been unusually warm, the sky a deep cloudless blue just faintly hazed with pollution for weeks; the sun an unblinking golden eye fixed on the city as we all dragged ourselves around like ants frying under a magnifying glass. That Monday, I staggered into the cool airy sanctuary of the shop, grateful for its air of oasis-like calm and felt the sweat dry on my forehead, courtesy of the two big stand fans Leckie had insisted on getting.

At first I'd laughed at the idea of needing fans in Bradford, like, ever, but she made a good case about keeping the atmosphere fresh for customers so they'd want to linger in the cool – and buy more stuff. As usual, she was right, but she needn't think that meant I'd let her have her New Age Bollocks Corner with the crystals and drony tapes of woodland noises or dolphins yodelling in close harmony that she wanted. 'Native American Dreamcatchers', tarot packs and bloody runes. Power beads. Books by silly mares who called themselves witches about casting love spells, and find-your-chakras manuals. Meditation accessory kits in genuine Tibetan-style cardboard gift boxes. Thought of the Day calendars. Jesus. Well, no actually, not Jesus – apparently He's not New Age. I'm sure He's pissed about that but hey, fashion is a fickle thing.

The scent of flowers and wood polish drifted through the air and a few customers browsed the card rack and the shelves, glad of the respite from the baking city heat. Leckie, looking daisy-fresh and unfazed, flapped her hand in welcome and I smiled. She was wearing a tight pink T-shirt printed with the words 'Babe With Brains' in gold glitter across her ample bosom. I stood with the Starbucks bag dangling from my wrist and wondered, not for the first time, where she got stuff like that, and also, fleetingly, why she wore it. Yesterday it had been an aqua-blue one with 'Wicked' written on it in silver foil print and a baby devil showing its bottom.

She shrieked and a ruminating customer looked round alarmed from the greetings card stand. 'Oh, Ess-bucks! Go it, girl! Fabby, did you get my fave?'

'Leckie, that T-shirt, where…'

'Hmm? Oh, *Leeds*, natch – want me to get you one?' She pulled the bag off my wrist and plundered it greedily for her Vente Chocolate Cream.

'No, thanks. Not me, really.'

'God, Bill, get out of black! Honestly, you look like a Mafia widow! I saw *The Godfather Two* last night on telly and when Michael's mum came on after Marlon Brando died I thought – Billie! Colour, Bill, colour – life, y'know? Live a little, try, oh, try – lilac! You're the artist after all, I mean, your pictures are *full* of colour; but clothes? How about a goldy-coloured scarf, it'd look lovely with your complexion, that'd be a start and…'

I smiled at her as I necked my sugarless, milkless double espresso. I'd worn black and only black for years now. For me to wear colours – though I loved colours in general, in fact I could get quite weepy at certain shades of pink when it came to roses, or a new box of pencils – well, it seemed wrong. What was that Leckie word? Oh yeah, *inappropriate*. It would be inappropriate for someone like me to wear bright clothes like Leckie, and that had something to do with the age gap, obviously, and a lot more to do with – other things. But I couldn't tell Leckie that.

'Yeah, OK, a scarf. I'll give it a go. Yeah, I promise. I do. Now, owt or nowt?'

I'd been late this morning, due to taking Ghengis to the vets with his latest fighting injury. The vet had been telling me for years to get him castrated and this time, though it made me feel unbelievably guilty, I agreed. Better that than him succumbing to yet another bite wound – he was getting on now and had lost his brawler's edge. Younger cats were muscling in on his territory. Time the old gangster hung up his pistols. Or in this case, his testicles. Anyway, Leckie had opened up as, fortunately, this was her full day off from Uni.

'Hang on.' Smiling, she slid behind the counter and served the bloke who'd jumped at her scream with a couple of cards. He was mesmerised by her chest and the acres of high-powered white teeth she flashed him, making him feel, like she made all our customers feel, as if he were the most important, interesting and valuable person on the planet for at least ten whole seconds. And she meant it, too. It was just how she was; nice, kind and efficient. With a bizarre taste in clothes. Well, I say bizarre, but like she always said, soon enough she'd be in suits and medium heel pumps for all eternity. Not, she'd add with a sideways glance from her velvety brown eyes, that anyone would know what she had on *underneath*…Frankly, my mind boggled at that thought.

The bloke wandered off, dazed, and Leckie came out and leant against the counter. Above her low-rider, Dirty Denim Brazilian-style boot-cut jeans (I'd had my fashion instructions) twinkled a diamanté belly-button bar and the edge of her fuchsia thong. She flipped one of her sequinned flip-flops and tossed her thick hair back while ticking off things of interest on her pointy fingers. Thirtysomething she may be, but staid – never. As she would say, way to *go*, girl.

'Rep from Hawkins rang – said those moonstone bib necklaces are in, do you want? No luck with turquoise though, or lapis – he says while the Afghani thing is still on we can all whistle, and how about some nice rose quartz waterfall rings or Tiger's Eye – he can get those big chunky raw stone beads you fancied if you like. He also said they're doing a new range of unpolished crystals with matching incense sticks and holders for meditation, all with a theme, like, Cleansing Quartz, Sensual Amethyst…Oh, go on, *please*…Oh, you big spoilsport. Anyway, I said you'd get back to him today. Umm, what else? Oh yeah I found that letter from the Inland Revenue you *hid*, Miss Wicked – and your baby came in and said he'll pop back later.'

At the last bit of information she rolled her eyes and puffed her cheeks, blowing the air out exaggeratedly and pretending to fan herself.

'Natty? Did he say what he wanted?'

'Er, like, *no* – but you should have seen – well, you will see – what he *isn't* wearing…Blimey, I know it's warm today but…Dungarees, is all I'll say. Faded baggy dungarees, Calvins and a pair of Nikes. That's *all*. Phew-ee. If I was ten years younger – no, make that five…'

'Leckie!'

'Well, honestly. He's to die for, the bad boy – oh, don't look like that. I know he's your baby but really, he's all grown up now, hmm-*hm*.'

I wasn't really shocked. Well, not much. Jasmine's plump baby boy had grown up into a tall, broad-shouldered, narrow-hipped, long-limbed, golden-skinned 'hunk' in Leckie-speak, with a rather long face, full lips, a neat freckled nose, high rounded cheekbones, a halo of short sun-faded dreads and a six-pack that he seemed to mysteriously acquire by eating chips fried in lard and sleeping until midday, every day. His eyes were his best feature though, they were quite amazing: long and deep-set, slightly slanted, the colour of dark honey; with a little twist, way down in their depths, of green fire. His eyelashes drove Leckie mad with envy and caused us to muse bitterly on why it was that boys always got the good eyelashes.

Everything that was stark and strong in Jasmine's archaic little face was there in Nat, but softened, smoothed by Terry's genes. Natty had his daddy's height but his mother's heartbreaking beauty. Only his strong, but rather crooked teeth, the front left one chipped diagonally on the inner edge, spoilt his looks – but I'd never been able to get Jas to take his teeth seriously. If he'd been my boy, I'd have had him in braces pronto to straighten those teeth, no problem; if he'd been my boy…

But he wasn't. I was just his Auntie Billie. His Guardian Angel, as Jas put it tearfully. His fairy godmother. And his beauty, which I was so proud of, which I drew over and over filling sketchbooks with portraits of him from babyhood onwards, was Jas's, not mine. His chaotic unschooled intelligence, his monumental energy, didn't belong to me. None of it did. As to his upbringing, I couldn't demand anything, only hint; I couldn't force Jas to feed him properly or get him inoculated, only plead with her not to forget. I was just there to protect him as best I could from her muddled, clinging carelessness and from himself: his own volatility, violence and his consuming rage.

I sighed. 'He'll be on about having that broken tooth capped in gold again. Well, I suppose if it's the thing, but…'

'All the boys want them, Bill. It's gangsta – but you're not going to pay for it, are you? Honestly, Billie, don't get me wrong, love, I know what a saint you've been to that poor family and I, you know, I think the world of you for it, everyone does, but the money! It's not like you're a millionaire – you waste…'

'Leckie, we've been over this. It's not a waste – he's my godson, the nearest thing I have to a real son. I don't mind, you know I don't, and he's a good lad, basically.'

'Oh, *basically*. Right. He's got a black eye, you know, a new one – Billie, he's going to get into real trouble one day if he doesn't learn to calm down…Sorry, sorry. I know, he's just a bit wild. I'm sure he'll grow out of it, one day. Oh, you know what I mean, I think he's great, I love him to bits, I do, but – you worry, Bill, God, *I* worry, it's, he's…Oh, you know. He's just *Natty*, I suppose. Oh, by the way, that gnome was with him – I had to watch him like a hawk.'

'Monkey? Is he out then?'

'Apparently. Though obviously a spell inside hasn't cured his sticky fingers, dreadful little object. He had that mother-of-pearl pen set in his pocket, I had to make him put it back – Natty's no help, either, he just laughed. They've got no sense of property, people like that, really.'

I felt a little wash of pale anger tighten my guts, then subside. She wasn't being cruel, just sounding off. She hated public 'scenes' and it had embarrassed her to tick Monkey off so despite all her flip talk about Natty, she was up on her high horse. Natty laughing hadn't helped, either; I'd have to have a word with him about that. He had to control Monkey if they came in the shop, and that was that. And be more respectful to Lecks. Normally he was – but if he was stoned…Oh, bloody hell, Natty. None the less, a word would be had, and a hard one at that. Leckie's sore point was her dignity, she couldn't bear not being taken seriously when she felt she had something serious to say, it freaked her right out and she'd nurse a grudge against Monkey for being the cause of her feeling of humiliation. And she liked to think Natty fancied her – which he probably did, in his lazy way – his 'siding' with Monkey would have tweaked her feminine pride.

People – God. A constant balancing act just to keep the peace. My mind flicked back to Carl and I sighed. Now, in my forties, I really understood and admired his talent for leadership; but he was dead, died in a smash up Malham way years back. The funeral had been tremendous, hundreds of bikers from all over Europe coming to pay their respects. Carl. I wished, not for the first time, he was still with us and I could ask his advice – about Natty, about poor Jas, about, well, all sorts. He'd have known what to do best, he'd have sorted it all out with a laconic observation in that Cockney drawl that years in the north never softened.

I don't mean to sound critical of Lecks. Don't get me wrong, I love Leckie, we'd hit it off the very first time we'd met at a friend's wedding. Well, I say 'friend' but strictly speaking the happy couple were customers. She'd wanted 'something special' in the ring line and I found them a lovely, unusual rose diamond and put them in touch with Ron Hudson, an artisan jeweller I knew, who does repair jobs for me or makes things to my designs. The resulting engagement and wedding ring set was exquisite. Bride and groom had been ecstatic and I got an invite to the big day; no expense spared at the Fellroyd Hall Hotel, out Bingley way. I went on a whim, really.

My boyfriend *du jour*, Ricky, was very keen to attend, thinking, it turned out, that seeing such a 'fairytale' wedding – the bridesmaids wore Bo Peep costumes, poor cows – I'd respond favourably to his proposal. After all, I was divorced, had been for years; my short-lived marriage to Little Buddha was seen by everyone I knew as a typical early marriage gone sour. Jesus, it made me laugh in my head when they pontificated about 'being too young' and 'that's what comes of rushing things' and 'you're better off out of it, thank God you didn't have kids'. It hadn't been anything like that and I'd loved Micky, it had broken my heart when we split.

I never heard from him. Not a phone call, not a holiday postcard, nothing, ever. It was if he were dead to me, the sweet boy I'd lain with in that icy flat while we laughed and kissed and planned our future together. Just like Dadda, gone forever. The nightmare come true. My marriage was like a ghost image in my mind, now, wintery and far away; faded, the details blurred. I barely remembered the way Micky's hair smelt and I had to remind myself: Fairy soap and burnt honey. And the exact colour of his eyes? Was it iris or cornflower? The whole thing was like someone else's life, like a weird film I'd watched or something. Not me. Had it really happened to me?

But no one else knew what I knew. So they'd go on at me; why shouldn't I get wed again? I was still young, still 'reasonable-looking' (gee, thanks). Ricky was very keen, he nagged and nagged about it like some blokes do who desperately want the comfort and security of their mum's house all over again. So the wedding was a godsend to him. I'd see how wonderful it could all be. Also, it turned out, his cousin was an old rugby mate of the groom, so it would be quite the family do.

Leckie was the rugger-bugger's date. When we were introduced I think we both had that little tingle that says, 'She seems OK, the right sort,' and despite our differing backgrounds and ages, we found we shared a sense of humour. Also, as Ricky and Tim got steadily drunker and drunker as the afternoon reception progressed and turned into a night-time disco, we discovered we had something else in common. We didn't really like Tim and Ricky-boy.

Does that sound hard? Well, maybe, a bit. But it's a sad fact of the dating game. You quite like someone, they're *kind* of alright, then finally you realise that a habit of speech, a tic, a lack of personal hygiene, their politics – something, anything, just puts you right off. I had a mate once who finished with a fella because despite the fact he was good-looking, solvent and reasonably well-behaved, she just couldn't stand his bitten-to-the-quick nails anymore. I know – poor bloke, not his fault, etc. But it works the other way round too. A male friend once jacked a girl who he said 'smelt of soap'. Duh. OK.

And that's what happened. When Ricky, arseholed and egged on by the scarlet-faced and sweating Tim, bullied the DJ into playing 'our tune' and wobbled down unsteadily onto one knee in the middle of the dancefloor, spluttering, 'Billee, wouldja marry…Fuck, I mean – Tim, Tim wha shoulda I say, mate, wha…' went white, then green then puked like a fountain while Tim laughed uproariously – Leckie and I shared a cab home.

We quietly finished with the lads.

Watching her deal with it so calmly and in such a friendly but final way taught me to be more patient with blokes, because I saw it worked. Before, when I finished with them I'd dropped the shutters and done the Devil's Own thing; the poor sods ceased to exist. Nothing personal. Nothing at all, in fact. Just like the club. Once you were out, that was that. You were a cabbage, like all the other straights. Possibly you might get minimum icy courtesy, possibly not. Leckie always says she can tell instantly if I don't like someone, I'm so, *so* polite. Not that I had a lot of fellas to finish with, not anymore. Ricky was the last, in a way. After that, it was just Johnjo, if that counts as an actual relationship. Leckie says not, and bridles. I don't know, it suits me.

I admire Leckie, you see. As a person. When we first met up she had a good job in local government with decent pay, prospects, the lot. Not like me, struggling with the shop, scrounging the money to do my cottage up, sometimes despairing of the whole self-employed thing. She was a bit of a golden girl, on her way to the top. I suppose one thing we had in common was the desire to succeed. We had – we have – ambition, in our different ways. We both wanted to get on, get secure, do well, show the people who griped at us (yeah, our families) that we could win. It's just she's logical, grounded and I'm not. She'll calmly plan her way to success, I'll throw myself at it until one day, I'll stick. Well, opposites attract, they say.

So Lecks was doing well, on the fast track. And then, when everything seemed unstoppably perfect, she met Tony. It was classic; so commonplace, a joke really, if it had actually been funny, which it wasn't. Tony was – still is for all I know – the Office Romeo. Tall, handsome and married. Now, sure, lots of folk are wed and they separate and divorce or whatever, and no one expects anyone to be a bloody saint during the in-between bit. I mean, Johnjo's still married, legally, but I know Lin, I know her from the old days and she knows about me and she doesn't care. It's all out in the open. She does what she likes, and Johnjo does the same. It's honest, even if it's not moral by some people's standards. But Tony – not an honest bone in his body. His wife, naturally, didn't understand him, boo hoo. They were on the verge of divorce, only keeping up a front for the poor kiddies. They hadn't slept together for years...

Sound familiar? It's happening while you read this – somewhere, to someone, maybe even you. Well, if it is you, read on and take heed, because this is how it will end up and that's a stone promise.

Tony set his cap at Leckie, probably because she had the rep of being friendly – but untouchable, a bit of an Ice Maiden. Not the kind of girl who lets her hair down at the Christmas party and photocopies her fanny, like some. The problem is, at first blokes are attracted to her prettiness, then frightened off by her huge brain. So she's more than a bit susceptible to a man who appears to be unfazed by her. So soon the apparently fearless Tony had her eating out of his hand. A mild office flirtation turned into a full-on wild affair. Snogging in the stationery cupboard. Car trysts up on Baildon Moor. Weekends at 'conferences'. Text messages that made her blush. Secret e-mails. I pleaded with her to be careful, but she didn't want to be. It was all so exciting, so crazy. She had a over-heated, feverish look all the time and all she could talk about was Tony, Tony, Tony. How he'd soon be free, how they'd get married, how they'd both have glittering careers, what a blast it all was.

Six months later she was pregnant and he'd been promoted and transferred – with the wifey and three kiddies, one a new-born – to Edinburgh. Lecks had clamydia, too, just a little leaving present, that. Oh, and the fact those 'secret e-mails' weren't in fact secret at all; Tone had shared them with his departmental drinking buddies. Hilarious, eh?

Leckie had to get rid; I went with her to the place in Leeds. We both cried. It's not something I'd want to go through, personally, and I'm glad I've never had to. She was very brave, very stand-up through the whole mess. She took it on the chin like a good 'un; but anyone who thought she was cold or heartless would be about as wrong as it would be possible to be. It changed her, subtly. She – well, she matured a bit. A hint of shadow in her eyes, a less girlish laugh, a thread of melancholy woven through her. I don't know, something.

She lost her job, too; I mean, she resigned. She had to, it was intolerable working in a place where people had seen the foolish messages she'd written to Tony, who knew about the golden girl's fall from grace and loved it, who sniggered behind her back, who grinned and made remarks, who pinned crude, anonymous cartoons up on the noticeboard and sent e-mails of her head attached to a porno picture round her co-worker's computers. The usual stuff, the weakling's revenge.

She already had a BA in Business Studies, so she decided to do an MBA and then a PhD in Marketing at the Management Centre at The Ridings University. It's very posh, very famous – students go there from all over the shop, apparently. It was Leckie's way of giving two's up to the bastards who tried to grind her down; they thought they'd ruined her, well, fuck 'em. She was going to really go places, not just in a safe little local way, but in the big world. She was going to go global. America, Saudi, Australia, you name it. Mars, if necessary.

But while she carried out her plan for universal domination, she would work for me; practise on my business, if you like. Give the shop, the whole thing a full makeover. She only had to be in the Uni a couple of days and in the evenings so my days of stumbling along chaotically stuffing receipts in a carrier bag and being arty were over. It was a done deal, no arguments.

I remember her standing there, arms folded, a fierce expression on her sweet face. No one, but no one, would crush Karwinder Jessica Kaur Smith, no one would break Leckie's spirit. This was her way of proving that.

Oh, Karwinder's Leckie's real name, by the by. She's half Sikh. That's why she's called Leckie. It's a stupid school nickname, but it's stuck. She doesn't mind, in fact, I think she quite likes it. 'Electric Karwinder' – electric car window – see? No? Never mind. It's very Bradford. She *is* electric, Leckie though, she's lightning in a bottle. Or rather, that particular afternoon, lightning in a nice lavender cashmere cardigan.

OK, I said, it's a deal. And it was. I wish I'd had a camera, I swear, just to get a pic of her face when I didn't even argue; it was half disappointment I wasn't bothered about her carefully marshalled arguments, and half childlike joy.

Now the shop is really something special, to my mind. And it's all thanks to Lecks. So you see, I have a lot to respect her for. It's just when she says knee-jerk stuff about Monkey, or Natty or Jas...It's not her fault, she simply cannot understand how folk can exist like they do. It's beyond her comprehension, outside of her experience. She has no idea what it's like to be born poor, to be in the underclass, to be the flotsam and jetsam, the useless trash of a society that despises such people's hopelessness and resignation and is offended by their frustration. I know Leckie doesn't mean to be cruel – but...It's instinct, I suppose. I react.

I mean, I know Monkey's a klepto pain in the butt sometimes, but if you'd had his life, you'd be too. There's many who can't understand why tall, handsome Natty Savage, a lad with a solid gold street rep and a string of girlfriends stretching to Manchester and back, lets pitiful, crippled, stupid Lee Moncke trail round after him '*like fucking Igor from Frankenstein*' as one wit put it.

Oh, Monkey, you poor little sod. Beaten so badly as a toddler by his stepfather his nose is pushed flat to one side as if it were made of Plasticine, the holes of his nostrils staring at you like an ape's. His skull is distorted – slightly, but along with his nose it's more than enough to earn him his nickname. Monkey was kept locked in the cupboard under the sink for weeks on end as a child by his pisshead mum in lieu of getting a babysitter so his spine is a bit twisted. He limps a little. Probably he's a tad brain-damaged, probably he's verging on the simple; he's definitely wholly illiterate, innumerate and utterly unable to function in a world of officials who are repulsed by him, despise him and demand answers to questions he can't begin to fathom.

There's plenty Monkey can't do but what he can do, he does superbly – he loves Natty. That's what Monkey does, what he'll always do, that's his raison d'être, his whole life. He loved my boy from the moment they met one afternoon bunking off school, with every ruined, pitiful cell of his body, with all his big heart, with all his destroyed mind. He loved Natty unreasonably and without hope of reward. He loved him so much it would flood his beautiful soft hazel eyes with the gold of the undying sun when Natty grinned at him and rubbed his croppy head 'for luck', it illuminated him, it made him whole. Love like that is a gift from Heaven, it's a blessing, it's pure. And it's irresistible.

And no, he didn't desire Natty, it wasn't sex, it was worship. Natty was everything Monkey ever wanted to be, dreamed of being as he wept, raw with loneliness and fear, in grim detention centres and Borstals, as he fidgeted, confused and panicky, in waiting rooms and cold hospital corridors. Natty was Monkey's living God. An incarnate Wonder. A perfect and immanent Deity. And faith, as we all know, is a comfort. And no one, no one in the world, needs comforting more than poor little fucked-up Monkey.

So what did Natty think? What did he feel about this passionate devotion? Oh, my boy took Monkey's love as if it were his due, his natural tribute. I'd told him, over and over when he was little, that the strong have to protect the weak; that he had to take care of people less fortunate than himself. I realise to a lot of people, that's a given, but in the places my Natty was brought up, the opposite was true and I didn't want him to become yet another hard, bullying fly-boy. I wanted him to be decent, honourable, a stand-up fella. I wanted him to care about people, about Jas, not just rip her off for whatever he could and spit in her face like so many I knew did to their parents. I had to teach him the rules because Jas wouldn't be able to show him anything other than her own colossal self-loathing and the soft, insidious litany of complaint and self-justification that embroidered her every waking moment with its convoluted design.

Did I succeed? Well, partly. Some of it sank in; he always had an exaggerated regard for his mother, that's for sure. He treated her – after he'd grown up and realised what she was and the bitterness had subsided – like a fragile, faded beauty, like a delicate, ruined creature he had to protect. And he insisted everyone else did, too. No one could even breathe a suggestion that Jas was what she was. A junkie, a drug-whore. We conspired to create a fantasy of Jas as the wronged woman, the deserted wife crushed by circumstance. No so far off, really, but with Natty, it was a Technicolor illusion he defended with the blind devotion of a knight in shining armour.

And like Gawain, or Perceval of old, he had his squire. To look into Monkey's pathetic little mug and see the devotion and loyalty there like a ripple of light on the turning tide was the way it should be for Natty, because his power was to be loved and to accept love. All love. Any love.

So Monkey trailed round in Natty's wake, running errands, getting in the way, being his own whiffy, chain-smoking, crumpled self, stuffing his rat-catcher's pockets with anything that stuck to his Velcro fingers. It wasn't that Monkey was a real thief, more that he stashed stuff for later, in case, because you never knew, for a rainy day, might come in handy, like, know what I mean?

Though what the fuck he thought he could do with a mother-of-pearl pen set when he couldn't even sign his name, no matter how often I'd tried to teach him, I do not know. Flog it for tuppence, probably, and buy fags or draw.

To my embarrassment, I realised Leckie was still talking to me while my mind had drifted off at a tangent. I fanned myself with my hand vigorously and pulled my damp T-shirt away from my chest to cool off a bit.

'Uh, what? Sorry, love, miles away. It's this heat, it's not natural – what do they call it, Indian Summer?'

Leckie narrowed her eyes speculatively. 'No, that's when it gets hot in autumn – it's not – you know – The Change, is it? Because...'

'No it is not. Jeez, Lecks, I'm only forty-six, give us a break, please...'

Looking at her I realised the 'only' part of that was incomprehensible to her. To be forty-six was to be beyond the pale. I might as well jack it all in and become a nun. Wear tweeds and sensible brogues, get a Labrador to walk, knit. I didn't like to tell her I felt eighteen in my head most days. Twelve, some days. And about a thousand and counting on the rest.

She shook her head briskly. 'Well, you don't look it – you don't. Your skin's marvellous, hardly a line. I suppose it's all that healthy living and not drinking or smoking, and up at that gym all the time. You put me to shame, you do really.' Then she spoilt it. 'Maybe when I get to your age I'll make an effort...'

Feeling like Methuselah, I crawled cronkily into the office and rang Hawkins. I got a couple of nice rainbow moonstone things and some green amber, very fashionable. They gave me a good deal on the 'Crystal Dreams Meditation Set' range, too. 'Citrine Glow'. 'Ancient Onyx'. 'Celtic Carnelian'. All with matching stinky joss.

Anything for a quiet life.

Chapter Sixteen

NATTY DIDN'T COME back that day; I rang his mobile a couple of times but just got the answerphone; not unusual for him so I left it alone. Probably he was with a lass. No doubt he'd crawl up to the cottage tomorrow evening, unshaven, bleary-eyed and smelling of some cheap body spray, a big cheesy grin on his face. He'd tell me I was his favourite, best Auntie Billie, honest, and beg for lots of food. Then he'd fall asleep on the rug in front of the telly like usual.

Oh well; I made a mental note to get some fresh pasta in, and some rocket for a salad. And a six-pack of Stella, his favourite, and fortunately, Johnjo's too. It's a shame they aren't exactly each other's favourites; like two tom cats, one older, tougher and wiser, one young and full of 'piss and vinegar' as Johnjo says, they circle each other warily. Johnjo thinks Natty is a waster with no respect, he thinks Nat takes after his feckless, runaway daddy and that I spend too much time on him and Jas. He and Leckie have that in common if nothing else. I think Natty's – no, I know Natty's secretly afraid of Johnjo, a silent, older man whose lankiness turned into sinew and whipcord, whose uncompromising bony face is a scar-map of his bike accidents and fights. So Natty sulks, and plays him up on the rare occasions they meet, and when we're alone, quizzes me for tales of Johnjo's adventures, then makes like he's not bothered.

Once Natty asked me if Johnjo was like his dadda. I didn't know what to say: how could I tell him his father was a tedious, ignorant, unlikeable fool and a petty criminal? Maybe I should have, but that's moot now. I never did.

The afternoon crawled by, gravid with heat and humidity and I yearned for a holiday, to get away from the rancid city summer that was having this last, mad burst of fever. We never did much business at this time of year anyway, what with the Uni being out and so many people being on their holidays – though the Costas or the Balearics in late August certainly didn't appeal to me. Those fried red people who returned boasting about how much booze they'd managed to neck in a fortnight and how they '*Dint bother with all that sun oil stuff, costs a bloody fortune – I just rub a bit of Nivea in, me*' didn't make me feel I'd missed a lot.

Lecks usually takes her break with her current beau, or sometimes, with her mum. I find the idea of going off with my mum wholly untenable, if not downright horrifying and I'm sure she'd be just as uncomfortable about it. Last year she sashayed off to Malta with her Silver Salsa Mafia. The blue-rinse Carmen Mirandas. They had a Latino dance theme holiday at some all-inclusive walled resort for the Irresponsible Old. You should have heard the scandal and gossip; who copped off with whom, who cheated (shocking) in the Bossa Nova contest, who was drunk every day by two in the afternoon. The frocks, the sequins, the face-lifts, the implants. Fortunately for Mum, Jen sends her American make-up designed for the Florida retired set that's guaranteed waterproof, smudgeproof and unmeltable; as Mum puts it, once on, her lippie stops on till death. And beyond, by the look of it. Forget Ibiza and Aiya Napa, Jesus. Them rave kids know nowt.

I exist as a kind of symbol of a daughter to her now, rather than a reality. I visit dutifully. I take her flowers, nice gifts but I can't say she's really bothered. Like, I got her a string of pink fresh-water pearls – good-sized ones, none of your rice-grain bits of nothing – for her birthday a while since. Even though I got a deal on them from my pearl man, they still cost a packet. They reminded me of her old string of cultured Mikimotos, those gleaming, lucent drops that had seemed the height of sophistication when I was a child. Those pink pearls were absolutely gorgeous, and all the rage; every women's magazine was raving over coloured pearls that year. Since Mum devours every mag going, I thought she'd be thrilled, I was sure this time she'd be really impressed. She unwrapped them and said '*Oh*,' in that disappointed voice, '*Pearls;*

I'm not really a pearl person anymore, myself. They're a bit ageing, aren't they? Still. Very nice, I'm sure.' She's never worn them. Pearls die, you know, if you don't wear them; they die of neglect. They need love and the warmth of your skin to survive.

So, I ring now and again. She never rings me. When I visit, she talks about Jen, the Girls and Eric the Chinless Wonder all the time. How successful they are, how well-off. What a thoughtful, considerate daughter Jen is. She shows me all the nice stuff Jen sends her. This Christmas she's off to visit them in Canada; they're paying. The thing is, Jen *is* thoughtful, and considerate. She never forgets to send a card on my birthday, or at Christmas, always with a cheery little note inside. But I'm out of the loop. I just stand outside the lighted window of Mum and Jen's cosiness looking in from the cold. Still, what's done is done. Maybe if Dad hadn't…But he did.

That's the trouble with life, isn't it? It's a one-way deal, you can't go back, you can't change stuff or undo what's been done. Jesus, if anyone knows that, I do. It's like people who try and live in the part of their life they loved the best forever. Ageing punks, old goths – I still see middle-aged, black-leather-and-lycra-clad biker chicks dawdling round town, their straw-bleached shag perms topping faces no amount of Max Factor can make fresh and foxy again. Soon it'll be forty-year-old clubbers still trying to be young and wild, going to special Ibiza Nites at the crappy pub dancehall because proper nightclubs will have been into something else long since, still wearing those wispy Kylie frocks and the blokes with silly sticky-up young men's hairdos and all of them going on about how shit modern music is.

If you live like that you'll break your heart. It really is Never Look Back, in my opinion, and stuff trying to stay young. Better that than be turned into a pillar of salt, preserved forever at that one defining moment of your little youth, pickled like a wretched old curio for the young ones to giggle at, like Lot's foolish, self-deluding wife. There's no point in trying to halt the inevitable; better to be cool about it. Better to go with it and keep your power. At least Mum has a good time and though she's mad for glamour, she doesn't give out she's younger than she is; I'll give her that. She'll go down fighting. I got that off her, if nothing else.

But going on a nice walking weekend in the Lakes with my folks like Leckie sometimes does is pretty much out of the question.

I thought about booking something last-minute for the end of September as I locked the shop up and said goodnight to Lecks, and again as I pounded the treadmill and wrestled with the Nautilus machines in the gym up at the Uni, sweat pouring off me in buckets. Maybe I could get one of those Internet cheap flight deals. Crete again, or Spain. They'd be lovely in late September. Just a week by the sea, the scent of jasmine, the warm breeze shushing through the old tamarisk trees, a terracotta courtyard littered with drifts of fallen bougainvillaea, their luminous purple-pink flowers shocking against white walls and a cerulean sky, the stars like diamond chips in the clear, soft nights. I could get a cheap little room in a guest house, walk, rest, swim, eat nice food; I could get a snorkel, go fish-watching – that'd be fun. God, how I'd like to spend a whole summer away. Six months out of Bradford. Jesus, it'd be a dream come true. Oh, don't get me wrong, I like town, it's home, you know, but Spain or Crete…A whole other world.

And I'd wanted to travel so much when I was younger. It had been the dream of my life. At art school, all the other students went on holidays roughing it in the Greek Islands, living on the beaches in tents, that sort of malarkey. But I didn't, partly because we didn't have the money to spare and partly because, like all young people, I thought I'd live forever, never get old and if it didn't happen this holidays, well, it'd happen the next.

There was no way I could have foreseen what would happen to my life; if I'd seen it in the tea-leaves, or had it spread out before me in the cards, or Gypsy Petulengaro had told me what my fate would be after I'd crossed his palm with a tanner, I'd have laughed in his face.

Sometimes, fury at how everything had turned out rose up in my throat and threatened to choke me; I'd feel its red heat in my face and in the steel yoke of tension in my neck and shoulders. I'd want to bang my head on the wall. But it was spilt milk. I'd just do another twenty minutes on the treadmill or put another five pounds on my weights and sweat it out until I got control of myself again. Like I'd done this evening.

I wished Natty had come round though. If he wasn't at a girl's he'd be with Jas. It was Johnjo's night at the pub with his mates in Skipton, so he wouldn't be round. I was alone, with the cats stretched like soggy dead things on the sofa, their lickspittle fur damp and tufty, worn out, like me, with the heavy thick heat of the night.

I could ring Jas, I suppose, see where Natty was, but I couldn't face her tonight. I was still mad at her after I'd caught her begging outside Waterstones last week. Begging – Jesus. Standing there, a lying whine about '*Food for t' babby, an' the rent money owin*' tricking out of her withered lips, her cavernous eyesockets housing the pinned, chlorotic gates to her dead soul.

I'd gone ballistic and the odorous husk of a fella – probably her latest flame – who'd been crouched by her dragging on a rollie and scratching his bleeding calves with yellow, broken nails as thick as horn, sloped off and left her to my fury.

'Why, Jas? Just tell me that – *why*? If you want money, for fuck's sake, come to me, don't do – this; don't make a bloody exhibition of yourself in the street…Oh, I see, it's not the first time, is it? Is it? For God's sake…'

'Don't, Billie, love, don't…Don't be cross wi' me, I dint mean owt wrong, I – it were Brian, he said we could get a bit o' spare, like, I'm a bit short, like…' She broke off, coughing. Another chest infection, I thought; why couldn't she take even the simplest care of herself? More trips to the doctor's to arrange, more hassle. Did it never bloody end? I tried to control my irritation, and failed.

'I give you fifty quid the end of last week, didn't I? Jesus, it's gone on that fucking poison already, hasn't it? That night probably – oh, Jas, Jas, look at yourself, begging in the fucking street – what would Natty have thought if he'd seen you?'

'I – I – don't be mad at me, Billie, you're my guardian angel, you are, don't be mad, I'm sorry, I'm sorry, I – just wanted some…You know. I'm sorry…'

And the easy tears of the junkie flowed down her bony cheeks, as meaningless as her constant promises to get herself clean.

It hadn't taken Jas long to set her little foot on the long slope down to heroin. Maybe she'd have walked that path anyhow, Terry's 'desertion' was just one of any number of excuses she'd have used. But I'll never know. What I do know is that Jas believes, to this day, that Terry left her because she's scum. And that's my fault.

No one missed Terry at first. After all, no one liked him, not even his mum. Only Jas loved him and no one ever listened to her. He quite often went off on jaunts without bothering to tell anyone and he especially enjoyed not telling Jas because he liked to fuck her up. A couple of weeks went by without anyone unduly worrying, or even wondering where he was, apart from the usual weeping and wailing from Jas. Then it was a month and the people who wanted to knock the cottage down contacted his mother. After much to-ing and fro-ing, she signed some papers and went to fetch his stuff. After all, he'd had the cash, he knew full well he was leaving the cottage. As far as everyone was concerned, if they even gave it a thought, he was just being his usual tedious self, making things difficult for other people.

But some conscientious soul from the building firm asked why he hadn't been reported missing. No doubt in their world, people didn't drift off for weeks on end without notifying their families or friends of their whereabouts. Or the mother of their new-born son. Terry's mother, always ready to get an attention fix and play the martyr, seized on this novel idea and with the kind help of the Citizen's Advice Bureau, reported Terry as a Missing Person. The attitude of the authorities was 'so what?' And frankly, I expect the coppers for one were glad to be rid of the likes of Terry for a bit. Everyone assumed, with his history, he'd turn up eventually full of lies about his exploits and stony broke.

Everyone except me and Micky, that is.

We knew where he was and we were with him.

In Hell.

Chapter Seventeen

VIOLENCE IS AN interesting thing, don't you think? I read a statistic in the paper the other day that said modern children are exposed to the details of over a thousand murders, via the media, before they're eighteen. Violence is on the telly, in our homes, day and night. All that fake blood and folk getting up after being shot in the arm by a sawn-off and fighting on for another fifteen minutes of prime time. I often wonder if the filmmakers naively believe people know, *really*, that it's not possible to do anything after being shot except collapse, lose copious amounts of blood and chunks of *meat* from your arm or wherever, suffer mortal and unthinkable pain, get shock and possibly die in a twitching, pissing, shitting heap of mangled humanity. Do directors think their ironic gangster gore-fest movies are watched, mouths dripping popcorn, by people who know it's a bit of theatrical fun, all that brutality? Witty, stylish post-modern voyeurism. Do they think people put a mental Post-It note on their viewing that says: *dont forget this vilence stuff not real, get bred an milk from spar.* Er, well, sorry fellas, they don't. That's why people get so confused when violence happens to them; why they get in such a paddy when they give in to a violent impulse and smack the person who insults their partner at the office Christmas party. It wasn't like this, all messy and shrieky and crap, when they went to see that action flick last week.

Violence isn't about third-rate actors or ridiculous characters in thrillers throwing punches; any bar-room brawler will tell you violence is not only the biggest adrenalin hit you can get but it's a state of mind. It does something deeply unpleasant to your brain. It's like shoving a blender in your head and pressing the button. Physical breaks, bruises and cuts heal, eventually, but the mind...That's a delicate thing. You can only really patch it up after it's been hurt, never make it like it was before. Violence hurts the mind in ways that leave you begging for a broken thigh, if God would only swap that for the hurt and disgust in your soul.

I've never denied I've been a violent person. I could, I suppose, seeing as I'm writing this. I could make out I was Mother Theresa if I wanted to. I could justify everything I've done, paint a rosy picture of a poor lass who sadly fell in with the wrong crowd and...But that's not the point. I want to tell the truth. Maybe it will help me understand my life; how I've thrown it away. So yeah, I've been in plenty of fights in bars and dancehalls. The usual kind of thing: black eyes, broken noses, swollen knuckles, hours in Casualty staring at the posters of desert islands while over-tired, over-worked nurses look at you as if you're shit on their shoes. I've started fights, sometimes, when the churning muck in my head made me want to scream and smack my way to oblivion. I know the hot iron stink of violence; I know it far too well.

But what I did to Terry was a universe away from punching some dickhead in the local disco. I ended his life; I unmade him; I lost my temper in the biggest way possible and I stopped his stupid, worthless heart beating; forever. Then, I vanished him. Like some fucking magician; oh, whoops, now you see him, now – well, now you don't. Funny, eh? Oh Jesus God, oh Mary Mother Of Sorrows, if you exist, if you're not a feeble lie made up to comfort us sorry little apes against the storm of our living – take me back to the day before it all went down, let me be back there and I beg you, I *beg* you, let it not have happened.

Ah, shit. Why do I pray when I know it's without logic or hope? Please excuse me, in my head, see, the fighting never stops. Me against me. Me against the past, the done deal, the unalterable.

So, yeah. You know what? I think those filmmaker boys are fascinated by violence because they've never been involved in the actuality of it. If they had, they'd do films about nice people holding hands quietly by the seaside and being very careful what they said to each other. That was me and Micky after what happened at Terry's, only without the nice, seaside or hand holding parts. We were very careful. Not about the police or forensics; we had no idea about stuff like that then. It would never have occurred to us to consider whether we'd left 'fibres' at the 'crime scene' or not. No, we were very careful with each other. Of what we said to each other. Of what we thought, of how we moved through the flat that held in its icy damp little space, the other person. The only other person who knew more about ourselves than we would ever, ever have wanted anyone to know. Who knew more about what we were than we wanted to know ourselves.

Oh, we were very careful indeed.

I've sat here for hours now – honestly, like, two or three hours, staring at the screen. I've sat here and tried my damnedest to think of how to describe the day after what happened. I can't even say it; can't think it. When I try to remember, a sort of woolly fog descends on my brain and I find myself thinking about getting the tumble dryer repaired or when I should do the weekly food shop at the big Asda. It's like my mind automatically diverts my thoughts away from the thing I mustn't, *mustn't* think about. It's been like that for years, ever since, in fact, and in a way, I've been grateful for that numbness.

I have a bag in my bedroom, a sports bag, not too big, convenient. It's packed and ready to go. Sponge bag full of necessities, change of clothes, knickers, box of paracetamols. A copy of Edith Wharton's short stories. A fleece, because I get cold when I'm nervous or stressed. A pen and a notebook with my lawyer's number written on the flyleaf. Over the years I've updated it, you know, changed the toiletries, put different clothes in. I'm all ready to go.

When they come for me I'll just say, OK, can I get my bag? I don't know if they'll let me, the coppers, but it's there, in case.

See? Anything but what I want to say. But it's part of it all, that bag. That's my reminder, my knotted hankie, it never lets me forget what I did and that I've been living a lie ever since. That it could all end in a second; the shop, Leckie, Natty, Johnjo, the cats, the cottage, my nice life – all gone in the time it takes to knock on a door. My conscience in the form of a dusty black vinyl Adidas bag.

I was so ill the day after, so was Micky, that's what I remember most. Every bone, every muscle, every sinew ached like fire and plum-black bruises blossomed all over my body like poisonous flowers. I was running with fever, and my tongue was swollen in my raw throat; raw from shouting and pleading and bullying Micky into doing what I thought I knew, I truly believed, was for the best. What would allow us to survive. To be safe.

Micky just sat on the sofa wrapped in a blanket, staring at the telly like a lobotomy case. He hadn't got into bed with me when we'd finally dragged ourselves back to the flat. After we'd each had a bath – him first, I drew it for him, his hands were shaking too much to turn the stiff old taps on – and put our clothes in a bin bag and sluiced our boots under the tap like automatons, I went to bed with two hot water bottles and waited for him. He never came. He never got in bed with me again. He never hugged me, kissed me or even looked me directly in the face, ever again. If I brushed against him by accident, he jumped as if I'd electrocuted him, then he'd mumble sorry and look away. I don't think he ever willingly touched me again.

He never forgave me for being stronger than him. For showing him his weakness. It – what's the old expression? – it unmanned him. I became a living breathing reminder that despite being a big, strong fella, an outlaw biker with a good reputation – when it all went tits up he couldn't hack it. He panicked. He wept like a child. Every time he looked at me, that's what he saw. Not his beloved Princess, but a screeching harpy who forced him to do things he wasn't really capable of. Who made him look into the abyss.

It was as if all the strings that held his big body together had been cut; he seemed somehow slack, his muscles jellied and useless. His blue eyes were empty of anything but a kind of childish disbelief, as if he couldn't, wouldn't believe what had happened. The joyful strength that had been so beautiful in him, the healthy, boyish glow that had illuminated his homely face was gone. I'd never see it again. My Little Buddha, my love, my Micky was gone and in his body, a senile old man squatted, listlessly gazing at the box, not even stirring himself to eat or get me water to ease my fever.

Three days we were like that. Then his work phoned. Where was he? Was he ill? Through cracked lips, both hands holding the receiver steady, I said we'd both been struck down with terrible flu and we'd barely been able to make ourselves a cuppa. The woman was cooingly sympathetic, Micky had joked before about her having a crush on him, he was a magnet for motherly middle-aged ladies. Micky had to have a sick note, she fluttered, otherwise she couldn't say what Mr Asquith might do – he was very strict about sick notes...

I assured her Micky would be back as soon as possible, and I'd personally post a sick note to the works. She twittered off and I rang the docs with the same story, asking for a home visit. We got the sickie no trouble; we looked so shit the fresh-out-of-med-school locum they sent hardly bothered to check us over. He just nodded sagely and stroked his beardless chin when I mumbled about our 'symptoms'. Micky barely acknowledged the doctor's presence and he never spoke the whole time, I had to turn the sound off on the telly myself. He just sat there while the doctor desultorily prodded and stethoscoped him, then wrote out a script for a 'tonic'.

As I showed him out, closing the living room door on the ghost of my beloved, the doctor turned to me with a concerned look.

'Mrs Er – um – I – well, I'm a bit worried about your er, your husband. Flu like this can be very nasty, you know. There can be mental as well as physical effects. Your, um, husband looked – you see, it's – I don't want to alarm you, but depression can sometimes follow something like this. Do you know what depression is? I'm not talking about feeling a bit down, you know, as we all do sometimes, but more – more long term problems. Depression in young men like Mr Er – yes – can be very difficult, very – awkward to treat. I'd keep a close eye on him if I were you. If you're worried, just pop in for a chat with me, or Dr Ellis if I'm no longer at the practice – I'll make sure Mr – ah – Kendal's notes are fully up to speed. Don't forget – depression is nothing to be ashamed of these days, not at all, hmm?'

It's a testament to how appalling I felt that day I didn't laugh in his poor, silly face.

I stood for a moment outside the living room, my heart pounding, my head a ball of pain. I leant my hot forehead against the thick, waxy-cool old paint of the door frame and tried to brace myself. *'Frame yersel, Princess, get the job done an' then it'll be break out the*

Jammy Dodgers all round, eh?' That's what Micky used to say if there was a tedious or difficult thing to do; the bathroom to paint, the bike to strip down, the gutters to unblock.

But there'd be no steaming cuppas and Jammy Dodgers this time. No big comfy cuddles and dirty-faced kisses to congratulate ourselves on a job well done.

I went in.

Legs quivering with fatigue, I sat on the end of the sofa opposite my Little Buddha. The viscous afternoon light slanted across his face from the dusty windowpane, bleaching him, fading him like an old photograph. The silent telly flickered insanely. Eyes still fixed on the screen, without looking at me, Micky drew his feet up, away from me. I felt my heart break, at that. Really, something broke, I felt it, real as a burn or a cut. Another pain, but so much worse than all the rest.

I'd done it. I'd destroyed his love for me. My greatest fear had become reality. My throat swelled with pleas and tears, but I swallowed hard, and wiped my forehead with my clammy hand, pushing the wisps of hair that had escaped from my ragged plait behind my ears. I had to talk to him. I had to get him to understand. I had no choice. If I didn't get his co-operation in this it was the end of both of us. I had to save him, protect him from his weakness, because I loved him so much, and I always would. And even though he loathed me now, maybe as much as he'd once adored me, Micky had to be my accomplice, for the rest of our lives.

'Micky love,' I tried to keep my voice calm, like you would if you were talking to a nervous dog.

He didn't look at me, didn't stir, but I knew – I felt – he was aware of me, was waiting.

I coughed, cleared my throat which felt like someone had shoved a tennis ball down it. 'Micky – I – look, love, we've gotta talk. We – I mean, what happened, I...'

In a convulsive gesture that made me jump, he jerked his hand up, palm outwards at me. A get-the-fuck-away-from-me thing, primitive, brutal. Hot tears filled my eyes and I breathed hard, trying not to cry. I wanted to throw myself into his arms, begging him to love me again, to make it all alright, to make it not have happened, feel him stroke my hair, tell me I was his princess, his sweetheart and everything would be fine, no worries.

But in my head, thick and silted, a dead whisper told me the truth: that would never happen and if I loved him, if I cared at all, I had to do this, I had to go on.

'OK,' I said in the same fake-steady tone, 'OK, I know you – you don't want to – to talk about stuff, but – please, just listen, just listen…We've got to keep this between us, we've got to – no one's got to know, OK? We can't be tellin' anyone, we can't – not ever…If we do, they'll do us for it, they'll do us…They're straights, Micky, they'll just see bikers and they'll freak, they'll say it were a drugs thing, we'll go down, I'll go down, and sure, I mean, I deserve it but you don't, you don't – ah, Micky, they'll blame you because you're a bloke, because they won't believe it were me, you know what they're like, an' they'll bang you up an' it's not your fault, I know, but they will…We can't tell, love, we can't. Never ever. Micky, I know it's – I know it's fucked with us, I know that, I'm not – I don't blame you, right? It's all my fault, it's me, not you, but see, you've got to promise me, love, just promise me you'll never say owt, and I won't, I won't, not ever, I swear. I'll protect you, I'll – I won't have you suffer from what I've done, I won't…If – if anyone ever asks, if the coppers – if anyone asks we'll just say yeah, yeah, we went to score some dope, about eleven o'clock, we got it an' we left. End of story. Done. Nothin' else, nothin'…Nothin' fancy, just that. An' we'll only say that if anyone asks us, only if they ever ask. We saw him, bought the gear an' left. Nothing else. Micky, Micky, swear, swear to me…'

My hands, my legs, my body were shaking, my mouth was numb and I could barely frame the words that bubbled out, glutinous and clotted with tears. *Say something,* I begged him silently, *for fuck's sake, say something – oh, Micky…*

He stared into space, silent, like a wax dummy of himself. Seconds seemed to stretch like taffy. Did minutes pass in that stuffy, airless room, all the oxygen eaten by the crappy gas fire, did hours pass?

I was just about to speak again when he said, 'Yeah. OK.'

It was little more than an exhalation; a breath that seemed to come from immeasurable distances, as if someone else, someone long dead spoke through his face.

He didn't turn to look at me. I put my head on my knees and wept until I couldn't breathe.

Three months later I got home from town laden with shopping for the weekend and he was gone; he took his saddlebags, 'Lady Blue' and our savings from the Building Society.

There was no note. No phone call. No letter. It wasn't necessary, I sussed straight off where he'd go. He'd be off to Bristol to the new chapter of the Devil's Own Sammo had set up when he'd moved there the year before. I saw Cochise in town a few weeks later and he let it slip, but it was only confirmation.

I was on my own.

Chapter Eighteen

I FELT LIKE A BUG in a jar; all alone in my glass prison I stared panic-stricken through the cloudy walls at the distorted mass of people swooping around outside. I could hear their booming and receding chatter, but half the time I couldn't understand what they were saying. Micky was gone, but even while he'd been with me I may as well have been by myself, struggling to heave the burden of what I'd done onto my back and walk, to go to work at Morrisons where I'd got a job stacking shelves to make ends meet, to deal with stuff like eating, paying bills, washing, brushing my ratty hair that no longer shone like a starling's wing but draggled limply in a heavy greasy ponytail.

And sleeping. That was the worst. I tried to stay awake as much as possible because the dreams...I'd wake up screaming, choked with snot and tears, my heart thudding with terror, the sheets soaked with sweat. Sometimes I was so terrified I thought I'd die, really die, all alone in that freezing stone meat-safe of a flat. I can't describe the horror of those dreams; sometimes I hear people go on about this or that scary film and I think: you should have my dreams – in fact, I wish you would, then you'd shut up about how gruesome some DVD you rented last night was.

And there was no one to comfort me, no calming voice to soothe away the terrors. No Micky.

At least while he'd been in the flat I'd known someone was there, another person was around even if he stayed out as much as he could. When he went it was like being buried alive. People were outside, but there was an impenetrable barrier between me and them. After all, I was a murderer. They were normal. I knew stuff they'd never know, I'd done something they'd never do, I was – different. Really different now, not just a maladjusted kid who couldn't fit in, but a person who had stepped through a dreadful gate into some kind of roaring, bloody limbo.

I had my hair cut off. It felt like a nun when they shave their heads to go in the convent, like I was going into a different place in my life where shit like hair or make-up or diets didn't matter anymore. I moved out of the flat to a cheap slum house in West Bowling. I took nothing with me, other than the basic necessities. I wanted to get rid of anything extraneous; I was carrying enough as it was.

Anyway, the hair – it was an 'urchin' cut, very short. The first time in my life I'd had short hair. Naturally everyone assumed it was because my marriage had 'broken down'. That phrase – like it was an old car or something. Mum saw me when I went round dutifully the following Sunday and tutted furiously, while Liz stretched her neck like an old turkey and looked elaborately away over her teacup. Then Mum said nothing I did surprised her anymore but why oh, why I had to ruin the only asset I had was beyond her. And just because I'd been unable to hang on to my husband – she and Liz were convinced he'd run off with another woman since All Men Were the Same – there was no need to let myself go – the state of me, where was my pride? Liz sucked in her cheeks and looked at the ceiling. I just knew after I left she and Mum would have a field day going over my shortcomings. The tension in my head notched up tighter still. Jen tried to defend me a bit, like she always did, saying short hair was this season's hairdo, all the stars were doing it and in *Vogue*…But Mum just said I'd look a right show in my bridesmaid's outfit with that croppy head and couldn't I ever think of anyone but myself?

That's why I wasn't a bridesmaid at my sister's wedding. In fact, why I didn't go to my sister's wedding at all. I told my mother to fuck off. In those words. *Fuck off, Mum, fuck off and leave me alone, I can't stand it anymore; yeah, and you too, Liz, yes, you, you fucking old witch. You don't want me, Mum? I'm a fucking disgrace? Well, fuck you, I don't want you either.*

Then I added the coup de grâce. *I'm not surprised Dadda fucked off, I'm not fucking surprised one fucking bit, the way you go on. He was well out of it and – and me too, me fucking too. I'm sorry Jen, I'm sorry, I'm sorry, but I can't I can't I can't...*

Mum didn't speak to me for five years. I don't think Liz ever did again, preferring if we met, to look away in a pained manner. It was Jen mended the rift between me and Mum eventually, she never could stand rows. But I missed the wedding. Fortunately, my frock fitted Adele from Jen's work and so Jen was trailed down the aisle of St Stephen's by Eric's chinless, chestless, charmless sister Irene and Adele, who when made up and coiffed, looked more like Jen's sister than I ever did. Matching enamelled blondes. Much more suitable, aesthetically. But I was sorry not to have actually seen Jen in all her frilly glory; I saw the pics, of course, the white and gold suedette album with 'Cherished Memories' in swoopy copperplate on the front and a corded tassel trim.

But as I left Mum's house that evening, stumbling, blinded with anger and pain, I felt like a fox who'd chewed its own leg off to escape the killing trap; I'd cut the last rope that bound me to my family, to my innocent past. Now there was only a life that began with Terry's death, and the future seemed unbearable. Adrift, alone, I began to sink into a desperate depression. There was a kind of twisted logic to it: after all, I certainly didn't deserve happiness after what I'd done, did I? The years of hopeless despair I envisaged stretching out before me in a dull, dank path would be an atonement not just for the murder, but for what I'd done to Micky and my family. Brokenhearted, desperately poor, with no career, no close friends now I wasn't part of the Devil's Own anymore, I couldn't see anything but my excoriating guilt and self-loathing. I fantasised about just dying in my sleep somehow: who'd miss me? No one. Who'd mourn? Maybe Mum and Jen might for a short while, but no one else and they had each other anyway. I was an infinitely small droplet in a vast ocean of gabbling humanity; what did it matter if I lived or died?

The days slid one into another with only the dreaded, lonely weekends a mark on the calendar. If I could, I worked overtime like an automaton to avoid Saturday and Sunday, numbed by the stupid repetitive work and the tape-loop of old Muzacked pop-songs played on the loudspeakers. I still can't listen to 'Stop in the Name of

Love' without feeling that despair wash back over me faintly, like a ghost wave drenching me in the past.

In the end, it was Jas who pulled me back into the land of the living. Jas, who I'd put out of my mind with a clammy shudder. After the fateful day Terry's mum finally reported him missing, Jas rang me and rang me, asking to see me so we could 'ave a chat, like'. I kept putting her off. The thought of seeing her and Natty make my stomach turn. But I reckoned without her irrational attachment to me, her belief I could always fix things for her because I was 'dead clever' and her blind determination, once she'd set her heart on something.

Eventually, she appeared at Morrisons with Natty strapped into a rickety pushchair with squeaky wheels and followed me round the freezer section like an imprinted duckling. Wherever I went the squeak-squeak-squeak of Jas, Natty and that sodding pushchair was behind me. She came every day for a week. I hid in the stock room – but she just waited patiently outside the plastic swing doors; I could see her blurry little form through the scratched opaque flaps. I got cautioned by the staff manager for 'chatting with my friends while I should be working'. How could I explain to him Jas wasn't my friend, she was the girlfriend of the man I'd killed and I didn't want to see her but she thought I was Miss Einstein and could explain the world to her? It was hopeless. I gave in and we had a cuppa in the store café on my break. I couldn't look her in the face. She thought it was because I was ashamed of being dumped, of no longer being a princess; that I was distraught at my headlong fall from grace.

She put Natty in my lap; it was a brilliant move, how could I resist him? While I held him and let him grab my finger she rambled on like one of those peat-brown moorland streams gurgling over rocks and dead trees that you see in the big old Victorian genre paintings up at Cartwright Hall. Inexorable in a soft, unceasing way.

'We're int same boat, now, love, int we? 'Bandoned; y'know, both our fellas fucked off, like. I don't mean ter be funny, but I feel right bad fer yer, that I do. An' I hope you don't mind me sayin', but I'm worried about yer, what wi no one seein' hide nor hair of yer since – since – you know. Micky goin', like. Here, I saw Carl up at pub last week an' he asked after yer he did, but honest, I dint know what ter say cos I dint know owt an' he scares me ter death, he does, an' he give me such a look, honest I coulda died. Billie love, don't be mad at me, but, you don't look right well, you really don't…'

And on and on. Her huge green eyes glowed with concern, the fine, satiny bronze skin on her rounded forehead creased, her soft lip trembled. The very picture of a Bradford Madonna, tender, compassionate, seated in the Formica hell of the café offering solace to the damned.

At Carl's name, I felt a sharp pain under my breastbone at the thought of what I'd lost, then the lead weight of guilt settled back in place: if I felt shit, I deserved it. I closed my eyes, but Jas was having none of it. She reached over and smoothed Natty's jacket which made him wriggle. I came back to myself for fear of dropping him and seeing it, she continued.

'I don't mean ter bother yer, you know, at a time like this, but I don't know where else ter turn. Thing is, see, you bein' so clever an' that, an' us bein' well, like I said, in the same way, I thought…Shush now, Natty love, just bounce him a bit, Billie, he likes that. So see, thing is, the landlord, he wants ter throw us out, me and t'babby – I don't know what ter do, an' I ent givin' that – Terry's mum, satisfaction of me askin' her fer help, cos she'll just hold it against me fer ever an'…Please help me, Billie, y'allus were a right pal ter me, an' now what wi't babby bein' yer godson…Billie, landlord ud listen ter you, what wi you bein' educated like, Billie, please…'

Natty looked up at me as I dutifully bounced him and smiled like a cherub. Maybe it was wind, I don't know, I'm childless, what do I really know about kids? But it looked like a smile to me. Something gave way in my heart; he needed me, it was bad enough what I'd done – but to abandon this child, the innocent victim of my crime to feckless Jas…I gave in.

On a sort of mindless reflex I sorted the landlord, a tedious wannabe Rachman. But it was only the start. Jas had found, instinctively, her new protector; much more reliable than a man, who might sod off like Terry and all the others before him had done, I had, in her mind, always been her best mate, her child's godmother. And now she knew what a massive bargaining chip she had – Natty. Nothing was ever for her personally, of course, it was always for 't'babby'. Her voice would be on the other end of the phone, a soft whine, pleading, irresistible; and after all, though she didn't know it, I owed her. I owed her as big as you could get.

Round and round my life she twined like the tendrils of the delicate white flower whose name she bore: sweet, clinging, powerful in its frailty. Maybe if I had still been with Micky, and Terry really had just fucked off, I wouldn't have got so involved with her. Maybe Micky would have put his foot down and Jas would have faded back into the non-people like an old sepia picture, distant and more ghostly with each passing year until she no longer existed for us.

But the vast crushing guilt and remorse I felt meant that anything I could do for her, I did. I kept on blindly 'trying to help'. I found myself sorting the unpaid bills, the dole and the social, the nurse's visits for Natty, his vaccinations and the broken fridge. Before I realised it I was seeing her and Natty nearly every day, or talking to her on the phone, reassuring her, comforting her. It was so ordinary, so everyday. It was as if my mind split into two halves. One half was working on a day-to-day basis, normal, just helping a lame duck, an unfortunate pal, someone who was terminally impractical. The other half of my mind was screaming '*You killed this woman's lover, the father of her child, what the fuck are you doing, get away from her*' – and I'd swear to myself as I lay tense as a board in bed, my head aching, my neck a fist of pain, to wean her off, get rid of her.

But then she'd come round, with Natty. It'd be tea and cheap, powdery biscuits from the Co-Op. She'd put Natty in my arms and we'd talk about him and his little ways, or about what was on the telly, or what the lads were up to – second-hand of course, now we were nobodies.

I'd take Natty on Saturday nights to 'give her a break'. Then I'd take him Friday nights and Saturday, and most of Sunday. She heard about my rift with my family – and wasn't it scary because, well, she'd bust up with her mum ages since, too, on account of her not giving Jas that pink vase with the flowers on what had belonged to her gran and Jas knowing, *knowing* mind, that Gran had meant for her to have it. She decided we were sisters, our lives were so similar. I was officially Natty's Auntie Billie. That's how she spoke of me to everyone, as her sister, without qualification, without explanation, despite the fractionally raised eyebrows and careful voices of the officials she chattered blithely on to. I think she came to believe it herself, in her Jas way. 'Jas thinking' I call it. Magic thinking. *I want it to be so, so it is.* It starts as an idea with her, then little by little, it becomes a fact. A lie becomes the truth. She believes it utterly, even when presented with evidence to the contrary. Push it and she'll cry and say *it int fair ter torment her, what with the babby an' all* – even when t'babby was sixteen and virtually a grown man. Natty was always t'babby to Jas. Her little lad. Her sweetheart.

The babby. My Natty. How can you explain the love you feel for a child? It's in the cells of your body, it's blood and breath. Their hands, their eyelashes, their tiny fingernails like miniature translucent shells. The first time he toddled up to me, arms outstretched – to me, not Jas…it filled me with an inexpressible golden joy. He was a gorgeous baby, folk would stop and coo at him in the street. He was such a flirt, too. Any excuse and he'd toddle up for 'kissis' and hugs, sweets and attention. He ruled us both with a rod of iron – because underneath that rosy exterior, was a will-power of steel and a sharp intelligence that showed him how and when to turn on the charm – and when he did, he was irresistible. Jas fetched and carried for him as if he were a little prince and he took that as his due, which she liked, it reminded her of his dad. With me he was more subtle, but the result was the same. I had respect for him – that's not daft, I did, I respected his bright grasp of things. He wasn't stupid, you could talk to him properly even when he was very little.

Was he spoilt? I suppose so, but not materially, both of us were truly skint. But saying that, even the health visitor and the social worker brought him little treats and I had to stop strange grannies in the park buying him ice cream. He was a sun-child, he couldn't get enough love. The more you gave, the more he wanted and he gave back as much as he got. There never was a more affectionate and funny little kid; his sayings had us in stitches, his expressions and childish observations were priceless. To us, at any rate. The temper tantrums, the childish fits of anger we thought of as growing pains. Just a phase. All kids got like that sometimes, maybe he was over-tired. To us, he was perfect. We doted on him.

He became the centre of my life and all the more as time passed because it became obvious that Jas was as much use as a mother as a peg-doll would be.

I suppose that sounds nasty but it's the truth. I'm not saying she didn't love him, she did. She always will. But the day-to-day caring, the remembering to feed him properly, not just crisp sandwiches, the washing, the getting him off to school and making sure he stayed there, the dentist – it was all too much for her. She didn't have it in her to do things like that, she forgot, got distracted, she meant to, but...

Eventually, I helped her get a council flat in a low-rise estate up Shawe Wood; her own place, and almost, sort of, in the country – if you walked fast for twenty minutes in the right direction. She was thrilled, and I spent hours decorating it in shades of pink, lavender and cream, her favourite colour scheme. We – I – put up heavy Austrian blinds and double nets I got second-hand from the small ads. In that flat, you didn't want to be looking out of the windows much.

All the centre blocks in Shawe Wood faced in towards a square, it was supposed to be neighbourly. Naturally, it was a filthy, syringe-strewn hell-hole, probably within months of its first tenant moving in. Dogs got thrown off the balcony walks, the stairwells stank of piss. Recently, it's become a dumping ground for care-home kids who've outgrown the orphanage – if they still call them that. The thud-boom of stereos are counterpointed by that kind of row characterised by incessant and monotonous screaming of the words 'you fucker', 'you cunt', 'you whorebag'. Sometimes the coppers lurch round and tell them to put their weapons down, sometimes the ambulance comes when they don't. Whoever comes gets pelted with half-bricks and dog-shit by the packs of feral children.

I tried to get Natty educated, tried not to waste his intelligence, but I failed, largely. He became a street-lord instead. A sharp lad. I did the best I could, under the circumstances and God knows it caused me enough grief. At least I taught him to read and write; they couldn't teach him anything at school, he was too easily bored and, I imagine, a teacher's nightmare. I can just see him leaning back in his chair, a man-child, the sun-bleached nubbles of his embryo locks studding his head, that expression of lazy contempt on his face. It was a wonder he wasn't expelled before he finally jacked it in for good at fifteen. It put paid to my futile dreams of getting him to college or even university, of him getting out of Bradford and having a decent life somewhere.

Jas wouldn't hear of it, you see. The idea of education, of him going somewhere to college or work frightened her and she'd get fuddled and weepy, saying she wouldn't be parted from him, he wasn't to ever leave her, she'd die without him. He'd kneel by her chair, put his arms round her, fifteen years old and he'd have his arms round her like they were an old married couple saying, *hush, hush, it's OK, Mammy, it's OK, I'll never leave you, I love yer, Mam, Mam, my sweetheart you are, eh, Mam…*

My fault, that, I suppose; I'd drilled it into him from being tiny what I thought was wrong and right; don't be a bully, be kind, be brave, be strong. Stick to your family, your friends; be loyal. Always tell the truth and hate a lie. Yes, even that; I told him that over and over. I didn't want him ending up like me, so meshed in lies I could hardly expand my ribs to get a breath.

I suppose, to be honest, I couldn't have sent him to university anyway – I mean, what with? Even if he'd got a grant, neither Jas nor I had anything to spare; he'd have had to get a job as well as study and there were much easier options available to him on every street corner. Over time, sure, I got better jobs until I could scrape together the money I needed to buy the shop off Lizzie, the old hippie who had it before me; Lizzie's Emporium and Headshop it was, took me months to get rid of the stink of patchouli, it had sunk into the woodwork. I had hardly any money and Jas has barely had two pennies to rub together all her life.

So I taught Natty what I could. Arty stuff, I suppose, like a good italic handwriting – he liked being able to write properly, do something his friends couldn't. Same as reading, he was proud of his little collection of books. *Treasure Island, The Hobbit,* stuff like that – all second-hand from Oxfam but he loved them. He wrote his name in them, *Nathan Terry Savage, Flat 15, Larch House, Shawe Wood, Bradford, West Yorkshire, England, United Kingdom, The World, The Universe, Space.* I've still got his copy of *The Lion, the Witch And the Wardrobe,* all dog-eared and held together with Sellotape. Old-fashioned, now, those books, kids these days don't fancy stuff like that, but he did, he liked old stories, fantasy. Jas used to say he was the spit of his dadda in that way; you know, clever, what with the book reading an' all.

And that was the problem. Well, OK, one of them – but a big one.

Natty grew up as I've described: handsome, strong, healthy. In that he resembled his father not at all; oh, maybe he had Terry's height and length of bone, but otherwise, no. But his dadda was in him alright.

Terry's ghost lived in Natty's head. Like the endless refrains looping on that supermarket tape, Natty's dreams of his absent father fuelled his belief that he was different from other lads, a bit special and it was only a matter of time before Terry came back for him. It drove him mad when Jas had 'friends', the endless succession of her waster pick-ups with their pisshead breath and thieves' faces, the dog-rough barrel scrapings she dragged home from the club – working men's, not dance – or the pub, the men she slept with because she was lonely and hoped for a cuddle after they'd done her.

What if Terry came back when Dave or Frank or Len were there, stinking the place up with BO, dope and fags, littering everywhere with empty cans of extra-strong lager? Natty, powerless at ten years old, would lock himself in his tiny room with his big old cheap Walkman on and dream. Or stay at my place and confide in me, never knowing what it did to me.

'Auntie Billie?'

'Hmm, what, love?'

'Auntie Billie, my dad, I think he's gone to be like, a spy – you know, like James Bond in the films with a car with rockets and a gun and…'

'Maybe, honey, you never know…'

'He's gonna come an' get me one day when I'm grown up, he's gonna come in the car an' bring me loads of stuff and we'll do spy stuff together an' go to America and…'

'Time for bed, sweetheart, come on, it's way past your bedtime and…'

'When d'you think he'll come back, my dad? Mammy says he could, he could come anytime but what if I were 'sleep an' I missed 'im?'

'Don't you worry your head about stuff like that, love, come on now – Natty, come on, love, really…'

Or Terry was a cowboy, riding the range, or an astronaut, or a gold prospector in Australia. Whatever Natty dreamt up, the story was always the same; one day Terry would come back, a suitcase full of presents, and take Natty in his arms and swear he'd only left him so he could make lots of money, or be a spy and serve his country. And he'd never ever forgotten his beloved son.

Then it would get a bit hazy over the details but we'd all live happily ever after.

After he left school, he stopped talking about it, but it was there, in everything he did. When Terry came back, he'd have a son to be proud of. Maybe not in the way some people see it – a nice white collar boy with a suburban home and a pretty, passive wifey. No, Terry the Hero's lad was a playa. Cock of the estate, a mover and shaker in town. Complete from his heavy gold chain to his £150 ram-raided Nikes, a beautiful girl on each arm. He'd be there for his old dad, and they'd bond straightaway because his dad would be that chuffed with him. And Jas, magically rejuvenated and clean, in a spotless house somewhere countrified, would fall into Terry's arms and they'd be a lovely older couple sitting at dusk under a rose bower in the garden.

Well, Natty was certainly a little king in the estate and around, that part had come true – but Jas, that was something else altogether.

As I put clean water in the cats' bowl and ticked them off for bringing their mates in through the catflap at night for parties, locked up and got undressed for bed, I shuddered to think what Natty would have done if he'd caught Jas begging for drug money. In fact, I'd go round tomorrow evening and have another word, try and make her see sense, see what she'd do to Natty if she didn't get it together.

After a few minutes, Ghengis jumped up and lay on one side of the sheet covering me, then Cairo got on the other, pinning my legs down. I tried to wriggle free but Gheng growled irritably. Mardy old devil; God, I might as well be married to him the way he grumped about.

Praying for sweet dreams and full of good intentions, I fell asleep.

Chapter Nineteen

'LECKS, I CAN'T – I'm not – dressed properly, I…'
Leckie's head wobbled and her face registered incredulity. 'Huh, like, yeah – what would you change into anyway? Something *blacker*? Oh, come on, love, *pleeeease,* pretty please – Tom's going, he's got a thing about you, you know he has – I'll lend you some make-up and that, duh, *black* evening cardi with the beading you liked, wear that new green amber pendant you haven't put out yet, we'll have a snack at mine, then off we go – Billie, it's *Friday night* – do you even *remember* the last time you went out on a Friday night? I mean, never mind a Saturday, or *any* day…'

'Well…'

'Yes! Result! Oh, it'll be a hoot, I swear – Teena B! *Oooo, sol y sombre, dum dum dum, my latin luvvvver…* D'you remember? Dreadful – I loved it! Have you seen pics of her recently? They did a thing about her come-back in *Hello* – her house, I laughed my head off. Not to mention the *enormous* new boobs and the botox! Those lips! She's a guppy! Like *inner tubes,* talk about collagen – and how skinny? All *yoga* of course – yeah, right…' Leckie mimed someone throwing up, her face lit with glee. 'She's a gaycon now, totally, I'm telling you, every queen in Yorkshire'll be there!'

'Tom has not got a thing about…'

'He *so* has – he said he thinks you're really deep, really interesting and he's got a *thing* about the Older Woman – I mean, not that you're that much older than him, he's got to be nearly forty now – oh, don't look like that, you know what I mean, Miss. He's nice, Billie, he's a nice guy; OK, he's divorced, but it was all friendly, there's no baggage, he's got good job, he *reads* for God's sake – he's not a dickhead and I think…'

'Yeah, I know what you think – no, I know, I know – oh, you're right – yeah, yeah, as always – go on then, you big matchmaking pain in the arse, it'll be a laugh…'

'It *will*…'

And it was, it was great fun. Buzzby's (formerly Swingers, formerly Rockafella's, formerly The Starlite Ballroom) was rammed to the giant mirror ball with a mixed bag of gays, drag queens dressed in outfits from Teena's chequered past – the Teena of the Jungle ensemble was my personal favourite (though Leckie went for the mini-flamenco dress and red glitter platform shoes outfit sported by a six-foot-two bloke with coal heaver's shoulders), scowling serious Teena B fans who didn't like having their idol (however fallen) mocked by shrieking camp blokes in skin-tight Teena T-shirts and people like our little group who just wanted a frivolous good time.

As I queued in the Ladies, I felt happier than I had for years. Leckie was right, Tom did seem like a nice fella and he was obviously interested. I was grateful Leckie had persuaded me to put on some make-up and I'd let her spritz me with her favourite new perfume. I felt – feminine, attractive. It was very pleasant indeed.

The faintly euphoric feeling even lingered when a pale, hung-over, but determined Leckie questioned me long and hard all the next day about Tom's every word and gesture. When she wasn't doing her impression of Torqemada she breathlessly recounted to all and sundry, delighted customers included, the details of Miss B's gigantic silicone bust, inability to move her botoxed face or sing with her grotesquely swollen lips – a feat she couldn't achieve when her lips were plain old lips anyway, as *everyone* knew.

It was nearly five and I was still laughing at her goings on when my mobile rang. It was Natty, I could tell from the ring tone. I went into the office and flipped the phone open.

'You gotta come round ter Mum's – Billie, you gotta come round…'

'Natty, what, what? What's the matter?' He sounded terribly agitated, and he never called me plain Billie without the Auntie bit, unless he was very upset. Suddenly, my heart thumped. Jas – it had to be Jas. An overdose? Oh God. I ran a shaky hand through my hair and tried to breathe calmly. A little voice echoed through my skull – *serves you right for being happy, now see what's happened.* Oh, Jas, Jas, don't for Christ's sake be dead or anything, please, please.

'Billie, you just gotta come, come now – Billie, *they've found me dad.*'

'What…' I sat down heavily on the chair, a dizzy, faint feeling surging through me, my stomach roiling.

'In the paper, in that *Clarion*, they – they're doin' some thing about missin' people, an' it's there, in wi' a lot of other photos, a picture of me dad.'

I could hardly swallow. 'But – you said they found…'

'Well, not yet, like – but they will, they will, Billie, they'll find him, you gotta come over, Mum's doin' her tits, me nan's here givin' her no end of grief, it were her sent the picture in when they did a story about how relatives should write to 'em about who'd gone missin' an' how t'coppers dint give a shit an' it were a national disgrace, an' they're gonna investigate it an' now she's sayin' Mum oughta done it an' it shows she don't care about me dad cos if she had she'd a – Billie, it's mental, honest…'

In the minute or so it took him to tell me, my world fell apart. Just like that. Tick, tick, tick. Done. Over. I swallowed bile as I shut my eyes, my head swimming.

'Billie? Billie? You there?'

I had to answer him. 'Yeah, yeah, sorry love, it's just a bit of a shock…'

'Too right it's a shock; man, it's mad, it's fuckin' mad – sorry. But you know, it's just – God, Billie, me dad, in the paper, ont front page…He'll see hisself, y'know? He'll see an' he'll know t'come home…'

'Natty, Natty – you've got to be calm now, love – look, I'll, I'll be over as soon as I can, just – take it easy, right? Look after Jas, put the kettle on or something – I'll – I'll be there, I will – OK? OK?'

'Yeah, but – be quick, right?'

'I will, I promise. Go on now – I love you, Natty.'

'Love you too, Auntie Billie.'

He sounded twelve years old again; the years had fallen away from him, and his childhood fantasy was coming to life, expanding in his fertile mind like one of those tightly folded Japanese paper flowers that you drop in a glass of water. I shut the phone and put it down, very carefully, as if it were dangerous. Then I sat, my elbows on the untidy desk, my hands steepled over my nose and mouth. I could hear the unsteady inhalation of my breath and smell the sour yellow fear on the palms of my hands. I felt freezing cold, despite the close heat of the windowless little room and a long shiver shook me from head to foot. Suddenly, my guts cramped and I needed the toilet. I ran to the loo past Leckie's astonished gaze and managed to undo my trousers and sit down before everything left my body in a hot rush. Shaking, I crouched, head in hands in the stink and tried to talk myself calm, like I'd always done before, only this time, it wasn't working.

There was a knock on the door. 'Billie? Billie, are you alright?'

'Yeah – yeah, I just – I – I think I ate something – It's OK, I'm OK, thanks, thanks, love.'

'Well, alright – I'll put the kettle on, there's no one in, I'll make some peppermint tea – are you sure you're OK? Do you want me to nip to Boots for you before it shuts?'

'No, no, it's OK, I'm better now, really – honestly, I'm fine. Tea would be good, thanks.'

I heard her heels tip-tapping away on the wooden floor.

I cleaned myself up, and washed my shaking hands. The cold water on my wrists and the clean, sharp smell of citrus soap revived me a bit. I washed my hands again, it seemed very important to be properly clean. I was about to do it a third time when I stopped myself and instead, breathed the foetid air slowly and deeply. Then I got sorted, wiping the cold sweat from my face and neck with a wad of damp loo paper. I felt wrung out, and horribly tired, as if I had trained past my recovery point and my muscles were refusing to obey me. Leaning on the basin edge, I paused to look in the dark little mirror to fix my hair.

In the dim light, above my funereal clothes, an ashy white mask floated, its eyes huge and sunken, its cheeks drawn, its lips a bloodless compression. I stared at myself for a moment then made a dry rictus grin.

'Come on now, you can do it,' I whispered. 'You can do it.'

I laughed, mirthlessly, silently. What choice did I have anyway? What choice had I ever had since it happened? This is what I'd waited my whole adult life for, the sword that had been hanging over my head by a single thread. Now the thread was about to break. I opened the door and walked out into the unravelling future.

Chapter Twenty

T O THIS DAY I don't remember a blind thing about the drive to Jas's place. I expect the only thing that saved me from having an accident was the number of times I'd driven there over the years; I must have done it on auto-pilot.

I pulled up on the street and parked like an idiot, the curb side front wheel rammed up against the pavement, the back end all skew-whiff. Normally I prided myself on my driving; now I couldn't have cared less. It didn't matter. Nothing mattered.

As I entered the rancid stairwell, I saw one of Natty's girlfriends coming down the stairs, her beautiful brown face like thunder, her mass of fine braids swinging out of the back of her Burberry check baseball cap like a flail. I didn't take her expression personally, it was standard for lasses her age. As I looked at her more closely, I saw that under the practised gangsta-girl mask, another face moved. Her lower lip trembled infinitesimally and her nostrils had that tight, slightly flattened look of someone trying not to cry. She was very young, not more than sixteen, if that; not for the first time I felt a sharp little flick of worry at the edge of my mind about Natty's taste for such young lasses. OK, girls grew up so fast now, but still – when this was all settled, I'd have a word. It wasn't on, he should make an effort to settle with a girl his own age. I sighed – what could I do, really? Girls adored him, especially girls like this one – he was their real-life, honest-to-God pin-up: they ran after him, hung over the balconies calling to him, hi-jacked him in the stairwells. It's hard for any bloke to turn down the attentions of a beautiful girl – but, no. No excuses. This one was far too young; poor little thing, she looked broken-hearted.

I could well imagine her trotting round to Natty's, eager to play tease with her lazy golden cat – her living doll – only to find a frantic, troubled man with no time for her. Neither woman nor child, she didn't have the emotional learning to deal with it – it would have been a cold smack in the face for her not to be instantly beloved. She was about to brush past me, but I put my hand on her sleeve.

'Now then, Venus, you come from Natty's?' I was amazed at how calm and normal I sounded.

Venus pouted and reaching up with her hand, twined a braid around her finger, her long, high C-curve acrylic nails were muralised to match her cap. She was embarrassed, because apart from being upset and struggling to control herself, like all teenagers, she hated talking to adults. Also, she never knew quite what to call me.

'Yeah, Miss – um, Billie – y'know.'

'So, your mum alright? And Grace? All OK?' I didn't want to climb those stairs, even if it meant causing this child grief by forcing her to chat with me. I needed a moment, I needed to get control of myself, too.

'Yeah. Uh, gotta go. Mum rang me, says tea's ready.' Venus looked mutinous at the mention of her sister, Grace, known for good reason in the estates as Amazing Grace, and one of Natty's previous love interests.

'Well, give my regards to your family, eh?'

But Venus was already gone, that bouncing ponytail her only goodbye.

I stood for a moment watching her striding down the road, then turned back to the stairs. I felt so tired. The stairwell stank of piss and was graffitied in layer upon layer of obscenities, schoolkid love-notes – Kerry 4 Mark True – and brainless tags. Sighing, I hitched my bag higher on my shoulder and climbed.

As I walked along the balcony, I saw Monkey slope out of Jas's door. Seeing me, his simian face brightened and he smiled. Not for the first time, I thought how his rare smiles showed the sweet-looking boy he would have been. He almost ran to me, his lopsided gait making him stumble slightly as he stopped in front of me and began to gabble ten to the dozen.

'Easy, love, come on, slower, what is it, Lee?' I never called him Monkey to his face. I wasn't that cruel.

'Natty said, Natty said I were ter come an' see if yer, when yer come, I was ter see an' fetch yer, an' then…' His forehead creased with the effort to remember.

'What, love?'

He brightened. 'Ter fetch yer, Miss, an' then go – go get him some fags, yeah, fags.'

'Well, it's OK, I'm here now, you don't need to fetch me – did he give you the money, for the cigarettes?'

'Did he…? Oh, no. I best…'

I fished out my purse and gave him a fiver. 'Go on, Lee – and Lee, it's Billie, love, not Miss.'

'Yes Miss, right Miss, Billie Miss.' He nodded vigorously, as he did every time I told him to call me by my name.

'Go on then, off you go, I'll see you in a bit.'

I went to the door. It was ajar and a strong smell of cigs bloomed out in a bluish haze. Natty had just wanted to get rid of Monkey for a while, he always sent him for fags when he wanted him out of the way. I shut my eyes for a moment, feeling that strange duality in my mind – one half of me simply being a close friend of the family offering help in its hour of need, the other – well. But I couldn't stand around putting the moment off forever; taking a deep breath, I knocked and went in.

'Jas – Jas, it's me, Billie.' I put my head round the front room door. The air was chokingly hot and stuffy, it reeked of beer, unwashed people, cigarettes, fried food and the strong cheap jasmine oil Jas still wore and Natty bought for her religiously every birthday and Christmas. I wondered briefly if I could tactfully open a window before I fainted but I knew it was unlikely. Jas had a medieval distrust of fresh air and hated open windows.

'Oh, Billie love, Billie love, thank God yer here – oh, Billie, I don't…' She coughed harshly, the spasm seeming to shake the very depths of her tiny, frail body; mentally, I noted the cough – back again, she'd had it on and off for months now, it never seemed to really go away. I must get her to the doctor's. With an effort, I pulled myself back to the matter at hand. Jas was curled up in a corner of the old sofa, a furry purple cushion clutched to her belly, a cigarette in one shaking claw and the floor around her littered with beer cans. She was both drunk and stoned. My heart sank.

'Oh, right, the bloody cavalry's come. I might 'ave fuckin' known *you'd* be round fast enough.'

Terry's mother, Mrs Skinner, sat bridling in the easy chair by the fire, like a gorgon gone to seed. As gaunt, hook-nosed and lantern-jawed as her son had been, at sixty-odd she dressed as if she were twenty and augmented her long, dyed yellow hair with luxuriant false tresses; like scruffy serpents, as she quivered indignantly, her fake locks twitched and writhed. She was, literally, plastered with make-up, which only served to make her resemblance to Mr Punch more obvious. Recently, as the price had dropped and the exclusivity vanished, she'd taken up cosmetic surgery; her coarse lips were ballooned with Restylene, her forehead paralysed with Botox and her silicone bosom was mesmerising, two footballs inserted into an acre of age-spotted, crêpy, tanning-bed-orange chest. My mind flicked back to Leckie and us giggling at her impersonation in the shop of another surgery queen, Teena B. Oh, Leckie, if you read this, I missed you so much; but you were a world away from this life.

'Mrs Skinner. Keepin' well, I hope.' No wonder Jas was in a state. Not only would she be terrified Terry would come home and find her in the condition she was, but his mother, who she loathed and was frightened of, was, from the look of the alcho-pop bottles and full ashtray, apparently in her house to stay for the foreseeable future.

'Oh aye. *I'm* well enough, thank you. Not like *some* I could mention. Some folk round here are in a right bloody condition. Let themselves go, if you get my drift. My God, a fine bloody mess my poor boy'll have when he gets home...' Her voice thickened with the conflict and aggression that fuelled her every waking moment. Like mother like son, as they say. I levelled a look at her and she flickered her ash on the floor and set her head back on her neck, pleating her chins. On the sofa, Jas clutched her cushion and tears tracked down her face silently; she still cried like a Raphael Virgin – no scrunchy face, no reddened nose, just fat crystal drops falling from those cloudy emerald eyes.

'Well, that's as maybe, Mrs Skinner. Jas, where's Natty?'

She coughed and snuffled. 'In his room, oh, Billie, I don't...' But I didn't want to hear what she was going to say. It would be more pleading and excuses, more junkie chunter. I couldn't succumb to the old lure of those huge, plaintive eyes; not this time, not now. I needed to know exactly what had happened and make plans accordingly. My head throbbed with the start of a colossal headache.

I went and knocked softly on Natty's door.

'Natty love, it's me...'

He came out and folded me into his arms. I felt how hot and tense he was, his neck corded with ligaments like a ship straining at anchor. He smelt strongly of the expensive shower gel and aftershave he favoured and he was dressed in his best clothes; baggie white trousers worn very low on his narrow hips and a long, loose white Aertex-type vest with deep armholes that showed his muscles to their best advantage. Everything he wore had cost a small fortune, all American imports and labelled with the name of a famous rapper. His heavy gold chain glinted in the dim light. His best kit: it was as if he expected his dadda to walk in at any minute and he wanted to look flash for him. The strange, observing, detached part of my mind thought cynically that if his dad had seen him dressed like that, he would have bullied him and denigrated him as unmercifully as he had Jasmine, all those years ago. Time would not have mellowed Terry, far from it if his mother was anything to go by. I felt a wave of nausea go through me and swallowed bile. I had to get through this, I had to.

Natty's wiry dreads tickled my face and when I pushed him back to look at him, I could see he'd been crying; probably with his mother – I'd seen those mutual orgies of emotion before, watching as they wound each other up to fury, or tears, or love. But Natty wouldn't let his nan see him crying; he knew her ambivalence towards him. You couldn't exactly say Mrs Skinner loved Natty; she couldn't love anyone, it wasn't in her. Months would go past without a word from her, at one point we didn't see or hear of her for over two years and I'd hoped she'd fucked off for good. But she always slithered back with some cracked homily about blood being thicker than water.

No, she didn't care for Natty as such, but she liked to have him around to gripe at and to aim her racist digs at: *pity yer mam's a nigger, int it, Natty? Pity my boy dint pick a decent girl to go wi – eh, eh? Still, yer my flesh an' blood, int yer? We'll ave ter do best we can...'* He'd stopped rising to her baiting when he was about thirteen. One day, when she'd delivered one of her fusillades he didn't respond, there was no furious, childlike burst of temper. He simply looked at her and said *'whatever'*, then walked out, his face closed and carefully disinterested. It was after that he stopped reading and making up stories about Terry's adventures. I still couldn't forgive the old bitch for that.

I hugged him back and sighed as I imagined the scenes that had gone on before I arrived. No wonder he'd been crying; not that I'd ever mention I'd noticed. Men like him didn't cry, naturally.

'Bille – aw, Auntie Billie, so glad you've come. Man, it's doin' my head in, I'm telling yer. Me nan's enough ter drive anyone fuc – sorry, mental and me mam – you seen her? What a fuckin' state – I don't mean ter swear, but I just...'

'It's OK, It's OK, love, never mind about that...'

'But I don't want ter disrespect yer, it's just...'

'Don't worry, Natty love, really. Look, let's set kettle on, make a brew, an' you can tell me everything, eh? Eh, love?'

He took me in his arms again. His thin, hard body was shaking. I hugged him back and patted him until he calmed a little. It was like a bruise on my heart to see him like this, so desperate, so wired.

The tiny kitchen was its usual filthy mess; the once bright and cheerful yellow-checked curtains were grubby and faded and the yellow Formica countertops were rubbed white in patches and seamed at the joins with dirt. In times past I'd tried keeping it clean, but it was pointless, Jas wasn't up to it and Natty – well, along with crying went cleaning. Sometimes one of his more domestic girlfriends washed up to impress him but I couldn't see Venus bothering. The place was strewn with empty tins of Nutrament and Dunn's River Nurishment, the sweet, milky protein drinks that were all Jas could stomach most days. Natty's idea of cooking was to incinerate something to charcoal in a frying pan then slap it between two doorsteps of bread and marge. If I ate like him, I'd be a balloon, but whatever he ate, he burnt off almost immediately.

I washed up two mugs and made tea – no point asking Jas if she wanted any, she never did when she was drinking and I wasn't going to ask Mother Skinner.

We went back into Natty's room. I sat on the end of his old single bed, cradling my tea, wishing I had some Ibuprofen. Natty kicked away the open shoe box and tissue paper that showed he had box-fresh trainers on – the mark of a playa. He sat carefully on the other end of the bed. The room was so small, there wasn't space for a proper chair. From the open window came the sounds of the estate drifting in on the heavy air; a radio playing, kids shouting, someone revving a bike. There was a faint smell of cut grass and exhaust fumes mixed with Natty's perfume. The dull light caught the dusty surfaces and made one side of Natty's face gleam like liquid bronze.

The detached part of my mind caught the image and saw it on canvas; a palette knife portrait in acrylics, impasto, perhaps even touched with metallic leaf like a Klimt…I shook my head. How could I think like that at a time like this? It felt as if my mind were being slowly, but inexorably, torn in half with a horrible fibrous feeling, like a bath sponge ripping. A sudden moment of sheer panic bubbled up in my chest, I had to run, get away, hide, I could simply go, not come back, ever – people did, didn't they? People ran away and…I clutched my tea mug harder. This was no good, I had to know what had actually happened, after all, maybe it wasn't so bad, a storm in a teacup, one of Jas's moments of drug hysteria. I looked at Natty and managed a tremulous smile.

We both started speaking at once. 'So what's…'

'Will he…'

I waved my free hand. 'Sorry, no, go on, you…'

Natty's head wove slowly from side to side in a sinuous motion of distress; his jaw tightened. 'I – I…' He palmed the damp tendrils of hair that escaped from his dreads off his forehead.

'Go on, love.'

'I just – I don't know. I – I can't get me head round it. Him – me dad – comin' back. Like I keep thinkin' – he could walk in any minute, you know? Any minute…'

I swallowed some tea to give me a second's respite. It burnt my mouth and the little pain cleared my mind. 'Yeah, I know, I know, love – but, look, what exactly – I mean, how…'

Natty picked up a much folded newspaper from the floor and handed it to me. 'See, see? A fella at the pub give Nan the paper when there were

an ad in it, askin' fer people ter contact 'em if you had family missin'.
Nan wrote 'em. They rang her an' said they were doin' some story about
people as go missin' cos it were a disgrace, like, how the coppers an' the
government dint give a shit about 'em. They only cared if it were a little
blonde lass, or some rich bastard's kiddie. So Nan sent a picture of me
dad, said how no one had given a shit about what happened to him an'
how Mum were driven ter drugs an' how I'd never seen me own dad.
Look.'

I looked. The banner front page headline read 'Britain's Vanished'.
Under that was a collage of small pictures of men, women and children,
all ages, all races. A smaller banner read 'Are You A Boy? Are You Working
Class? Are You Black? If You Are – Don't Go Missing – No One Will Care'
and a short paragraph about the corruption and apathy the Clarion
saw in the authorities responsible for finding missing persons and the
general disinterest there was in the fates of the thousands of Britons who
vanish each year – but no longer. The Clarion was launching a nation-
wide search for The Vanished. Pictured were only a few of the many...

The blurred grey print swam in front of my eyes. One image, a small,
rather indistinct old photograph of a young man with long, greasy hair
and a fuckwit smirk on his long face coalesced out of the mosaic of
pictures and imprinted itself on my aching brain.

Terry.

Terry...

Jesus fucking God: Terry.

I felt my gorge rise and fought a short, hard battle not to throw up.
Sweat beaded my forehead and a feeling of weakness spread through
my body. It was true then. There was Terry, my own personal nemesis,
grinning at me from the front page of a national newspaper.

'See? It's me dadda – there...Here – you alright? You look funny...'

'What? Oh – it's – I think I ate summat bad last night, just got bad
guts, it's nothing, love, thanks anyway.' I drank some more tea, glad of
the stewed, bitter taste that took away the sour bile in my mouth.

Natty nodded – which for a lad like him was an expression of deep
sympathy – then went on, his voice strung with adrenalin. 'So he's gotta
see it, his picture, hasn't he? I mean, if he don't, someone he knows'll
show it him, right? I mean, like, even if he's abroad, y'know, they get

English papers, y'know, posh ones like this un anyway – in Amsterdam or wherever. That's what I think, I – I – oh, Billie, me mam, me mam, what're we gonna do about me mam?'

His voice cracked into a groan and he shut his eyes, pushing his dreads back with the spatulate tips of his fingers.

I looked at him and sighed. What would we do with Jas? God knows I'd tried to get her straight, I'd done everything bar drag her bodily to the scruffy, underfunded NHS detox clinic – and I'd considered that option on several occasions. But Jas was a devout junkie. There was no glimmer of the genuine desire to get clean in her, despite her rambling monologues about how much she wanted to be straight; that was just doper cant. The drug, the culture, her skag-mates, even the sorry little rituals surrounding her use of it were the cental pillars of her life – take it away and the perished remnants of her personality would collapse into dust and blow away in the breeze. She could never be the tidy, sweet-faced mother singing in her neat yellow kitchen Natty wanted her to be. The monkey on Jas's back was heroin. The monkey on Natty's back was Jas; clinging, pitiful, heartbreaking, those long, knuckly brown fingers, so like his own, fixed like steel hooks into his soul.

'Natty love, the main thing is to keep calm, right? I know yer mum, well, she's got her problems, we all know that – but – hang on, right, let me finish – if yer dad comes back, *if* he does, I know – I mean, Natty, he'll understand, he'll see how hard life's been for her – for you both – an' it might be just the thing to get her off the stuff, eh? See what I mean? It might be what she needs to get her right.'

The lies slid out of my mouth easy and fluid. The detached, observing part of me nodded in satisfaction. The other part wept savage salt tears that burned like acid. The refrain from an old Clash song tagged in my mind *'Straight to Hell, boys...'* Oh, I was bound straight to Hell alright, if there was any justice in this world or the next, right enough.

'Yeah, yeah. I know. Yer right – as always.' Natty smiled at me ruefully. My heart contracted painfully with love. 'Just gotta stay cool, yeah? I mean – I -I – y'know, prob'ly I shouldn't say this – but sometimes, I get so fuckin' angry about me dad, y'know? I get so mad. I mean, how could he 'ave just *gone,* left me mum, me – he musta known how

– what is it – how – well, how she int strong, in herself, like. Mebbe he had his reasons but – it weren't right, you know what I mean?'

'Yeah, love, I know. Of course you feel like that, it's only natural. But, see, that's why you gotta keep cool, hmm? It won't solve anything, us gettin' het up. You know what yer nan's like, she'll have a field day over this.'

'Oh, aye, right enough. There's some reporter comin' up from London ter talk to her an' all. She's made up – it's a fuckin' nightmare.'

My mouth went dry. It was bad enough having Terry's picture in amongst twenty others – but a reporter? Why on earth would a reporter come to Bradford – from London, mind you – to talk to Mrs Skinner? It didn't make sense.

Natty continued, rolling his shoulders to ease his tense muscles. 'Stupid, I call it. They rang me nan, that's why she's here, she wants to lord it ovver Mum, now she's gonna be a celeb, she reckons…'

'But Natty, I don't understand, why…'

'Oh, they want ter do a thing on her – on us. I don't fucking know. Er – I don't – yeah; a human interest story, the lass said. They're gonna – I don't know – write some stuff about how me dad goin' missin' fucked us all up or summat. Like they do, you know. Nan loves it, reckons she'll be goin' on telly an' everythin'. Had her nails done special, silly old…'

'Natty – don't. Don't, she is your nan after all. I know, I know – but that's the way it is. We just have to live with it and…'

Natty's phone trilled, and taking it out of his pocket he flipped it and answered with the unconscious rudeness of his generation. I sighed, then mimed at him I was going to the other room. He nodded, and as I passed him, I rubbed his dreads. Without interrupting the flow of his conversation, he put his arm round my waist and, pulling me to him, butted his head against me, then let go. Just like Ghengis, I thought, when he wants to tell me he loves me but doesn't want to compromise his machismo. What would Nat's phone-pal have thought after all, if he'd said 'Hang, blood, I jus' gotta hug me auntie, know what I'm sayin'?'

As I turned into the living room, my mind bruised and numb, Monkey ran full tilt in the front door and nearly knocked me over. I staggered and braced myself against the layers of coats hung up in the tiny hall.

'Lee – easy, tiger.' I straightened up as Monkey, a crumpled packet of fags in one hand and a bag of strawberry Campinos sticking out of his pocket, looked horrified and burbled an incoherent apology.

'…Soz, sorry, Miss – but Miss, Miss, at shop they sayin' Natty's dad's int paper – int paper, Miss, an' I don't…I said I dint know nowt, I don't know nowt an' they said Natty's gonna be famous and they said Missus is a – they said summat bad, Miss, they said…'

I knew what they would be saying about Jas – or 'Missus' as Monkey always called her. 'OK, it's OK, Lee. Don't worry, don't worry, love. It is true about the paper, it's a story 'bout why Natty's dadda went away, see? Everything's cool, Lee, really. Tell you what, love, you go give Natty his fags, eh? Mebbe make him another brew, hmm?'

As Monkey ducked away into the kitchen I heard the rusty gate of Mrs Skinner's voice grinding away at one of her favourite themes. 'Is that that fuckin' little freak? Ugly little weirdo, if I had my way, rubbish like that'd be put down, wotsit, you know, exterminated…'

I heard the sound of Jas protesting feebly that Monkey was a nice lad, a good lad, it weren't his fault he weren't nice-looking. She always said this, because he fetched and carried – probably drugs as well as fags and beer, but I didn't ask – for her and he loved her son. In reality, he could have been Hannibal Lecter crossed with Quasimodo, Jas wouldn't have cared, he was a shadow to her, like most people she knew. She wouldn't have noticed if he'd dropped dead one day and never came back to the flat: '*Oh,*' she'd say in that wavering voice if someone had mentioned his demise, '*shame, poor little fella.*' But then, that's heroin for you, leaves you nice and numb, makes all the nasty stuff go bye-byes. I rubbed my temples, trying to ease my headache; if Jas offered me some of her precious gear, I'd have been seriously tempted. How in God's name did I come to be here, listening to Mrs Skinner, the estate's answer to Eva Braun, with my head throbbing and my life ravelling into tatters around me? Why? Why had this happened to me? The old childhood plaint rang in the back of my mind: '*It isn't fair, it isn't fair.*'

Mrs Skinner's drivel dragged me back to the reality I couldn't avoid. Fair or not, it was how it was and I had to deal with whatever the old bitch had dragged down on us.

'…Well, that's as maybe, *Jasmine*, but what use are retards like that, I'd like ter know? I mean, God help the race if he breeds wi some other mental case, it'll be more money the government 'ave ter spend on keepin' em alive an'…'

'Lee isn't retarded, Mrs Skinner, he's got a few problems, that's all – who hasn't?' I tried to keep the acid out of my tone, I needed to know what she'd done, not set her off into one of her famous tirades.

She bridled furiously, her chins quivering. 'Problems? *Problems?* Trust the likes of you ter come out wi summat daft like that. Bloody do-gooders. That's why the country's gone ter t'dogs…'

I interrupted before she could set her usual rant in motion. 'Well, we'll have to agree to disagree, eh, Mrs Skinner? But this newspaper thing, pretty amazing – it, er, really shows how determined you are about Terry, doesn't it? And they're sending a proper reporter up to talk to you about it – that's great, isn't it?'

The spit curdled in my mouth, buttering the hag up like that and it pricked my pride, that deadly hubris that had got me into this in the first place. Everything I'd felt about her dickhead son I felt for her. I had a sudden flashback to the old days, when I'd been somebody and a cabbage like Pauline Skinner would have been beneath my contempt. Carl's face swam before my mind's eye – how had he kept his temper when the likes of Terry had caused him grief? I tried to emulate his calm, his control – Mrs Skinner was a means to an end, that's all. Nothing personal. I set my face into an approximation of friendly interest.

It fooled her; her vanity overcame her aggression for a few moments. 'Agree to…? Oh, aye. Well, I daresay – but you're right enough about the paper. Soon as I saw the first bit of a story, I though, right – an' I wrote 'em an' sent in my lad's picture. Like the reporter lass said, a mother's love, Mrs Skinner, strongest thing on earth…'

'And she's comin' to talk to you personally, then? From London? Well, that's a result, I'd say, wouldn't you? When's she comin', then?'

Mrs Skinner smirked and was about to speak when Jas, who had appeared to have nodded out on the sofa spoke up, her voice a dreamy slur. 'I loved 'im. I loved my Terry. I doan know why he left us, me an' Natty…When she comes, that lass, I'll tell 'er, like, tell her I loved him an' I'm sorry, I'm sorry fer whatever it were I done wrong ter him…'

Blood mottled Mrs Skinner's sagging cheeks and her thickened lips pursed as if someone had pulled a drawstring tight. 'You'll do nowt ut sort, you bloody junkie – state of you. You're a fuckin' disgrace, you are – no wonder my boy run off, shackled to fuckin' nigger jun…'

'That's *enough*, Mrs Skinner. I mean, it wouldn't do to argue in front of that reporter, would it? They might not be so interested if they thought the family dint stick together, like – you know how they like everything sorted, folk like that. And honest, what you've done – it's astonishing, isn't it? You wouldn't want to spoil it. Just my opinion, like, obviously, I'm not family, but I like to think of myself as a *friend* of the family, if you see what I mean.'

She subsided somewhat, mollified by the thought of herself being in the papers as a loving mother, fighting to the death for her lost boy, a pillar of strength to his vulnerable partner and a doting grannie to his beautiful son. You could see where Terry had got his cunning from; you couldn't say either of them was clever as such, but by God they were quick when it came to seizing an advantage to themselves.

'Well, I'll not deny you've helped a bit ovver the years. Babysittin' an' such. She's comin' termorrow as it happens, that lass. I says, what, on a Sunday, like, but she says it don't make no odds to her, when it's summat this important.'

She smirked, Queen of the Shitheap. She'd dine out on this for the rest of her life. I wondered briefly if the journalist girl had any idea of what she'd let herself in for.

On she went, like a mangle wringing the last drops out of a worn washcloth. 'Sophie her name is, Sophie James. Very posh ont phone, very polite, like. Says she'll get to the bottom of things, you know, find out what become of my Terry. Sounded very caring. Says she'll stay a couple of days till she gets it all sorted out. I daresay she'll want a word with you, since you were mates with our Terry an' yer allus hanging round, but mostly she wants ter talk ter me. Only natural, seeing as I'm his mum. She's stoppin' at the Great Northern – oh aye, nowt but the best it seems – I offered her ter stop with me, but she said it's all expenses, like; well, you know these London types…'

She ground on but I stopped listening. The main thing to do was not to panic; OK, this wasn't exactly a brilliant situation, but it wasn't as bad as it seemed. After all, I thought grimly as I watched Mrs Skinner pontificate, an Irn Bru Alcopop dangling from one hand, a fag from the other, Terry wasn't exactly going to walk in through the door going, '*Surprise, surprise, did yer miss me?*' All this girl from the papers would find out was that Terry was a wanker disliked by most people and missed by no one except his nightmare mother and poor little ruined Jas. And Natty, of course; Natty was the one who'd come out of this worst, choose how; but there was nothing I could do about that – no use crying over split milk. I'd deal with the fall-out as it came. The thing now was to sort out this newspaper stuff.

I read the *Clarion* myself sometimes, it was marginally better than the *Mail*, or the *Sun*. Anyway, they had a big review section and I could keep up with what was fashionable in the arts. Generally they jeered at people from 'the provinces' and did sarky, ironic photoshoots in their Sunday supplement about pissed-up lasses on a night out in Newcastle. Sometimes, though, they appeared to have a fit of guilt and did a story about 'real people'. Gritty, authentic, crusading, you know the kind of thing. That's what this was all about, a quick ratings boost in the silly season. They'd run with it for a bit then drop it when something more interesting happened. There really was no need to panic; none at all.

'…Anyroad, I can't be wasting my time here – Bobby'll be wantin' his tea an' unlike some, I like ter look after my family.'

Mrs Skinner dropped her teetering column of fag-ash on the floor and kicked her empty bottle away as she heaved herself to her stiletto-clad feet. Adjusting her low-rise, baby-blue velour joggers and matching skinny-fit zip-up mini-hoodie whose V-neck displayed the leathery, ginger acres of her torpedo cleavage, she turned the gaseous glare of her dog-yellow eyes on me. Reflexively, as always, I felt a brief pang of pity for poor deluded Bobby, her fella. He was a pallid, wizened shrimp of a bloke with greasy, fingerprinted, thick-lensed specs who did everything in the house and worshipped La Skinner who he apparently thought was Bradford's very own Marilyn Monroe.

'I'll be off then, you're welcome to that 'un.' Mrs Skinner jerked her head viciously at Jas, dozing, mouth open, on the sofa. 'Say tat-ta ter me grandson for me – the lazy little bastard. Oh, when my lad gets home, there'll be some changes round here, don't you fret.'

With that, she clumped off, slamming the door in her wake. Jas jumped in her sleep and her eyelids fluttered heavily, showing the whites, but she didn't make it to consciousness and slumped back into her dreamworld. I sat on the spindle-legged plastic kitchen chair by the telly and put my head in my hands. I was exhausted and my head still throbbed painfully. After a moment of trying not to think, I got up and raggled myself together. There was no point hanging around here; I'd be better off going home, taking some painkillers and getting an early night. Then tomorrow at least I'd be rested. Things would look better in the morning; like Dadda used to say, *'Get a bit of daylight on it, that's the ticket, my darlin'.'*

As I shouted goodbye to Natty, still on the phone, and walked down the stairwell hoping my car was still there and intact, I felt the old hook of despair bite into my heart. The Black Dog snuffling at my heels; you went missing, Dadda, didn't you? Only no one cared what happened to you, did they? No reporters searched for you, no papers got filed in Missing Persons Bureaux. You just slipped away, dark, elusive, like a black fish sliding down, down into the depths of an old tarn, the sepia peat-water closing over you, hiding you from view.

My whole life was a tapestry of the missing, the dead and the ruined survivors. Back and forth the bone-white shuttle flew, dragging the threads of us behind it whether we liked it or not. And the pattern grew and grew, generation after generation...

I wanted my home, my cats, my pictures, my own bed.

No more people; not until tomorrow, anyway. Tomorrow I'd be better, tomorrow I'd cope.

Chapter Twenty-one

'I'LL BE BACK soon, this job's summat an' nowt – look, don't you talk to no fuckin' reporter if you don't want to, right? It int your responsibility – them lot int your blood when it comes to it…Yeah, yeah, I know, an' you know what I think of that. Yeah, yeah – well, you gotta do what you think best, just – tek care of yersel first, right? Right? Look, I gotta go – I'll come round, we'll watch a vid or summat, eh?'

'Yeah, OK, that'd be nice…' But Johnjo had gone already, the muffled buzzy thread of his cheap pay-as-you-go mobile clicked into nothing. Still, it had been comforting to hear his matter-of-fact voice even for a few minutes. Sunday had been hellish. The reporter girl hadn't turned up – then she'd rung Mrs Skinner full of apologies and rearranging her visit for Monday. Apparently, she hadn't been able to get a photographer. Mrs Skinner's fury at being 'disrespected' as she saw it evaporated at the hitherto unconsidered idea of a photographer; that meant pictures – and the whole day disintegrated into her ransacking TK Maxx for 'summat decent' to wear and Jas feebly trying to 'tidy up' her flat. Natty and Monkey had vanished like water dropped on a hot skillet as soon as the reporter begged off. Normally, I wouldn't have noticed, but this time it worried me. Natty was so wired, so volatile, I didn't want him going on some dreadful bender and ending up coked off his tits in the cells. At least he didn't like crack, I knew that because he'd often told me he and his pals, the estate elite, considered it 'loser's dope'. That was a blessing.

I'd spent the day helping Jas and trying to ignore her increasingly obvious desire to 'get summat for her nerves'. By tea time, the flat reeked of bleach and Jas was shaking like a leaf. I put out what I thought was a reasonable outfit for her to wear the next day, and left. As I walked out the door she was on the phone. There was nothing I could do. Oh, I know some folk would say I should have stayed, kept her off it, seen her through 'cold turkey'. There are dickheads out there who think like that, hard though it is to believe. I've spoken to people who think getting off a lifetime's heroin addiction is no worse than exerting a bit of will-power and suffering a night of the flu. Next day, up you pop, bright-eyed and bushy-tailed, singing 'Spring Is Bustin' Out All Over' like Doris Day, fully re-integrated into a caring, loving, forgiving society. They honestly think that. It used to make me angry, but now I think they have to believe crap like that because they're so scared; they elect to live in La La Land because real life is so fucking desperate. And they're right, it is – so I don't get mad any more, what's the point?

Sunday evening was a blur, frankly. I remember making an egg sandwich, then lying on the sofa with Cairo on my chest and Gheng on my legs and wishing Cairo didn't dribble so much since the vet took her teeth out, poor little baggage; I remember some bizarre film on Channel Five about cowboys with Will Smith in it – then nothing. I woke up at midnight and crawled into bed, a big crick in my poor old neck that made a sound like someone crumpling up cellophane. The alarm rang at seven like the crack of doom.

So I'd phoned Johnjo as I drove into town through the stuffy heat, just to hear a sensible voice. The humidity was terrible; sun I could stand but this wet heat…My clean T-shirt was already stuck to me with sweat and my newly washed hair looked like a damp duckling.

Along the Leeds road, what Leckie called 'Leeds Road Girls' wheeled their latest babby out in the pushchair, fags sticking out of the knuckles of their paws as they flapped down the hill in three-quarter chinos and halter tops, their luminescent white skin welted with strawberry-red patches of sunburn. How could they smoke in this weather? And why were the babies hatless and swaddled in kiddie-jeans and fleeces? As I drove past the motorists' discount shop, I spotted a toddler, not more than three years old, stumping down one of the back alleys that led off the road, wearing nothing but a dirty vest and an adult's full-face motorcycle helmet, sucking an ice lolly through the aperture. Jesus, Bradford in summer, you couldn't invent it.

But still, as I crested the rise and looked across the valley to the opposite hill, the old illusion of driving down to the sea caught me; that glimpse of strangeness, of hidden things, of puzzles in mazes in carved stone boxes that made Bradford such a weird place. How often I'd heard visitors say, 'Oh – it looks like...For a minute there, with that view, it looked like you could be at the coast, how funny.' Yeah, funny. If only it were true, the sea – oh, what I wouldn't do for a week by the sea. High on the heather-clad slopes, across the bowl of town, the wind turbines stood sentry-still in the breathless heat and the sky was a hazy iris-blue. I thought longingly of Leckie's famous fans in the shop; the cool, sweet scent of wood polish and lilies – unfortunately tinged with joss, probably.

I had woken, after the shock of the alarm, feeling oddly cheerful. The more I thought about it, the less I had to worry about. Sure, it would be a bit rough for a while, but I'd had worse. Even if there was a bit in the papers, it wouldn't change anything – how could it? I'd seen to that, right enough. It'd be bumpy, then everything would subside back to – well – normal.

And something else had occurred to me as I showered. This was a kind of turning point. Yes, I'd done a dreadful thing, a terrible thing. But I'd done my time – and more. If I'd gone to prison, I'd have been out years since, a free woman. Even if Terry hadn't – if I hadn't – he probably would have abandoned Jas anyway, he was that kind of guy. That wasn't an excuse, it was reality; OK, I couldn't prove it, but it was a reasonable bet. I had paid, over and over, for what I'd done – and it was time to let it go. I only had one life, this wasn't a bloody sketch for a bigger, better painting to come, this was it. Like Japanese calligraphy, you had the one shot at the perfect line.

When this blew over, I'd make some changes. Get someone in to manage the shop, go away, an extended holiday – one of those round-the-world air tickets. This whole stupid newspaper thing would be a sort of – what was it Leckie said? Oh yes – closure. I'd effect closure. I'd known for years I couldn't save Jas; it was hard, very hard, but I had to be real about it. I loved Natty but he was a grown man now, I couldn't be hanging round him like a wistful spinster auntie all his life. I'd always be there for him, of course, but I had to breathe, I had to *live*.

Leckie was full of the news when I got in. She'd almost bust a gut when I told her a reporter was coming to talk to Mrs Skinner, Jas and Natty. Then to tell her it had been called off – but was happening today – just drove her nuts. She so wanted to be a fly on the wall; well, she was welcome to that, I wanted the opposite. I played it all down, of course, but Leckie was such a hound for gossip, I had to tell her in detail the awfulness of Mrs S's reaction to the idea of a photographer and what she ended up buying at TK Maxx at least three times while she did exaggerated mouth-open goggles. After she finished goggling, I told her I was thinking of a long break when this was all over, and to my surprise, she got tearful and rushed round the counter to hug me. When she recovered, she went to get us a treat from Starbucks and brought back a sheaf of travel brochures. Personally, I fancied Hawaii – but then, who wouldn't?

Anyway, speculating about holidays kept my mind off things to a degree, though Natty calling what seemed like on the hour, every hour, tended to remind me of the whole mess, as he recounted the mayhem that was happening at Jas's; the bloke taking pictures and the reporter girl coming round with Mrs Skinner, and what a cowbag his nan was, and what should he say to the lass, and oh, everything relayed in detail. Not for the first time, I longed for the days when mobile phones were something off *Star Trek*. I did my best to keep him calm, but it didn't help when I could hear Mrs Skinner yelling at Monkey in the background and what I was sure was Jas crying. I had to force myself not to drop everything and go round – because that wouldn't do, not at all, seeing as I was only a 'friend of the family'. I had to stay cool; not seem to be too into everything, too nosy, too – suspicious. I had to be balanced – interested, yet not obsessively so. Have you ever tried to seem normal? It's the hardest thing in the world and the more you try, the less *normal* you appear. I decided that the only way to do it was to think concertedly about something else; in this case, the shop, so I ran around furiously rearranging the displays and putting out the new stock.

We had a bit of a rush after lunch, did some good business which distracted me somewhat – the new green amber was proving extremely popular. I was bemoaning my inability to source decent turquoise and scribbling a list of stock to re-order, when the bell tinkled and a man came in.

'Leckie, love, will you see to this gentleman, I want to ring Bettlestein's about the silver chains...'

'Billie...' It was the man. His voice sounded – I knew that voice – I...

Suddenly, the world narrowed to the dark sun-edged doorway, to a tall shape silhouetted in the sequinned haze. I blinked. I heard my voice coming from a long way away and the hair rose on the back of my neck.

'Micky? *Micky?* Is it you?'

He stepped into the light. It wasn't him, it was his dad. Oh – I'd really thought – oh, my God, it *was* him. Something like a trapped bird fluttered frantically in my heart, my throat closed like a fist. Jesus, I thought, he – Jesus, he looks so *old*. Speechless, I searched his face for my sweet boy, the youth I'd loved so desperately. In his place stood a man whose face was a map of bitterness and caution, whose faded cornflower eyes were cold and suspicious. His broad shoulders slumped, his beer-belly rounded his cheap T-shirt; the once shining fall of chestnut hair was still thick, but untidily cropped to utilitarian shortness, lustreless and coarse. Deep lines scored his face either side of his nose to his lips.

From the corner of my eye I could see Leckie gawping: was this wreck of a middle-aged man the handsome outlaw I'd told her about? I signed to her silently and she busied herself ostentatiously with the card racks.

I cleared my thickened throat. 'Er – well, this is a surprise...'

He grunted. 'Yer mam told me where you were. I want a word. In private, like.'

'Yes – yes, of course. Come into the office.'

He seemed to fill the tiny room as I stood behind my untidy desk and motioned for him to sit down. He didn't – and he wouldn't look me in the face. Just like old times. We stood there, silent. His jaw was stuck out, in the way it did when he was uncomfortable about something, and his red, battered fingers plucked at the seams of his cheap baggy jeans like they did when he was nervous and...Oh, where was my love, where in this ruined flesh was my young husband, my...

I suddenly realised why he'd come. It was screaming from every line of his body. Just as quickly, knowing him, seeing the signs, I was terrified he'd blurt out everything and Leckie would hear.

'Micky – er, well. Would you like a coffee? Some wa...'

He made that warding off gesture with his hand, like before. I got the feeling, very strongly, the sight of me was repulsive to him. I don't know if that's ever happened to you, but believe me, it's crap. I felt – diminished by it, weak, and steadied myself on the edge of the desk.

'You know why I'm here,' he said, as if it cost him a great effort. 'You know – I seen it in that newspaper – fella at work had it, student – I saw – *him* – I…'

I had to get control of this, and fast. 'Yes – yes. I know. Micky…'

'Don't call me that. No one calls me that no more. I'm Michael now.'

'I'm – sorry. OK, Michael then, look, this is not the place to talk about stuff. Do you understand? Not here.'

He grimaced. I wondered if he was in some kind of physical pain. 'Mic – um, are you alright? You look…'

He made that gesture again. 'I done me back in at work, liftin' summat. It's nowt, nowt for *you* ter bother with. It were a long drive, that's all. Look, I'll not be put off, y'know, I've got a family, kids, I'll not…'

'I'm not trying to put you off – just, not here, OK?' My mind worked frantically, I should drop by Jas's, dead casually of course, after work, but – shit, this was more urgent. Micky – *Michael*, could destroy everything if he got himself in a state. Just like before, I had to do what was best for us both, despite him. I felt, so, so tired, so exhausted again. It was a battle to gather my wits. I shut my eyes for a split second, then blew out the breath I hadn't realised I was holding. 'Um – you – you'd best come round to my house this evening, after work, say – oh, half six. Here, I'll write the address down. It's by the church.'

He took the scrap of paper and looked at it. 'I'm stoppin' at me mam's. She int well. That's what I told folks. That I were visitin'. You'd best say the same.'

And he turned, slowly, and walked out of the shop. He didn't look back.

Feeling for the chair behind me, I sat down hard. It was as if my brain had been sponged clean; I sat in a thick bubble of nothing and all I was aware of was the thud of my pulse and the rush of my breath. I had a feeling that if I wanted all that to stop, if I wanted my blood to stop moving, my lungs to stop working, I simply had to go: *No more, finish.* I just had to…

'My God, Billie, are you OK? Was that – you know who? Talk about everything coming at once! What did he want – what did you say? I mean how long has it been since...'

The bubble ripped and the world zoomed back like someone tuning in the radio. As it did, my mobile rang and the shop door opened. Leckie mimed that she was going to serve and I flipped the phone.

'Hello,' my voice said, in a normal way.

'Oh, hi. Um, my name is Sophie James, Mrs Morgan, you don't know me and I'm so sorry to bother you, Nathan gave me your number, I hope you don't mind me ringing you, but I'm doing...'

'Yes, you're the reporter. From the *Clarion*.'

'Oh, yes, yes I am. Of course, you'll know all about it. Sorry. Well, you see, Jasmine's told me what a tower of strength you are to the family...'

'Oh, I wouldn't say that, I'm just a friend...' My voice sounded incredibly calm, it was amazing. I was internally amazed at myself.

'Oh, not at all – Jasmine calls you the family's guardian angel! They think the world of you. I was wondering, do you think it would be possible for us to meet? Have a little chat? Your insights would be so invaluable, really, I mean, no one knows the situation like you do and...'

'I'm sorry, I don't...'

'Please, Mrs Morgan – it would be such a help, really. I've spent all day with er, Mrs Skinner, and she now seems convinced there's some question of foul play and I wondered what you, as a – as a family friend – thought because...'

Foul play? What the *fuck*? I coughed convulsively as the air left my lungs and a cold sweat clammied along my spine.

'Mrs Morgan? Are you alright?'

foulplayfoulplayfoulplayfoulplayfoulplayfoulplayfoulplayfoulplayfoul playfoul

'Yeah, yes, I'm sorry, I – swallowed some tea the wrong way. It's, erm, not Mrs by the way, it's Ms. I'm divorced. Morgan is my family name. Just call me Billie, everyone does...' I was burbling. With an effort that seemed to rip my head in two, I got myself together.

foulplayfoulplayfoulplayfoulplayfoulplayfoulplayfoulplayfoulplayfoul playfoul

'Oh, OK – Billie. So would it possible...'

I wanted her to fuck off so much it made my teeth ache, but I had to be sensible. If I refused to see her it might look odd since everyone else was falling over themselves to be involved. This was the age of the celeb; no one in their right mind refused to be in the papers. If I did see her, at least I'd be in control of what was said about my end of things.

foulplayfoulplayfoulplayfoulplay – stop it, stop it *now*; concentrate.

'Well, ummmm – you'd best come to my house, say...' I thought frantically; Micky wouldn't stay long, not loathing me as he did (*go away, go away, pain, not now, don't think about that now*), if I spend half an hour with this lass I could then zoom up to Jas's and check if they were alright and...'around seven thirty?'

'Oh – yes, that would be fantastic, thank you so much.'

I gave her the address and directions and hung up.

I heard a tapping noise; looking down at the desk I saw my nails drumming convulsively on the chipped Formica. With an effort, I stopped and tensing my hand straight, laid it flat. The surface was cool against my palm. I felt a terrible calm drop through me; unnatural, like a kind of death. I felt that if I breathed on the pot plant on the desk, it would die. That made me smile.

The absolute worst thing about this whole situation, the most horrific, repulsive thing, was that I knew I could deal with it. I was that person. And what, I wondered, the chilly little smile still on my numb lips, did that make me?

Chapter Twenty-two

'Look, you get off early, love – I can lock up, no problem. Billie, go on, you've had a shock, seeing – *him* like that. And all this stupid newspaper business – my God! I can't believe you're actually going to *speak* to this reporter! Just *be careful*, that's all I'll say. They twist stuff round, you know, make out you've said things you haven't. Jackals, the press are, you can't trust them.'

Leckie nodded sagely, pursing her MAC pink lips; she had that I-know-about-stuff-like-this expression on her face, like she did with computers or celebrity gossip, subjects which in actuality, she knew no more about than the rest of us plebs. But she liked to think of herself as terrifically worldly, and I liked to let her. Her innocence was something I treasured; something I do treasure, Lecks, if you're reading, if you've got this far and not chucked the pages across the room in disgust at what I really am. I treasure you, love. Your beauty, your cleverness, your big heart and yes, your naiveté. All those things are a charm, they're your luck, a totem that wards off the dark, keeps you clean.

Clean was what I wanted to be, more than anything. The dirty stain of regret spread through me like ink spilt on blotting paper. I regretted everything; I would have sold my soul without a second thought if I could just have had my life back, to start again, to tear off the old page, sharpen my pencils and do it again – only this time, right.

When I trailed in, the cottage smelt a bit catty and musty to my mind, so I threw all the windows open and binned the bunch of garden flowers that had gone to sticks. I got the Shake n' Vac and the Dyson out and tested its claims to the limit with the overlay of cat hairs that Ghengis in particular liked to rub into the rug and his favourite spot on the sofa. I faffed and fiddled at housework for half an hour, then gave up and showered. I stood under the lukewarm blast for as long as I could and lathered copiously with some tea-tree wash, its sharp, pungent odour more satisfying than fake fruit or chemical flowers on a hot evening.

Putting on some loose cotton drawstring pants and a clean T, I flip-flopped out to the garden with a glass of cranberry juice and sat on the tiled bench, turning my face up to the thick golden light of the sun; was it my imagination, or was there the faintest hint of autumn? There's always that moment when the season starts to turn. It's not exactly visible, but there's something in the light…

Things chased at random through my mind. I tried to do that meditation thing that Leckie always advised and listen to the sounds around me, bring myself into the here and now. I could hear wood pigeons, a lawn mower, children laughing, music playing faintly – something classical – Mrs Leach calling her insane Jack Russell, D'Arcy, sounding like an extra from a Jane Austen adaptation on the telly, and D'Arcy snuffling and yipping in the cemetery over the wall. I tried to listen to all that and forget the other things, but I couldn't.

Frivolous thoughts would rise to the surface of my mind and repeat and repeat, then vanish. What to get for dinner. Should I deadhead the roses. Laundry. The window display. Then, suddenly: Did I look as old to Micky as he looked to me? Did I look that old to everyone? Was it totally over, my – well – attractiveness? Was I now the sort of middle-aged, invisible, unsexed, woman that no man in his right mind looked at twice in the street? The sort young comedians poked fun at on telly? I started to panic – stupid, but I couldn't help it. Despite all the serious things that were going on, it seemed terribly important that I'd never flirt again without people thinking I was a stereotypical sex-starved old cow, never be whistled at again, never be the object of any man's desire, ever again. I tried to be reasonable – what about Leckie's pal, Tom? He'd seemed so nice; but, what if he was only being sociable, polite, and I'd taken it as personal? How mortifying that would be, but how would I know if I didn't pursue it and if I did, what if he laughed in my face and said, *'Oh, you're too old for me, God, I mean, my last girlfriend was eighteen! I was just being pleasant because Leckie asked me to…'*

That would kill me, it really would and I – I…My heart seemed to scurry round inside me, frantic, trying to find a place to hide from this overwhelming triviality. Oh, Jesus, oh, Jesus – I was all alone; there was only Johnjo, and much as I cared for him, how much of that was habit – and from his point of view, was I just his other wife? Oh, it was so unfair – all gone and I'd thrown it away, chucked it down the drain and now it was too late…What was the point of life? What was the fucking point? To be young and stupid, then be old and consumed with regret and then be – dead? Over. Finished, and no second chance? How coldly cruel; how brutally sad.

Thoroughly stressed, I got up and accidentally knocked the tumbler of juice over. It ran into the grass like blood. I put my hand to my chest and felt my heart knocking like a jackhammer. Calm, calm, I had to get calm. Micky was due any minute, I couldn't see him like this. A thin voice in my head screamed shrilly *'Don't see him at all – run away.'* Then everything seemed to swirl around me like the tile mosaic on the bench and the next thing I knew, I was sitting on the grass.

Dizzy, I lay back and tried to breathe slowly. A mini-faint. OK, not surprising, under the circumstances. Stay still for a minute – and, when did I last eat? Yesterday evening? Tea and toast then. The great cure-all. Wobbly as a new chick, I scolded myself into the kitchen and made toast out of three-day-old bread. Walking around as I ate, I glanced in the mirror; white as a sheet, worse than ever. I'd look a hundred percent better with a tan, even though it's supposed to be so bad for you now. At least I wouldn't look so peaky and ill. I fed the cats with tiny, expensive tins of gourmet catmeat as a treat, then flipped the telly on mindlessly and watched the local news. Then it finished and I realised the time. Where was Micky?

At five to seven, I heard a car pull up. It was him. I went to the window and looked out, watching the middle-aged man who some evil fairy had substituted for my young husband clamber stiffly from his dirty old Ford. That cheap, crappy car; it seemed to sum up what he'd become. The other Micky, even if in time he'd brought himself to get a car, wouldn't have been seen dead in a neglected heap of shit like that. His mechanic's skills and his pride wouldn't have allowed it. This man didn't care.

But I was being harsh. After all, as he said, he had a family, from what he'd let slip he seemed to be working in a factory, not making use of his qualifications and his talents – maybe jobs were hard to come by where he was, God knows they were round here. Kids are expensive – it caught in my heart. Kids. What had we dreamed of calling our children? Oh yes – Hester, Emerald, Dylan, Rory. Foolish names, perhaps, but they still sounded nice to me. What were his children called?

I opened the front door before he knocked and watched him struggle to control his worn face. A wave of pity drenched through me and I wanted to reach out and put my hand on his arm, the freckled forearm, still roped with muscle under the sun-pinked skin that was so familiar to me. The shape of his nails, the turn of those ruined hands...I looked away quickly.

'Well – come in then – would you like...' Again I as I offered him a drink he averted his face slightly and grunted a refusal. 'OK – in here then.'

I showed him into the living room and gestured for him to sit. He perched uncomfortably on the edge of the armchair, his hands hanging between his knees and his head thrust out furiously. I searched for something to say but it was if my admittedly small stock of social conversation had dried up totally. I felt so sorry for him, that was the problem. I wanted to reach him in some way and comfort him. There was a lump in my throat and we both started speaking at the same time. I shook my head and told him to go on. He cleared his throat convulsively; I didn't think it was because he was choked up and felt for me as I felt for him. Sentimental I might be about our lost past, but you only had to look in his face to see love for me wasn't making him nervous. Far from it. But somehow, I still felt that if we only got talking, properly, like the old days, then at least we could go someway to making amends, become friends again, however distant. After all, we'd meant so much to each other once, and time heals all as they say.

'I 'ave to know – what you gonna do? Cause if you, like, you think you're gonna – talk – about – what 'appened – I won't – I won't 'ave it, see? I've got the wife an' kids ter think of now, I won't 'ave you messin' it all up, I won't. All this stuff in the papers – I – I'll do what I 'ave to, I'm warnin' you – I...'

He sounded livid; iron-hard and choked with anger. Side-lit by the low golden light from the window his face looked mask-like; the deep hollows of his eyes rayed with wrinkles looked like holes behind which something twitched and gibbered, biting its own flesh. I had the sudden strange feeling I wasn't talking to Micky but to whatever was inhabiting his worn-out frame; it was him, but it wasn't, all at the same time. The fury seethed off him in an almost palpable fume. It was infectious, I felt my own anger spark off his. This wasn't right, this wasn't how it should go, but honestly, I couldn't believe he was going to be so intractable. He knew me, he knew I was sound – what in the name of God did he imagine I was going to do? Spill my guts to the coppers? Go public in the papers and confess all? Did he imagine I'd gone through everything that had happened just to fall at the last jump and wreck everything? Anger boiled up through the pity I'd felt. Look at him – look – sitting there and threatening me. What did he think he was going to do? Smack me silent? Kill me too?

Jesus. Jesus. I got up and walked to the window, my back to him, struggling to control my fury. Dear God, when this was all over, nothing was going to keep me here, *nothing*. I'd be on the first plane possible and that was that. As if I didn't have enough to cope with without this. I knew from the first he'd come to check things out, but to threaten me – in my own home? Fuck. I could feel the blood burning in my face and laid the back of my hand on my cheek. It was freezing cold – despite the close evening warmth. Freezing cold – I shut my eyes. So tired. So fucking tired of all this. I took a long breath.

'Micky – OK, Michael. You can't just come back here and I don't know – what? Threaten me? Don't start, because – I know you've got a family, I know that, right? But it's out of order. I've protected you all these years, I…'

He snorted with ironic laughter. 'Protected me? You ruined my fuckin' life, you bitch. I 'ave nightmares – I wake up screamin'. Joanne – my wife – don't know what ter think. I told her it was from being in the club. She don't know, Billie, an' she won't ever know. She's decent, a decent woman. Not like you. Protected me? Fuck. You took everythin' away from me, it's took me years ter get even a bit right an' now…I know you hang around with that fuckin' smackhead Jas, with *his* fuckin' family, the lads told me. They said it were a fuckin' Ex-Wives Club, joked about it. Yer sick, you are. Sick. I won't 'ave you…' He stopped, panting like a dog that's run too far.

Sick, was I? Oh, right. How could he come here after all these years and throw this in my face when I'd – I'd loved him so much. And I had, I'd loved him and loved him, a dream, an ideal, made all the more precious because I'd driven him away, and because I'd sacrificed myself to save him. Or so I thought. I just hadn't thought, somehow, that through all that time he'd been brewing hatred of me like a poison, a black oily venom that oozed from behind his white, straining lips and corroded the bright memory I'd kept of him. How could he? How could he? I felt nauseous with the roiling brew of feelings that chased through me one after another.

'That's enough, Micky, d'yer hear me? I've done what I had to. Yeah, I look after Jas an' the boy – at least I didn't fuck off into the wild blue yonder an' wash my fuckin' hands of it all an'…'

'Look after 'em? Spy on 'em more like. Try an' control 'em, that's you all ovver. Don't you fuckin' try an' boss me round like before – you int Carl's little pet no more, you're no one, like me. No one an' fuckin' nothin'. No wonder the lads laughed at you – so fuckin' high an' mighty you were, an' now look at yer – a dried up old bitch. They hated you, y'know – *oh* yeah, it were only Carl kept 'em off yer – did yer fuck him too? Eh? I allus wondered about that. Yer did, dint yer? You'd do owt, you. Disgustin'.'

I stared at him in astonishment. Did he really think I'd slept with Carl? 'I never…With Carl? No – an' they dint hate me, what d'you mean? I…'

'Oh yeah, they fuckin' did. They all hated you, stuck up little cow. They hated you an' they thought you was a right little whorebag. Times I had ter stick up for you an' you never knew. Fuck me – you lived in a fuckin' world of your own, right enough. The little fuckin' princess. The lads couldn't stick yer – a mouthy cunt like you. An' the lasses – Christ. Only Carl wouldn't have it, wouldn't hear a word against yer. Even blacked his wife's eye on account of her bad-mouthin' yer. Everyone thought you was fuckin' him, *everyone*. I had to stand that too – but back then, you had me fooled, I was well under the thumb, fuckin' idiot I was. But not

anymore, oh no. Why the fuck did I ever get in with you? You're a fuckin'
jinx you are, bad luck, a fuckin' curse – a fuckin' disgrace to women, the
likes of you; an' if you think…'

I could hear him chuntering on but it seemed as if he was talking
with the sound off. Hated me? All the Devil's Own hated me? But – I
– no, it wasn't like that, I got on with everyone – I – sure, I was mouthy,
I know, I admit it, but…No. It wasn't true. *Don't take that away from
me too.*

'…I'll not be put off. I know what you're like, lordin' it ovver folk,
bossin' folk around, allus knowin' best. This newspaper stuff, I won't…'

'I'm talking to the reporter tonight.'

He stood up, fists clenched. 'You mad bitch. I won't have it, I won't.
You don't…'

How cold I was. In the heavy heat of the room, I was ice inside. I
looked at him and it was as if the reality of him, of what he'd become,
broke through the waxy carapace of my dream-memory and he stood
there, about to hit me and I wasn't afraid, because he could kill me and
he wouldn't have hurt me more than he had. He looked in my face and
dropped his fist. He always had been weak.

'Oh, go on then, big man, you thump me. That'll look good when
the reporter comes – an' she's due any minute. Yeah, I thought not. For
Christ's sake, get a grip of yourself. If I don't talk to her, how weird would
that look? I've got to – to control this, surely you can see that? God – to
think all these years I – oh, never mind. I'll do what I think best, Micky,
an' I'll thank you to fuck off now and let me get sorted so everything
looks normal when that lass gets here. D'you hear me?'

'Christ, you're a hard cow. But I'm warning you – if I think you're
gonna drop me in it – I'll make sure you never fuck around with anyone
else, ever again. I'll shut that fucking mouth of yours permanently. You
might have nowt, but I've got…'

'Your family. I gather that.'

'That's right, take the fuckin' piss. What would you know about
family? Even your own mam can't stick yer, you should have heard what
she said to me about yer – askin' me – *me* – where she went wrong with
yer. Born bad, she said – an' she's right. You were born fuckin' bad, bad
blood. Well, be warned. I'll not stand for it, I'll…'

There was a knock at the door, we both froze, united in that, if nothing else. He opened his mouth as if to speak but I signed for him to shut up.

'That'll be her, the reporter. Shut your mouth, Micky, if you love your family like you say. Just – just go out, don't say owt, I'll say – I'll say you're just a neighbour, borrowin' summat.'

'Don't you fuckin' tell me what ter...'

I looked at him, hard. He dropped his eyes. I felt a queasy mixture of grief and disgust lurch through me. 'Ah, go on, go. An' Micky – don't – don't come back, ever. I swear no one will hear of – what happened – from me. Not ever. Think what you like of me, Micky, but I haven't told so far, so why the fuck would I now? Go on, go – *go* – I've got to let her in.'

I took a breath and went to the door, Micky behind me. I opened it and he shouldered past me, out into the lane, to his car. For a second, I watched him, he was haloed by the late sun, a golden drift of dust-motes dancing round him.

Then he was gone.

'...So sorry, am I interrupting anything? You must be Mrs Morgan, I'm Sophie, from the *Clarion*? You said I might have a few words?'

I pulled myself together. The young woman stood looking at me questioningly. I managed a smile. I don't know what I'd been expecting, a hatchet-faced London It Girl, I suppose, but Sophie was a tiny, thin young woman in her middle twenties. She was pale, her high-bridged nose pink with sunburn, dressed in a crumpled cream sleeveless blouse and cropped grey linen trousers. A little cotton cardigan was tied round her waist, her fine mousy-brown hair pulled into a short ponytail, a strand hooked behind one ear. Brown-tinted shades were pushed back on her head. Little oval silver ear studs set with blue topaz, I noted automatically. A matching delicate pendant. Not cheap, not flashy. No wedding or engagement rings, just a plain fine silver band on one finger. An enormous bulging canvas briefcase was slung over one frail shoulder. She looked worn out.

'I'm sorry, yes – an annoying neighbour, he can be a bit of a pain, you know how it is. Not exactly a neighbour from hell, but...You know. Don't mind him. Come in – and please, call me Billie. Look, would you like to sit in the garden? It's nice out there – I could get you some tea – juice? Cranberry? Sure, just go through, I'll be right out.'

As I fetched glasses, ice cubes, juice, I watched her perch on the bench and turn her face to the sun, eyes shut, while she eased one foot out of her brown leather flattie sandals and rubbed her heel. She looked like she never ate enough, or saw daylight; what must it be like to live in London, I thought, if it made you look so knackered at her age, poor thing. The curious, cool detachment I'd felt earlier still lingered; nothing seemed to touch me, not even this.

'Here you go – you must be exhausted.' I smiled and sat next to her. I found it amazingly easy to be still, and fold my cold hands in my lap as she took a sip of the juice.

'Hmm, yes – well, a bit. You know – this heat. Thank you, delicious. What a nice little garden – and are those your cats? I love cats – and dogs too. All animals really, I suppose.' She smiled too, as Cairo twisted round her bird-bone ankles.

'Have you got any pets, then?' I could talk about nothing too.

'Oh – no, sadly. London life, you know. I live in a tiny little flat – it wouldn't be fair. Um, do you mind if I record our talk? I'll take notes too, but it does help...'

She took out a recording Walkman and set it down between us, pressing record before I answered, then sat, notebook unfolded, pen poised. I wanted to laugh: she wouldn't look so unruffled if I told her the truth, would she? Sitting next to a real murderer, in a cottage garden, sipping that blood-red juice. I took a deep breath, and grabbed the thought, stuffing it down inside myself hard.

'The thing is, Mrs – *Billie*...Mrs Skinner seemed quite set on the thought that Terry's – well, his involvement with the Hells Angels...'

'Devil's Own. The club was called The Devil's Own. Still is. Not Hells Angels, that's a whole different thing, different club, everything.'

She scribbled something. 'Oh, OK, I see – well, the gang, you know – that you both belonged to...'

'Look, I'm sorry, I don't know what Mrs Skinner told you but Terry was never in the club – the gang, you'd call it. He hung around, but he was never a member – he – well, he wasn't suitable. And I wasn't, women can't be members, it's not possible. It was my – my ex-husband who was a club member.'

'Oh. Right. Uhh, OK – Mrs Skinner seems to think that Terry, well, he wouldn't have gone off without contacting her unless something suspicious had happened, she says they were very close. Frankly, she suspects – well, foul play. The gang, perhaps drugs, she's not clear but these things do...'

'No. It was nothing like that – I mean, I'm sure it wasn't. I'd have heard something. A rumour, whatever. No, he just fuc – went off. He did it all the time, off for weeks sometimes, without a word, then he'd appear again. Look, I'll be straight with you, Pauline Skinner is full of, well, she's got her own ideas, about Terry, Natty, Jas – me. She's that sort. Likes to stir stuff up, likes excitement. I wouldn't put too much store by what she says, really.'

Sophie sighed, and laid the notebook on her knee. 'Well – yes. She was rather – challenging. Not really the angle I was trying to get. I mean, it's devastating, when someone goes missing, really devastating. The more people I've spoken to, the more awful it becomes. Fathers, wives, sons, daughters – pouf! Gone, vanished and not a word, ever. Awful. I tried to speak to Mrs Savage, but she was so stressed, and honestly, as you know, not terribly *well*...'

I nodded. Gnats flitted in the soft golden light, the sound of a soap opera theme tune drifted from next door. *Not terribly well*. Yeah, right. 'Was she stoned?'

'I – er – well, yes. I felt so sorry for her, she seems so fragile, you know? And she must have been quite amazingly beautiful before – I mean, when she was – the photographer took loads of pics of her, said she was a fabulous subject.' She reddened slightly and fiddled with her pencil.

'Have you done much stuff like this, love? I don't mean to be awkward, but...'

'No, that's OK. I have done features, obviously, lots – but this one – it just seems to be getting to me rather. My uncle – well, he went to France, for a holiday, walking, when I was a child, and never came back. The family were devastated. It's why I wanted this job, I thought, I don't know...'

'You thought it might help you make sense of stuff.'

'Yes – yes, I think I did. But it's just so mystifying. How can anyone – just *go*. Terry, my uncle – Mrs Savage said your husband went, too – she said it made you sisters. Is that why you look after her, and – Nathan?'

Her voice changed when she said Natty's name. You didn't like my Natty, did you, Missie, I thought. Well, well. 'My husband and I split up, you know. We got divorced – it wasn't the same as Jas and Terry, I mean. But Jas – well. I try, you know. You're right. Jas is fragile and yes, she was a looker alright. Very lovely, Jas was, like a flower, but aye – not now. Not anymore. I do my best with her. What about Natty? Did you talk to him?'

She bridled slightly, her body language mirroring an uncomfortable memory.

'Er, yes – he certainly had a lot to say about his father. His – you know, his ideas about Terry and where he might be. What would happen if Terry came home, that sort of thing. His friend – the disabled chap…'

'Lee?'

'Lee? No, they called him Monkey, I don't know what…'

'Lee. His real name's Lee. What about him?'

'Well, he – took – stole – Pete's, the photographer's, camera bag. It was – odd, I mean, so obvious, he hid it in the bathroom. There was a bit of a row, Nathan was very upset with him, and Monk – Lee – it was very unfortunate. Mrs Savage got very upset too, and Mrs Skinner…'

'I can imagine. Lee doesn't mean any harm, stealing's a sort of reflex with him; he would've given the stuff back, probably. I should've been there, I meant to get over, but work…'

'Oh yes, Mrs Savage said you run a card shop, in the town centre. She says you're very generous to her, financially; isn't that something of a burden?'

'Not really. I do what I can, you know, I mean…'

'Of course – but, well, she – I don't want to be rude, but doesn't she spend what you give her on drugs – and if she does, how do you feel about that?'

How did I feel? To gain a moment's respite I took a sip of juice and looked at the girl, sitting bunched up next to me, her face intent, her pen hovering, the red light on her Walkman steady as a devil's eye. How did I feel? Tired, mostly. Of everything, of this conversation, of explaining things. An overwhelming feeling of being very, very tired of being polite to straight people whose experiences and blinkered canter through life left them unable to begin to comprehend how I felt or how I'd lived. It occurred to me I'd be better off telling this to a copper than Little Miss Sophie. A copper would understand, they'd have seen it all a thousand times; fished nodders out of public bogs all over town, seen what smackheads would do for a fiver, know what lengths those of us not blessed with the protection of the straight world did in order to survive. Yes, a copper would understand alright. The thought made me laugh, but I turned it quickly to a choking fit.

'Are you OK?' She looked concerned.

I coughed theatrically and mumbled something about my drink going down the wrong way. Then I told her how it was: if I didn't give Jas money, she did what she could to get it and that was worse. I told her how it was on the estates. I told her at least Natty loved and cared for Jas, and for that matter, so did poor Lee, who knew no other family. I said we all might have problems, but we had something most of the others in those places didn't – we loved each other. I tried to explain the honour codes of the outlaw gangs and why I'd stuck to them as best I could. I attempted to make her understand that we did our best in circumstances that were unlikely to ever change, or improve, even if Terry did come home, unless of course he came back a millionaire. Even then, really.

There was a short silence. I don't mind silences, myself; I think of them as a rest from talking so you can think about what's been said – but I know others find them difficult. Sophie did. Her face was like a screen on which I watched her emotions – distaste, disbelief, pity, revulsion and finally, a kind of inward shutting off – chase each other in an impressionistic blur. She was so easy to read in that way, I wondered how she'd fare on the streets, with everything on her pale little mug for any predator to see. But she was the product of her upbringing and soon had herself in hand; her expression settled back to one of polite enquiry.

'I see, yes. You've all been through so much, I mean, that's what we want to convey, really. The suffering – the damage done by the event of someone disappearing, you know.'

The event of someone disappearing. Did people really talk like that? Obviously, some did. 'Would you like some tea? We could go in…'

She nodded, and put her things into the enormous bag. As she manfully struggled to shoulder it and follow me, I thought how weak, how fragile she looked. No muscle tone – her arms looked like white marshmallow with sticks in it. I doubted if she could walk two miles or lift even a small set of weights. How could I have been afraid of anything so soft-looking? Poor little thing, she looked done in.

I made tea in the good pot while she sat on the sofa and played with the cats. Well, Cairo, anyway; Ghengis as usual did his Satan-in-a-catskin routine and regarded her with his sulphurous glare from the windowsill.

We drank the tea and chatted inconsequentially about Bradford – much nicer than she'd imagined, and a Starbucks! – cats, art and what the best route out of the city was by car. She wasn't staying, she had to get the 'piece' in straight away, so it would be out in the forthcoming Sunday supplement. I got the impression of terrifying editors breathing down her fragile neck making impossible demands that only by intense efforts of will-power she managed – against all the odds – to deliver.

As I waved goodbye, I felt quite grateful for her visit. It hadn't been that bad and at least it had the effect of distracting me from the awfulness of Micky for a while. But I couldn't think about that now. I had to put him out of my mind until this whole thing was over and – buried. I realised, with a little shock, that's how I felt; as if I'd found out he'd died. In a way, he had. Whatever it was that walked about in his body had completely replaced the lad I'd known. He was dead to me now, the boy I'd loved all these years was dead. It made me feel both terribly sad and yet, in a strange way, free. Who was it said all change is good? Maybe out of this mess *would* come Leckie's favourite closure and my freedom, at last.

I slept soundly that night, and dreamt of a garden full of plumy grey-green trees, great masses of brilliantly coloured flowers like hibiscus and bougainvillaea and huge old terracotta urns filled with masses of lavender and geranium; there were butterflies dancing in patinated flashes just outside my vision and a heavy scent of lilies. I walked and walked, almost floating, through an unending series of gentle, curving paths as the silvery sound of a fountain playing into a tiled basin seemed to create spangles of light in the blue shadows. It was warm, and the air was soft, hazed in gold-dust. I knew, somehow, that this was the garden of my house, and that the sea was close by and any time I liked I could walk down to it and bathe in water that shaded from cerulean to turquoise over white coral sands. It was perfect and I knew, in the way you do in dreams, that I was finally happy and I cried, but it didn't matter because everything was alright.

Best of all, nothing happened. I just walked in the garden. It was so beautiful, so ideal, I've never, ever forgotten it.

Chapter Twenty-three

FIVE DAYS. Hardly a lifetime, you'd think. Anyone could stick anything for five days, surely. Yeah, right. But then, not everyone had Jas, Mrs Skinner and Natty ringing on the hour, every hour – well, to be fair, La Skinner didn't ring but she was virtually a permanent fixture at Jas's – '*in case our lad comes 'ome*' – and this even before the article came out. How I didn't smash my mobile into tiny pieces, go mad and run screaming into the street I'll never know. I turned it off on Friday night, call me heartless, but I was exhausted. I couldn't bear to hear Jas crying, pleading, having the shakes, throwing up, getting smashed, vowing in that skaghead mumbly slur to be '*a good girl*' in future and repeating endlessly her undying love for '*her little boy*', '*her sweetheart*', her '*baby*', like a warped record wobbling round and round a ruined turntable, anymore. And that was just the phone – you should have been at the *flat*.

That sounds like I'm taking the piss. I don't mean to, but God's honest truth, if you can't find humour – albeit coal black humour – in shit like that, you're doomed. I turned the phone off partly because on Thursday night, driving back after a marathon row and weeping session, I found myself laughing uncontrollably at the memory of Jas, poor little bitch, her face literally smeared with a ton of old make-up – '*I'm jus', jus' tryin' ter to look nice*' – cack-handedly trying to bake a cake for Terry's imminent return. There she stood, the sorry scrap of fucked-up humanity, shaking in every limb, panda-eyed, sobbing, and covered in flour along with the entire kitchen, while Natty raged around the living room smashing things and Lee hid behind the sofa whimpering. Frankly, I wanted to join him.

It took me three solid hours, with the unwanted intervention of the neighbours on both sides hanging out of their front doors screaming 'Shut up, shut up, you fuckin' junkie cunt' and other helpful remarks, to get them calm – and that only after Natty flung himself out of the flat and into the roaring car of a blood he'd called up to come get him.

I put Jas to bed, and sat with Lee as he lay curled up, shivering and crying on the sofa wrapped in an old blanket. Anything like that – shouting, rows – brought on what I can only assume was some kind of post-traumatic shock syndrome attack. I never have found out the half of what had happened to Monkey in his childhood, and if I'm dead honest – I don't want to. Oh, if he ever wants to tell me, I'll listen, you'd have to be a heartless bastard not to, but it won't be a confession I'd want to receive and that's no joke. But whatever – arguments, his god deserting him – Lee can't take it. I've seen sick dogs look better than him that night.

But when he finally slept, thumb in mouth, twitching, I left and halfway home, pulled over to try and stop the convulsions of inappropriate giggles that spewed out of me against my will. I suppose it was like the reaction some folk have at funerals; there goes your beloved family member into the grave, or more likely these days, behind the dreadful blue velvet curtain to the oven, and out it all comes in an hysterical gale of helpless laughter. I sat there, my head resting on the steering wheel and let it go until shaking like a malaria victim, I stopped. Just stopped dead.

I was so cold again. I stared out of the windscreen like a zombie, random shivering twitching through me. It was as if I was staring at a surrealist landscape, some Dali-esque horror, not Bradford. I couldn't seem to recognise anything, to connect with it. Even the car seemed weirdly unfamiliar and for a strange, brief moment, I wondered if I was dead and this was Hell, like in those old films where someone's died but they don't know it and wander around until some angel comes to fetch them.

I was on the verge of getting ill; even in my deranged state I could sense that. The cold I felt was unnatural on such a muggy night and it seemed to pierce my bones to the marrow. Still shaking, I turned the key and drove home very slowly and carefully; if any copper had seen me he or she would have got out the breathalyser pronto. Only drunks faking sobriety drive like I drove that night.

So after I was woken from a stuporous sleep on Friday morning at 6.00 am by Natty, still high as a kite, jabbering and begging to be allowed to come over and well, hide, and then the following calls to say no, he was OK, 'some chick' had taken him in (*quelle surprise*) and he was in Leeds somewhere, then Jas ringing, mumbling something and putting the phone down mid-conversation, then doing it three more times – you get the picture: mobile off.

Thank Christ for Leckie, is all I'll say. If it hadn't been for her I'd have had to shut the shop because I could barely function. I knew she was bursting with questions but she didn't let on. For all her gossip-hound chattering when stuff gets leary, she knows how to behave. All that you-go-girl ditzy Miss Pink malarkey is only skin deep with her, an amusement. She's a real warrior at heart, you'd definitely want her at your back in a crisis.

So yeah, I turned the bloody phone off. I watched crap TV, I ate chocolate, I played hunt-the-screwed-up-tissue with the cats. I rang Johnjo on the land line – and talked about nothing, and after a brief question about the interview, he let me ramble on; but it was weird – I got the feeling, one of those phone feelings you can't explain – that he wasn't listening. I tried that thing where you stop suddenly and go '*Are you there?*' and it took a spilt second too long for his husky '*yeah, yeah, course I am, love*' to come back. I didn't need to ask him if he was mad at me about stuff, I knew he was. He wasn't the shouty type, far from it, he's positively zen, but that's worse as any woman knows. That sort just *go* – they fade out of your life like the sun burning off morning mist when they think it's all too complicated for them. Not for the first time I meditated on our so-called relationship. Perhaps it would have been better if we'd stayed pals and not become lovers, perhaps it had run its course and had become a habit like Lecks always said. But how could you end a relationship like that when there was no passion, no fire? It was easier to drift. Go with the flow and see what happened. I genuinely didn't want to lose Johnjo's friendship – or his respect: I didn't want to be a weepy, clingy tedious saddo. But I could feel the past stretching away from me, the fibrous bonds tearing loose, the great mass of it dragging behind me as I struggled onwards. Was Johnjo part of that past, a sweet relic, and if I were honest, nothing more?

Trying to organise my thoughts about it all, I got my photo-box out. Nothing so organised or grand as albums, just a black cardboard storage box full of snaps. I sifted through the layered past, looking at faces, places, parties and outings. Me, Jas and baby Natty at Whitby. Johnjo and Micky at some Easter run to Malham. Mum and Jen at Christmas, the scorched image of Liz looking like a sepia insert next to their twinkly party outfits. A picture of Dadda; dark, a lock of hair falling into those runaway's eyes. Me clowning it at a Devil's Own party, Micky caught by the camera looking at me, his homely face transfigured by love. The paper strata of my life, falling through my hands back into the box, back into the past.

But the past wouldn't stay where I wanted to put it and it rose up through me like a mist, smelling of musty jasmine perfume, tasting of cheap speed and midnight curries. I remembered – I remembered – no; nothing. Nothing. I shut the box and tied the old bootlace round it tight. The past was dead, over. I had to think of what was to come and deal with it. I felt stronger now I'd rested and it would be OK.

Chapter Twenty-four

THE PICTURE WAS fabulous; if the photographer didn't win some prize for it, there was no justice. Even now, I think that. Despite everything, there was that picture, that morsel of beauty, like a diamond dropped in a cesspit, glittering in the shit and horror.

They'd given the whole of the front page of the colour supplement over to it. The C2 logo had been reduced to a small insert on the top left. Jas's face, an exquisite ruin, gazed out with those enormous, liquid green eyes, pinned pupils fixed directly on you – it reminded me of that famous picture of the Afghani refugee girl in that it had the same instant, connecting human power. Jas's ragged afro of grey-shot curls was fringed with golden light from the sun filtering through the tatty yellow curtains of the kitchen as if she were about to ascend to heaven. The same light gilded the glorious archaeology of her cheekbones and the puckered curve of her full lips, parted slightly, the glint of her gold-capped incisor faintly visible, adding to the rich, jewelled, renaissance look of the photograph. It was a masterpiece of a portrait; she looked like an icon, a despoiled Madonna, the mask of a primitive saint cased in a twenty-two carat reliquary.

Across the bottom of the cover ran the tag-line: *This woman is a junkie. Her son is a gangster. Her husband is one of the Disappeared. What went wrong?*

It didn't sink in at first, I was too caught up in the photo. It was the silence that brought it home to me. My phone was on, it was past ten o'clock and no one was ringing me. With a sense of foreboding amounting to barely controlled panic I turned, fumbling, to the article.

It was monstrous. Not in an abusive or malicious way, there were no actual insults but the whole piece was soaked in a thick brew of arrogance, patronage, lazy preconceptions, wilful ignorance and spin. It recounted what Sophie had seen, filtered through her own tight vision of our life, though not what she'd been told, and it was designed entirely to put the *Clarion* in a good light as the defenders of the hopeless, feckless, useless underclass. Us, in fact. There was a certain feeling of distant, cool sympathy for Jas; more, I felt, for the loss of her youthful beauty than for her personally, but that might just be my interpretation.

Sophie detailed Jas's fall from grace in a way that implied she had been unwillingly dragged into her present deplorable condition by the crushing brutality of the – yes – Neanderthalic, degenerate, knuckle-dragging Hells Angels gang her adored and adoring 'husband' had been a member of, despite his 'well-known' intelligence and self-education. He had, as it were, foolishly fallen in with a bad crowd and the results were devastating. Drugs. Orgies. Violence. Finally, his mysterious disappearance. There were questions – questions that demanded answers. The authorities should act, discover the truth and remove these gangs from the streets of Britain once and for all, whatever it took. They seemed to think outlaw biker gangs were as powerful and out there as they were in the Seventies – it was weird, as if the *Clarion* was in a time-warp, still blathering on about Altamont and unaware that gang-life had moved on like everything else and new warlords ruled where the Devil's Own once rode unchecked. Anyway, the article continued with a diatribe about the authorities obviously not giving a toss about the powerless and vulnerable, and how it was left to the *Clarion* to be the champion of justice Britain so badly needed in these dark times.

Plug for the *Clarrie* over, the story ground on, now focussing on Jas. Distraught and pushed to her limit by the cruel fate that befell her, she'd turned to drugs not because she enjoyed them, but as a way out. Now she was yet another helpless pawn in the hands of the drug-barons; devastated, her only dream was to see Terry again before she died and make amends, to beg him to forgive her weakness, which she knew in her heart he would because of his sensitive and loving nature. The sub-text screamed homicide and Jas's tragic chemically-enhanced delusions of a dead man's return. It continued with the now *Clarion*ised Jas; fragile, dependent and terrified, she had been unable – a woman alone – to control her brutish wayward son, who contributed to her decline by breaking her heart over and over as he grew up to become a callous, hardened street gangster. Natty was portrayed without mercy as a drug dealer and a crack-coke-speed-freak abuser of under-age girls (Venus, I imagine) who kept a deformed, mentally disabled boy as a virtual slave and who probably supplied his own mother with heroin. His dreams of Terry were re-interpreted as a drug-fuelled, bling-bling, playa's fantasy world and he himself as a predator and a vicious, stupid, ignorant bully.

Sophie dwelt long and hard on Natty. She really didn't like him one bit. She had nothing good to say about him. Even Mrs Skinner came out better, re-fashioned into the *Clarion*'s favourite stereotype: the decent, working-class grieving mother – in this case, struggling to keep her hopeless daughter-in-law Jas on the straight and narrow, despairing of her monstrous grandson.

All that was bad enough. But then I came to my bit; OK, selfish, I suppose but there you are. Seeing yourself in print for the first time, it's weird, to say the least.

With oddly old-fashioned courtesy, Billie, as she anxiously begged me to call her, ushered me into the ragged wilderness of her tiny garden. With her stocky, bruiser's build, ex-gang moll past and all-black attire, she should have been a frightening prospect, but the pathos of her life – the tumbledown cottage she shares with her many cats, the feuds with neighbours, her obvious unhappiness – soon creates a sense of sympathy and indeed pity. It's no wonder she tries so hard to be a part of Jasmine Savage's family. As Jasmine herself says, she and Billie are sisters under the skin. Both have had their lives destroyed by the cruel phenomenon of the Disappeared…

Etc., etc. There wasn't much. Some stuff about me pathetically sticking up for 'the Hells Angels' with the implication that I did so because I was sadly deluded and morally bereft and how I bought my way into Jas's affections by giving her drug money on demand. I was used as a kind of wailing, hand-wringing Greek chorus to add to the impression of how devastated people are when their loved ones sod off. Sophie neglected to mention the fact I was divorced, like millions of other people, and had not been, as such, deserted. That would have spoilt the effect. So I came out of the article as a little higher up the chain than pond scum. A crawling, pitiful creature, witchy and isolated in my cat-stinky hovel.

There were some more pictures – good, but nothing to match the cover photograph. There was one of Jas with Natty, whose nervousness gave his expression a sullen, brooding cast and one of Pauline Skinner taken so you couldn't see her plunging, jacked-up décolleté and spike-heeled leopardette ankle boots. She looked old and saggy; God, she'd be livid. There were a few mock-ups of Missing Persons posters featuring various of the Disappeared as well, by way of illustrations – there was one of Terry using Mrs Skinner's favourite photo of him. It looked suspiciously retouched to smooth out the ill-tempered sneer, unshaven grubbiness and narrowed, mocking eyes. The article finished sketchily with a trumpet call to end the scandal of the Disappeared and save lives ruined by the disinterest and general corruption of the authorities – all of them, whoever they are, the *Clarion* wasn't specific on that – some contact information for suitable helplines and organisations ('*If you have been affected by any of the issues raised in this article*') and another, final big pat on the back for the good old crusading *Clarrie*.

I put the magazine down carefully, and looked again at that magnificent photograph. Then I got up in the deadly silence and looked at myself in the kitchen mirror. I knew it shouldn't matter, I shouldn't care – but was that how people saw me? A lumpy, eccentric old bitch in bloke's black clothes living a lonely, barren spinster's life? And my nice house – was I deluded and simply couldn't see how crap it was? I couldn't believe how much it hurt and cursing that silly little cow of a reporter in my head didn't help.

As the silence continued, stretching out like worn elastic waiting to snap, I began to realise the terrible destruction Sophie and her bosses had unthinkingly wrought on us all. What in God's name had I been thinking of to allow this? I must have been mad. I should have put my foot down, stopped it as soon as I got wind of it. But oh no – I thought I could control this just like I controlled everything. What a fool I'd been, what a stupid, egoistic, bloody *fool*. I was hurt, in that my feelings and my pride were bruised, but Jas – and my God, Natty – Natty would be

– it didn't bear thinking about. The enormity of what would result from this trash appearing in a national newspaper was horrifying and it got bigger and more overwhelming by the second.

Jas would be notorious, a kind of negative celebrity; famous for fifteen hellish minutes while the whole estate – the whole of fucking Bradford because it was bound to be covered in the local paper too – jeered and hooted at her exposure, cruel as only a mob could be when targeting a weak and helpless victim. She might need to move, she might need to go into rehab double-quick; I thought furiously, trying to sort things, trying to anticipate what could happen so I could deal with it pronto and not be taken by surprise. Would the council re-home her? Could I bear to have her here until things died down? Would the police big-wigs decide to make an example of her in view of the publicity? I knew the street coppers couldn't care less about small fry like Jas but their bosses, always under orders to clean up the streets from dickhead MPs with an eye to the media – they might seize on something like this and…Jesus, it was like trying to get toothpaste back in the tube; the more I thought about it the more it escaped and expanded and swallowed up the light.

Through the din in my mind I could hear the old dark chant beating time with the rhythm of my blood, the cruel song that chained me to the Black Dog forever: stupid, stupid, you *stupid* girl – if people can go off you when you just do something little like break an ornament, what will they do when you do something this destructive? *Worthless, that's what you are, selfish and worthless just like your father…*Shakily, I sat at the table and buried my head in my hands. It was hopeless, I wanted to wind time back and make it not have happened, to stitch that foul old cow Pauline Skinner's mouth shut, anything, just so this had never existed.

Chapter Twenty-five

ACROSS THE FRONT of the flat, in wonky red spray paint, were the words 'junky horbag'. What a struggle it must have been for the illiterate perpetrators of this fascinating comment to have mumbled and picked their way laboriously through the article – but worth it to them if they could generate a bit of excitement on a hot, boring, overcast Sunday. A mess of eggs and dogshit was splattered over the fractured window and the door. The paint was still tacky when I touched it gingerly, and I could hear stifled sniggers from the clot of teen fuckwits who were congealing round a flat four doors down. They were drinking and I knew they'd try more fun and games later, as the stifling heat and the booze misfired whatever braincells they had left into action. I stared at them, and heard the usual riff of insults – *fat bitch, fuckin owd cunt, fuckin lezzer* – rise to the surface of their garbled yattering. We'd met before, sadly. I knew it was pointless to confront them because although I could hold them off for a few minutes by confusing them with proper sentences, eventually, they'd just clump together and stick me, or stomp me. Not for the first, or last time, I longed for the security of the Devil's Own. Or a gun. I toyed with the idea of ringing Johnjo and getting him to organise a crew, but in the end, I decided to save that for if it got worse.

Finding a reasonably non-dogshitty space, I knocked. There was no answer until I wrapped my fingers in a tissue and pushed the letter-box open to tell whoever was in it was me. Monkey opened the door.

'Hi, Lee. You alright, love?'

He nodded dumbly, bereft of speech, his ruined face stark white. He stood in the doorway, the hand not holding the door jerking and twisting, a tic he had when he was frightened.

'Can I come in, Lee, eh love?'

He stood back immediately, flinching. 'It's OK, Lee, it's OK, everything will be OK,' I said in what I hoped was a comforting voice. In my head, I wished savagely that the *Clarion* could see the great work they'd done with underprivileged, vulnerable, underclass Monkey. I walked past him as he pushed the filthy, stinking door shut and slid down the wall to huddle in a heap of coats and rock back and forth to some internal rhythm of his own.

The flat was silent, except for the sound of Jas's weak, thready sobbing coming from the front room, Monkey's adenoidal breathing and the inane buzzing of a fat bluebottle. The air was thick and hot, stinking of fear, booze, spoiled food and dirty bodies; a sickly twist of coarse Jasmine oil twined through it all from the open door of Jas's room where I could see a smashed up mess of clothes, bedlinen, bottles, talc, fragments of a broken mirror and ancient cosmetics, all her bits and pieces trashed and spilt on the carpet. Someone had gone through the place good style, alright.

It was the same in the kitchen where I went to put the kettle on: everything smashed to bits. Drifts of sugar and instant coffee, stalagmites of jam and Nutrament oozing off the work surface. The cooker was flooded with rancid black-specked cloudy grease from the overturned chip pan, the rusty fridge door was ajar with the shelves half wrenched off, the meagre contents either teetering on the brink or on the floor. Sighing, I found a couple of cheap enamel mugs and a plastic beaker still intact and fished out teabags from the back of the cupboard.

As I looked around at the mess, I felt exhausted. Automatically I started clearing up, knowing that if I didn't no one would – but then I stopped. I couldn't be bothered. How many times had I cleaned up only to find it as bad as before when I came back a few days later. It had become a habit, a reflex, like when you live with someone slovenly and you get in to silent wars about the waste bin in the bathroom or the washing up. You get sick of nagging them about their untidiness, so you think you'll leave it and leave it until they can't stick it anymore and they'll be forced to clean up for themselves. But you always lose, because they really don't care or even notice the overflowing bin or the greasy heap of plates. Truth be told, no one cared about the flat except me, they never had. It was me who'd decorated, who'd painted, who'd got a new shower curtain when the old one went mouldy, me who'd bought new kitchen curtains – the curtains that hung half-ripped from their wooden rings, the yellow gingham curtains that had lent the golden aura to the light that illuminated Jas's beautiful wreck of a face in that amazing photo.

I put the dustpan and brush down and did the tea. I didn't need to ask who'd created this chaos. I'd seen Natty's rage before. It was that uncontrollable, unthinking fury that boiled through him occasionally that made me worried stiff now, wondering where he was and what he could be doing.

I went through to Jas. 'Jas, Jas love, here, drink this tea, c'mon, sweetie…'

'Oh, Billie, Billie, Billie…' She broke off, coughing. She looked a hundred years old. Her skin was ashy, withered with dehydration and her hair was a dry, frizzled mass, the ends popped white, grey streaks crawling through ragged curls that were clumped and tangled. Her dirty brown hand, nails chewed to the quick, shook like a dead leaf in a breeze and her eyes – Jesus. There were no pupils, just a milky-hazed burning emerald iris that glowed like hellfire from the sunken, veined caverns of her sockets. I'd seen her bad, but never this rotten. She kept moaning my name, over and over.

'Come on, love, here, I'll help you, try to sit up a bit – Jas, you've got to drink something, I put lots of sugar in, please, love.'

I put the tea down and lifted her up against the sofa arm. She didn't weigh anything, no more than a bundle of sticks. There was no flesh on her and she'd never had a lot to lose anyway. A child would have weighed more.

I got her to sip at the tea, between coughing fits, while I held the cup. I could hardly bear to look at her; pity ran through me in a hot rush and I had to close my eyes against the prickle of tears.

I put the cup down. 'Jas, don't move, I'll be right back, I'm just going to take Monk– Lee some tea, OK? OK?'

When I got back, having failed to get Monkey to move from his hiding place, but at least having got some tea down him, I sat at the other end of the sofa. My foot slipped on something and glancing down, I saw the magazine – or the ripped bits of it.

'Jas – Jas love – where's Natty? Where's Natty, Jas? Jas, come on, come on, try, love, please, where is he?'

She moaned again, the yellowed whites of her rolled-back eyes showing in a fluttering slit. I thought about calling an ambulance, even though I knew it would get bricked and the crew pelted with rubbish or worse, if it came. Again, I decided to hold off in case things got worse. This wasn't a nice, smart neighbourhood, where you called for help and it came in moments, everything neat and tidy. This was the Wild West. We were on our own, to all intents and purposes. I got her to drink some more of the sugar-thick black tea.

Coughing, she tried to speak. 'Billie, Billie – he – he – he went mental when he saw that – that – the paper. He read it, but wouldn't read it me, like. He said they made us out ter be idiots, said it were – bad, really really bad. He just – he's broke everythin'…Then they come an' were outside – people – I don't know – chucking stuff an' shoutin' sayin' I wor – I wor…'

'Oh, Jas love, never mind that now, don't worry about that, we'll sort that – but Jas, where is he? Where's he gone?'

'Dunno, dunno – he just run out, went after them that had been shoutin' but they run off when they saw him, like…He dint come back. Mebbe he's gone ter Hudd– or Leeds, to a lass, I doant know. Billie, Billie – I seen the pictures – I look so old, so old – I don't feel old, tired mebbe, but in them pictures…What did they say, them reporters, what wor it – he wouldn't tell me proper an' I can't – me eyes is a bit funny, I can't…'

It wasn't her eyes, Jas couldn't read. She never learnt – past recognising her own name and stumbling painfully through simple sentences like a six-year-old – and try as I might over the years I couldn't get her interested in the idea. I thought when I'd tried to teach Monkey the rudiments she might learn with him but though she encouraged him, she wouldn't have a go herself. At the time I'd wondered irritably if it was another of her 'poor helpless Jas' control devices. Now I thought it was a blessing in disguise. She lay back on her beloved purple furry cushion, the one Natty had given her last Christmas, a happy day that seemed an incredibly long time ago now.

I couldn't tell her. Call me a coward if you like, but I couldn't tell her a national newspaper had printed a story telling the world in no uncertain terms she was a worn-out junkie prostitute and the son she adored was an evil thug. Whoever's reading this – are you, Leckie? – ask yourself what you'd have done? Yeah, I thought so. Jesus, we're all liars sometimes, we're all fucking *human*. Someone once said '*evil is the absence of empathy*'. Well in that case, only an evil bastard would have read that article out word for word to the pitiful, wasted creature lying in front of me.

'Well, love, see – the paper, they were really – really snobby; yeah, you know, that lass you talked to? She was a bit posh, wasn't she? So you see, um, she wrote stuff about – oh, er, us not having much money, or living in smart houses, stuff like that, you know? She kind of looked down on us for not being – well – not being posh types like her. Not having a proper education, going to university and things like her and her lot. And see, Jas, she didn't understand about how we live, or you having to have your – your medicine, and stuff – you know what them type of people are like, they live in their own little world and they don't understand how the rest of us – what we've got to do to survive. D'you understand, Jas?'

She was silent for such a long time I thought she'd fallen asleep. I was about to say something else when she coughed and spoke so quietly I could barely hear her husky whisper. It was as if she were talking to herself as much as me. 'It int right, her being that way about us. Writing stuff like that. It int my fault I can't – I dint get no schooling. My mam were on her own, Billie, like me, she wor – there weren't no one ter help her an' she were – Billie, she were a prossie, straight out, on t'Lane like. But what else could she do? There were four of us, me an' our Stevie an' Rick an' Tony. We never had no dads, not that I knew of. Just Mam an' us. Stevie an' Rick's dead now – did yer know? Both gone, aye. I int heard owt of Tony fer years. Billie, I dint want ter be like this, I dint – y'know, when I were a lass, I wanted ter be a singer, like Diana Ross, I could sing lovely I could, an' do all the dances…I use ter practise an' then sing ter Mam and the lads – 'Baby Love', 'You Can't Hurry Love' – all them hits…We used ter turn the lights off int room an' Tony'd shine a torch an we'd give out it were a spotlight an' – oh, we had a right laugh, honest…'

She smiled, her hands moving slowly to a song she could hear in her mind. Then she sighed and a tear trickled slowly down from the outside corner of her eye into her matted hair.

'I loved Terry, Billie, I dint want him ter go off, like. I'd 'ave done owt for him to have stayed, owt, honest – but mebbe he dint love me like I loved him. I'm not daft, I know how that goes sometimes, I just wish…I'm not much of a catch, I s'pose…I dunno. But Natty, oh, oh Billie – I love him ter bits, you know that, he's my sweetheart, my angel, he's bin everythin' ter me, everythin'…Do them newspaper people think I don't love him? That I dint want him ter go ter school proper an get a proper job? I did, I did…'

She coughed hard – a strange, harsh cough – and the tremor ran through her, shaking her convulsively. I laid my hand on her forehead; she was very feverish. Two rounds of hectic red bloomed on her cheekbones. I made a mental note to get her to the doctor's as soon as I could. And Monkey, come to that; he could do with a check-up. Natty, as well. Bloody hell, all of us – maybe I should just hire a sodding mini-bus.

'Shh, shh, Jas, course you love him, course you do. We all know you did your best, it int your fault, don't cry, love, don't…'

'I'm poorly sick, I am, I'm so tired, so…Billie, Billie…' She suddenly clutched my hand, with a wiry strength surprising for someone who seemed so frail. Her hand was burning hot and dust-dry.

'What, love? What? I'm here, don't worry.'

'Billie, look after Natty, look after my boy – you promised, you – you're his fairy godmother, remember? When he were little? Remember? You promised, Billie – Natty…'

'Shh, there there, love, don't fret, I'll look after him, you know I will, haven't I always? Hmmm? Shh now, love, try to get a bit of sleep, eh?'

Her great eyes were already closed and her mouth relaxed. If you looked closely, in the wreck of her, you could see the giggling twelve-year-old singing Motown chart-toppers to her mother while her brothers tumbled around the damp little room, Tony shining his spotlight torch as Jasmine Pearl sang and sang.

I cleaned the flat – yeah, well, it had to be done – while she and
Monkey slept, each in the only place they had where no one could touch
them. I threw the thin, lumpy duvet from her bed over Jas as she slept
and some more coats over Monkey and left a big plastic jug of water
and some tins of Nutrament next to the couch. There was no sign of the
balcony gang and their dogshit-and-spraycan activities but I stayed on
anyway and watched TV mindlessly with the sound down low in Natty's
room. I stretched out on the narrow bed that smelt of him, his sweet
male body smell, and his latest aftershave, something by Calvin Klein
that smelt of chemical lemons. The modern, jaunty odour, designed for
funky, carefree young people who live funky, carefree lives, seemed like
a joke, an aromatic irony.

I repeatedly re-dialled Natty and left six or seven messages on his
mobile. I texted him two or three times as well: *Nat cm hme NOW or
fone me URGENT!!! BM*. I waited for his call – for anyone's call, to be
honest, but none came.

In my head, the Black Dog howled, the sound ringing like an iron
bell in the hollow tunnels of a deserted barrow: the burial mounds of
Celtic kings, my dark inheritance. The noise had a savage, brute finality
– I could hear the ghost of Jas's words thread through the clangour: *'You
promised, you promised ter look after my boy...'*

I put my hands over my ears and bit the inside of my lip until I could
taste blood: but that deadly resonance echoed and re-echoed round my
skull. A life sentence.

A life sentence.

Chapter Twenty-six

I MUST HAVE DOZED OFF, because I woke with a start as someone banged loudly on the front door with what sounded like half a brick. I jumped up groggily and catching my foot in the loose quilt cover, twisted and fell onto the floor, banging my hip painfully. Swearing under my breath and rubbing the place where I knew a huge black bruise would appear, I staggered up and listened – but the jeering voices receded so I sat back down, shaking my head and stretching my jaw. The telly was subsonically burbling – a programme about antiques. Someone with a truly hideous vase I wouldn't have given house room to looked delighted when a bloke told her it was worth ten grand. Ten bloody grand for a twisted mess of finger-painted clay; I thought about what good could be done with the money folk paid for antiques – kidney machines, toys for the kids' home, giving some poor terrified bastard of a refugee a decent place to live. Naive, idealistic, old-fashioned stuff like that. Jesus. What a fucked up world we lived in. I turned it off. My ear was numb where I'd slept on it and I rubbed it to try and get the feeling – however painful – back into it.

Yawning uncontrollably, I staggered into the hall and burrowed into the hot, smelly felted layers of coats hiding Monkey – he was sound asleep, snot crusting his nose and upper lip, tear tracks the only clean bits on his face. He smelt like a cage full of hamsters. The fabric packing him into his nest was excellent soundproofing, as he intended, so I covered him back up and went to check on Jas.

She was still boiling with fever. I half woke her and made her drink some water, most of it drooling from her slack mouth as she coughed reflexively. I soaked a clean tea towel in cold water and bathed her face and hands, debating with myself whether to move her to her bed or not. She was so tiny, the sofa was plenty big enough so I decided to leave her there for the time being. I didn't want to think about how she'd be when she woke up wanting her 'medicine' and there was none to be had.

I went back to Natty's room and tried him on the phone. 'Welcome to Orange Answerphone...' I left a message telling him to get in touch urgently which I had no particular hope he'd reply to.

I phoned Leckie and told her how it was at the flat; I can't say she was impressed. You weren't, were you, Lecks? What I couldn't tell you was how much I wanted to run away from the mess of it all and hang out with you – like a normal person. I did, I really did – I suppose I wanted to say I loved you, I do love you and what a good friend you are because even though you were narky, there was none of that *you can go off people* shit in your voice. I can't say how much that means to me.

But thinking about that phrase made me realise there was someone I had to phone, however much I might not want to. I'd spoken to Mum last week – or was it the week before? It had been the usual, perfunctory conversation in which she recounted at length – having just got the photos – and in detail Jen's wedding anniversary party which had been a catered affair with a band and a special cake – 'a designer cake' apparently, featuring a sugar sculpture of twin hearts being garlanded with roses by the bluebirds of happiness. Jen wore a pastel peach chiffon layer dress and matching beaded wrap. Big surprise; if she'd worn ruby red I'd have fainted. The Girls were in matching pastel ensembles and Eric – dear God – wore a powder-blue tuxedo. I didn't need to see the pics to imagine what they looked like.

The sound of Mum's voice, an uneasy mixture of pride, boasting and judgment of my failings echoed in my head as I dialled her number. I tried breathing slowly and deeply as Leckie recommended I did when I had to do a stressful phone call: that was fine for annoying wholesalers but it didn't touch the gigantic screw turning in my belly at the thought of what Mum would say about the article.

I wasn't disappointed – no, that's not true. I was disappointed like I always was, always had been, that she wasn't on my side. In fact as the conversation ground on, it became obvious, to her at any rate, that I had done the interview solely to upset her and probably to get back at her for some past imagined slight. I was always giving out she had been a bad mother and making mountains out of molehills, a trait I inherited from my father's side of the family; always exaggerating, always so dramatic.

'But I don't expect anything else, Billie, I really don't. I just hope you're satisfied now, my lady, now you've made a guy out of me, shown us up to everyone – Mrs Atkinson showed me the newspaper, her son gets it and you should have seen the smirk on her face, the old cat. Oh yes, thank you *very* much for that, putting me on the spot with the likes of the Atkinsons. No, I did *not* read it, I don't read rubbish like that – I skimmed it, thank you, and I saw more than enough to show me the way you've lived your life – drugs, carrying-on, the lot. Well, don't expect me to come weeping and wailing after you anymore, I've washed my hands of you and I told Mrs Atkinson that. Thank you, Joyce, I said, but no thanks. She's not my daughter, not any more. It's the final straw, it really is. Oh, when I think how I've struggled with you, I could – but not anymore. I'm off.'

'Mum, I didn't – it's not…Mum, please…'

'Oh it's "Mum please" now, is it? You can stay and ruin yourself with your drug addict friends to your heart's content now, Billie, I'm going to stay with Jen and the Girls, yes, you heard me – Eric's done up the extension as a flat for me and I'm going for six months to see if I like it, then if I do, I'll stop. I'm renting the house – a nice professional couple – there's an agency deals with all that. I admit, I did have misgivings at first – Jen love, I said, what about your sister? But she said I had myself to think of, my health – my nerves – and after this! You've never been anything other than a burden and a disgrace, my girl; you drove your father away and then your sister and now I'm off too. Well, it serves you right, you're selfish, selfish, selfish and always have been.'

'Mum, please – stop crying, Mum, I didn't mean to hurt…'

'Oh, you didn't mean to hurt my feelings? But you never did, did you? Well, don't come whining to me, you've made your bed, now you can lie on it for all I care. I've boxed your things up, such as they are. I'll thank you to fetch them before the end of the week and if you don't, they'll be in the bin with the other rubbish. And I'd rather you came in the afternoon, after three and before six because I'm saying my goodbyes all week at that time to folk, *nice* folk, not that you'd understand *that*. You've got your key.'

'Jesus, Mum, how long have you been thinking…'

'Of going? Not that it's your business, but I've *thought* about it for years. Then Jen said last Christmas come to us for Christmas this year, don't spend another dreadful, lonely Christmas on your own, Mum, with no one to care for you and I thought, why just Christmas? *They* want me, you see, *they* care – unlike some. I got it all sorted months ago, I was just hanging on for the right tenants. Well, I've got them now and that's that. I never said anything to you because what do you care? And now this awful…Oh, Billie, how could you do it? How could you disgrace us all like that? I don't understand you, I really don't. You've had every advantage – a loving home, devoted sister, an education, college, everything – but you're no better than a drop-out. Well, I read in *Woman's Own* about children like you and how they ruin everything for their families and it said parents have to be tough, 'tough love' they called it. Stand up to your kids, they said, show them they can't get away with that sort of thing. It's for their own good. I've had enough heartache from you, so I'm doing what it said.'

'But, Mum, I…'

'No, don't give me any of your excuses, you're no child of mine, you're all your father's. And don't ring me anymore, I don't want to speak to you ever again. D'you understand? Never, ever again. As far as I'm concerned, you cut yourself off when you put that story in the newspapers for all the world to see. You're cold, you are, Billie, cold and selfish, just like your father.'

And the phone went dead in my hand.

You'd think I'd have cried my eyes up, wouldn't you? I mean, that's what you'd do in a film or a soap on the telly, right? But I didn't, and I didn't want to. Maybe I am like my father, cold and selfish, but something dried up inside me. Like a bit of paper thrown in a fire is itself for a second, then you can see all the moisture go out of it, it goes brittle and then it disintegrates. What I felt for Mum fluttered away in an ashy tatter. She hadn't even given me a chance to explain, to apologise for upsetting her.

But maybe she was right, too. I hadn't thought of her, or Jen, or Uncle A, or any of my blood family, however distant, when I'd got into this mess. The fact was I seldom did think of them and when I did – apart from Mum and Jen but even them to some extent – I didn't feel much at all. My life had drawn apart from theirs so much, there had been so little contact between us over the years, they meant virtually nothing to me. So I hadn't thought about them and I hadn't thought about Mum and this was the price I paid. Mum was sodding off half-way round the world and disowning me.

I have to say it was in the back of my mind that she might well be blustering on, like she always did when she was pissed off, but in time, as usual, she'd come round and things would go on as before: not perfect, crap in fact, but what we thought of as normal. We'd speak, send cards. But, as I write this, she's been as good as her word – I haven't heard a dickey-bird from her since that phone call. Now, I think it was a relief to her – though she'd never admit it – to have a good reason to cut me loose. What is it they say? You can pick your friends but you can't pick your family. People usually say that when they find out they don't like their mother or father as people, they don't often think their mother or father might not like *them* for the same reason. Mum, well, she never liked me, woman to woman. Jen she loved and understood, me – no. The cuckoo child, the changeling. I think it was a weight off her mind to – how can I put it? – to divorce me, if you see what I mean.

So I didn't cry – I was too fucking tired to cry. Like Micky, I filed it away for later, I'd deal with it later. I'd cry later.

Chapter
Twenty-seven

APPARENTLY, I'D GOT Jas to the hospital if not in the nick of time, pretty damn close to it. When I dragged her to the triage desk they took one look at her and whipped her into a cubicle. We waited, me and Monkey, the blood drying on us, watching the soundless shadow-play of the wall-mounted telly, listening to the babel of voices from every part of the globe, for what seemed like hours. I think we slept a bit, exhausted – I know Monkey did, poor little sod. Eventually, I got called to talk to a harassed over-tired young doctor. He was a nice enough lad, but the despair in his red-rimmed brown eyes as he talked about Jas was palpable. I knew how he felt.

'You say she's a heroin addict, Mrs Er…For how long? Oh, I see. And cigarettes, alcohol, does she…oh, OK. And she's been like this for how long? The fevers, the coughing, I mean – well, approximately…? Right… I've had a look at her and obviously we'll have to run some more tests, but initially it looks to me very much like TB. Oh, yes, it's rife again, really, especially among – among people with Mrs, um, Savage's, er, lifestyle. I'm admitting her immediately and she'll be put in an isolation unit, of course, so I'm afraid you won't be able to visit her in the normal way. We may have to move her to a special unit later, but at present I don't want to do anything that might add to her stress. There'll be detox issues obviously and we'll have to get consent forms signed…Next of kin? Mmm, mmm. Oh, you're a friend of the family, well, under the circumstances you'll be the best person for us to keep informed…You'll contact the son, excellent. Good. Well, you'll need tests, chest X-rays, etcetera – yourself, the son and Mr er, Monk. As I was saying, you'll have to be tested, but I'm sure…If you go with Nurse she'll see to everything and…No, no, that's perfectly fine, really.'

And he flurried off, his over-sized white coat billowing behind him. The nurse wasn't much better, age-wise, but being plump as a pouter pigeon, she looked motherly at least.

I tried to ask the nurse useful questions, things I might need to know, but my brain felt like a lump of congealed porridge. I took the information leaflet she gave me and tried to remember the details of where to get the tests done. I could barely take in the idea Jas was so ill – I'd thought, a heavy chest cold, maybe bronchitis – but TB? no one had TB, it was Victorian.

The nurse soon disabused me of that idea; the thing we had to hope for, apparently – and frankly, we didn't have much hope left – was that Jas didn't have the multiple drug-resistant strain that was creeping through the country. I didn't understand what she meant, so she explained – you got the disease, but it was immune to all the current drugs. Nothing would work, the docs had to try cocktails of allsorts to knock it back. The 'White Death' they called it. Jesus. Jas had holes in her lungs the size of teacups; she was terribly run down and the drug abuse – all that was bad enough. If it was that type of TB…The nurse seemed to see me as a sort of social worker, rather than a relative, so she was pretty frank, or as frank as medics ever are. I didn't understand why at first, then I twigged. Jas is black, I'm white. She assumed I was from a different class from Jas because of my speech and my clothes, however filthy and bloodstained. So many years of being Jas's 'sister' – I'd half forgotten how ridiculous that might appear to outsiders.

Then the nurse looked at me, a different kind of look, and I twigged it – I might have it, too. And Monkey, and Natty. We could all be seething with this unkillable bug. I sat down, heavily, while Monkey crouched by the chair like a bloody gargoyle. I felt like shit.

I thought I'd better fill the nurse in with the newspaper thing in case anyone came to try and bother Jas. At first, she didn't really understand, people like us being in the papers, but I persisted and she finally seemed to get it.

'Oh, you're famous, then? Should I ask for your autograph?' She smiled brightly. I suppressed the wave of foul irritation that rose up in me. Poor little cow, she didn't know any better.

'No – I mean, it's not like that. It wasn't a good, not a nice article. It made Jas – Mrs Savage – out to be…'

I stopped. It made Jas out to be a junkie and a whore. But that's what she was. But at the same time, she wasn't just that, she was real, herself, a human being, not a cheap media tag. How could I explain in the ten seconds of small talk I had with this busy girl, that it wasn't as simple as being a bit of a celeb, like in those magazines you read in the dentist's waiting room?

I swallowed bile. 'I mean, it wasn't complimentary, they said some pretty cruel things.' I tried to appeal to her. 'The media, you know, the way they hound folk…I don't want them at her, stressing her out even more, or people saying things to her.'

A brief expression of sympathy passed over her round face. I could almost see the image of Princess Diana rising up in her mind. 'Oh, I see, well, don't worry, nobody gets into the isolation unit. But I'll make a note…' She frowned and wrote on her clipboard, reciting as she scribbled. 'Details of Mrs Savage's progress to be given out strictly to relatives only. And yourself, of course – really, don't worry, we'll take good care of her.'

She bustled off, leaving me and Monkey sitting in the corridor like cases waiting to be seen by some phantom consultant. What would he say, the ghostly medic? Not a good prognosis, Mrs Morgan, I'm afraid it's bad news. I let out a short, humourless laugh and Monkey looked at me questioningly.

'Sorry, Lee, I'm knackered. Come on, love, let's go back to the house, I'll get us summat to eat, eh? Come on.'

As I drove home, I replayed the evening's events in my mind and wondered how I could get Pauline Skinner killed for a reasonable price. I'd given the nurse the impression that the stress of the newspaper article had brought on Jas's crisis, but that wasn't true. Pauline fucking Skinner had.

She'd appeared, like a screeching harpy, piss drunk and dragging poor old Bobby in her wake like a human poodle. We were alerted to her presence by the sound of her cries and the fact she was apparently trying to kick the front door in with her pointy-toed, spike-heel slingbacks.

'Open this fuckin' door, yer fuckin' – open the fuckin' door, y'skaghead bitch – Bobby, Bobby, get the fuckin' door open…'

Before I could stop him, Monkey had opened the door – on a sort of reflex, I suppose. La Skinner's forearm slammed him into the wall as she staggered past and tried to shove past me too as I stood braced in the living room doorway. She attempted to wrestle me out of her way in a flailing strop, all slappy hands and stinking booze and fag breath; going for my eyes with her square-tipped, inch-long, acrylic nails hooked like claws. Fuck, she could have stripped paint at forty paces with that breath and mixed with her foul body odour, the unmistakable stench of a liver unable to metabolise any more alcohol, and copious amounts of whatever fake knock-off perfume she had on; it made my sinuses buzz.

'Ya fuckin', ya fuckin' cunt, get the fuck – Bobby, Bobby, she's 'urtin' me, Bobby…Where's tha' fuckin' nigger bitch, where…'

I slapped her. Not very hard, on account of her advanced years, but hard enough. It was so satisfying, I had to stop myself doing it again. She sat down suddenly on the floor like one of those little wooden toys whose base you press and they flop or stand up. As I was waving my hand to cool the sting, Bobby tried to go for it.

I looked at him and he subsided, chuntering vaguely, poor git. I got hold of Pauline's greasy false hair and dragged her up by it. She twisted and wriggled until it all but tore out of its mass of pins. I shoved her backwards into the hall. I was shaking with adrenalin, but the pure rush of it was exhilarating after the long hours of depression. There was a kind of bright, white-hot joy in discarding reason, breaking out of the chitinous carapace of control, of ceasing to be endlessly polite to straight people, to the wilfully ignorant, the malicious and the mendacious. It was a power surge that struck out of my congested heart in a lightning burst; for a mad split second I was an outlaw princess again: savage, barbaric and free of all the niggling constraints of society. In that moment, I could have killed Pauline Skinner myself, broken her scraggy neck in my hands and not given a damn. I knew I'd pay the usual price for my temper, but I didn't care. Nothing mattered except the cresting wave of my anger. I don't say it was right, or good – it was neither. But I can't, and I won't, make excuses or try to simper and cavil my way out of it. It was just a fact, that violence was as much a part of me as love, honour and pride. It had given me iron strength of will over the years, but sometimes it demanded a price for that daily control.

'Shut the *fuck* up, Pauline.' Bobby made a tremulous move towards me. 'And you – don't you even fucking think about it. What do you want, you old cow? What? Christ, you stink, did you know that? You fucking stink.'

Pauline's gas-yellow eyes flared with a napalm burst of fury. 'I fuckin' stink, *I* fuckin' – wha' about that cuntin' nigger? Eh? Eh? She's fuckin' ruined everythin', the fuckin' slag, the fuckin' – I'm a fuckin' laughin' stock thanks ter her, folk fuckin' laughin' at me fer havin' a – a junkie nigger pross fer a daughter-in-law...'

'Shut it, you fucking old bitch. Get out of here, get out now. You, you fucking goon, get her out of here before I do her some real damage, I mean it, go on.'

'I'll get the law on you, you 'saulted me, you did, dint she, Bobby, you 'urt me – I'll get the coppers...'

I laughed. There wasn't any humour in the sound. 'Go on then, get 'em. What'll you tell them, eh? That you bust in here screaming filthy racist abuse at a sick woman? That I tried to stop you? Go on, you disgusting slag, ring 'em and let's see who they take down.'

Momentarily confused, she shut up. Her face, the pink mark of my hand imprinted palely on her cheek like an old brand, seemed to crumple into a thousand cacky wrinkles and her yellow eyes, with their broken palisade of claggy mascaraed lashes filled with the easy, oily tears of the habitual drunk. She moaned and stumbled back into Bobby's arms.

'I 'ate you, d'you hear? I 'ate you – you're a right hard bitch, you are, hard as fuckin' nails. It int your boy is missin', my son, my little lad – mixed up with the likes of *her*...The stuff they put in the paper, I can't hold me head up no more wi' all the world knowin' what she is...Oh, Bobby, Bobby, tek me 'ome, oh...'

Bobby wrapped his skinny arms round her juddering form. He looked at me, his eyes hugely magnified by the thick greasy lenses of his big specs.

He spoke. It was the first time I'd ever heard him say a word. 'Y'dint 'ave ter be like that with her. You're cruel, you are, cruel. You got no feelins. She's delicate, she is, you don't understand.'

The love in his face as he gently steered the loudly sobbing Pauline out of the door was palpable. Poor, poor deluded Bobby; transfigured by love. I felt a sharp pang of guilt and the adrenalin started to ebb coldly from my body. I was about to say something to him when Pauline whipped round and spat in my face like a cobra.

'Cunt,' she hissed, 'I int done wi you – or her, I int, just you fuckin' wait, I'll burn this fuckin' place wi her in it, I'll do you all, I…'

Wiping the thick, smelly gob from my face, I lunged forward and shoved them out, slamming the door and snecking it. As I stood there shaking, trying to pick Monkey up off the floor and attend to his bloody nose, I heard a sound, a sort of guttering breath, and I spun round.

''As she gone, Billie? So scared of 'er, all these years, so…' Jas gasped hoarsely, standing in the doorway, clinging onto the frame like a skinny, panting spider.

'Jas, Jas love, forget her, I sorted her, she's gone, come on, back to…'

She looked at me with those great eyes, an expression of puzzlement on her face and suddenly, a terrible sound, like cough but worse; a fibrous, wet, tearing noise shook her whole frame convulsively and a fine, aerosol-like spray of bright blood spewed out of her mouth, glistening on her chin, spattering her corded neck. She fell forward, fainting, and I ran and caught her before she hit the floor.

Monkey screamed, like a hare caught in a barbed-wire fence, shrill and panic-stricken; I would have screamed but I was too busy trying to pick Jas up, not throw up at the sight and smell of the warm blood that was soaking into the front of my T-shirt, and get her dead weight back to the sofa.

Then it had all been a mad rush of paramedics, the crowd who'd gathered outside spitting, jeering and lobbing beer cans; I watched them with a kind of sickly detachment, their round, gaping, yelling mouths and blurred faces like an oil painting of a mob that had got smudged before it was quite dry. Late Degas chalk drawings of people: vivid, unreal, snapshots of Hell. I knew some of them – that girl with bleached white hair was Mandy from three doors down, who was always borrowing milk, that whippet-skinny lad in the filthy outsize jeans hanging perilously low on his hips was Gaz, who had hero-worshipped Natty when he was a kid. Now they were united in the buzz of persecuting someone, all the jugs of milk, high-fives and borrowed CDs forgotten. All their individual humanity forgotten. For a second I felt a terrible sadness steal through my heart because their lives were so shit and debased – this was what they'd sunk to for entertainment.

But feeling sad didn't help when it came to hustling Jas, Monkey and the paramedics past the hail of missiles, gob and filthy abuse. Then there was the jolting, terrifying ride in the ambulance, with Jas nozzled in an oxygen mask, the paramedic woman looking worried but trying to be cheery and Monkey, who shouldn't have been in there but couldn't be left, sobbing like a child and shivering like a beaten cur. Finally there'd been the hospital, and the diagnosis, which I still couldn't take in properly.

Monkey was still shivering when at last I pulled up at my house. There had been no point in going back to Jas's place – the coppers had been notified of the disturbance, as they put it, and said they'd keep an eye on the place. Then they advised me not to go back there 'if I had anywhere else I could go'. I didn't need telling twice.

Shovelling Monkey bodily out of the vehicle while he gibbered and muttered about being sorry, as if it were all his fault, I made him take a shower (with Wright's Coal Tar soap) and stuck all his rags in the washer at sixty degrees plus a good dose of lavender-scented disinfectant. I found one of Natty's cast-off Nike sweat-shirts and some old joggers and left them outside the bathroom for him. When he was clean and dressed – looking, in Natty's too-big clothes, like a rag doll that had been put in the washer on boil wash and shrunk – I gave him some painkillers, made some hot chocolate and after he'd drunk it, his hands shaking like an old man with palsy, I put him to bed in the tiny spare room. He was asleep by the time I turned the light off, snoring like a train through his wreck of a nose. He'd slept there before, often, and I knew if I went into the room later, I'd find him wrapped up in the quilt under the bed, like a big cocoon; only, Monkey never emerged a glorious butterfly, just crawled wonkily out from under the bed in the morning the same old Lee, the same old Monkey-boy.

Exhausted, I made myself a cuppa and sat at the kitchen table, Cairo on my lap, kneading my legs to make me softer and purring almost as loudly as Monkey snoring. I rubbed the beautiful, soft, downy fluff behind her ear and mindlessly studied the swirling pattern of short fur on her nose; like an Op Art print in shades of dun and tawny. I felt my eyes closing but I forced myself to flip the phone and ring Natty again. I had no hope he'd answer but on the fourth ring, he picked up.

He sounded smashed. Beyond smashed; ruined. His usually resonant voice was slurred, hoarse. 'Yeah, whose, wassa…'

'Natty, Natty, it's Billie, it's…'

There was a sound like a scuffle and another voice came on the line; a woman, with a harsh, Leeds accent. It snagged in my mind, I'd heard it before but I couldn't quite place it. Before I could speak she shouted down the phone.

'Fuck off, fuck off, right? Right? Fuck you, bitch, fuck you, y'hear? He's mine now, you – geddit? D'yer geddit? Jus' fuck right off, yer little slag, go back ter yer mam, yer fuckin' – Natty, don't – I won't – I'll say what I fuckin' well like, I will an'…'

The line went dead. As I stared hopelessly at the phone, the voice assumed a face: an older woman by Natty's standards, a girl in her early twenties from one of the Leeds' estates – which one? I couldn't remember. Her name was – Charmaine, that was it. Shar. One of those white girls who act black, with stiff, streaky braids and a huge, gold-jointed clown pendant hanging, winking, in a mass of chains round her neck. She drew on her eyebrows, was leathery from sun-beds and had a sharp, vulpine face. She did that annoying head wobble thing girls like her copied from the black American women on the Jerry Springer show: *Talk to the hand, sister, 'cos the head aint listenin'*. I hadn't liked her the couple of times I'd met her and I fucking hated her now. God alone knew who she'd thought she'd been speaking to. Venus? Possibly.

I dialled again, got the answerphone and wearily left a last message. As I plugged the phone into the charger on the worktop, I saw the magazine and the photo of Jasmine.

The ineffable, timeless beauty of the image was like a cruel joke. The picture was a relic, not a living thing; the tarnished image of a ruined saint. The glowing halo surrounding Jas's head looked like the gold leaf of a renaissance devotional; I remembered some article I'd read in an arts magazine about the origins of haloes – aside from all the crap spaceman theories, of course. Apparently there was a curious phenomenon, rare but possible – people in the last stages of TB were sometimes witnessed with a haze of phosphorescence surrounding their heads. Early saints were obsessed with inflicting terrible physical suffering on themselves, mortifying the flesh, starving themselves and staying outdoors, practically naked, in all weathers, literally making themselves ill for God. Often they had symptoms that would now be diagnosed as TB. Hence the saintly halo.

In my lifetime, I never imagined I'd know anyone who had tuberculosis. That article had been a weird little thing I'd stuffed away in my brain. Now it was as if thousands of years had been stripped away in a second and the idea of some great Western civilisation was an arrogant delusion. Oh, look, we've got power showers, mobile phones, computers, DVDs, blenders, the Internet – but the peasants and the holy still die of ancient diseases we can't cure.

I shivered and stuffed the picture into a drawer. Jas might die. I hadn't really taken that in. She might actually die – in fact, there seemed to be a good chance of it. Oh, God, poor little fucked-up Jasmine, poor little hopeless scrap. What a shit way to end up; coughing your lungs up in a hospital where your loved ones couldn't even hold your hand in case they caught your disease. Jas, who was so terrified of being alone, was about as alone as a person could get; in the care of brisk, disinterested strangers, with none of her pitiful bits and bobs around her, her beloved son crashed out in the stinking flat of some hard-faced cow who thought *she* owned him now.

I locked up, but didn't sneck the front door. Natty had his key, he might come in during the night. I got in bed and both cats jumped up and lay next to me, Ghengis pushing his broad old head under my hand so I could scratch behind his battered ears. I must have been giving out terrible vibrations if Gheng stirred his stumps to come and, in his own fashion, comfort me. After a while, he got bored and scratched me – but not very hard.

I lay in bed, thoughts whirling fast and crazy in my head; plans, scenarios, re-plays – I willed myself to be still, breathe slow and watch the patterns that coalesced, gold against black-blood red inside my eyelids. It was a kind of self-hypnotism I'd perfected over the years because some nights the memories went at me like a swarm of biting insects and I knew

I was cranky and non-functional if I didn't get enough sleep; I couldn't afford to be that weak. I concentrated – soon the shifting, crackle-glaze shapes would send me into the dark.

And they did, but I jerked myself awake involuntarily. It was too steep a slope, I felt out of control as if instead of sleep, it was a kind of dying, unconsciousness, oblivion. As ever, a picture flashed into my mind – Degas again, no, that French bloke who painted nightmares – no, not – *Goya*. That was it, Goya – 'Chronos Devouring One Of His Children'.

In a terrible black void, that still suggested titanic shapes moving in slow terrifying nothingness, the gigantic mad old god Time half crouches, his hair wild, his appalling eyes staring at the viewer as he grasps the limp, pale body of a normal-sized young man. His head is gone because Chronos has eaten it, blood and gobbets of flesh dripping from his slack lips.

Time eats us all in the end, the picture says; young and old, beautiful, ugly, whole, impaired, insane, sane. We all go into the dark, we all dwindle, we all die.

I sat up, trembling. That picture had always put the shits up me: Goya's genius was in showing us the true nature of our own personal, irrational fear. By God, he did it for me right enough. I reached and got a tissue from the bedside table, and wiped my damp face.

Then I lay back again, exhausted.

And sleep ate me up.

Chapter Twenty-eight

I DIDN'T SLEEP very well – in fact I woke up around three with a raging sore throat. Gagging on the raspy dryness, I staggered into the bathroom and groggily drank a glass of water. Even half asleep I took care not to look in the mirror; I knew at some cellular level I'd look like complete shit. Everything was bad enough without that too. Vanity – it gets you every time.

As I drifted back into a coma, I thought longingly and probably feverishly of cool, white sand beaches and blue sparkling seas. Floating lazily in turquoise shallows embroidered with drifting veils of foam like wet bridal lace; a marriage of the blue water and the bluer skies above. As my over-heated blood thumped through my veins I dreamt of dozing in a hammock strung between two coconut palms. Paradise names fluttered through my mind: the Seychelles, Hawaii, the Maldives... Christ, I needed a fucking holiday – but I'd be lucky if I got a day trip to Whitby in October at this rate. Sighing, I turned over into the foetal position and tried to get back to my personal Shangri-La.

I was woken for the second time by the bedside phone, which seemed unnecessarily loud. I grabbed for it, dropping the body on the floor and dislodging Cairo, who sprang off the bed, outraged at the disturbance. I wrestled the receiver to my ear.

'Natty? Natty, is that you? Look, you've...'

'It's me, Billie, Leckie – it's half ten, love, I'm in the shop, I've been here for three-quarters of an hour. Are you alright?'

I checked the clock and with a groan, fell back on the pillows, which appeared to have had their fillings replaced with concrete during the night. I felt awful. Not absolutely incapacitated rotten, just fairly filthy. Fantastic.

'Jeez, Lecks – I'm sorry, I forgot to set the bloody clock.'

'OK, OK, don't worry – but love, but it's Monday, remember? My Uni afternoon? I really can't miss it, this week of all weeks – I told you, Ben Thorby is giving a lecture – the marketing guru, the American bloke who wrote the book I showed you and...'

I groaned again, louder. I did remember her enthusing like a star-struck teen over the fella – he'd written some business book global best-seller called *Screw Your Competitors into the Ground and Make Colossal Wads of Cash*. Or something like that. Leckie wanted to re-make our business in the Thorby mould.

'Of course you've got to go. Get his autograph for me, eh? Look, I feel dreadful – I was at the hospital all night with Jas – Leckie, she's been taken in, she's in an isolation ward.' I took a deep, phlegmy breath. 'She's got TB. Had a crisis or something – she's in a pretty bad way.'

'Oh. My. God. Ohmy*god*. TB? *TB*? Jesus Christ, Billie, are you...?'

'Yeah – I mean, I've got to be tested, but I was immunised at school, we all were – they stopped doing that, didn't they? Anyway, no, I've just got a cold, from the hospital, probably, you know what these places are like – look, did you get immunised?'

'I don't know – I think so – I'll ask Mum...God, Billie – God, I can't believe it, it's like...'

'Something out of the bloody Brontë sisters, I know, I know, that's what I said to the doctor; fuck, Lecks, I'm knackered, just knackered, I can't do it today, I – look – just go inside, and put a notice on the door saying – oh – shut due to ill-health, open soon. Or no, fuck it, just go home. It's only a sodding gift shop, Bradford can do without it for a couple of days. Yeah, yeah, I know, business, business; business – but Leckie – we're all only human, we're not bloody machines. Go to the talk; enjoy yourself. Look, I'm sure you'll get so many great hints an' tips we'll more than make up for being shut.'

'Well, if you're sure...I'll ring tonight and see how you are – or shall I come round...'

'Thanks, darlin', but there's no point two of us getting sick. Ring me though, give me the goss.'

'OK – Billie…?'

'Yes, love?'

'I'm – I'm *very* sorry about Jas, it's *awful*, it really is.'

'Thanks, Lecks. Look, go on – pick that fella's brain, enjoy yourself – and don't worry, normal service will be resumed before you know it, honestly. Ta-ta.'

I fell back onto the lumpy pillows. Then I reached out and grabbed a handful of tissues and tried to unblock my nose. No use. I crawled out of the sweaty raggle of sheet, throw cover and the cat's hair-felted, paw-print fleece blanket and went to the bathroom, standing under the full force of the power shower until I was scoured, reeking of tea-tree wash and gasping. That should incapacitate the bloody virus: also, it got rid of any lingering smell of hospitals. I hated that smell – no, I hated hospitals, end of story. That made me think of Jas and I stopped, suddenly shivery, and wrapped myself in the bath sheet. Jesus – Jas. TB. Christ Almighty. I'd worried about Aids, about Hep, about an overdose – but TB? Never, ever crossed my mind. Over the years, I'd dragged her to doctors and to NHS shrinks with her various illnesses and attempts at rehab – no one had ever even breathed a dicky-bird about *TB*. Her face coalesced out of the steamy mirror at me, blanched and insubstantial, a ghost already. I saw again the terrible disbelieving panic and terror in her great eyes, the whites visible all round those misty emerald irises, as the bright blood sprayed from her mouth…I shuddered all over, like a fly-bitten pony, like my skin was crawling on my flesh.

But there was nothing I could do at present, nothing more I could do for her until the docs gave the all-clear, or she – she died. Better face it, better face the things I'd need to do for her – if that happened. The things I'd have to do for Natty. I sat down heavily on the toilet seat and felt worry clench in my chest. I leant my forehead on the cool of the washbasin. First things first. Step at a time. You can do it. I can, I can do it, I can…

Cairo miaowed at the door, wanting food and love. Wearily, I cleaned up and trudged into my room. I pulled on clean black joggers and a T, and stripped the sour bed. Then thanking God I had short hair and no especial interest in make-up, I fed the cats and made tea – Yorkshire Tea, three bags in the pot, stewed until it was as black as Ghengis' temper. I did some toast for myself and breakfast for Monkey. Futilely, I tried Natty's number about a dozen times – standing there pressing that sodding little green telephone icon over and over as a crushed-looking Monkey snuffled through boiled eggs and Marmite soldiers washed down with a pint of tea. I was getting frantic; it was in my mind to go cruise round his favourite haunts looking for him, even though I knew in my heart it was pointless. But what else could I do?

Anything, really. I phoned the doctor's and made appointments for blood tests for us all. I settled poor, exhausted Monkey on the sofa in the front room with a DVD of *The Jungle Book* (his favourite) and put more washing in the machine. I flea-combed Ghengis and got scratched to fuck. I deadheaded the climbing rose by the back door. Finally, after more useless ringing, I glanced at the clock – it was nearly half-two. I decided to go and get my stuff from Mum's on the grounds that I may as well get all the shit out of the way on my enforced day off. I didn't relish it, especially with sinusitis and a thumping headache – but it had to be done. I felt fairly calm about it; after all, Mum wouldn't be there so there wouldn't be any sort of showdown, I'd just get my things and come straight back to wait for Natty. Knowing Mum, they'd be all bagged up and waiting so I'd be in and out in a flash.

I told Monkey I'd be gone for about an hour, and if Natty came, to tell him to stay put; if he rang on the landline, to tell him to come over sharpish – but not to say anything else.

Monkey's squashed face concertina'd into wrinkles of puzzlement and worry like one of those Sharpei dogs.

'But, Miss, what if he asks me, what if he asks about Missus…'

I sighed. 'He won't, love, and don't you say owt, eh? Just tell him ter come round as fast as he can, tell him I need to see him.'

'But, Miss Billie, Miss, he'll go mental if he…'

'Lee – it's alright, love. Honest. Don't worry – look, I'll be back dead quick, you just watch yer film, and there's *The Jungle Book Two* on the shelf there if you want it, and listen, there's a big bar of Fruit and Nut in the fridge, you can have that if you like. Just *wait here*, OK? Wait for Natty, wait for me.'

He nodded, his face smoothed out by the thought of seeing his beloved again – and possibly the orgy of chocolate and Mowgli that he could look forward to undisturbed.

I felt proud of my calm and what I fondly thought of as mature, attitude: of my cool behaviour in going calmly to Mum's and quietly, and with dignity, getting my stuff and what was it? Yeah – effecting closure.

The drive over was swift and uneventful. I was perfectly fine, perfectly in control.

Chapter Twenty-nine

I FOUND THEM LAID neatly and conspicuously – posed, almost – on the top of a box of old papers Mum had put on the kitchen table. The letters my father had sent me over the years, that Mum had kept from me. So like Mum to do that: subtle, passive, poisonous – a very feminine kind of revenge for the newspaper article and for all the other hurts I'd done her. She'd never confront me with them openly, just put them where I'd find them and then, if I said anything, toss her head and say it was my fault for nosing around in other people's things, I'd brought it on myself. But the gleam in her eye would be there. She'd know what it would do to me; they had been her final weapon, her Doomsday device.

They were bound together with an old tartan hair ribbon, one of the dogs' probably. I recognised the handwriting on the top envelope immediately – how could I not? It was so like my own. My dadda's handwriting, in that black, black fountain pen ink; proper calligraphy, italic, quick. Dozens of letters, dating from the very week he left. Disintegrating, compressed as fossils. At first he must have written every week, then as time passed and he got no reply, it reduced to birthdays and Christmases: long letters tucked into cards. But it had never stopped, until he died.

She'd hidden them from me. She'd fucking hidden them from me. I thought he'd deserted me, that it had been my fault he'd left – that he'd gone off me. She'd let me think that, let me twist in the wind, let me suffer. My father's daughter, the very picture of my dadda. If she couldn't get at him, she had his spitting image to hand instead.

I sat at the table and read the letters at random, wiping the snot and tears from my face with a tea towel I pulled from the rag bag.

…and when I saw you first, Billie my love, such a little thing, so red and strong and screaming the place down, bach, let me say, I thought, this is what the poetry means, this is the green fuse, this is what it's all for…

…and so a very happy birthday to you, my dearest daughter, I hope you like the dolly I got you, she seemed very pretty to me but I'm just a chap after all! The man in the toy shop said her name is Bella, which is Italian for beautiful but you can call her whatever you like, my sweetheart…

…don't think you're getting these letters, I want to think you aren't, my petal, my dove, because if you are and you hate me for running off I swear my old heart would break because I love you so much and I always will, you must remember that, love, and when you're older I'll…

…so tired, bach, sometimes I wonder what the hell it's all for. I rang your mum last night, did she say? No, probably not, I suppose. Billie, you've got to promise me you won't blame her, promise me that because you don't know how hard she had it with her own family and she just wants to be safe, that's all, to be secure and I'm not the chap for that. My stupid head is full of useless dreams of poems and pictures and songs, like those songs we used to listen to together, do you remember, songs by your namesake, Lady Day? I'm not all that with money and your mum needs money, love, she needs pretty things…

And the last one, the day before he died.

…I love you, Billie bach, my child, I love you and I've never stopped loving you. I hope to God you're alright, that you're happy. Forgive me for what I did, it was the worst thing I ever did in my life, was leaving you. Forgive me, little love, if you can. You're in my heart now and always. Your loving father, Bill Morgan.

I wiped my face and threw the cloth on the floor. I couldn't tell Dadda I forgave him because he was gone – but I'd never forgive Mum. I'd try to understand why she did what she did, but forgive her, no. I'm not such a good person as that. I'm not a good person at all, really.

As I drove through the narrow streets of Saltaire to the main road, I felt as if I'd done a shedload of whizz. My heart was pounding and my vision unnaturally acute: sharp, like looking through the wrong end of a telescope. As I went past Salts Mill, I saw a woman in a pink velour leisure suit, not a trendy belly-baring sports combo but an older ladies' outfit: I thought it was Mum. Everything seemed to misfire in my nerves, jangling and shredded by adrenalin and I yanked the car over and stopped before I blacked out. Through the shifting veil of metallic spots that shimmered sickeningly in front of my eyes, I realised it wasn't Mum, but the damage was done. I knew if it had been her, I'd have been out of the bloody vehicle and at her like a pit bull. That's not a nice feeling, believe me – wanting to shake your elderly mother like a rag doll and call her a fucking bitch. I sat back, gripping the wheel with sweating hands, trembling.

Everything seemed to be gathering some sort of unstoppable velocity: a train out of control, a car skidding towards a tree, a bike siding it down the asphalt, screeching towards the van that nothing on earth could prevent you slamming into. I was losing control and it frightened me: I don't do frightened very well, it's another thing that makes me angry, not pathetic and helpless. I put frightened away that night so long ago, when we went to Terry's cottage. There had been no time then for being scared and since then, fear was the path to panic – and that was a place I must never, ever enter.

They say the word panic comes from the Greek root *panikos,* meaning something that emanates from the old god, Pan. Something irrational, chaotic, ancient. You can feel it a little if you've ever been by yourself in deep forest, or walked through an unlit alley in the city late at night. You jump at noises, your heart flutters at a shift of light, a chill breeze. Shadows seem to thicken and clot: the familiar world fades into something darker, something stranger, and those myths and legends you read as a child come back to you, only they don't seem childish anymore – far from it. You remember the woodcut illustrations in your picture books, the ones that seemed so quaint and old-fashioned. In your mind's eye, you see again that bold, familiar leering face, the shaggy, goatfoot god come to play his pipes, come to make that weird, disorientating, crazy music, come to rob you of your senses and remind you we're not as far from the old ways as we like to think. That we're not rational, not *civilised* at all, really. The spinning, frantic madness of the bacchanal crawls bloody and panting just below the surface of our skins, waiting for the signal from those wailing pipes to turn us into beasts – and worse.

I know what tune Pan plays; I know it in the cells of my body, in my DNA, in every twisting neural pathway of my aching brain. I know his true music; not his little daily melodies that set you dancing like a puppet with cut strings when you're late for that important appointment, or the car breaks down as you're on your way to pick up your kid from school.

That's nothing, that's a bit of paper skirling in a dusty summer breeze. You think that's stress, you think that's the end of the world: well, forgive me if I smile.

I've heard Pan's real song, you see. I've smelt my own brute terror rising from my armpits and groin in a sour, yellow stench: I've heard myself screaming like an animal until I tasted blood from my torn throat. I've seen the god's clever, slanted bronze eye, lozenge-shaped pupil contracting in amusement, glinting in the night as he played and played a rising, spiralling riff that built and built until it crashed into a destruction so total, so cruel, it was like dying and being reborn because nothing of what I was remained. And nothing of what my poor, sweet Micky was, remained. And Pan laughed then: God laughed, and shook His fucking dice for another Game.

Those of us living, who have heard that hideous music will tell you that there's not much we wouldn't do, including suicide, to avoid hearing it again. We don't brag it up into pub war stories, we don't make ourselves out to be hard cases, we don't whine and plead for sympathy, we don't *talk* about it at all. But other people smell it on you, they sense it, like animals sense a wolf before they see it. So they say you're 'scary' and 'intense' because they've lost the proper words for what you are. They're frightened but they don't know why, they couldn't tell you why.

But I know why: the god put his mark on you and they see it with that part of their brains they've forgotten they have; it's an overlay, a transparency with *damnation* written on it in a dead tongue. People smell it without knowing what they smell, it makes the hairs on the back of their necks and their soft little arms rise and they rub themselves and say, *'Oh, someone just walked over my grave,'* and they don't think for a second what that means. And us – the Fellowship of Pan, struggling to make sense of our ruined lives, withdraw into whatever makes us feel safe and never, ever open the door with the old god's face on it, never even touch that gleaming bronze handle made in the shape of his mask, never look into those carved eyes, those wicked, undying terrible eyes that know more about you than you can bear even to think of.

So, that was the threshold I stood on as I shook and tried not to throw up in the car. So I *stepped back*. I genuinely don't have the words to tell you how much energy and effort of will that took. Just to do that thing in my mind, to turn away, stopping my ears against the desperate temptation of that soul-killing music.

The drive home was a fractured kaleidoscope of colours whirring and shattering past the car windows; sometimes I'd jump out of my skin at some fluttering rag of an image seeming to hit the windscreen. My nose was so stuffed up I couldn't breathe through it and my eyes were sore and gritty. The weather had turned heavy and humid, the sky bellying down with thick, sulphurous clouds. Sweat shimmied down my back and my hair clung lankly to my forehead reminding me to get it cut, very short this time, very short…Something was over, something was beginning, but I wasn't sure which was which.

I was driving so badly that as I threw the car into our lane I nearly squashed Mrs Leach's silly terrier, D'Arcy, as he skittered about chasing imaginary rats in the bleached-out grass edging the cemetery wall. I got out, slamming the door and glared at him, poor doggie fool. He yelped and bounced off; if he could have talked, I don't doubt Mrs Leach would have been round knocking at my door with a face as thunderous as the clouds above. This sort of weather made everyone narky, it was like an electrical disruption in the nerves.

Chapter Thirty

NATTY WAS LAID on the sofa, sleeping.

Monkey sat cross-legged on the floor by his head, a beatific smile illuminating his face; his precious had returned to him, his faith was rewarded, all was right in his world again. *The Jungle Book* played silently on the TV screen, Baloo masquerading as an ape, King Louis flirting with the beautiful simian pin-up he thought he saw.

I leant against the door frame, a wave of relief surging through me, leaving me washed out as it sucked back into nothingness. Thank you, God, for bringing my boy home safe; the oldest of prayers chanted in my mind, atavistic, reflexive. I looked at Monkey; how happy he must be, how great it would be to be plain old happy like that. I managed a smile at him and he nodded vigorously, giving me a thumbs up. I beckoned him to the kitchen. He came, with a couple of backward glances to make sure the beloved still slept and didn't vanish again in a panto puff of smoke.

He couldn't wait to share his good fortune with me, the other guardian of the shrine. ''E come back joost after you went, Miss Billie Miss, he come an' I made him a cuppa an' he drank it an' he had a bit of chocolate an' he went ter sleep straight off, like. I dint say nowt, like yer said not ter, I dint, Miss, honest.'

He beamed. That had been an impossibly long speech for Monkey, but joy possessed him. I smiled at him. 'Go on back, then, Lee, we'll just let him get his sleep out, eh? We'll sort stuff out later. You did good, love, honest. Well done, Lee, good lad.'

I shut the door on them and put the kettle on; as I did so I noticed Natty's jeans jacket in a heap on the floor by the table where he must have dropped it. I bent to pick it up and as I did, his phone rang, muffled, in the pocket. Quickly, I pulled it out and as it wasn't the same make as mine, pressed a couple of buttons before I got the right one.

'Hello? Hello? This is Natty Savage's ph…'

'Which one are you then? The fuckin' mother or the fuckin' guardian fuckin' angel? Eh? *Eh?*'

The voice was familiar: Charmaine, the Leeds' girl. Her tone had the catgut tension of amphetamines. I wasn't going to deal with a coked-up bitch banging on about some whizz-induced lover's tiff, not now.

'It's Billie Morgan, Charmaine. It is Charmaine, isn't it? Natty's sleepin'. I'll get him to ring you back when…'

Her shrill laughter was like cheap fabric ripping. 'Ring me back? Ring me fuckin' back? I don't fuckin' think so, you fuckin' old cunt. Not after what he done, no fuckin' thank you. That's why *I'm* ringin' *him*. You tell him my brothers are gonna do him, they're gonna find him and do him, you hear? Good thing he run off home to his mam and you, you…That fuckin'…He's trashed my flat, the fucker, trashed it, everythin' – an' he smacked me up good style, you should fuckin' see my face, you should fuckin…Your fuckin' wonder boy, your fuck…'

'That's enough now. I'll tell him to ring you or whatever but…'

'But what? But what? You another like his fuckin' whore of a mam, are you? You another one like that? You lot, you should be fuckin' ashamed, you made him like this, you – I…'

She was screaming incoherently into the phone; I could almost see her, curdy white speed spittle flying, her braids lashing, her hands shaking. I pressed the little red phone sign and she vanished into the void. I turned the phone off, for good measure. I could see her alright and I didn't want to see what Natty had done to her.

Because I knew she wasn't lying. I knew he'd knocked her around. Well, I'd known it was only a matter of time before I'd be forced to confront him about something like this. His bouts of temper were incandescent and as time had passed, they'd increased in frequency and intensity. The coke didn't help, and all the other shit he took. They were a druggy generation, programmed to excess and Natty was proud of his lifestyle. What could I say to him? Me who'd taken everything, done all the things I'd done? Me who was so full of rage myself? So I'd hoped against hope while he was growing up that his tantrums were just that, childish fits of frustration. But he hadn't grown out of them, far from it. He was like quicksilver, one moment he was the most loving, charming, adorable lad you could wish to meet – the next…Fury ripped through him in a brute, boiling wave.

But this was well out of order. Of course the lovely Charmaine was a piece of work; I could imagine the coke-induced ratcheting crank-up row they'd had, grinding tighter and tighter until he'd lost what little there was of his control. But still; a nasty bitch she might be in my opinion, but that was no excuse for him, a man, to hit her, a woman. It wasn't right. Not by anyone's standards.

I made the tea and took it upstairs to my room. I drank half then took a quick shower, turning solutions to Natty's, Jas's, Monkey's – even my own – problems over in my mind as I scrubbed myself with tea-tree gel from head to foot. Then I put on my old djellaba and took two strong Ibuprofen tabs with the remains of my cooling tea, Dadda's letters spread out on the pink cotton bedspread.

Selfish, selfish – but those letters and cards were so precious to me. I couldn't do anything for anyone until the morning; I couldn't even tell Natty about Jas, or confront him with his behaviour until he woke and, coming down off a binge, he could sleep for twenty-four hours. He had before. That caught in my heart. I failed you, lovely boy, didn't I? I fucked it all up for you way, way back. Oh, not now, not now. Now I wanted to read and re-read the letters; to touch the words with my fingertips, to find something of my dadda caught in those tight-pressed folds of fragile paper. The light was fading outside, you could almost smell the storm coming; I turned the bedside light on as Ghengis jumped arthritically up onto the bed. He hated thunder and lightning nearly as much as he hated Fireworks Night.

'Careful, careful, babba, don't squash this stuff, my old darlin', settle down, good fella.'

He grunted disdainfully and curled up at the foot of the bed as I read. Slowly, as the drug spread through my system, the words blurred, the phrases ran into one another in a black river of pain and loss. I was asleep before I realised it.

I woke to the sound of the shower. Groggily, I put the bedside light on and looked at the clock. When had I fallen asleep? Jesus, it was gone midnight. I rubbed my face and yawned.

Natty came in from the bathroom – he didn't knock, he never did unless Johnjo was visiting, we were family after all – dressed in old faded blue joggers that were going threadbare at the seams and a clean white vest. His gold chain lay like a heavy snake round the sinuous curve of his neck, the skin flushed from the hot water and the humid heat of the night. He brought a veil of steam and the sharp smell of coal-tar soap with him. It made me smile – he hated tea-tree, saying it smelt of dirt, but he loved the old-fashioned coal-tar soap I kept in the house for him, because he thought it was clean-smelling and it reminded him of being a kid. Funny things, people.

Rubbing his damp dreads with the towel, he sat on the edge of the bed. I looked at him, searching for the words to tell him everything I had to say. It struck me again, as it always did when he sat still long enough for me to look at him, how beautiful he was; his face, neck and arms were perfectly moulded, like a bronze kouros. I couldn't look at him without wanting to draw him, to try and capture that feral grace, those gleaming colours. Maybe he was too strong-featured, his face a little too long for the current fashion and I don't suppose everyone would have thought him good-looking, but what did they know, fed on a diet of surgically bland celebrities? I thought he was marvellous; a marvel, a gift to any artist, a son to be proud of.

I sighed, and patted his hand. If only he'd been my real son. If only I'd been able to get him a decent education. If only…But it wasn't too late, it wasn't. There were courses he could take, he was intelligent, a quick learner when he wanted to be, he could pull himself out of this mess. I'd help him, I'd do anything for him: he was my boy, my dear, good lad; we'd sort him out, get him proper help, get his temper under control, get him off the drugs and out of the Life. Never give up. As long as you never gave up, there was hope.

He smiled at me, his chipped front tooth only adding an urchin charm to his face. He had his 'sorry-I'm-a-bad-lad' look on. Oh, Natty.

It worked when you were ten, but you're a grown man now. Jesus, this was hard. I wanted to hug him and pet him like he was a kiddie again, but I couldn't.

He gestured at the letters still spread out where I'd put them. 'You got a secret admirer, Auntie B? These your old love letters? I'm jealous.' His voice was hoarse and as he smiled again, the lamplight showed the fatigue in his face, plum shadows discolouring the fine, silky skin under his eyes, too sharp an angle at the curve of his jawbone.

'Not love letters, darlin'. Well, not that sort of love. They're letters from my dadda; you remember, I told you he ran off when I was little...'

'Jus' like my dad. I remember. I used to feel sorry for you, y'know, cause we were in the same boat, like. You don't mind, do you? You don't mind me bein' sorry for you? I don't mean it nasty, jus' – oh, you know. I wanted us ter be the same, then it meant we'd allus be together.'

'Oh, Natty, sweetheart...'

And I told him everything.

He cried, not bothering to hide it this time, the hard man dissolved in the cauldron of his pain. The tears tumbled out of his amber eyes just like the tears fell from his mother's green ones – crystalline, clinging like diamonds to his eyelashes. No red swollen face, no snotty gasping. Just those pure tears falling onto my neck as I held him close and rocked him like I'd done when he was a child. He cried and cried, clutching me tightly, his strong hands digging into my back as he called for his mother and begged me to make it all alright. I listened to him swearing he'd do anything, everything if only Jas didn't die, if only everything would be OK: I heard him cursing his grandmother for getting us all into this mess with the newspaper and pleading with God to send his father home so he could help him carry this burden. It was like a dull blade sawing at my heart.

Children cry and you kiss it better, put a sticky-plaster on their knee even if they don't really need one, put them to bed with a hot water bottle. Your child that is now a man cries and it breaks your heart because there's nothing you can do anymore, except love him. And I did love him, I loved him so much it eclipsed everything else, time stood still, the moon covered the sun and in that still, heavy dark

I kissed his sweet face and told him the loving lies every mother has ever told their child, even though he wasn't my child and I should have been his mother.

Eventually, he lay back, exhausted. I moved my letters and put them on the chest of drawers; Ghengis jumped down crossly and padded out, disinterested in these petty human dramas that disturbed his rest. I lay beside Natty, stroking his hot forehead, pushing his damp dreads off his face.

'Poor Natty, poor baby. It'll be OK, love, it will, we'll make it OK, Jas will be OK eventually. It'll just take some time, is all.'

'Billie? When it's all over, when me mam – can we all go live somewhere else? All of us? Monkey too? We got ter get away from this shit hole, it's killin' us; we'll never get right if we stay here, never, I know it. Can we go live by the sea? Do Mam good, sea air. Get her away from all this shit, away from them lot she hangs around with. Can we?'

It was his old dream of a life in the country, the cottage with the roses round the door, the bluebirds in the garden. I looked at his face; under the man's mask a boy looked out, exhausted and hurt.

I patted his cheek. 'Sure, baby. All of us. An' Gheng and Cairo too. How about a big house out Whitby way – or even Cornwall, how about that, hmm? A big old farmhouse near the sea, room for everyone. We could go swimming and you and Monkey could learn to sail a boat an' take Jas out, I could have a proper studio an' I could paint all day; an' we could grow our own veg…'

'The Good Life, eh?' He smiled and butted his forehead against me softly. It had been a longstanding joke, springing from when I'd made my garden, that I'd really wanted to grow my own vegetables and have a goat to milk like a 'right old hippie' as Natty put it; not true, but the gag had run and run. I was pleased he remembered the old tease.

'Yeah, *just* like that. Only no snobby neighbours, eh? We could do the garden, do the farm up nice, with a flat-type thing for everyone and a big communal kitchen with a long table where we'd eat our dinner with stuff from our garden, and…'

'Me an' Monk could catch fish…'

'Yeah, love, you could, you could…' My own tears started then.

'Don't cry, Billie, we'll do it, we will. I'll be good, I swear, I'll not go on like this no more. Don't cry, I love you, Billie, I love you, you're my guardian angel, you are, we're family, don't…'

I reached for a handful of tissues and wiped my face. 'I'm sorry, love, I'm alright, I'm just tired, you know.'

'Yeah. Me too.'

We lay together on the bed, as the night thickened around us.

Chapter Thirty-one

I WOKE WITH THE first thunder; I woke to the tearing white of the lightning and I woke to a man kissing and sucking at my nipple and a hand between my legs, pushing at my flesh, pushing into me.

As I lay, frozen and unbelieving, not daring to move or breathe, the man stopped kissing my breast and moving down my naked belly, began slowly licking me, his strong hands curving under my buttocks, lifting me to his mouth. A savage brew of memory flooded through me like acid: a great jewel made in the shape of an insect devouring a woman; light splintering on yellow lichen, snick, snick the old clasp knife notching the wooden bed head. The feeling of a tongue on me made me frantic with fear; I never could stand that, never, not after that other night so long ago now; but it was here again, happening again, I hadn't escaped, I hadn't and...

Did I scream when the lightning tore the dark again and I saw who it was? I don't remember if I did or not; I don't think I did, I don't think I had the breath for it. I remember bile spilling into my mouth and the savage, churning revulsion; how I suddenly found my strength and twisting, kicked and clawed myself away, huddling against the bedhead, pulling at my djellaba, dragging it down over myself so I wouldn't be naked and exposed in front of the man who should never see me that way, should never touch me that way, should never taste, smell or know me that way.

I remember how he looked at me, his face a sketch of devastation in the dim light, a thing conjured out of copper and sepia, the liquid gleam of his half-closed eye, the ragged tousle of his locks.

He wiped his mouth with the back of his hand. I remember that. I can't forget that. Then I heard my voice, not shouting, but tight and compressed, suppressed into a brute whisper, the sound of the unthinkable; your voice saying things you never thought you'd be made to say; to speak words you would have cut your own tongue out rather than utter.

'Natty, Natty, for God's sake, what you doin'? Are you awake? Are you? D'you know what you just…'

I hoped then, it crept into my heart on dirty, pallid feet. I hoped he was dreaming, didn't know what he'd done, or maybe was still stoned, the drug confusing him, making him in his half-asleep state think I was someone else. I could get over it then, make like it hadn't happened. Forgive him. I hoped; but it was a lie.

He looked at me, his long eyes gone dull, like a dog beaten for a crime it doesn't understand.

'I love yer, Billie.'

'Natty…'

'I love yer. I love yer; it's only what I do fer me mam, it's what I do fer her when she's upset, like. I allus have, allus. Since I were little. It's nice. It's a nice thing ter do. We're sweethearts. She says that. We're sweethearts. We can be sweethearts too, Billie, I love yer, I never want ter lose yer, I want ter make it nice for yer…'

My skin crept on my bones, I exhaled a juddering breath as I felt my stomach turn. Oh, Jesus God in Heaven, no. Not that, not that. Haven't we had enough? Not that. No, it's not fair, it's not fair. But I knew he wasn't lying; for all my lies over the years I knew the still cold truth when I heard it and it was far too late to stop up my ears against that penetrating voice.

'God, Natty, what has she fuckin' done to you? What has she done?' I sounded weak and pitiful to myself, my voice trembling.

He looked at me as he knelt on the end of the bed, his arms wrapped round his belly, like a man holding his guts in. I was shaking; really shaking, tremors running through me uncontrollably. I wanted to piss, to run to the bathroom and scrub myself raw but I couldn't move from the bed. In front of me the child I'd loved, the boy I'd owned as a son in my heart fell slowly into fragments; words tumbling out of his mouth in unconnected spurts, like an abscess breaking.

'...looked like me dad, was the spit of me dad...I saw what that bloke done to her – she showed me, she were black an' blue, I were only nine, she showed me an' she were cryin' then she said come here an give me a kiss, kiss yer poor mammy, an' I did an'...She said now we were proper sweethearts you love me, don't yer, don't yer, you'll never leave me now, we'll be tergether forever, like real...I dint fuck her till I were twelve but then we did – not always but sometimes – I did it she said it were good fer me would mek me relax...It were like I were two people two people in my head an' when I got older I knew it were wrong but it weren't wrong in the flat when we were together then it was how it was, don't yer see? It were how it was but I knew it were dirty I knew it were wrong an' it bust me up in my head an' I get so mad, I get so angry an' I can't tell, I can't tell, see or they'll tek me way, I'll go in a home fer bad lads an' they'll lock Mammy away an' we'll not be sweethearts no more an'...I told that bitch Charmaine, it were everythin' that happened and the gear, it made me say, an' I told her an' she said I were a dirty pervert an' Mammy were a filthy paedo whorebag an' I hit her till she shut up but I had ter run cause I dint want ter stop hittin' her and her face was Mammy's face an' it were all wrong...Now you hate me too, you do, don't yer? You think I'm filth, I can see, I can see, you do – you hate me, you hate me...Ahhh, God, ah, God, God, God, Billie, God, I'm dyin', I'm dyin'...'

'Natty, Natty, no, Natty...'

But he ran. He half jumped, half fell off the bed and he ran, the thunder breaking round us like a great wave, the lightning illuminating him as he ran out of the room and down the stairs and as I stumbled after him calling his name he was out of the back door and over the wall into the cemetery and he was gone. Gone. My boy was gone and the night closed round me in a pounding curtain of rain.

Chapter
Thirty-two

I DIDN'T WANT TO go in to the shop, but it occurred to me, after hours searching the cemetery, and the village, that he might go there; not very likely but I'd run out of other options. Also, I couldn't stay in the house: I had to get out for a little while. I'd showered again, scrubbing myself until my skin was red, stripped the bed and thrown my djellaba in the rubbish bin: but it didn't make me feel any cleaner. I wondered if I'd ever feel clean, if I ever really had; layer upon layer of dirt felting up my soul, ingrained and foul, a dirty silt of lies and brutalities.

Monkey had woken at the sound of all the commotion, but I'd managed to get hold of myself and calm down enough to tell him Natty had had a temper tantrum and run off like he sometimes did: Monkey was worried, but it wasn't that unusual so he settled down to wait for Natty to come back. I suppose I could have told him the truth. Technically he was a grown man, but what good would it do frightening him when he carried enough baggage like that anyway. No, I wasn't that much of a bitch. When I left the house, *The Jungle Book* was on again; Monkey was laid on the sofa wrapped in the blanket that had covered Natty, breathing in, and comforted by his residual smell. But nothing comforted me and I drove to town like a zombie. Really, like the living dead, numb and cold despite the warmth of the storm-washed day.

I had begun to seal the secret in, you see, to wall it up in my heart; brick by relentless brick. That's what I did with stuff like this, I put it away. I wasn't disgusted by Natty, I wasn't shocked. The – I hate even to say it – sexual part had been foul, but I'd get over that; I had to. I wasn't a kid; I'd had worse, in that way. Natty wasn't Steveo, the bastard who'd raped me – Natty was much more the victim in this than me. I genuinely thought that and still do. I don't blame him and for what it's worth, he had my forgiveness from the moment he told me the truth of it, and normally, as I've said, I'm not big on forgiving.

I was horrified, yes, and full of a white-hot rage at the thought of Jas and the wicked thing she'd done out of desperate weakness, selfishness and ignorance. It was a blessing, I thought grimly, that she was in hospital, because I would have done her some serious damage if I'd got hold of her. Some part of me that I couldn't rationalise away wished her dead. I wished her dead from the horrible disease she'd contracted because that would be fitting, that would be a raw kind of justice. Not nice, I know, but I couldn't stop thinking it.

I knew stuff like that went on. Incest. Child abuse, whatever. I can't imagine any adult not being aware of things like that happening. I know lots of folk try never to think of stuff like that and deny it when it's bang in front of them, but they're just pathetic. Worse really, they're cruel, because it's that kind of wilful blindness that allows it all to go on. Fathers at their daughters, brothers at their sisters, uncles, grandfathers, you name it. There's much more notice taken of it nowadays than when I was a kid. But most people still think it's only men that do it. Women couldn't, mothers couldn't – it would be the most unnatural thing possible, surely. Jesus, I tell you what – think of the worst thing one human being could do to another. The very, very worst thing. Thought of it? Right; as I live and breathe, I swear to you now that at this very moment, someone is doing something twenty times worse than that to someone else. A child, a woman, an old person, a prisoner of conscience, a slave – yes, a slave, because that's not gone away, either. Men to men, women to women, women to children, men to babies, anything, anyone; we're the cruellest species, the most inventive predators ever.

But still, a mother using her son for…It was vile. The ultimate taboo. With all the things I'd seen and known and smelt and swallowed, this – this stinking foulness Jas had done to Natty was a spike in my mind, as cruelly painful as a deep glass cut – if I had been his mother, you see, this would never have happened, this would have been impossible.

I thought of Jas's wheedling voice, those spidery fingers touching Natty in that way, the awful parody of their being 'sweethearts' – my God, how many times had I heard her call him that? It made me shudder. How many times had I heard her say they were 'real sweethearts' and tell me how much she loved her boy especially now he was 'the man of the house'. I had a sickening thought that if I'd said straight out to her '*Are you fucking Natty?*' she'd have rolled those great eyes under her fluttering lids and moaned on about how lonely she was and how she missed Terry and how Natty had wanted 'the comfort' of it as much as she had, they loved each other, it wasn't a crime to love each other...I'd have hurt her, then. I know I would have.

But so much made sense now. How Natty was, the rage, the moods, the violence. What had he said? – '*I'm two people in my head*' – the tension of carrying that around day in, day out for all those years must have been appalling. I knew what carrying a secret was alright, no one knew better than me the galling weight of it, the way it spread to every part of your world, tainted everything you did; the way it made you lie all the time to cover it up until you'd half-forgotten the truth.

But the truth would always come out, sometime or other. It would rise up like a blue-white tide of ice out of the dark cold depths of your ruined self and crush you out of existence. I knew that because I'd spent the last twenty-odd years waiting for it to happen to me.

I got into the shop before Leckie arrived and took a few moments to get myself together, to make myself into a normal person; another lie, of course, but in this case, Leckie and Monkey shared the same space in my mind – how you would have hated that, Lecks – but I mean that each in your own way, you were innocent and I didn't want to be the one to spoil that. Anyway, as anyone whose had shit happen to them will tell you, life has to go on. Like it or not, we're none of us characters in some beach-book thriller where when the victim dies horribly the hero wanders off doing detective stuff and never seems to worry about money, his job or his family and friends. He just puts it all on hold until he's solved the fascinating mystery. Well, sorry, but it's not like that in real life; so I opened the shop fifteen minutes early, sold three cards, a sheet of expensive heavy art wrapping paper and a leather-bound notebook.

Then I set the kettle on. My hands hardly shook at all. I was proud of myself, then. It proved that I could cope.

But by three that afternoon, I was flagging, physically. I still had the remnants of a cold, I was exhausted from lack of sleep, worn out from jumping every time someone came in the shop in case it was Natty, and knackered from plain old worry; I was, as they say and in this case quite literally, worried fucking sick. I retired to the office to shuffle papers around.

Leckie brought me some tea and stood in the doorway enthusing about her new guru Ben Thorby. She'd been practising her 'customer culture' (one of his amazing marketing concepts, apparently) on every poor sap that trundled in and frightening them half to death since Bradford isn't Los Angeles and Yorkshire folk aren't used to megawatt smiles and glad cries of '*You're so, so welcome, have a really great day, now*' when they buy a one pound fifty greetings card. I usually save that kind of thing for the ones who buy a matching rainbow moonstone necklace, earrings and bracelet set, such as the one in the window going for a hundred and fifty quid. But apparently, the Thorby Method is to make every customer, no matter how minute the purchase, feel they're really, really special so that in comparison to the non-Thorby trained surly indifference of your competition, the punters long for an excuse to revisit you and buy something else so they can bask in the warmth of your undivided attention. Yeah, right.

Leckie was beginning to frighten me, never mind the customers. Her plans for our expansion were astonishing, we were going to be not merely a gift shop but a 'wellspring of human contact', a 'source of authentic exchange' and 'a hub of community communications networking'. That last bit referred to sending someone a birthday card.

'...so what it is, really, I mean, you know, basically, is that Ben thinks we need to put the *warmth* back into sales, what's missing in the, duh' – Leckie did that finger-squiggly quotes thing – '*millennium culture* – the modern world if you like, are values, real human values. Ben says...'

'Oh, it's *Ben* now, is it? I see. Did you get his autograph, then?'

'Billie, really. You are dreadful – you're not even listening, are you?' She bridled, tugging at the straps of her turquoise lace-edged strappie vest and flipping her hair. I didn't like to tell her she looked cute when she was narky.

'Soz, sweetie. I am listening, I am – well, sort of, I'm just – I'm just knackered, it's great, what you're saying, I agree with you – and *Ben* – but I'm dead beat, honestly. Natty came round last night and…'

Suddenly, I was crying. It came out of nowhere, a great gulping, heave of tears. Leckie rushed in and hugged me while I fumbled for a tissue and mumbled about being over-tired and everything that had happened and Natty running off – and part of me longed to tell her the truth, the awful, unsayable truth. But I couldn't.

'Billie, *go home* – no really, go. Get a proper night's sleep. Take tomorrow off, get well. You're worn out, love, and no wonder – my God, it's been completely *mad* the last week or so, really crazy, *anyone* would be exhausted after what you've gone through. No, I insist – come on, it's not like you ever dump on me usually, you're as straight as a die – I mean, when did you last take a holiday? I think I can put up with looking after things here for, like – duh – a few days on my own. I'm a big girl, you know, I can manage perfectly well.'

She shook her finger at me, and rolled her eyes. Underneath the cheery act I could see she was genuinely concerned about me, God love her. I sighed, and wiped my face with the soggy tissue.

'Yeah, you're right, I know you are. Just don't bloody Thorbyise the whole shop while I'm gone, OK?' I managed a wavery smile.

I got my stuff together and trailed off, waving goodbye to Lecks as she was Thorbying a customer by the New Age section. She was right. I had to get some sleep, I'd be no good to Natty in this state and I had to be one hundred per cent on the ball when he came back – and he would come back, I was sure of that. He knew in his heart I loved him and that I always would, no matter what. He knew I was his refuge and I'd get him the help he needed. He might be in a state now, but he'd cool down in a bit and where would he go? He couldn't go back to the flat and he'd hardly go to Charmaine; possibly he'd crash with one of his buddies for a night or two but in the end, he come back. Tomorrow I'd take the opportunity of being off sick to ring round some places, get some idea of how to go about sorting Natty out.

As I drove back home, I saw that the leaves were starting, faintly but definitely, to turn. Maybe someone else wouldn't have seen it but colour means so much to me and I like to notice stuff like that. The deep summer green was tinged with yellow, autumn was on its way.

As I turned into my lane, I saw the police car. I saw two coppers get out and go towards Monkey, who was running back and forth in front of my house like a rabbit trapped in a dead end by dogs; frantic, he tried to get past the male copper, who got hold of his arm, not unkindly, but Monkey freaked. I think it was then, at the sight of Monkey's face, that I knew. I don't know how, or why, but I knew. I parked and scrambled out of the car. As I ran towards them I heard Monkey gabbling, terrified. The copper told him to get calm, but it was useless, Monkey was petrified of the police at the best of times and he began to struggle wildly, his T-shirt twisting in the copper's grip, as he tried to wriggle out of it and escape. Then he saw me.

'Miss, Miss Billie Miss, Miss Billie Miss, Natty, Natty come, Natty come but he locked me out, Miss, he's in an' he locked me out…Summat wrong, Miss, summat…Natty, Miss Billie, Natty…'

The female copper turned towards me. She was little, blonde, with a child's peaked face, her stab-vest giving her a clumsy bulk. I couldn't seem to hear what she was saying; I could hear Monkey alright, but not anything else. The copper frowned and spoke again. Suddenly I heard her, as if someone had turned the volume up. She sounded distorted and unreal, I could understand her words but they meant nothing to me. I was flooded with irritation, she was between me and the cottage. Between me and Natty.

'You know this man? We had a call to say someone was trying to burgle this property and we…'

I opened my mouth and words came out. 'Do I know . . ? Yes, yes I do – this is my house, please, let him go, he won't go anywhere, please, he's frightened, I'll explain, only I've got to…'

It was as if the sound had been turned off completely then. It was as if I was in a weird film. I saw everything, slightly skewed and far away, but all I could hear was my blood pounding in my ears and my breath rushing in the tight cage of my chest and everything was slow, very slow and I couldn't get the key in the door. I knew the coppers were talking to me, and I could see Monkey still in the copper's grip and there was Mrs Leach saying something with D'Arcy struggling in her arms but…I couldn't get the fucking key in the lock and then I did, and the door opened and I ran in knowing, knowing that something was wrong, and a voice in my head started screaming *Natty, Natty, Natty* only it wasn't in my head, I was really screaming, and I ran to the stairs because I thought, he'll be in my room, he'll be there, just sleeping or something and he'll jump up, startled by me yelling and we'll hug and I'll tell him how much, how incredibly much I love him and how everything will be alright and then we'll laugh at all this and stupid Mrs Leach ringing the cops and…

Chapter
Thirty-three

THEY WERE VERY NICE, the coppers. Years back, I used to be like everyone else I knew, spouting knee-jerk guff about pigs and fascists, but they were decent with me throughout the whole thing, they did their best. Ironic, really – if only I'd thought they'd be like that all those years ago, none of this would have happened. But that's sour, spilt milk and I've cried enough over it, I've got no tears left for that.

Anyhow, he'd been – gone, for a while, apparently, before I found him. There was nothing any of us could have done. Nothing I could have done. They assured me of that, I couldn't have saved him or anything. He'd done a proper job of it, but they couldn't say if he'd been in any pain – he must have been, I suppose, he must have suffered but they said it had probably been very quick. I don't believe that, myself. But I don't dwell on it, because – you don't. That's all I can say. Anyone who's had similar will understand. You can't. You'd go mad.

He must have watched me go – at least, that's what I think. He must have watched then let himself back in, got the old climbing rope Johnjo used as a tow-rope, and after chucking Monkey out – you see, I think that shows he loved Lee really, that he didn't want him to see what he was going to do – he went upstairs, pulled the attic ladder down, went up, tied the rope to the joists, pulled the ladder back up out of the way and – I can't. I can't.

So I found him, and I tried to push him up, I tried to take the weight off the rope and Monkey tried to help me but he was screaming so hard he was no use. I was – I tried so hard to – but it was no use, of course, and there was the smell and the – look of him, the dreadful, swollen, ruined look of him who had been so beautiful and the coppers came and they checked, you know, to see if he was still alive but I saw it on their faces and so did Monkey and if I live to be a thousand, I will never forget poor Lee's face, because you could see him dying too. He ran, then, and I've never seen him since, though I would have been glad to, some nights. It would have been nice just to sit, not talking, but remembering Natty.

I don't suppose there are many people in the world who haven't lost someone they love. Everyone tells you you'll get over it, that you must get on with your life – in one stupid magazine I read they said you shouldn't mourn for longer than six months because it wasn't healthy. Jesus; I'll mourn the rest of my life and not a day passes when he isn't in it. I don't care if folk think I'm morbid or all those other stupid words they use when you don't grin like a chimp all the time and dribble out the usual platitudes to make them feel comfortable.

The hardest part for me was that for ages, the image of him in death kept intruding, overlaying the memories of him I wanted to see. I'd think of him – maybe see a lad whose swaggering, youthful walk reminded me of Natty, maybe read about a film I think he'd have liked, and I'd see my boy's smiling face, as a child, or as a man, and like a stain, the image of him so cruelly distorted by what he'd done would bloom like a dirty weed and cover everything. It's passing a bit now, but for I can't tell you how long, it was a real torment.

And the nightmares, of course, they were – still are – bad. The doctor gave me some pills, but they made the dreams worse. I'd struggle and struggle to wake as the tears choked me but the drug would keep me asleep, always trying to hold him up, to take the weight off the fucking rope. So I stopped taking anything like that and I refused the Prozac too, which made them think I was totally weird, but sod them. Everyone deals with things how they can; I'm not going to be one of those glassy-eyed robot women off the estates you see in the doctor's waiting room; nothing changes, they still want to drug us into submission.

At least all the official things are over now; the inquest, the funeral. I won't go into the awfulness of the service at the crematorium; that squat brick building that looks more like an old public toilet than a place to honour the dead. The bloody priest or whoever she was who droned on about Natty – who she didn't know from Adam – cut down 'in the flower of his youth'. Just the three of us were there, Pauline Skinner in a leopardette fur-trimmed coat looking like a 1940's French hooker gone to seed, faithful old Bobby and me, at the back, in black because I didn't have anything else. I've been in mourning all my fucking life. Pauline had a go at me, of course; she loved every minute of it, yelling, screeching and pretending to faint when Bobby gathered her into his wobbly stick-thin arms. She got her revenge though, she got Natty's ashes and took them off with her, back to her flat no doubt, though I wouldn't put it past her to tote them round the pub in order to get drinks bought while she played the grieving granny. God knows what she'll do with them in the end.

I would have scattered his ashes up on the moors out Baildon way on a cool, bright golden day. We'd gone there often when he was little for walks, picnics, an ice cream from the old dairy. That's where I'd have left my wild boy, with the foxes and the kestrels, his energy feeding the heather and the bilberries he loved to pick and eat until his little face was smeared with purple – ah, it hurts, you know? Still, forever, it hurts so much, so much. It makes me desperate with the pain sometimes, that I'll never see him again, that he did such a terrible thing. I love him so much, never to see him again is beyond any pain I've ever known.

At least I didn't have to see Jas. I couldn't have borne that. I rang the hospital of course, to have them tell her. She's not dead yet; in fact, they said she's improving slowly. They asked me if I'd be caring for her if she survived, came out of hospital. I put the phone down. Let them think what they like.

So anyway, I'm all packed, ready to go. Ghenghis and Cairo are living with Leckie's parents – such good people. Gheng is having a whale of a time tyrannising Leckie's mum, poor woman. She even makes mushroom gravy and freezes it into cubes in the ice-tray so he can have individual portions with his dinner. Crazy; I've told her he's an old bastard but she loves to look after animals, people, any creature in need. I miss them, my cats, my old loves, my pals, but the cottage is gone, sold near enough straight away for a huge profit, apparently. People from Leeds moving out into the villages because prices in that terracotta mini-London have gone through the roof. Whatever, I don't care. I took the first offer and banked it. Leckie's got the shop – I'm a sleeping? silent? whatever it is partner. She can Thorbyise it to her heart's content. She'll do well, better than I did, I don't doubt. As long as she's happy, that's all I care about.

It's raining outside. Chilly. I rented this place without really looking at it – there's no central heating, just a gas fire in every room. Typical Bradford, that. Freeze your arse off every winter. I'll be glad to see the back of it, truth be told.

Christ, it's sileing it down, the rain's beading the window, I can see my reflection in the dark glass, covered in tears. It was like this the night we went to Terry's. Raining, cold, me in my old black jumper, pictures in my head, and a big gaping hole in my heart. Poor Micky, you did your best with me. You tried to save me but it was fucked from the minute Terry opened the door. If God really is a gambler, He'd rolled the dice in the slant of light that cut into the night as that idiot opened his door to more than he could ever have imagined.

Terry stood there in his leather jacket, check shirt and filthy Levis, dirty, mud-crusted steelies unlaced over grubby fisherman's socks. He smelt terrible, a thick sweat-sour funk overlaid with the whiff of rancid bacon fat. My nose wrinkled at the odour and something prickled in the back of my mind, something…I knew that smell, what was it? I mean apart from BO, no, it wasn't just that, it was…

Terry grinned mirthlessly like a death's head. 'Fookin' hell. Royalty, eh, eh? Fook me. Ha ha fookin' ha, well, well, don't fookin' stand there, come in, welcome ter my 'umble fookin' abode, yer majesties, don't mind the mess, I say, don't mind the mess, it's the maid's day off! See? The maid's day off! Fookin' hell…'

He was speeding off his tits, his weaselly face blanched to a bloodless fish-belly white and drawn, his nose red raw, his eyes brilliant and pinned. He must have been up for days; spending his compensation money, no doubt. That's why he smelt like that, it was the typical whizz-head's stink, the by-product of his liver and kidneys overloading, unable to process fast enough. I coughed. Jesus, to smell like that he must have been on a king-size bender and no mistake. Faintly, at the back of my mind a warning bell sounded and I heard Carl's voice: 'Never trust a speed freak, eh? Fucked up bastards, all of 'em – you never fuckin' know what they're gonna do next…'

'Now then, Terry,' Micky tried to sound affable. 'You gonna ask us in proper, like?'

Terry wiped his nose and shook his matted yellow hair. His hand was shaking and he jerked and twitched, unable to keep still. 'Yeah, yeah, don't mind me, man, fuck, just a bit – just havin' a laugh, y'know. Come in, come in, eh. A brew, fancy a brew, gotta cold 'un int fridge, got all sorts, wine for the lady, fancy a bit of wine, then, lasses like wine, don't they, eh? Eh? Summat sweet, like, summat tasty…'

I looked at Micky and made a what-the-fuck face at him as Terry stumbled off to the fridge. The room was a shambles, filthy beyond belief. It looked like one of those mediaeval paintings of a peasant's hovel and it was freezing cold mostly due to the uncarpeted stone flags and the defunct Aga. Dirty clothes and boots were jumbled everywhere mixed with engine parts and tools; the stink of shitty keks, rotting inner soles and rancid engine oil made a pungent and repulsive incense. There was a rickety table covered in bottles, ashtrays overflowing with tabs and roaches, and surprise surprise – a mirror tile still dusty with speed, a razor blade and a rolled tenner beside it. A half-empty baggie of whizz lay open, its contents – and there was enough there to get an army going – drifting out in a powdery veil. Terry had been having himself a ball, alright. I shifted an old leather coat and perched on the edge of the knackered sofa that was patinated with grease and food stains. Micky sat next to me, not so bothered about the dirt since his jeans were nearly as filthy anyway.

I grabbed Micky's arm and hissed in his ear, 'He's wasted – come on, let's get the gear and fuck off, he gives me the creeps.'

Micky patted my shoulder. 'No probs, Princess, he don't do much fer me neither.'

'Now then, now then, what you two lovebirds whisperin' about, eh?' Terry leered at us, showing his brown stumpy teeth and an awesome cold sore in the corner of his mouth. It looked painful, but it wasn't as painful as his disgusting, rotten breath. I gagged and covered it with a fake cough as he leant over me, shoving a half-empty bottle of British sherry into my hand and a cold Budweiser – the new style American beer just coming into fashion with the lads – into Micky's.

'Here's to yer, here's to yer then, eh? Eh? Drink up, go on, let's have a party. My leavin' do, I'm off, I'm off me, goin' ter the Dam, that's where it's at, man, that's the place ter be fer a guy like me, movin' an' shakin', gettin' some good gear an' some o' that Dutch bird action.' He sniggered, snorting through his nose. Bubbles of bloody snot bloomed from his nostrils and he wiped them away with his thin fingers. 'Wot yer think of that Yank brew then, Mick, piss weak ter my mind, still, that's Yanks fer yer, int it, no bottle – get it? Get it? No bottle, fuck me…' He bent double, wheezing with hoarse laughter at his joke. I looked at Micky again and raised my eyebrows.

Terry saw me. With the startling mood change of the speed freak he snapped out of hysterics into paranoia. His face seemed to collapse inwards, as if it had been sucked back onto his skull, his sulphurous eyes igniting.

He leant towards me, his scrawny neck extending in a horrible, unnatural way, and he hissed at me – really hissed, like a cat.

'Wot you come 'ere for? Wot? Eh? Eh? You…'

Micky put a restraining hand on Terry's arm. 'Come on, mate, leave it. We come ter get some downers off yer – if yer can't oblige, well, no harm…'

Terry subsided, grumbling. 'Oh, right, right. I get it, yer come ter me when yer need summat, otherwise…' He got up, still mumbling and scrabbled around in a kitchen cabinet standing by the Aga. I could hear him talking to himself and tugged at Micky's sleeve.

'I should never have asked yer to do this, I'm sorry,' I whispered desperately. 'Look, let's just go, eh? Let's just…'

Faster than I would have thought possible for a man in his state, Terry whipped round and shot across to Micky, an old World War One bayonet in his hand, the steel of it dull grey, the edges nicked. I knew that blade, it had been traded round the lads but no one had wanted to keep it for long, there was something about it, something bad; we had superstitions like that, bad blades, devil bikes, inanimate things that had a kind of cursed life. Terry had been made up when he'd finally got hold of it in exchange for some engine bits. He'd held it in the pub, weighing it in his hand, going on about how many men it had gutted. Now he held it pushed up against Micky's throat.

Thick white spittle flecked his lips and his yellow eyes bulged, shot through with red. 'Ya fuckers, ya fuckers – too good fer the likes of me usually, aren't yer? You an' little Miss High An' Mighty, that fuckin' Carl's bit on the fuckin' side – oh, yeah, we all know, we all know he's givin' it one. I'm not worth yer spit in the pub, am I? Am I? Won't pass the fuckin' time of fuckin' day wi' scum like me normally, will yer? But when yer wants a bit o' summat then it's all *Ooooh Terry can we come in, Oooooh Terry, I'll 'ave a fuckin' drink wi yer…* Oh yeah, yer come ter me, ter *me*, when yer want a bit of gear – bastards, bastards, I seen yer whisperin', laughin' – well you int laughing now, are yer, eh? Eh? I could do you, you fucker, I could do yer an' that cunt an' no one would ever find me cause I'm off an' I'll never come back, me never…'

The heavy blade wavered in his hand and through the awful thudding of my heart and the shock of adrenalin, I could see Micky shifting, about to throw himself sideways – but so did Terry and raising the knife he shrieked and started forwards…

Then the blinding rage flashed through me like a bomb detonating; the fucker, no, he wouldn't hurt my Micky, the stinking bastard – I flung myself at him, my whole weight crashing into him, shoving him sideways and back and he fell hard, me on top of him: without thinking, reflexively, I grabbed his shirt front and slammed his head onto the stone floor with a sickening, crunching thud.

Simultaneously, I started to clamber off Terry as Micky grabbed the bayonet from his outstretched hand and dropped it onto the sofa. Terry didn't move. I turned to tell Micky we had to get out of there, when Terry started to fit. I know now he was fitting, then I had no idea what was happening, why he was arching and juddering uncontrollably, his eyes rolling back in his head as if he was being electrocuted. I screamed and clutched Micky as we both stepped back, out of the way of those flailing, thrashing limbs.

Then it stopped. Micky and I stood there, holding each other in horror, in that filthy, disgusting room while Terry lay still on the floor and we both realised something was wrong and for a second, we both seemed to hear a terrible roaring sound, as if a whirlwind had come into the cottage and I buried my face in Micky's chest while we both cowered at whatever it was – and then it was gone. The room was still and utterly silent; as cold and quiet as a high country tarn.

We stood, frozen, and looked at Terry. Then, cautiously, I knelt and gingerly pushed Terry's shoulder.

'Terry, Terry – are you…Terry, I'm gonna phone an ambulance, Terry, can you…' I looked up at Micky who stood, unmoving, his face stark white. I patted Terry's shoulder again and his head suddenly lolled on his neck; startled, I scrambled backwards and crouched there, waiting for Micky to speak, to do something, but he just stood there, staring.

It was then I first felt panic. It began in my guts, twining up through my limbs, hot, like simmering oil. I felt couldn't bear to touch Terry again, but shakily, talking myself through it, I felt for a pulse in the outflung wrist. Nothing. I must have done it wrong. I tried again.

'Micky, Micky, is this right? Is this the right way…?

He stood there, silent, beginning to shake and I knew with a dreadful feeling in my guts that I'd have to deal with this. For a moment, I fought against it: it wasn't fair, I couldn't, why should I? He was the bloke, he was supposed to be the one who…It was no use, I had to. It wasn't Micky's fault he couldn't do stuff like this – but I could, I knew I could. I had to get control of everything, and quickly. I struggled to my feet and grabbed the mirror tile, wiping the speed off it with my sleeve. I knelt again and held it over Terry's parted lips. Nothing. No breath clouded the surface. I wiped it and tried again, my hands shaking now, hot tears welling up in my eyes, my throat constricted. Nothing.

He was dead. I'd killed him. I'd killed a man.

I dropped the tile, which broke; seven years' bad luck I thought stupidly, as I stood up, my hands over my mouth to stop myself screaming.

'Micky, Micky – I think – I think he's dead, he's dead…' My voice was rising to a shriek and I wanted to howl like a dog; what had I done, what in the name of God had I done?

Micky stumbled backwards and sat down heavily on the sofa, then he looked at me and shook his head dumbly.

'Micky, what shall I do? What shall…'

'Phone the coppers.' The words seemed to have been heaved out of his mouth.

Then it hit me and I staggered slightly, my knees gone to jelly, my guts griping: the coppers? Everything crowded in on me, suffocating, as image after image tumbled through my head. I'd be arrested – no, we'd be arrested because the coppers would never believe Micky was innocent; one of the Devil's Own, an outlaw biker, a gang member? They'd have him down the cells quick as a flash. I could see with awful clarity how it looked; a drugs deal gone wrong, Micky's fingerprints all over the bayonet, signs of a struggle everywhere, speed and God knows what all else stashed around the house. We were scum to the coppers, how many times had we been harassed, persecuted and generally given shit by policemen all too willing to believe the worst of the likes of us?

We'd go down; life imprisonment. No one would care what really happened. Our lives would be over and while I could face that on my own account, if I had to, I couldn't bear the thought of my beloved Micky in prison, forever, for a crime he'd had no part of.

'We can't call the coppers,' I croaked, my throat tight and sore.

'What? We have ter. He's – he's dead. We have ter.' The look of desolation on his sweet face was unbearable. Micky in prison? Christ, he wouldn't last a month. I seemed to see Carl's face and hear him say '*He's weak. You remember that, he's weak an' one day you'll know it, see.*' And I did know it; I knew it in the deepest part of me: Micky was weak and I wasn't. I had to save us both, I had to find the strength from somewhere.

It was then I made my biggest mistake. I gave in to panic; that wheedling music snagged my brain and I stopped thinking and danced to that mad archaic tune instead.

Turning to the table, I licked two fingers and stuck them in the bag of speed. Great lumps of the coarse whizz adhered to my wet flesh. I sucked the bitter powder down, then did it again, rubbing it round my gums, waiting for the buzz to start, the hit to climb my bones and give me that savage, glorious strength I desperately wanted. I had loved speed, and now I needed it. That's what I thought. *I needed it.* Speed would be a tool and a weapon to help me get us salvation. Pan laughed, then; and the world yawed out of logic, time and space.

And it came like God kickstarting my brain. Hot and heavy, the chemical flared in my blood. Terry had got some good stuff, alright, it was monstrously strong. I shuddered, and then almost immediately I knew what I had to do. It was the only way out, but we had to move fast. We had to get rid of the body, of Terry, and forget any of this ever happened. I felt my whole will concentrate to a diamond point of light as the drug surged through me. I dabbed some more and told Micky my plan.

He started crying, then. In some faraway part of my mind I felt desperate pity for him, but the rest of me paid no heed. Terry was about to vanish anyway, I argued, no one would look for him, no one would care. I pulled Micky up, cursing, and while he stood shivering I found a ragged candlewick bedspread from the other room and made Micky help me pull Terry's boots and leather jacket off, and roll him up in it. There was no blood, nothing, but when I accidentally touched the back of Terry's skull as I manoeuvred the bedspread over his face, it gave slightly and I felt a wave of nausea pass through me, and I had to stop for a moment and get myself back together.

I put the baggie of speed in my pocket and sent Micky to reverse the van up to the door. I freaked a little then, frightened Micky would take off. But he didn't, and we lumped Terry into the back. It was easy. Amazingly easy. We went back in and I stood in the middle of the room and looked round frantically. We needed tools to get rid of the body. I spotted what I needed by the window in a jumble of other stuff.

'Micky, get the fuckin' pickaxe – over there – an' that spade, the big one. Don't argue, just get it, get it for fuck's sake…'

'Billie, don't, don't do this…'

'*Get the fuckin' stuff*,' I screamed at him, my face burning hot in the chill of the unheated room. In my head I could hear a voice saying save him, save him and he'll forgive you. You can make it alright tomorrow but tonight you've got to save him.

I looked around. There was no way, in that mess, you could tell anything had happened. I hustled Micky out and shut the door behind us. We drove away, and I told Micky – no, I forced Micky – to drive out towards the country. It doesn't take long, round here. People don't realise how close the country is to Bradford. The rain was still falling, but behind the scrim of clouds, the full moon was bright, making the night slightly bleached, with a strange, numinous quality; you could see pretty clearly. *I* could see everything in brilliant, drug-fuelled detail and I rocked back and forth in the passenger seat refusing to think about what lay in the back of the vehicle. Finally, I saw a small road turning up through two big fields thickly hedged with hawthorn and beyond, a copse of trees and more fields. I made Micky pull up in a passing place by a field gate. The land beyond the gate was ploughed, it would be easy to dig.

'Get out. We'll do it here – come on, for fuck's sake, we gotta be quick.'

He turned to me, misery pinching his broad face, his eyes imploring. 'I can't, I – don't make me, Billie, please, I love you, don't…'

I slapped his face, as hard as I could. I'd never hit him in anger before: I'd had no cause to. He dropped his gaze and I pulled his face up by the chin. 'Get. Out. Of. The. *Van*. D'you hear me? There's no time for this; God, I love you, I love you with all my heart and soul but not now, not now, Micky. Come *on*.'

The fresh air woke me even more and I helped Micky drag Terry to the gate and then inside. I found a place by the hedge that I thought looked neglected. The pale bedspread looked leprously white in the dimness and I was jumping with terror in case anyone should drive past and spot it somehow, or wonder what the van was doing in the lay-by.

'Dig – dig there.'

'No, I won't, I…'

'Fuckin' dig – Christ, it's too late, Micky, it's too late to stop now, they'll do us double if they catch us here like this, please, please, baby, come on…'

I fell to my knees in the soft earth and the smells of dirt, wet scrubby grass and the strange, pungent scent of the hawthorn leaves filled my head as I scratched and scraped at the ground with my bare hands, the rain soaking me through, wetting my face as I looked up at Micky. He couldn't see my tears because of that, and he couldn't hear my heart breaking.

He fetched the pickaxe and the spade, and dug, then. Love is a two-faced thing, dark and light; maybe he was thinking the same as me, that when this was over, we'd make it alright again. I don't know, I'll never know. But I think he still loved me at that point, so he did what he had to do to make it be over fast: he stopped thinking and gave himself over to his physicality, doing what he knew he could do best – be a strong man. If only that strength had been in his mind, too, but if wishes were granted, I wouldn't be writing this for you to read, would I?

I don't know how long it took, an hour? Less, I think, I really don't know. Micky dug and unable to keep still, I kept pushing the loose dirt into a muddy pile, trying to stop it from crumbling back into the diggings or crept along by the hedge to the gate to see if anyone was watching us. I was terrified we'd be seen and kept thinking I heard cars coming, or dogs barking. But it was a cold, rainy night. No one was about. I heard Micky grunt sometimes as he struggled, but we didn't speak; what could we have said?

Only the top layer of the ground was really wet, underneath the rich soil was just damp. I piled the earth up ready to put back in the big hole that Micky had made, his muscles and his broad back flexing as he shovelled the muck like a train; a golem, animated clay that looked at me with dead eyes and did as I bid him. Finally, I judged we'd done enough and sucking another finger full of mud and speed, I stopped him. He stood in the hole, soaking wet, his T-shirt stuck to his body, waiting – for what? For orders? I couldn't bear it. I looked away, that pitiful mantra chanting in my head. Tomorrow you'll make it alright. He'll forgive you if you save him; but counterpointing it was Carl's voice whispering *He's weak, he's weak*…And I'm strong, I thought as the drug hit again, I'm *so fucking strong* I could rip the stars from the sky to save him and I will if that's what it takes.

Grabbing hold of Terry, I dragged him, my back cracking, to the side of the pit. Micky crawled out and lay on the ground, exhausted.

Taking hold of the edge of the bedspread, with a grunt, I pulled it and rolled Terry into the hole. He landed face up. I wiped my sore eyes in relief and looked.

It was too short. The hole was too fucking short. Terry's long, skinny legs rested grotesquely up at an angle, ankles on the edge of the grave. The bedspread had twisted away as he'd fallen in and his legs in their dirty jeans were straight as sticks. I could see him, his neck bent, head pushed forward, rain falling on the insensate jelly of his staring eyes, mouth gaping, smeared with mud, clotted with mud…

I laughed, then. It was funny, it was a joke. The laughter chopped through me harsh as the drug. His legs, his legs, fuck me; I laughed until I fell on my knees, coughing like a hag, a thin acid bile burning my throat. Then suddenly, I was serious again. No time to fall apart, no time, no fucking time. Gotta move, gotta get a move on. I got up and staggered over to Micky.

'Get up, get up, get the spade, it's too short, the hole's too short, he don't fit.'

Micky groaned and rolled into a shivering ball. 'I can't dig no more, God help us, Billie, don't make me.'

The world was a white electric dazzle; I was completely calm; as cruelly pure as a fighting angel. My voice was still, but intensely concentrated in the wet air. I felt as if I was in a bright glass capsule, suspended a little off the churned earth, the rain bouncing off the hard, shining thing I was. I was exultant and terrible, there wasn't room for mercy in the place I was.

'I don't want you to dig,' I said. 'Break his legs with the spade. Make him fit.'

There was a silence then like the cessation of everything that moved and breathed on the earth; Micky got up, the rain plastering his beautiful hair to his head and he looked at me. I saw him looking and I saw *him*, his soul, his spirit, whatever had made him the sweet, loving lad he was, dwindle down through the savage night into Hell.

He picked up the heavy old spade and walking to the edge, swung it high over his head, the great muscles in his back and arms bunching; he brought it down with all his strength and Terry's leg broke just under the knee with a sound that brought all sound back into the universe; an appalling sound – rotten tree branches cracking under a climbing boy, or the noise pack ice makes as it splits in the high Arctic and the black depths embrace you. Micky swung again and Terry's other leg shattered, bending back at a cruel unnatural angle, like a bird's leg; inhuman, repulsive beyond reckoning. The body crumpled slightly into the hole and Micky flung the spade down. Stumbling to the hawthorn, he vomited into the grass, over and over, emptying his body until there was nothing left.

I was drawn out like an infinity of silver wire, my eyes so wide they felt lidless, my mouth drawn into the speed freak's rictus grin. I picked up the spade and pushed the legs down, folding them over until the body – until Terry – settled at the bottom of the pit. Then I started shovelling dirt in; clods and stones dropping in little sodden explosions. I felt nothing except the trance of rhythmic movement, I didn't feel the muscles in my shoulder tearing, the blisters rising then ripping on my hands, the freezing cold; I couldn't see the fields, the night or Micky. I shovelled and shovelled until the pit was filled in and then I tramped the earth flat, shovelled on more earth and tramped that flat too. Then I scattered the remaining dirt on the field and letting the shovel fall, stood like an arrow notched to fly, in the rain, with my face to the sky, my bloody hands stretched out at my sides. Opening my jaws I screamed silently until my raw throat closed and I staggered, the weight of what I'd done settling on me, a burden that would only grow, not diminish, with time.

That's what I did. That's what I made Micky do. No one ever found Terry's body, but then, no one's ever looked for it. I could take you there and show you the spot, if you liked; I've never gone back there since that night. Maybe one day the farmer will dig it up by chance, but that's a fate I can't control.

So you see, I am a murderer; but it's not Terry I regret killing, in the sense of taking his life. His life was worthless but his dying was devastation and despair. I'm a murderer because I killed Micky that night. I truly believed, because I was young and didn't know as much about the world as I thought I did, that I was saving him, but I was wrong and it cost me everything. The lies that started spawning that night grew into a mass so choking, so irredeemable that everything I touched forever afterwards was tainted, and I could never stop making more lies, and more and more, each one covering another rip in the fabric of the mass, each one adding to the weight.

That night is as fresh to me as if it had just happened, even now after all this time. I go over it in my head trying to re-make it and believe me, there are a million better outcomes than the truth of it. I could blame the drug; it's the usual cop-out, but it was a tool, it only made more of what was there in me anyway. I could blame Terry, say he provoked me, which is true up to a point, but I didn't have to react. Most people go out of their way to avoid conflict, I could have played the girl and stayed passive, no one would have blamed me for that, far from it. I could blame society and say I was terrified of prejudice and had no faith in the law, which is true enough too, but many would say I should have put those feelings aside and taken my chances with the system like everyone else. I could blame my family and say the rage born in me from their handling caused me to do it. True also, in some ways, but lots of people have difficult childhoods and they live normal, ordinary adult lives and don't go around killing people. The excuses are endless; but so what? I did it, and there's an end of it.

I made a decision and it was the wrong one. I was arrogant and proud of my strength. I was so young; I look back now and I weep for the girl I was, because now I'm old I pity her.

So here's the rub: here's the question. You reading this, whoever you might be, put aside for a moment all the crap society dumps on you from the moment you're grown, all the judgments, the morals, the rules and regulations, the better-than-them self-righteousness, and ask yourself: What would you have done, if you'd been me? Not what I should have done, not what I was supposed to do. None of that shit.

What would you have done and more – what would you do now?

Here's a story to help you decide: after Natty's inquest, more dead than alive, I found myself outside the Central Police Station in Bradford. It was the afternoon, a dull day, nothing special, the town was quiet. I walked up the side to the double doors and as my reflection formed in the dirty glass, it was as if I were a swimmer, rising through the mucky waters of a polluted pool to the meniscus, the surface tension, of the water. As I put my hand out to push the door the tension broke and I moved through into the building in something approaching a state of grace, because I had come to confess.

I approached the counter, winding gently through the barriers put there so the public could form an orderly queue; and the desk clerk, a pleasant-looking girl in a white blouse looked up expectantly. I opened my mouth to speak.

And around me rose up a choir of living ghosts and behind them, the distant figures of the dead; all my people, their faces, their hands reaching out to me, all asking me the same question: why are you doing this to us? Isn't it bad enough what you've done without ruining our lives, too? My mother, Jen and her family, Leckie and her parents, Micky and his new family, all hurt, some destroyed if I let the weight drop, just to make myself feel better – because that's what it would be. It wouldn't bring Terry back, it wouldn't save Natty, it wouldn't help Jas. I must have looked odd, because the girl asked me if I was alright and I said: 'Yes, yes – sorry, miles way – I – I've been having nuisance phone calls, what should I do?'

You see, I couldn't do it, I couldn't betray them. So I told another lie, yes. But the truth is in me, I see it every night, replayed in dreams that never cease. And that temptation to confess, to be punished in the light of day and be absolved is there all the time and I crave as much now as I ever have; more, really. Oh God, to let that burden down, to be free of it; the thought is unimaginably wonderful.

But I can't, I mustn't, ever. Carrying it, keeping the secret, is the only way I have to show I love them, all of them, even those who only live in my memory, now. And I do, I do love them; I love them so much. Yes, even Mum, and Micky and Jen – they might not love me but it doesn't matter, I know that now. You see, everything I did, I did for love. That's the terrible – and the beautiful – thing. All for love; and I thought love would make everything alright, but that's not how it works, you can't expect a reward because you love someone. Dadda knew that, I think; it killed him in the end. But like they say, just because you love someone doesn't mean they have to love you back, it doesn't mean they owe you. You just feel what you feel and that's the gift of it, it's of itself, alone.

I love them and the best thing I can do now is put as much distance as I can between me and temptation.

So I'm running; I'm running.

Epilogue

Ms. B. Morgan
c/o Rooms Minoa
Sougia
Crete

Dear Leckie,

At last, a proper letter. I'm typing this on Mr B's ancient machine – he's the owner of this pension and a cat-lover so we get on – Cretans do love their cats, must be the Egyptian influence. Mr B has a huge, battle-scarred old ginger tom, that I call Marmalade and he calls Achilles, we conspire to over-feed him dreadfully. Makes me miss my babies, but your mum is a saint, the way she's looked after them, especially Ghengis. I hope your dad feels a bit better now, stuff like that can knock you back: give him my very best love, and your mum too.

There's so much to tell you, so much has happened since I left – it's over a year now, isn't it? I'm sorry not to have written before – I don't count e-mails, they're useful, certainly, but you can't really get stuff down the same. I couldn't fit it all in a letter either, so you'll just have to come out here and see me, OK? You've done so well with the business, I can't believe my bank balance: a triumph of Thorbyism, I take it? About the redecoration thing, just do what you think will look nice, the stuff you said about red and darker wood sounds good, mellow, if you see what I mean. I take it you got the last lot of stuff I sent from Morocco? Maybe you could use some of that.

I'm going to be staying here in Sougia for a while. Really, that's why I wanted to write to you; things are looking up at last. I mean it – good stuff is happening. I can't pretend it's been an easy time this last year, but I think it's all going to be alright, finally.

Lecks, it's beautiful here: the village is tiny and fairly unspoilt and the Cretans are really sound people. I can see everything from my little veranda: the gnarled, fuzzy old tamarisk trees are hazed in gold and the sea. Unbelievably gorgeous. Tonight it's a kind of purplish sapphire, and the sky is like an indigo velvet scarf just dotted with tiny diamonds. It's warm, even so early in the season; I can smell pine trees, night jasmine and the flinty, earthy scent of the hills behind the village mixed with a hint of wild thyme. To be honest, this is as near to heaven as I can imagine. I looked at some places to rent today – maybe even buy. I'm seriously thinking of settling here, if not the rest of my life, for a good long time. The last three months here have been like living a dream; an old dream I used to have about being in this kind of place.

But onto the good news. You know I told you I was doing a bit of waitressing at the German-owned hippie café here, just to have something to do more than anything else, well Uwe, the owner, let me hang a few of my Cretan paintings – he likes to think of the place as a bit of a gallery, European-style. So, there I am scurrying about with coffees and feta salads as per usual yesterday, and a fella asked me who the artist was. When I said it was me, he asked to see more work. We chatted a bit, and got on very well – he's English, from Stoke originally – I showed him some more stuff last evening and guess what? He's offered me a job teaching painting to groups that come to his hotel for art holidays; 'Art Crete Holidays' it's called, you know the kind of thing. He says the type of people who come want a bit of painting, some walks, visit interesting sites, churches, etc., nothing strenuous. But he said he loved my use of colour, it was 'vibrant' and 'really masterful', just what's wanted apparently. So, I'm going to do it. I mean, if it doesn't work out, so what? I've lost nothing.

Now, one of the paintings I'd hung was of Yev, sitting on a white wall, a fall of brilliant pink bougainvillaea behind him and a slice of blue sky. I've done a lot of portraits – Kirkos, Irina, Yanni, Uwe's partner Monika. I don't want you to get all over-excited, but Yev is my – what does someone my age call it, for God's sake? – he's my boyfriend. I have a boyfriend, a manfriend, whatever. A bloke. We've been seeing each other for about a month, properly, if you get me. I know it's not long but we've really connected. He's Russian, not Greek, there are quite a few 'invisible' immigrants here, Serbs, Croats, Romanians, and Russians. They drift here, or are running way from the ruined places they come from, or like Yev, just want a chance at some decent life before they die. He does odd jobs, collects glasses, bar work, helps Kirkos at the Mini Mart. Anything, really.

His proper name's Evgeniy, he's forty-two (toy-boy, eh?) and he's from an area of Moscow called Presnya. It's pretty rough by all accounts and I think Yev was a bit of a bad lad when he was younger. He was in with a gang, that sort of thing. It might put some people off, but to be honest, it was something we had in common. He's not had an easy life, far from it – a bit like me I suppose. He wanted to go to university, be a writer, but his family didn't have the cash or the influence so there was nothing but the street for him. He educated himself, though, despite everything, and I've read his poetry; it's tough stuff and perhaps it loses a bit in translation but it's got a kind of spare, haunting feel, like a winter forest. I like it and I don't think that's only because I like him. How he got the money to get out of Russia, I don't know – he'll tell me if he wants to. That's all it was at first, just talking about our lives, drinking coffee. He doesn't drink alcohol, either; says he left all that craziness behind in Russia. He was married, but it ended years ago. He has a daughter he misses very much but she went with her mum and that was that, basically. I told him about Natty. He was good about it, quiet. He understood, Leckie, and he didn't freak out or push me away.

I've enclosed a snapshot of him for you – that's me, in the <u>blue dress</u> in case you wondered – yup, out of black – sometimes. I've got a pink sarong, too, don't faint. I'm very girlie now, with my long hair and suntan; or as girlie as I'll ever be. As you can see, Yev's not exactly a pin-up, a bit bony and battered-looking, in fact, but what you can't see in the picture are his amazing pale grey eyes, like a wolf's and his hands, which are big and square, with long, knuckly fingers. He has a great sense of humour too, very dry, very clever; he has me in stitches sometimes at the things he says – and that accent – very sexy. I do like him a lot, but I don't ask for the moon anymore, so what will be, will be. You understand.

So, that's me, lady. All done and dusted. I'm doing pretty well. Of course, sometimes it still gets to me, you know – I think wouldn't Natty love it here or something like that, and it rips me up, like someone had torn my heart apart. But it's easing a bit every day, I can think of him without crying and without those awful memories, just with love, which is good. All I need now is to see you here, in the sunshine, and it'd be perfect – so, promise you'll come out? I'm off now to see if Kirkos has any bread left, then me and Yev are going for a walk up to the little chapel on the hill. I'll send you lots and lots of good wishes from there, eh?

Love,

Bill
XXX